TEMPEST

Calista Robbins

For Neal,
Once more unto the breach, dear friend.

THE KINGDOM OF ALYRIA

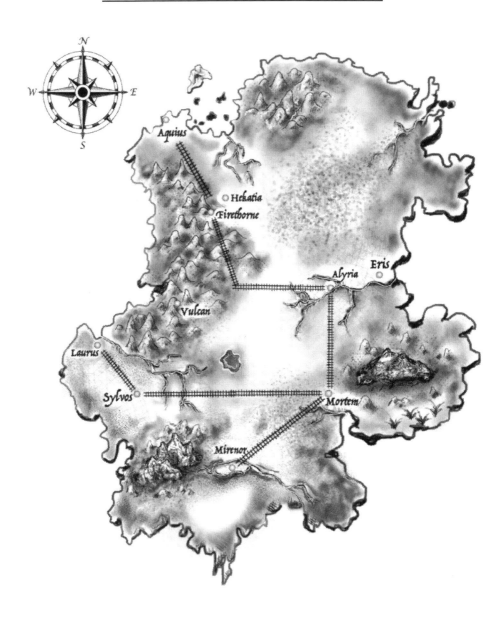

1

orridors of bookshelves stood like a labyrinth around the table where Dasha sat. Concealed in their depths were stories of conquest, prosperity, and despair. They were fantastic compilations of historical tales recorded from numerous storytellers that had traveled the land.

Dasha often read these stories, hoping someday soon, her parents would let her explore the world they described. Maybe, in her exploration, she'd discover an adventure worthy of its own story.

She was next in line to be Queen, so someone was bound to write something. She hoped it would be something good. Her parents ruled well, and she intended to do the same.

There were stories in these corridors that told a less fortunate journey. The realm would prosper through the entire reign of a king or queen, only to fall when their heir took over the throne. Peace was lost, wars broke out, and thousands perished. They made for wonderful stories, but it was a life Dasha never wished to live.

She stared blankly at the book laid open before her, but rather than focusing on the aged writing within it, she fiddled with her mother's ring, lost to thoughts unrelated to the text at hand.

Her magister slammed yet another book against the wooden tabletop, jolting her back to reality. She'd nearly forgotten the woman was there. "Dasha, answer the question," said the magister.

"Could you..." Dasha paused, unsure how to begin. In the end, she decided on simplicity. "Could you repeat it?" she asked, bracing herself for the scolding she knew was to come.

The magister exhaled through pursed lips. "Have you lost your head this morning, child? Which god rules over the second month of the year?"

Dasha couldn't say whether she'd lost her head or not, but her mind had certainly gone elsewhere. She'd started reading a most grievous book this morning that'd been gifted to her by the squire boy named Prince, and she wished desperately to return to it.

"Odemus," she replied before the magister's impatience grew. Her thoughts, however, remained in a time long passed. The story Prince had given her was one that'd taken place in the era of Dragon Hunters.

Reading about those days brought an ache to her heart that she couldn't shake. She'd always loved dragons, despite having only ever seen a few.

Dasha hadn't seen much outside the castle walls. She'd walked around the city a few times with her father, but exploring was an ordeal. Guards must be summoned, and travel arranged.

She knew, though, that once she enlisted into the Royal House, she'd be given more freedom to wander. She'd need to know what was out there if she ever intended to lead. Her father had told her as much. She figured there'd be more books to read out there, too. She was quite tired of these books.

"Correct. Why is this name important to know?" The magister asked, pointing a bony finger at the face of the god on the page, the fuchsia ring on her hand twinkling in the candlelight when she moved.

"Because the god of each month controls the conditions of each month," said Dasha, quicker this time. She'd already read this book, and she thought if she answered fast enough, the magister would end the lesson early.

"That's right! Tell me this as well, what does the month of Odemus hold in store for us?" The magister paused. "What is Odemus the god of?"

"Death... Odemus is the god of death." It was a dreary thing to rule, thought Dasha.

"What month is it currently?"

"The month of Wynris, goddess of winter and ice."

Dasha grazed her thumb over the metallic curve of the ring in her hand. It had an amethyst stone lodged in its silver hold, and there was an intricate design of a dragon engraved along the side. She liked the look of it and imagined that the dragon would come to life and flee from its silver cage. It kept her mind busy as boredom threatened. Perhaps one day she'd join in its freedom.

"Which means?"

"Many will fall ill from the Touch of Wynris in preparation for Odemus," Dasha said. It was a process often recited to her. Every winter, the warnings came. Wynris claimed souls for Odemus, and Odemus led the souls to the realm of the deceased, where Xudor, child of Death, ruled. It was in that realm that the souls lived out their days in the afterlife.

"And how many days are there before Odemus takes charge?"

"Seven."

"He's on our doorstep, child, so stay warm and stay healthy. Don't let Wynris claim you for the dead."

It was a message with good intentions, but one Dasha had no need of. People recorded gruesome details of the illness within their books, and she'd read a good many of them. She had no intention of suffering the same way they had.

"Yes, ma'am," Dasha assured.

"Good, next question. Which god or goddess—what do you have in your hand?" The magister pointed to her clenched fist. The ring had been spotted, and she wasn't supposed to have it.

Dasha tried to hide it, shoving it beneath her leg, but the ring clattered to the floor, and the magister snatched it up. "Why do you have this?"

"I found it."

The magister looked down the sharp angle of her nose, dubious. "Where?"

"In my mother's jewelry box."

"This doesn't belong to you yet, and you know it. It is a great shame to walk around without one's ring. Your mother's reputation would be ruined."

Dasha nodded. It wasn't like her mother planned on going anywhere anyway.

"Your ring is your identity," said the magister, arms flailing about in hysteria. "It represents who you are, your occupation. Without it, you're no one. A convict who's escaped their shackles. Convicts are the only ones without rings. Gods, child, what will your mother think of you for stealing such a thing."

Dasha looked at the band around her finger, a thought brewing in her head. "Why do children get rings?" she asked, trying to diverge the conversation. The rings for the youth were empty; there were no engravings and no crystals. She hated hers.

"Children haven't reached their enlistment day, so they have no trade to claim as their own. When you turn eighteen, you'll get an amethyst ring like this one." She held up the ring. "But, for now, go return it to your mother."

Dasha grabbed the ring and made her way out the door, dragging her feet along the way. Her footsteps echoed off the long, empty halls as she wound her way through the castle.

The door to her parents' room stood slightly ajar. Maybe they weren't there, she thought, hoping she could sneak the ring back into its box unnoticed. She peered through the crack, and the door creaked open. Her mother stood on the other side, arms crossed.

Dasha lowered her head, cowering from her mother's glare. "Sorry... I was going to return it," she said.

"And what would have happened if you'd lost it?" her mother asked.

"I would have searched the castle until it was found. This is the only place it'd be."

"Why do you insist on taking mine? You'll get your own soon enough."

"I would hardly call it soon," said Dasha, passing the ring to her mother, eyes falling once more to the beautiful dragon on its side.

From what she'd been told, the dragon reflected the period of her mother's life when she'd trained with the Dragon Keepers. Her mother had been a member of their guild before her father asked her to marry him. According to stories, her mother even had a dragon of her own, but it had been killed a long time ago.

Dasha longed for the freedom of choice her mother had had in her youth, and her thoughts broke through her lips. "What if I don't want that ring? What if I want a different one? Why can't I choose my guild like everyone else?"

Her mother looked down upon her with pity. "I know you want adventure, Dasha. I was just like you, but the amethyst is in your blood. You'll find it bears its own adventures in time. It is also a gift only a few can ever dream of. You mustn't say you don't want it."

"I want choice!" She didn't mean for her voice to raise, but it did so unbidden.

"Alas, you were born with duty instead."

"It's an obligation."

"It's a chance!" her father chimed in, silencing the room. "It's a chance, Dasha. A chance to be somebody, a chance to make a difference, and a chance to leave your mark in history. With the amethyst ring on your finger, you have the power to change the world. Your job will be to serve and protect the people of this nation, and you'll do that without further complaint." His voice rumbled through the air. "I never want to hear you say you don't want it again. It's not for you, it's for the people. To say you don't want the ring is selfish, and selfish people cannot lead."

Dasha retreated into herself, regretting her words but also angry. "Isn't this castle selfish?" she asked. "We have all this space; all these empty rooms and empty halls, and we need none of it. Is that not selfish? We could be living amongst the people in hovels and huts, but no, we're stuck up here, watching the commoners below." She'd thought of this often. The halls had grown lonely. Down in the city, she'd at least have had a friend.

"Believe it or not, these rooms were needed at one point," said her father. "When your mother and I first took office, Alyria was in need. The streets abounded with homeless and penniless citizens. This castle was filled, housing hundreds of people each day until circumstances bettered. We live in a time of prosperity now, and the halls have fallen silent. For the sake of the people, I pray they stay that way." He took a long breath and lowered his voice. "Go tell the magister she is done for the day. You're to study elsewhere for now. There's only so much that can be taught in that library."

Dasha didn't move. "Where else am I supposed to learn?" she asked, and the king smiled.

"The city. Your mother and I have decided you're ready. I did it when I was your age; I figure you can manage too. Go out and learn from the people. Books can only say so much, but looking into a person's eyes, seeing their life story play out before you in the small glimpses you catch of them, that is the thing that teaches you most about the leader you will be." He placed a hand on her shoulder and gave it a comforting squeeze. "Someone, a momentary friend in a far off city, once told me the world was our greatest teacher. I didn't believe him until I opened my eyes to actually see it. It's amazing what lessons you can find hidden in the rarest of people."

"I'll go!" Dasha said, eager to explore.

Her father grabbed a quill and parchment, and he wrote out his orders for Dasha and the magister. When finished, he handed her the paper, and she bounded to the library, shoving it at the scholar upon arrival. "I'm going out!" she beamed. "Father's set me free."

The magister sat there in utter confusion, eyes flitting between the paper and Dasha, who gathered a pack and slid a few books and a pencil inside. Within seconds, Dasha was gone again, leaving the magister behind.

Her father held his arm across the front entry, stopping her before she crossed. "We need to establish a few ground rules," he said, brow raised.

Of course he would, thought Dasha, annoyed, but she listened regardless.

"You mustn't pass the walls of the city while you're out, and I expect you to return by night fall. Your purpose of exploring will be only to study. I want you to record what you see. Write down trades you witness, stories you hear, and discussions between common folks. You will do this every day for the rest of the month. I expect to have your findings in hand by the end of the week when the month changes."

A black cloak was draped suddenly over Dasha's shoulders by the squire who'd given her the Dragon Hunter book. She'd seen him around the castle on occasion but never long enough to say more than a few passing words. He'd be off to claim a guild within the next month, so her chances of forming a friendship were slimming. "Tell no one your identity and keep away from the Touch of Wynris," her father said before lowering his arm so she could pass.

"Yes, sir."

Cool air rushed in as the doors were pressed open, and she stepped out, pausing a moment when they closed once more behind her. The crisp wind brushed over her skin and sent a chill through her spine. She pulled her cloak tight around herself as protection against the winter goddess, then she started down the path to the castle gates. They opened at her approach, and the guards ushered her through.

Beneath her feet, the carefully laid cobblestone path slowly faded into scattered gravel and dirt, and the iron gates to the castle disappeared behind her.

2

*S*mall houses and shacks formed in clusters near the edge of the city, but the closer to its heart she walked, the more crowded her surroundings became. The scattered hovels quickly changed from isolated clumps to tight fit shops mashed together with houses. The street bustled with activity, and a fresh layer of snow coated the ground, decorating the rooftops and icing the roads. Amongst the chaos was the occasional sound of laughter that followed the mishap of a person slipping on the sheets of ice that invisibly gathered on the pathway.

A small group of children had taken claim of a large ice section and skated around it. Frequently, they crashed into each other and knocked their friends over as they passed a large stone back and forth, kicking it with their feet.

Dasha watched the stone shoot from the crowd, heading towards a single boy on the edge of the ice sheet. The boy dove for the sliding stone, but it flew past him and into the street. He hit the ice hard and slid a few paces before coming to a stop. Half the children cheered in triumph, but the others grumbled and muttered under their breaths.

The boy lifted himself to his feet, brushed himself off, then went to fetch the stone. It was smoothed down flat and carved into a perfect oval shape. He threw it once more to the center of the ice, and the game continued. Dasha pulled out an empty, leather bound notebook and a charcoal pencil, recording what she saw of the game; the objective, the players, the rules, and anything else she could pull from it. She'd seen the guardsmen play a similar sport in the castle courtyard when time allowed for such activities, and she wished she could join in on the fun, but she could not disobey her father's bidding.

In time, the game came to an end, and Dasha was forced to move on. Down the road a bit, she found a small ladder that led to the rooftops where she knew there'd be a much better view than the one she'd had in the street. She scaled the rungs and pulled herself onto the roof, scanning her surroundings while she walked along the edges of the buildings. The roofs grew slanted when she reached the more centered, larger buildings of the city, so she chose a small butchers shop with a flat top, cleared a section of snow, and sat to watch the happenings below.

The man and woman behind the counter just beneath her bore the burgundy crystal rings of the Merchant guild. A man stood on the consumer end, digging through his purse of coins to pay for the meat. His hands were worn and calloused; burn marks spotted his skin, and a black diamond crystal rested in his ring, marking him a Blacksmith.

Dasha jotted down the exchange, noting the coins paid, the meat given, and the Blacksmith status of the consumer. When the man left, another shortly took his place. This one was younger, yet carried a presence with him impossible to ignore. Bystanders' attentions were drawn to him, and people stared from all around. Something about the way he walked, the way he stood, it drew one in.

He was tall and solid, a determined fire in his eyes. When he moved, he strode with power and confidence, and when he spoke to the Merchant, his voice was deep and strong. A thin scar traced down the center of his right eye that evoked curiosity in Dasha's heart. Everything about him fascinated her. He was one of those people that carried such a presence that you knew he was there without ever having to see him. Her father carried a similar presence. She made a note to learn how to walk with the intensity that he walked with. She wanted to be able to draw the eyes of everyone around just by simply having the confidence to be herself.

Something that was draped over his shoulders began to move, glistening an emerald green that matched the man's ring. The creature stretched, revealing a dark, forest-green set of leathery wings and a beautiful green scaled body. Its length equaled the width of the man's shoulders, and the tail coiled around his arm, slithering like a snake with each movement of the beast. It hissed at a child whose curiosity betrayed her, a spark forming in its mouth at her next step.

A dragon. Dasha realized. The man stroked the shoulder blades of the creature, and it curled back up, retreating into a slumber. "Back away, child. Just because he's young doesn't mean he isn't dangerous." The child listened and took a step back, but she kept an awestruck gaze upon the dragon.

Dasha quickly sketched the man and dragon in her notebook, not wanting to forget a single detail of this encounter. The strength of the man, the mystery of the beast, and the spark of curiosity in the eyes of the child. She captured it all with the strokes of her pencil, then the man walked away, a path parting in the crowd as he moved through the gathering, seemingly oblivious to the hundreds of eyes that glued to him and this magnificent creature. Eventually, he disappeared from view, feeding a small chunk of meat to the dragon.

Out of what seemed thin air, a boy plopped down beside Dasha, and she jumped, startled by his sudden appearance. "Apologies, miss, I didn't mean to frighten you," he said. "The name's Patch... or at least that's what people call me. No one knows my real name, y'see. My parents took that secret to their grave." His face twisted with a mix of sorrow and something Dasha couldn't place. "Anyway, enough about me, what have you got there?" he asked, reaching for the notebook, deep green eyes staring into hers.

"Nothing," said Dasha, slamming it shut.

"Oh, come on now, let's see it please. Does it hurt to be curious?"

"Yes, actually, didn't you hear? Curiosity killed the cat," she replied.

"Well it's a good thing I'm not a cat, then, isn't it?"

He looked a bit like a cat, though she dared not say it. His scruffy black hair lay in shambles atop his head like the ragged fur of the stray cats she'd seen wander the city. He grabbed the notebook while she was distracted and flipped it to her drawing. "A mysterious girl in a black cloak, drawing pictures of random civilians. Fascinating. What, may I ask, is your name?"

"Uh..." Dasha hesitated, not sure what she should say. She couldn't tell him the truth. She'd promised her father secrecy.

"Or don't you have one?" He spoke fast, not giving much opportunity to process what was being said. "What're you doing up here anyway?"

"I'm studying," she said, glad for the topic change.

"What are you studying?"

Dasha thought for a moment, trying to conjure an explanation. A quote from her father seemed to do the trick. "My surroundings... The world is our greatest teacher."

"But why study it when you can live it?" he asked. "Here, come with me." He grabbed her hand and dragged her down to the street.

Dasha's feet tangled beneath her, but she managed to keep her footing. "Where are we going?" she asked, glancing back to the rooftop they'd been sitting on only a moment before.

"Don't know yet. We're being spontaneous," he said.

Dasha huffed, struggling to keep up. "I've got to write some of this down, you know," she said, hoping it would suggest a break from the running.

Thankfully, he stopped. "What for?" he asked.

"My father," said Dasha, using the moment to catch her breath. "He let me do this instead of sitting with the magister all day."

"So you have a father... can afford a magister," he thought out loud, mumbling his conclusions to himself. "So must be upper or middle class. Black cloak indicates secrecy, and you hesitated to give your name. You're hiding. And! You're studying the city as if you don't walk these streets every day, so you must live in the outskirts... or perhaps not in the city at all... perhaps that castle over there. See, we're getting to know each other, princess." He bowed, and she stood like a fool with her mouth agape.

"Could you really tell from that alone?" Dasha asked.

Patch gave a wry smile. "No," he said. "I saw you a couple years ago when you went with your father to the docks. It's a pleasure to meet you, your highness." He held out his hand in greeting, head bowed ever so slightly.

"Don't call me that," said Dasha, a bit flustered from the encounter.

"Why not?" he asked.

9

Dasha lifted her hand to show the silver band of a child on her finger. "No stone on the ring means I'm technically not part of the Royal House yet," she said, though that meant nothing with her being the only heir. She was more fearful of others noticing her presence than anything as trivial as rings. That was the true reason she wished to avoid the title. His courtesies would surly draw attention.

"How long until you get yours?" he asked.

"Half a year."

"Same," said Patch.

"Which guild will you join?" Patch had been given choice, and she wanted to know what someone would do with it.

He thought on the inquiry for a good minute, then said, "I'm not sure. I don't really fit into a guild. Not yet at least. To be honest, I never thought I'd make it to my enlistment day. A life on the streets isn't one of luxury." That thought silenced him for a bit, and they continued forward. "If I had to choose, though," he said once they were further down the street. "It'd be a guild with power, one where I could make a difference and help the kids like me."

"Maybe one day, I'll have the power to do the same," said Dasha.

After some time of wandering, they found a small alcove wedged between two buildings. It was concealed in a way that it was difficult to see in but simple to see out. They cleared a patch of snow and sat, getting comfortable on the ragged, rocky ground.

Together, they watched the people that passed for a short time. Some walked hurriedly by, others lingered for a moment, speaking with another, or just gazing upon something that had caught their eye in a shop. Dasha recorded anything that sparked interest. Most of her entries were small pieces of stories heard at a distance. She liked the tales, real or fake, they gave her a glimpse into a world that wasn't her own. Patch had a few stories to tell as well, things he'd heard on the street and the spread of rumor going around the city.

Amid one of these stories, a woman stopped in front of the entrance to their alcove. She had long, dark hair, pulled back with a leather strap, and she was garbed in black, slim fitted clothing. Even the ring on her hand held a jet crystal. Patch fell silent, backing further into the shadows.

"What is it?" Dasha asked.

He pointed to the woman. "Necromancer," he said. "First one I've seen this year."

"So?" Dasha had rarely heard of them. She knew it was one of the guilds but had never learned much about what it was they did.

10

"Servants of Odemus and Xudor... ringing a bell? They speak to spirits. Terrible omens. I've heard people say that if you see one, someone is likely to die."

The woman's head turned towards them as if summoned by the mention of death, and her eyes met with Dasha's for what seemed an eternity. Then, as quickly as she'd come, she turned and walked away. The Necromancer had a strange presence to her, sort of like the Dragon Keeper, but it was different. Rather than drawing the attention of everyone around, she went unnoticed. No one looked at her, but they all parted when she neared. She was like a phantom that no one could see, yet they all adhered to her movement. She walked straight through the crowd without having to dodge a soul. Patch relaxed as the woman grew distant, engulfed suddenly by the sea of people.

"It's just a guild. What makes them so different than the others?" Dasha asked.

Patch looked at her with disbelief. "Dasha... they have the ability to raise the dead. They could make an army out of them if they wanted to. You can't tell me that isn't at all terrifying to you."

While it was a grand idea, Dasha didn't think it was a likely thing to happen. "The Mages could just as easily turn the ground beneath our feet against us, but no one cowers from them," she said. "It's an outlandish fear. There's no reason for them to do it."

He blinked slowly, deep in a thought. "I'd rather have the ground turn against me than face a battalion of ghosts."

"It isn't that terrible of an idea if you think about it... an army of the dead with the backing of Mages and Dragon Keepers. It'd be unstoppable, wouldn't it?" She smiled at the thought, imagining the power behind such an army.

"I dread the day. Remind me not to be here when it happens."

Dasha, having dismissed the notion of the army, returned to the topic of the Necromancer they'd encountered. "I wonder who's dying," she said, and she peaked her head out, searching the surrounding households for signs of distress. Somewhere behind a closed door, someone was slipping out of this world and into another.

"It could be anyone with the reign of Odemus approaching," said Patch, looking Dasha in the eyes for a fleeting moment.

Shortly thereafter, the sun sank behind the buildings, cuing Dasha to return home. "Will I see you again?" Patch asked as she gathered her things to leave.

"I'll meet you here every morning when the sun hits its peak until the first of Odemus," she promised.

"Sounds like a plan, see you later, then."

"Bye." She scampered off, making it back to the castle just as the sun kissed the horizon.

3

$\mathcal{T}$he week continued similarly. Each morning, Dasha would set out into the city, and as promised, she'd meet Patch in their alcove. They'd start the afternoon with a small feast of foods she smuggled from the castle kitchens, watching the people that wandered about while they ate. When nothing but crumbs remained, they'd move their studies to the streets, walking alongside those that intrigued them until the people either reached their destination, left the city, or caught the two following them.

Necromancers and Medics bearing amber rings grew numerous within the city as the Touch of Wynris began to take effect. It seemed a battle between Ides and Odemus; a war between life and death. Many residents remained hidden in their homes to keep away from the spreading illness of the icy season, but some still mingled, unable to halt their daily lives.

Occasionally, Dasha would see a Necromancer trailing a congregation of mourning families as they paraded down the streets, honoring the recently deceased. Sometime mid-week, when the sun had set and she returned home, one of those Necromancers lurked in her own shadow, following her back to the castle. The fear-stricken look her father gave her when she told him about it left her terribly paranoid of the illness around her. She wanted to lock herself behind closed doors like so many had done with the reign of Odemus nearing, but the week was so close to being over, and her time with Patch was decreasing each passing day, so she decided to press on, hoping she wouldn't be the next one marked for the god of death.

The sun retreated towards the horizon on her final day of studying, and with it drained her curious spirit. Dasha sat perched atop the crow's nest of a Naval ship with Patch at her side, watching the men and women below who bore aquamarine rings that reflected the color of the river waves gleaming in the sun. Alongside the Naval guild members was a line of convicts, chained together and restrained by iron shackles around their wrists and ankles.

The convicts were likely being transported to another location, where they'd work on a renovation project in the city. All had been stripped of their rings and held no source of identification. Their rings would never be returned, and the shackles never removed, even after being released from the cells. Had they not been guilty of the most heinous crimes, Dasha would have felt bad for them.

"Hey!" came a voice carried by the breeze from below. "Get down from there!" the stranger shouted.

Dasha and Patch scurried down the mast of the ship, giggling, hearts pounding. They were not meant to be there. When their feet hit the deck, three Necromancers locked their gaze on the pair. Patch tensed up and leaned close to her. "Don't let me get word one of these folks took you to dine with Odemus, you hear?"

"I'll do my best," she assured. "Promise me you'll do the same?"

"Well of course. How am I supposed to help you with your studies if I'm dead?" Patch smirked and nudged her with his elbow.

"Maybe at the end of the month, when Izasel reclaims the throne for spring, we can see each other again," said Dasha, hope surfacing in her heart.

"Perhaps," Patch said, "but for now, it's goodbye."

Dasha frowned. "It's not goodbye, it's see you later."

With that, the two made their separate ways. Dasha flipped through her notebook, reliving the events of the week, a smile creased upon her lips.

The cities beaten path shifted back to the neatly placed cobblestone bricks, and the gates closed behind her. A wave of disappointment struck with the thought of the gates remaining closed for some time, but a spark of hope remained within.

Her mother greeted her at the door. "Supper will be ready shortly. Would you like anything to hold you off until then?" she asked, words oddly spoken, almost seeming nervous.

"Where's Father?" Dasha asked. She wanted to know the verdict on further trips as soon as possible.

"He's... in the bath house... I can take your notebook to him if you'd like."

"No, thank you. I'll give it to him later," said Dasha, then she started down the small hallway that led to her room, trying to piece together her puzzled thoughts.

A breeze drifted in from a door that sat slightly ajar, spreading its cold winter fingers over her exposed skin. She moved to close it, but a sound on the other end caught her attention, so instead, she stepped through and into the wooded garden.

A blanket of snow had draped over the trees and the dirt path that wound through them, glittering a pale blue under the full moon light. In the center of the woods, Dasha's father sat perched on a bench carved from a fallen tree that looked over a shallow pond. He was wrapped in a plethora of furs, trying to stay warm in the bitter night wind. She wondered why he was there instead of in the bath house like her mother had said, but as an answer to her curiosities, his lips began to move in silent prayer. When he finished, his eyes shot open. Dasha feared he'd noticed her, but he made no action towards it.

A chill swept through his body, and he stood to go inside. Every movement he made was shaky and weak, and the color slowly drained from his skin. Each step he took seemed to expend too much of his energy, every breath seemed labored. Dasha took out her notebook and began writing what she saw.

The way he looked matched the many people in the city who'd fallen ill from the winter, and the words she used to describe it matched those of the books that'd explained the nasty disease. A daunting realization dawned on her like the shadow of a great beast. Wynris had claimed her father.

He fell to his knees, a coughing fit overcoming him. His body writhed, and he struggled to regain control of his breathing. Dasha wanted so badly to run to his aid and lift him to his feet, but if she did, she risked Wynris latching on to her as well, and fear of the illness held her paralyzed in the place she stood, so she waited in the shadows, watching her father's strain.

Dark-red blood stained the cloth he held to his lips, spattering across the snow beneath him. He carefully rose to his feet and dragged himself inside. Her mother met him in the hall to help him to a seat, and Dasha took her own seat on the bench her father had previously occupied, sketching the image that burned in her mind. She felt that if she could get it onto paper, then perhaps it wouldn't haunt her.

Lost in thought, the pencil danced over the pages, creating the image of the previous event. Its tip snapped under the pressure of her grief fueled grip and she slammed the book shut, blinking away the tears that brimmed in her eyes. The smell of food beckoned her back to the dining hall, and she wiped the tears from her eyes, brushing off the snow that'd landed upon her shoulders.

"Have you been outside?" her mother asked when she stepped in.

"Yes. I was in the garden," Dasha admitted, the answer obvious by her still flushed face.

Her father stiffened, likely realizing the possibility that their paths had collided. Some of the color had returned to his face with the fire's warmth, but his complexion was still paler than normal. "How long were you out there?" he asked, failing to hide the tension in his voice.

"Not long," said Dasha, and he slouched in relief. She was glad she could offer him that much ease... at least for a short while. She took her seat and set the notebook on the edge of the table, chair scraping across the floor with a sharp sound that burst through the silence. He reached over, eyebrows raised in question, silently asking permission to read her work. She nodded, and he took it, opening it to the first page.

"Tell me, the man with the emerald ring, what was he?" her father tested.

"Dragon Keeper," Dasha said with effortless confidence.

Her mother smiled at the speed of her response. "Good, and what is it the Dragon Keepers do?" he asked.

"Protect dragons?" She wasn't solid on that particular answer. All she knew was that she'd rather be one than a Royal.

"Correct. They are the breeders and trainers of dragons," he said, then he continued through the book, quizzing her on small details of things she'd written down. "It's good, but all I see are simple observations. Next time you go out, go into more depth of what you're looking at. Add background information to what you see, and if there's something you don't know, talk to people or continue to observe until you know all the facts. Get multiple people's opinions on subjects. The more perspectives you get; the greater information you have."

Dasha sat upright, delighted by the phrase 'next time', but her joy faded fast when his muscles suddenly tightened. He'd seen the final page and fallen silent, sorrow burning in his eyes. "I never meant for you to see that." His voice was soft and defeated. Dasha's mother took the notebook, curious about the change of atmosphere. They both stared blankly at the pages, searching for something to say.

"When were you going to tell me?" Dasha asked, anger and hopelessness clashing in her soul.

"We didn't know how bad it was…" her mother said, a similar expression in her voice. "We thought he'd get better."

"Was I to find out on the day it took you?"

"We planned to tell you soon," said her father. "We just weren't sure what it was yet, so we decided to keep it quiet. There's a Medic coming later. She'll be arriving in the middle of the night so as not to spread panic amongst the people."

Dasha fell silent, understanding the situation. He could be severely ill, and come one morning, death might appear to escort him to the underworld. If that were to occur, she thought he would need time to set things in order, but if it was something small that would last only a few days and word got out, there would be unnecessary chaos.

One of the servants came and took the dishes from the table once the family had finished, and Dasha's mother excused herself to help. Dasha rose to join, but her father's voice stopped her.

"Dasha?" he asked. "I have a meeting with the guild leaders tomorrow. I think it's time you learned to deal with matters such as these in the chance of my absence," he said. "It would also give you a chance to learn more about each guild. Will you join us?"

"Yes, sir," she said, saddened by the details that made this meeting necessary.

"We'll meet in the keep first thing in the morning."

"Then I best get some rest," said Dasha with a half-hearted smile. "I'll see you in the morning. Good night." With one last glance at her father, she turned and retired to her bed chamber.

She felt heavy, the knowledge of her father's illness weighing down every step. Thoughts prowled her mind, unwilling to succumb to sleep. The fading torchlight crept from the room, leaving only the light of the moon, stars, and the faint burning wick of a nearly extinguished candle to outline her surroundings.

Hushed voices echoed off the stone walls; their attempt at silence in vain. There were three voices, one belonging to her father, another to her mother, and the third to a woman she didn't recognize. Eventually they faded to nothing, and Dasha was alone with shadows and silence once more. Soon, however, exhaustion got the better of her, and she drifted off to sleep.

~~~

Thirteen men and women sat around the table in the great hall with Dasha's father at the head. She looked around to each of their faces, reading the emotions that the lines and creases of their features told. There was worry in their eyes. They knew, as she did, the weight of the meeting. Depending on the fate of the gods, it was possible to be the king's last.

Each person bore a separate colored ring that represented the guild they led. At her father's right sat a man with the olivine crystal ring of the Army. "We are lacking in recruits, sir," said the man. "Very few join our force on their enlistment day, and those who do are green and only know tales and fantasies of battle. People are more interested in the societal guilds than they are in defending a nation that has no threats. I fear if they are put in a situation of war, they will not live to see the morning."

"We're in a time of peace, in which I hope we stay. Unless a civil war breaks out, these men will never see a battle," her father said in response. He had a collected wisdom in his posture and a tone of voice that demanded authority.

"A civil war isn't as unimaginable as it may seem, sir, you are unwell, it is plain enough to see. You bring your heir to your council, your eyes are hollowed, and your skin is paled. The Necromancer sits uneasy. Death is lurking in this hall, and she knows it, don't you, Sepora," said the soldier, and the Necromancer nodded. She had pale white eyes that made Dasha's skin crawl. "What is to happen if the peace dies with you? My men need to be ready," he said, bold and passionate with his claims.

"I have every faith in my wife and daughter's ability to maintain the peace if I'm taken," her father replied through gritted teeth, a flare of rage in his eyes. With a breath, he composed himself. "But if it comforts you, spread word of your need of soldiers and train them, harden them."

The Army's guild leader wasn't satisfied. "How do I harden men who have never tasted war? They don't fear death, not out of strength, but rather because there is nothing left to kill them."

"Then make them fear death," the king answered, no longer the man Dasha knew as her father. Now, he'd stepped fully into his role as King. He gnawed on his lower lip, some dilemma brewing in his head. "There's a system my father used to use. He was a cruel man but brilliant in warfare. Line two soldiers up, one defensive, one offensive. Put the defensive with their backs against a cliff. This will put them on death ground. If they're not victorious against their opponent, then death awaits them off the ledge.

"They will win, or they will die, or so they will think. Find a way to keep the losing defensive alive without the other soldiers knowing. Perhaps a system of nets and baskets. Keep them scared of death. The moment the others know their lives are no longer in danger is the moment they stop fighting."

From stories Dasha had heard about her ancestors, she imagined that her grandfather hadn't kept the losing soldiers alive. There'd be no point in keeping the weak, but there was no humanity in letting them die.

"Yes, sir." The soldier nodded, and sat back in his seat, retreating from the conversation.

"Sepora, what's the tally of the dead?" her father asked, transitioning the group to the next topic.

"We've lost about fifty in the city, probably around fifty thousand in the nation. Odemus has not been kind this winter. Many lives have already been lost or will soon be lost..." Her voice trailed, and Dasha sat in silence, digesting the numbers.

Other matters were brought up and discussed between the guild leaders after Sepora's words. The Farmer told of the crops and how much food the cities were to expect for the rest of winter. The Medic listed off preparations for healing once the icy months were over. The Naval officer read reports of expeditions and trade routes from the sailors of the land.

As the conversations progressed, a feast was brought out to entertain the guests. A singer sat across the room with songs of ancient wars. Dasha found her ears straying from the monotonous conversations of the guild leaders to listen instead to the magic and wonder of the music. The singer bore a clear diamond ring, marking him as undecided. His trade didn't fit under a guild, so he chose not to join one. She wondered if Patch would do the same when it came time for him to make his choice.

The feast fell silent when the king stood, and all eyes turned to him. "I have one last request for the lot of you before you return to your guilds," he said. "I would like each of you to show my daughter what it is that your guilds do. After all, what better way is there to teach her than for her to learn from the masters of trade themselves?"

An energy washed through the hall. They each seemed eager to show off their skills. "I understand that many of you can't successfully represent yourselves in this room, so you may lead us wherever you please," he offered.

A man in a red robe stood from his seat, a fuchsia ring, like the one Dasha's magister wore, on his finger. "If I may stray from the castle, I'd be honored to begin," he said.

"I'll arrange for an escort," Dasha's father replied, nodding in approval before sending a guard to gather the horses.

As a group, the guild leaders rose, and with the king's direction, they flocked to the stables. A troop of guards waited with the mounts, and Dasha's father helped her into a saddle, mounting the palfrey behind her.

The Priest took the lead, and they made their way down the streets to the temple of the graces. Eyes peered from behind the wooden shutters that protected the windows of every house. It was rare to see the king in the streets. A parade of this magnitude was unheard of. Children marveled from behind their parents, and adults all stared.

Luckily, the ride wasn't long, and without much delay, they were secluded within the temple. Dasha dismounted from her father's horse and stepped through the ornate doors. She'd never been inside the temple before. Great columns stretched from floor to ceiling, carved into them were stories of the gods. In a circle at the center of the room, there stood twelve statues. They were small replicas of the sculptures outside that resembled the supreme deities. Around each statue was an array of candles left by worshipers. In the middle of the circle was a fire. Written in stone beneath the fire were the words, *Eternal Flame*.

The Priest approached her, pulling a book from his robe. "My job is to spread the knowledge of the twelve supreme gods displayed here, along with all the other lesser gods. These lesser deities are the ones we pray to who never claim the throne.

Dasha accepted the book, but her eyes focused on the domed rooftop. It was covered entirely with magnificent and ancient paintings. In them were depictions of every god, supreme and lesser. Her eyes locked on one. Ides. She stood before the statue of the life deity and took in the artwork above her. Pictured in the brushstrokes on the ceiling was the goddess that could save her father.

"Ah, the goddess of love," the Priest said with a smile. Dasha's face twisted, but understanding came when her gaze shifted to the woman beside Ides who held an infant in her arms. "Is there a boy that keeps you praying to her at night?" the Priest inquired.

"No," Dasha responded coldly. She found it revolting that the Priest expected her to be focused on love in the midst of her father's illness.

"Ah." He sucked in his breath and changed his direction, reaching for the book he'd just given her. "May I?"

Dasha nodded and passed the book back to him. The Priest held the binding in his palm and flipped through the pages until he had passed the supreme twelve. Written in careful calligraphy at the front of the page was a dedication to the lesser gods. He turned each page with grace and showed Dasha the tales inscribed inside.

"Each of these gods hold power," he said. "They may not rule the heavenly realm, but they control the smaller aspects of our lives. The sea god aids the sailors in their paths. The war god puts courage in the hearts of our soldiers. The god of the night sky paints speckled stars for all to see, guiding the traveler to their destination—"

Dasha listened, intrigued. She'd never heard of most of the gods he spoke of, but some she'd read about in the books of the castle. The Priest returned the book to Dasha when he finished his lesson, and Dasha thanked him for his gift.

Another man moved swiftly to replace him, this one wearing the burgundy Merchant ring. "This may be the domain of the gods, but let me show you a place far more lively." With a gesture to follow, Dasha trailed behind the guild leader, and he led the group back into the streets. He stopped at the top of the grand staircase that connected to the courtyard where the temple met the city. Looking out from the top of the stairs, Dasha could see an array of markets and inns. "Anything you could ever dream of having, I could get you with a fair trade. A few coins here, and out comes the finest jewelry in the nation."

"Anything?" Dasha asked, testing his bold claims. He had a vain confidence that she found unnerving.

"Within a fair price, of course. Is there anything m'lady wishes to have?" The question dwelled in the air for a short while as she processed her answer. Dasha wanted her father to be well. She wanted to roam the city with Patch. She wanted many things, but none of which could be bought.

"A dragon," she finally said, unsure of where the idea had come from.

The Merchant's eyes widened, taken by surprise, so she deemed her answer successful. She had stumped this boastful man. "My dearest apologies, m'lady, but that I cannot give," he mumbled. "If there is anything *else* you wish to have—"

A woman with dark, olive skin and sleek, black hair pulled up with a leather bind touched the Merchant on the shoulder. "You heard the girl, she wants a dragon." The woman's hand bore an emerald ring, and she held the ringed hand forward in greeting. "Sagua; guild leader of the Dragon Keepers," she said.

Dasha shook her hand, a smile creeping to her lips, and the woman continued speaking. "A dragon I cannot give you, as you aren't a member of our guild. However, I may show you mine if you would like to meet him."

She gave a whistle, and a creature spiraled from the clouds. At the height the dragon flew, it looked no larger than a raven. It quickly grew in size as it approached, and soon, a red beast stood before her, its scales flickering like flames under the sun.

"Dasha, meet Zauryn," Sagua said, and Dasha stepped cautiously towards the dragon. It was much larger than any she'd ever been near. Sagua, with a smile, took Dasha's hand and put it on Zauryns neck. "He's still young, so be careful with your movements. He can sense the fear you show and will turn it into a game. You must stay confident."

Dasha nodded, staring into the black eyes of the beast that bore into hers. They seemed so dark and endless, yet full of life and focus. After a moment of inspection, Zauryn relaxed. "Well done," said Sagua.

Dasha stepped away from the dragon to get a better view of its body. "How big will he get?"

"About thirty feet in length, once he reaches his peak age," Sagua answered.

"How old is he?"

"Recently hit twenty years."

"What's their life span?" Dasha had many questions. This was, after all, the first time she could recall being this close to a dragon.

"If not killed by means other than a natural death, they generally live to seventy years."

"Enough about this dragon," said a man, stepping forward with a black diamond in his ring. "M'lady still hasn't gotten what she wants. Now, I certainly can't give you a live dragon, but I can give you one born of fire and steel. I'd simply need access to a forge," he said, looking at the king for permission to leave.

"Anything you need," said her father, gesturing with open palms to the path that led through the city.

"This will take some time, so I'll leave you here to continue speaking with the others while I work," the Blacksmith said before departing.

A woman stepped forward who wore a siam ring. "I'm Vitani; guild leader of the Mages. We study magic in the form of the major elements: earth, water, fire, and air," she said. "Would you like to see?"

Dasha nodded eagerly.

The group relocated to a garden that surrounded the temple, and Vitani crouched down, placing her palm to the dirt. Her eyes rolled back, exposing the white underside. Shortly thereafter, a sapling sprouted from the ground. When grown into something resembling a tree, Vitani pooled its roots with water. The water quickly dissolved, and the plant shriveled up and caught on fire. Once the fire burned out, the wind carried away the ashes.

Dasha stared in awe as each deed was performed. "A physical thing, I unfortunately cannot give, but if you're ever interested in learning more about my trade, feel free to speak with any Mage you see. They will be happy to show you a few things," Vitani offered, standing to meet Dasha's eyes. Dasha thanked the Mage, and she stepped back.

"Come over here, m'lady," the guild leader of the Army prompted. Dasha turned to find him standing on the edge of the stairs where the Merchant had been before. "Come look at this."

Dasha obeyed and stood by his side, looking out over the city. It was the exact same thing the Merchant had shown her. Her father came up beside her and asked, "What do you see?"

She looked around, searching for something new. "I see shops and inns." Dasha replied.

"That's what you were told to see. Clear your mind of riches and material things. Look again," said her father.

Dasha looked past the shops and the buildings and looked instead at the people. Following each of them was a life she would never know. "I see stories," she finally answered. "A child chasing a cat. A mother holding an infant. Two lovers enjoying the city… In all of them, there are stories." The king smiled.

"It is them that my guild protects, said the Army's guild leader. "The collection of people from all over the land united together. It is their families, their homes, and their stories that we guard. But it wasn't always like this. There was a time when war reigned the land. Luckily, that time is gone now. When the land united as one body, so too did the militaries.

"In this time of peace, we lack in numbers and purpose, but we continue to train in case the peace should fail to hold." His final words seemed a clear message.

"My guild holds a similar role to the Army," said a woman who'd yet to speak. She wore white garb, and a sapphire stone rested in her ring. "We protect the people and the land as well, just on a lesser scale. We are the keepers of the peace, or the Law Enforcement. We seek out criminals, and step between any conflicts that may occur."

A man stepped forward, drawing Dasha's attention to him. In his ring was a fire opal. "My guild is one of the most ancient organizations of humankind. It formed in the origins of civilization. When Zalder gifted man the power of flame, humanity knew it needed contained. It tore through forests and consumed cities, but there were many benefits to it as well. It is the duty of the Fire Keepers to protect people from the flames when they wander out of control."

When the Fire Keeper fell silent, another stepped forward. It was a man with an aquamarine ring on his finger. He pointed over the city to where the docks stood, water lapping at the ships anchored inside. "I lead the Navy," he began. "We manage all water affairs, including navigation of trade over rivers and seas, and the transfer of convicts to their necessary locations. A lesser known fact of ours, however, is that we currently have several ships out in the seas, searching for new lands. If there are no other lands, then perhaps we'll discover the edge of the world," he said.

"What's past the edge of the world?" Dasha asked.

"We may never know," the Naval commander answered.

"The realm of the gods perhaps," Sepora pitched. "Unfortunately, you know my job all too well. Necromancers take both the souls that Wynris tags and the souls of the murdered and dying to the throne of Odemus. Come the tenth month of our year, we merge the spirit world with the mortal world. Each spirit gets a single day of the month of Xudor to walk as men again. Once the month is over, every spirit must return to Xudor's hall," she explained. Dasha was grateful for the one day each year she would be able to see her father if he failed to fight off the illness.

"And it is our job to keep as many people away from the death gods as possible," the Medic chimed in. She was a bold woman. Dasha could see it in her eyes. "We are servants of Ides, who sadly doesn't hold the throne right now, or saving the ill would be much easier," she said. There was a certain bitterness in her words, and the atmosphere of the room darkened. But as always, the king knew how to lift their spirits.

"The two eternal lovers." A smile touched his lips. "Life and Death. Ides and Odemus. Life brings us forth into the world, and when our mission is complete, Death brings us with him. Please, continue." He gestured to the final guild leader.

A man with a jonquil ring stepped up. "Guess I'm the last one. I could give a demonstration, but my trade is something you see daily. All the food you eat, all the clothes you wear, they come from members of my guild. We produce fruits, vegetables, grains, and more. Any wool articles of clothing came from our sheep. We sell our produce to the Merchants, who in turn, sell to the people."

When he finished, the Blacksmith returned from the forge. In his hand was a small, sheathed dagger. A dragon with amethyst eyes wrapped around its quillion, and its tail coiled around the hilt. "There is an art to weapon making," the Smith said, handing her the dagger. "A proper blade will have perfect balance, be ornately designed, and reflect the soul of its owner." Dasha gazed at the patterns engraved into the beast. The blade was stunning. "There's a dragon within you, Dasha. Never lose sight of it."

Dasha thanked him and the others for their gifts and words, and soon they were dismissed.

4

$\mathcal{T}$he days passed slowly, each bringing further deterioration to her father's condition. By the final week of the month, he was bedridden and incapable of moving about. Dasha hated to see him in such a way. He'd always been so strong, but now he could hardly eat.

She looked down at the tray of food in her hand. On it was an array of broths and biscuits, fresh from the kitchens. She'd picked it up only a moment before and carried it now into the room where her parents rested.

She and her mother had been advised to distance themselves from the king so as not to catch the illness themselves, and Dasha tried her best to do so, but her mother dismissed the notion. Gods be damned if they kept her from her husband. Not even Dasha could stop her from visiting him. Even now, she sat in a chair beside him, holding his hand in her slumber.

Looking at their interlocking hands, Dasha noticed something off. Her heart skipped a beat, and cruel realization settled in. His fingers were stiff and seemed almost transparent. The discoloration had been common in recent days due to the illness' tendency to slowly kill the pigmentation in one's skin, but something was different now. An unsettling aura radiated off him, and he lay eerily still.

"Mother..." Dasha said, worry cracking her voice. His face was ghostly white, and his features looked as if they'd been chiseled from stone. "Mother!" she screamed. The Medic ran into the room at the sound of her shout, a Necromancer trailing behind.

Her mother's eyes flew open, startled into waking. The look of confusion on her face suddenly morphed into a deep horror when she looked towards her husband. She leapt to her feet, eyes wide and mouth agape, tearing her hand from his hold. "No," she whispered. It was a silent cry, a mournful kind that came with crippling pain, one that echoed in Dasha's own soul. "No," she repeated, as if it would make his death untrue. "Wake up. Please, wake up." Tears streamed from her eyes, leaving lines like rivers down the terrain of her skin.

Dasha dropped to her knees, wanting to wipe away her mother's tears and comfort her, but despair and shock held her frozen in place. The tray she once held lay on the floor with its contents strewn around her, steaming soup spilling into the wooden boards.

Through waterlogged eyes, she watched the Medic cross the room to her father, trying numerous things to revive him, but the attempts were in vain.

With one last apologetic glance to Dasha and her mother, the Medic stepped aside so the Necromancer could prepare the king's soul for the journey to the underworld.

The door slowly pressed open, and a guard stepped inside to inquire over the commotion. Dasha hardly paid him any mind, lost to her own thoughts of grieving, but his presence comforted her. She knew he'd bring others to the scene, and when they came, she wouldn't feel quite so alone. Her mother had the Medic's aid, but Dasha had been left with only her sorrows.

Several minutes passed before the other guards arrived, and she was summoned back to the harsh truth of reality by the clanging of the metal tray she'd dropped a moment before. One of the guards had taken to collecting the contents of it from the floor. He set the stack of bowls and cups aside and waved down another guard that'd entered with fresh food and drink.

"Are you okay?" asked a voice from behind her. Dasha turned her head, eyes locking with those of the squire boy, Prince. She couldn't find an answer in her grief, but the tears that welled in her eyes told plenty.

Warm cloth touched her skin. He'd wrapped something around her shoulders. Familiarity of the action drew recognition to her mind. Draped around her body was the same cloak he'd given her the month before when she'd left the castle to study in the city.

"Something's coming," he whispered, handing her a cup of water from the tray the guard had carried in. "Trust nothing."

Dasha looked cautiously down at the liquid in her cup, wondering if Prince had meant for her not to drink it. She held the cup tightly in her hand, finding comfort in the simplicity of holding something. Her eyes danced around the room, trying to foresee what was coming.

In the corner, her mother sat with a similar cup, lifting it to her lips to drink. Dasha opened her mouth to protest, but her mother had already taken a sip before she could. Nothing seemed to come of it, so Dasha figured she'd mistaken Prince's warning. The moment she dared to think it safe, however, her mother began to choke. The queen's face turned purple, and tears of blood ran from her eyes.

White foam sputtered from her lips, and she slumped against the wall, life expelled from her being. Dasha cried out but was hushed by the squire beside her. She watched, horrified, as the Necromancer reached down, adding her mother's name to his prayers, sending both of her parents to Odemus.

When he'd finished, his eyes opened, and he locked his gaze with Dasha. "Go," he mouthed, but Dasha didn't think he was talking only to her.

A tight grip clamped around her arm and dragged her to her feet, and the Necromancer stood to join the Medic's side. It all happened so fast. The two guards whom she'd thought meant safety pulled objects from their side that Dasha had never seen before, though she knew it was nothing good.

The last thing she saw before Prince pulled her from the room was the interlocking hands of the servants to life and death. They faced the mutinous guards together with an unyielding defiance.

Two thunderous cracks echoed from the room. Dasha wondered if it had been the gods punishing the traitors, but the panic in the eyes of her companion said otherwise. She stumbled, tripping over herself in attempt to keep up with Prince as he ran.

The two guards burst suddenly from the room, each holding the thunder-producing objects. Dasha and Prince dove around the corner to avoid the small projectiles the weapons flung, and a deafening crack echoed through the halls every time they let one loose.

Prince pulled one of the weapons from a leather pouch that hung at his side. He pointed it at one of the pursuers and pressed on a small lever. *Crack!* One of the guards fell with a small hole in his chest, his chain mail turning crimson at the impact point.

The other guard fired back, and seconds after the shots, a burning rod sliced through Dasha's flesh. No flames were present, but Dasha could feel the searing heat raging across her arm. Two more cracks, and the guard was killed, but the fire was spreading. This time the flames licked at her thigh.

Prince picked one of the weapons up from the floor and handed it to Dasha after reloading it. "Keep this. There will be more guards at the gate," he said, then he tore off two strips of cloth from his shirt and handed one to her. "Tie that around your leg to stop the bleeding. I'll tie up your arm. Make sure it's tight. Once we get out of here we'll need to split up. Kaburem will be looking for the pair of us if word gets out that you're alive. It'll be harder for them to find you if we're separated," he said.

"Kaburem?" Dasha asked, seeking recollection of the name.

"I'll explain once we're safe," he said, securing the cloth tie around her arm.

Once satisfied with her bindings, Prince continued towards one of the lesser known exits. It was one mostly used for water collection. Dasha followed, limping close at his heels. He propped the door to the path slightly open, peaking around the corner for more guards.

"There's two men at the gate. They don't know I've turned on them yet, so I'll distract them while you hide." He placed the handle of the weapon he'd given her into the palm of her hand, pressing her index finger to the lever. "Point the barrel," he said, gesturing towards the hole at the end, "at the guard on the left. When I whistle, pull the trigger." He demonstrated with his weapon, not fully pulling the lever so as not to set it off.

"What will you be doing in that time?" Dasha asked.

"Praying that you hit your target," he said.

In any other situation, it'd have been a humorous response, but at present, Dasha felt nothing but dread. "What if I don't?" she asked.

"Then, we both die." With that decided, he walked out.

Dasha stayed behind the door and waited for her chance to leave. The two guardsmen met him in the center, and he continued walking. The guards turned their backs to the doorway she was in, gazes following Prince's path. She slipped out from behind the door, desperately searching for something closer to hide behind.

A small ditch followed the side of the path, so she dove into it, dead leaves and twigs snapping under her weight. One of the guards spun and drew his sword at the sound, but Dasha was well concealed. she propped up the weapon and aimed it at the approaching guard.

"Who's there?" the guard asked, and Prince shifted to stand in front of the other man, then he gave a piercing whistle.

Dasha pressed down on the lever, and thunder ripped through the air, leaving her ears ringing. The ball shot from the weapon and struck the left-hand guard in the stomach. He fell to his knees, clutching the wound, shock in his eyes.

Prince was now behind the other guard. He had a small blade pressed against the guard's throat. Blood trickled down his neck at the pressure of the blade, flowing more when it dragged across his skin. Within moments both guards were lifeless.

Dasha stood up and returned to Prince's side, hands trembling. He took her arm and pulled her through the gates. "Hide your weapon," he said, sliding his own back into the leather pouch attached to his side. Dasha did as he asked and attempted to conceal the weapon beneath her cloak. "We need a place with no eyes or ears," he said when they'd reached the bottom of the hill where the city began. "Know anywhere like that?"

She pointed up to the rooftops where she'd once sat to watch the citizens; where she'd once met Patch. She hoped he was alive.

They scaled a ladder and found a seat above a Merchant selling beads and jewelry. The adrenaline was beginning to fade, and questions flooded Dasha's mind, buried under the heavy weight of grief.

The boy held a finger to his lips, silencing her before she could say anything. "A lot just happened, and I promise it will all be explained. Just please, let me tell it from the start," he said quietly. "I was on my way to the kitchens last week to get your father some food. Two men grabbed me and pulled me into a vacant room. I didn't recognize them, but I recognized those around me. All of them were guards or other staff I'd seen about the castle, including the three that lay dead on the floor. The two men held these *things* in their hands." He lifted his weapon from its pouch. "They called them guns. They're vile things, and very lethal, as you've witnessed.

"The men were citizens of a country called Kaburem. It was discovered by one of our Naval ships. The ship was overrun by the inhabitants of this strange land and sailed back to Alyria.

"According to the survivors of the ship, Kaburem has power much greater than this," Prince looked down at his gun. "They brought these guns with them and slipped into the castle during the night, demanding that we yield to them. Those who opposed were killed. They overpowered us. We were forced to submit."

"You joined them?" she asked, disgusted at the prospect of him being on their side.

"I had no choice," he said, eyes begging forgiveness.

"You could have gone down fighting."

"Then we'd both be dead, and where would that get us? No, I had to join them. That was the only way I could get you out. I planned to save all of you, but when your father died, plans were uprooted. They seized the opportunity of it, attacked too early.

"One day, we'll have our chance to stand up against these foreigners, but now isn't that time. Now is the time to hang low, gather our strength, and wait for the right moment. When that day comes, I'll always be loyal to you and your family. Your father took me in when I had nothing left. Until that day though, we should part ways."

He took his dagger to her hair, and chopped a few inches off the ends. "Your name is Tempest now. You're an orphan girl trying to find a home. If you can find a place out of the city to hide, that would be best. Dasha was killed in the castle alongside her parents," he said. He seemed to have thought this through, so she listened, soaking in the life that she knew would now be hers.

"What will you do?" she asked. "How will you hide after the guards know you turned on them?"

"Anyone who saw didn't live long enough to tell the tale," he said. "I have two identities now. One, a member of Kaburem." He held up his hand to show a bloodstone ring resting on his finger where the metal band that had marked him as a child once sat. "And I can be a commoner when I want to be," he said, pulling out the ring of a child. You, however, must make a new identity for yourself. Learn what the common folk learn, join a guild, make your own family. When it's time for your return, I'll be waiting."

"How will I know it's time?" Her voice rose in pitch, heart suddenly afraid. "What if it's never time?" She frowned. Her father had believed in her, but he was no longer here.

"You'll know, and when the opportunity comes, you must take it. If you miss your chance, it will never come again." He held out a pouch of powder packets and lead balls, then with careful instruction, he taught her how to load and prime the gun. When he finished, he descended from the roof and disappeared into the streets.

Tempest stayed perched atop the building and watched the people pass below. The city was slowly beginning to wake. Children ran about, playing in the crisp morning air. The markets were setting up shop, and customers flowed through the streets, going about whatever business they had. No one knew what world they'd woken into, no one but Dasha and the person she was to become.

She sat down on the edge of the building and tucked her knees to her chest. Cold air numbed her senses, and she retreated into herself. The pain of loss settled in her chest like a stone. Her thoughts were soon interrupted, though, when another boy sat beside her. *Patch*.

"What brings you back to the rooftops so soon, princess?" he asked, but Tempest pulled up her hood and gave no response. "You may have cut your hair, but a girl sitting on the roof in a dark cloak with a face as striking as yours, it's impossible to mistake, Dasha,"

She would have smiled if she could and thanked him for the kind words, but she couldn't bring herself to do so.

"Who's Dasha?" she asked with a quavering voice.

"As far as I know, you are... unless you've forgotten your name again." His lip twitched upward, humored by the thought. She wished she could join in on his amusement. She wished this was all a game.

"Dasha is dead," she said more confidently. "My name is Tempest now."

"Ah, I must admit, that's unfortunate to hear. I quite liked Dasha. What warranted the change? Why call yourself Tempest?"

She thought for a second on his question, then replied, pulling her hood back down. "Because a storm is coming."

5

A troop of men and women marched down the street. Unfamiliar faces with unfamiliar clothes. Each had a gun resting at their hips, and each bore the bloodstone rings of Kaburem. The man that led the procession stopped the group, slid out his gun, aimed it to the sky, and pulled the trigger. Its echo made the heads of all who were in the area turn to the sound.

Tempest ducked behind a nearby chimney, dragging a disgruntled Patch along. She lifted her finger to her lip and begged him to keep silent. Down below, the Kaburem group leader began to speak.

"Now that I have everyone's attention," the man said, voice thick with an accent Tempest had never heard. "We have arrived on your shores at a grievous time, and thus must come to you with tragic news." He paused, waiting for absolute silence, then he began once more. "The Royal family is dead."

A soft murmur washed over the crowd, and the man lifted his hand to silence them. "Quiet please!" he said. "Your king and his daughter fell ill, and your god of death claimed them both. In her grief, your queen took her own life to join them. There was nothing that could be done."

"Lies!" Tempest hissed.

"Spread the word of this tragedy and let it be known that a new king sits the throne," said the man, then he continued down the street to deliver the news further on.

Patch looked down at Tempest with pity. "It's true, then, isn't it? Dasha is dead, but Tempest is born. A storm is coming, indeed."

Tempest nodded, bracing herself against the side of the chimney. Her head spun, and her leg throbbed with a terrible pain. She reached down and touched the bandaged wound, hand coming up coated red with blood. Splotches formed in her vision, accompanied by a deep ringing in her ears, and she cursed beneath her breath, legs growing weak. "I don't feel well," she muttered.

Patch moved quickly, scooping her into his arms just before she surrendered herself to the void of faintness. It felt like she was drifting through a dream, floating in some deep abyss for only a moment of time.

When she woke again, she found herself in a dark and foreign place.

Slowly, she recollected her thoughts, and the memory of the previous events returned to her mind. She dared to hope it'd all been a dream. Perhaps if she just kept her eyes closed, the nightmare would go away. She knew that wasn't true, though. Her eyes fluttered open, and her senses worked avidly to make sense of her surroundings.

She could hear voices in the distance, and she seemed to be lying in a feather bed piled high with furs. Just above her was a window, sunlight blocked from entering by a dark cloth.

"Hello?" she asked, voice unable to raise above a whisper. When no one gave response, she decided to take matters into her own hands. She moved in small, laborious increments, but eventually, she managed to sit up and dangle her legs off the edge of the bed.

The room was empty except for the bed she lay on and a small fireplace across the room. The voices she'd heard came from behind the door, masked by the crackling of the flames. She couldn't hear what they said, but she could tell that one was a woman's voice, and the other was Patch's.

After numerous attempts, she managed to pull herself to her feet, and she took a precarious step. To her dismay, her legs buckled, and she fell once again to the floor, groaning in agitation. The door opened, and footsteps approached, Patch's face looming overhead. "Welcome back," he said, holding out his hand to assist her. "Best not to try walking yet. Liz sedated you for the surgery."

"How pleasant," said Tempest, using Patch's aid to pull herself to her feet. "Who's Liz?"

The answer stood in the doorway, watching with careful eyes. The woman seemed kind but looked also to be a person who'd never let anything get in her way. She lifted her hand, showing the amber ring of the Medic's guild on her finger.

"Patch has told me everything he could," said Liz, "but I need you to fill in further detail. I already know who you are, so I ask there to be no secrets between us. I'm here to help you, Tempest."

With a deep breath, Tempest turned her gaze and gave Patch a fearsome glare. She hadn't permitted him to drop her identity so freely, but there was nothing to be done about it now. Besides, Liz had used her pseudonym instead of her real name, so there was at least the promise of secrecy. She looked between the two of them and nodded. "It's a bit of an odd story," she admitted. "I'm not even certain I know the entirety of it."

"Tell us what you can," said Patch, helping her to a seat on the edge of the bed.

"I suppose I ought to start from the last day I saw you," she said. "That was the day I found out my father was ill." Her gaze fell to her hands. She could think better when there were no eyes to meet.

Over the next half hour, she told them everything that'd happened from that day onward. She told them of her father's death and her sudden rushed escape. She told them of Prince, and she told them of the guns. When she got to that part, Patch pulled out the gun Prince had given her and set it on a nearby table.

"We found it attached to you just before the surgery," said Patch. "I remembered seeing the foreigners carry something similar and figured it must be the same." A nervous smile touched his lips. "After some experimenting, we knew enough about it to know it'd caused your injuries."

"Can you tell us anything about the people?" Liz asked. "Do you know who they are?"

"I only know what I've been told," Tempest said. "They boarded one of our Naval ships that'd been sent out to explore the waters. The ship must have found land and docked on unfriendly shores. The foreigners that took it call their nation Kaburem, and it is apparently quite a powerful place."

"Have you seen their newly appointed king?" asked Patch.

"Not yet."

"Good. That means he likely hasn't seen you either," said Liz "They'll find out you've escaped as soon as your body isn't found, though. You'd do well to leave the city while you still can."

"Where would I go?" Tempest asked. She had no one left in the world but Prince and the people in this room.

"Anywhere," said Liz. "You ought to join a guild, hide in plain sight. Have you given much thought to enlisting?"

"Quite a bit, but I've never really dwelled on it. You don't have a choice when you're a Royal. I never expected that I'd be faced with one."

"Well, now's your chance," Liz said. "If you could join any guild, which one would you go to?"

Tempest didn't have to give it much thought. "The Dragon Keepers," she said confidently, remembering Sagua and her dragon. The day she'd met the guild leaders had been one she'd remember fondly for many years to come. They'd each been so kind to her, but Sagua had tapped into something rarer than kindness. She'd sparked Tempest's passion, and the Blacksmith had fueled it with his gift of the dragon hilted blade.

"Could you do me a favor?" she asked Patch, and he nodded hesitantly. "I was introduced to the guild leaders before my father passed. Some of them gave me gifts, and I don't want to lose them. They're memories, some of the last ones I have. Would you be willing to go to the castle and ask Prince to find them? I'd go myself, but I'd be recognized. The objects are all by my bedside. It's just a few things: the book of the gods, a dagger, and my notebook."

"You met the guild leaders?" he asked, hung up on the first sentence she'd spoken. There was sudden worry in his eyes, and Tempest feared it meant he'd refuse her request. "What if they recognize you and turn you in? You can't possibly join a guild!"

"She can still join, Patch," said Liz. "Don't worry. It's a large world out there. I've been a Medic for a decade now and have only seen the guild leader a few times. Tempest will be safe."

"What of my things? Can they be safely obtained; do you think?" That was all Tempest wanted in this moment, not them worrying about who might see her once she'd fled.

"How would I get to Prince?" Patch asked "They'll wonder what my business with him is. I'd need an alibi." He paused. "Is it even worth the risk? How can Dasha ever die if you never let her go?"

He made a valid point, but she wanted those memories, so she pushed on. Something drove her to demand success in this. They weren't incredibly valuable items, but to her they meant home. To her, they meant a life that was whole.

"Tell the guards he's a distant cousin of yours. A family member has passed away, and you wished to deliver the news personally. I understand that I need to let go, but I can't fully release my past… All storms must come to an end eventually. I'd like to have bits of myself left when this one is gone."

"What if they found out he helped you? He won't be there, and I'll walk into a trap."

"If he was caught, then he's either wandering the city as a commoner, or he's dead. My things will never return to me, and I'll be in greater danger than we thought. If he was caught, they already know I'm alive. Please, Patch, I beg of you. They're all I have left."

There was doubt in his eyes, but his denial never left his lips. "If it's truly that important to you, I'll go."

Tempest wanted to fling her arms around him in gratitude, but she settled with a reserved, "Thank you."

"As soon as he returns you must be off," said Liz. "I suggest you go to Firethorne. It's the Dragon Keeper city. It'll be easy for you to blend there. When you come of age, join the guild. Patch can escort you there, so you won't have to travel alone."

"I can?" Patch asked, taken by surprise. "What about the—"

"I'll manage well enough without you for a bit," said Liz. "Tempest needs you more."

He bowed his head, accepting. "We'll leave tomorrow, then. I'll send word to Prince tonight to warn him of my coming. With luck, I'll be able to get your things before we go."

A warm smile spread across Tempest's lips. It was the first time since the events of the morning that she'd felt any sort of joy. The first time, also, that she'd felt hope.

"Now," said Patch. "If I may excuse myself, I best notify your friend."

"Make it quick. You both need rest," said Liz. "You've got a long journey ahead."

"That we do," said Tempest. "Good night."

Patch retired through the door, but Liz lingered for a moment, head turned to watch Patch until he was gone. Once they were alone, she placed her hand on Tempest's shoulder.

"Something to keep in mind," she said. "Morning marks the first of Izasel, goddess of spring. After her, Ides will claim the immortal throne and hand it back to life. A new life is beginning for you, Tempest, and it is for him too. Choose the paths you take wisely."

~~~

Dreams typically evaded Tempest in the night, but occasionally one would come that stayed vivid in her mind, even upon waking. This had been one of those dreams. She could still see it play out in her mind's eye over and over again. It started in her parent's bed chamber with her father lying dead in the bed. On the floor beside him was her mother, poison chalice pressed against her lips.

No matter what Tempest tried, her mother still drank the poison, and when the cup fell, it landed with the jolting crack of a gun, shot by a guard with dead eyes who stood over the bodies of the Necromancer and Medic. The guard lifted the gun towards her and fired once again, but it was not her who suffered the wound. Instead, the guard morphed into another, clutching his stomach after having been shot by Tempest. Behind this man stood a young boy and his mother, weeping in each other's arms.

It was their cries that stayed with Tempest most prominently. A chilled realization came with its sound. She'd not been the only one to lose family that day.

Her palms were cold with sweat, and the dark room around her felt as though it were closing in. She didn't know the hour, but she had no intentions of returning to sleep if all it would hold were images of the dead.

She untangled herself from the furs and stood, hoping to find peace in the exploration of the halls. She'd yet to leave this little room and wanted to know what else was here.

Upon exit, she found herself in another, slightly larger room. Liz lay asleep in one of two beds that sat on either side of it. Hot embers remained in the fireplace, and moonlight seeped through the windows. Other than that, no light touched the room. Everything was dark and made of shadows.

A silhouette shifted in front of a doorway across the room. There was a person sat, leaning against it. "Tempest?" Patch asked in a whisper.

Tempest made a sound of affirmation and moved towards him with care. He scooted to the side, making room for her to sit beside him.

"Couldn't sleep?" he asked.

"No," she said, laying her head back against the door. "You?"

Patch shook his head. "What's keeping you up?"

"Bad dreams."

"What of? If you don't mind my asking."

"The dead," she answered truthfully. "First of my parents dying... then of the Medic and Necromancer who helped my father, then of the man I killed. He had a family, Patch. I killed a boy's father." A tear rolled down her cheek, and she wiped it away with her sleeve.

"Have you met his family before?" Patch asked.

"No," said Tempest.

"Did he ever speak of his family?"

"I'd never met him before... I don't know," she admitted.

"Perhaps he had no family and these people were just figments of your dreams."

"But what if he did..." she said, voice trailing. "Even if he didn't, that doesn't justify what I've done. I still killed a man. What else lay ahead of him that he will never experience because I simply pulled a trigger? How is it right for a man to die from so easy an action?"

"It is never easy to end a life," said Patch. "At least it shouldn't be. Every life is as important as another, and the faces of the dead will haunt you for quite some time, but they remind you that you're still human. Once you can kill with ease of heart as well as ease of action, you've lost every last trace of humanity within."

"Have you seen it happen before?"

"I'm told my father was such a man," he said, "but the dead haunt me too. I've seen more death this month helping Liz at the hospital than I could ever wish to see in a lifetime."

"Do they linger in your dreams too?" Tempest asked.

"Most every night," he replied. "None of these deaths were caused by my hand, but I can never forget their lifeless faces. Maybe I could have done something different and saved them."

"Is that what's keeping you up tonight?" Tempest asked.

"Perhaps it will if I ever allow myself to sleep. I'd rather not see the faces tonight. As of now, there are other things haunting my mind." His voice was wary, uncertain.

"What things?"

"Fear of what lies ahead," said Patch. "I finally found a place I belong, but now it's all going to change. What am I going to do if this king takes it all away?"

There was something in his eyes that made Tempest's heart ache for him. It was a mixture of fear and vulnerability he rarely showed voluntarily. She looked into his eyes, really looked, and shared the burden on his shoulders.

"He took everything from me," she said. "Everything but hope. Hope is something we can't forget in times like these. Whether it be a small spark or a raging fire, latch onto it, and never let it go. Without hope, we can never expect to get through this."

He relaxed a bit, closing his eyes from the world so all he needed to focus on were his words. "Forgive me... I forgot myself and who I spoke to. He's taken all you've ever known or loved. My complaints must seem melodramatic."

"Don't be sorry," said Tempest. "You have every right to be upset. But, we've dwelled enough on uncertainties, I think. Will you tell me about this place? I've been wondering how you ended up here."

Patch stood and held out his hand. "Come with me," he said. "Let me show you."

6

*T*empest took Patch's hand, and he helped her to her feet, opening the door behind them. They were exposed to a long hall, crowded with beds and pallets. Men, women, and children lay within these beds, all showing signs of illness. Some looked as if they were recovering, but most seemed barely alive. Their eyes were hollow, and coughing echoed through the hall.

Tempest followed Patch past bed after bed, each one labeled with a name. *Janus, Kat, Parthena, Cypher,* she read them each to herself, then Patch stopped, and Tempest read the tag on the empty bed in front of him. It bore his name, not yet repurposed for another patient. She slowly looked up to him, and he began to speak.

"A few days after you left for the castle, I fell to the Touch of Wynris. I thought for sure I was going to die. I'd given up hope and found a spot in an alley to ride out the rest of my days." He paused, remembering. "That's when Liz found me. She took me in and nursed me back to life. She gave me hope that maybe, just maybe, things would be okay.

"Once I had fully recovered, Liz taught me her trade. She knew I had nowhere to go, and she needed an extra hand at the hospital during the season. I've been training to be a Medic since."

A smile curved Tempest's lips. She was happy for him. "Will you join the guild?" she asked.

"I plan to," he said, and the pair started back to the door, not wanting to disturb the ill while they slept.

Liz stirred in her sleep when they entered the room, waking to the sound of the door closing behind them. "Where have you two been?" she asked, voice groggy.

"In the hospital," Patch said. "I was filling Tempest in on what's happened over the past month."

Liz shook her head. "You'll have all day tomorrow to do that, but you won't have time to sleep. Get some now."

"I'd rather not sleep," said Tempest. "Sleep brings things I don't want to live through again."

"I understand," Liz said, and by the look in her eyes, Tempest knew she truly did. "Come on, then. You can share my bed. That should take the terrors somewhat away. Just close your eyes and don't open them again till morning. Sleep will inevitably come. If the dreams return, remember that's all they are. Dreams, not reality."

"They were reality not too long ago," said Tempest.

"It'll haunt you for many days to come if you let it," Liz said, patting the foot of her bed. "Against all our wishes to do so, we can't change the past. The sooner you accept that, the better. What you can do, however, is change the way it affects you. You *must* keep moving. Learn from the past and keep going. Never let it control you. I need both of you well rested for tomorrow's journey, so please, sleep."

Tempest curled up on the edge of Liz's bed, and Patch returned to his own. She closed her eyes and allowed herself to fall prey to sleep. Luckily, no more dreams came in the night.

~~~

Tempest woke to Liz tapping her on the shoulder. She had collected a trunk of clothing from a closet in the corner, assuring Tempest the items wouldn't be missed. According to Liz, they'd belonged to her daughter, and her daughter had left on a Naval mission and never came back. Tempest gratefully took the items and changed into a pair of black riding pants, a white shirt, and her cloak. The rest, she stored in a pack.

In about an hour, there was a rasp at the door, and Patch stepped in with a messenger bag strapped to his side. He opened the bag and displayed the contents for Tempest to see. Inside was everything she had asked for.

She thanked him repetitively as he passed the bag to her. She hadn't really expected him to succeed, but she was glad he had. "I have one more thing to give you," he said before she turned to stow the items away, "They say a new king sits the throne. That means they have no need for a queen's ring. This belongs to you." He took her hand and slid the amethyst ring onto her finger.

Tempest stood in silence, not trusting herself to speak. A tear slowly crept down her cheek. "A little something to remind you of who you are whenever you find yourself wanting to forget," he said, and she smiled, mouthing a thanks. "Ready to leave?"

"Not with that on her finger!" Liz exclaimed. "Come here."

Tempest whined but obliged nonetheless, unsure what was to happen to the ring. Liz pulled a thin, chain necklace from her jewelry box and held out her hand for the ring. Reluctantly, Tempest gave it to her, and Liz slid it onto the chain, then clasped the hook around Tempest's neck.

Tempest tucked the ring under her shirt, relieved. "There, now it's hidden," said Liz. "You best get going. Take this for the journey." She handed Tempest a small pouch of coins. "It isn't much, but it's all I can spare. I hope our paths cross again someday."

"As do I," said Tempest. "Thank you for everything. I'm indebted to you,"

She grabbed her things and followed Patch to the stables, watching as he saddled the two horses. Once secure, he helped her mount the smaller of the beasts. She took the reins awkwardly, not confident in her ability to ride. No one had ever taught her. She'd only ever ridden with her father. She gave the reins a little tug to see if that would get the creature moving, but the horse whickered in annoyance, shaking its black mane.

Patch chuckled. "First time?" he asked, and Tempest nodded. "Get her walking by gently pressing your heels into her sides. Use the reins to guide her. You'll want to be careful, though. She seems a stubborn mare."

Tempest dug her heels, and the horse took off, much faster than she'd intended. It galloped down the road completely out of her control.

"Tempest!" Patch shouted, leaping onto his horse to ride after her.

The mare bucked its head and threw Tempest off balance. She reached for its neck, desperate to find something to latch on to, but there was nothing. Next she knew, she was on the ground, breath struck from her lungs.

With a groan, she sat up, gasping and coughing. Half melted snow seeped through her clothes, setting a chill through her body. She looked around for Patch and found him holding the reins of her horse, trotting back towards her with a grin plastered to his face. "Shall we try this again?"

"No," Tempest muttered, but she stood regardless. "I'm done with horses."

"You want to train dragons, but you fear to ride a horse? That doesn't make much sense, does it?"

"I'm not *afraid*. It just doesn't like me." She brushed the dirt from her cloak and took the reins from Patch's hand.

"That's because it has to get used to you first. Come on, we should get out of here. We've drawn too much attention."

Patch helped her back onto her horse and tied its reins to his own. At his lead, the pair of them continued down the road. Up ahead, the city wall grew larger, looming above them in challenge.

Three guards rode forth to meet them just before they reached the gate. "I need names and cause for leaving," said one with the bloodstone ring of the foreigners on his finger. No accent thickened his words, though, so Tempest assumed he was from Alyria. The other two bore the sapphire rings of the Law Enforcement.

Tempest waited for Patch to give answer, but he just stared back at the guards, seemingly lost in the fear of failure. There was no time for hesitation, though, so Tempest answered for him. "We're off to Vulcan," she said. "My brother here wishes to be a Blacksmith like our father and his father before him. His enlistment is next month."

"Why are you taking him? Where is your father, lad?"

Patch opened his mouth, but words stayed frozen in his throat, so Tempest answered again. "He was claimed by Wynris, as was Mother, but many years ago. I'm the only family he's got left."

"Can the boy not speak for himself?" asked the man. "I believe *he* was the one I asked, not you."

"Ask all you want, sir, but you won't ever get a response," said Tempest, throwing out answers on a whim. She hoped he wouldn't pry. "My brother was born mute. He sometimes speaks with gestures, but he doesn't like to do so in the company of strangers. He's a mighty hard worker, though. You can trust me on that."

"I apologize, miss, but orders are orders," said the Kaburem guard. He seemed a forgiving sort, and Tempest knew he'd have let her through on any other grounds, but he would not be wanting to disobey the orders of a new king. "No one leaves the city," he said. "Not until later at least. There's a ceremony being held at the temple tonight as a remembrance of the fallen Royal family. Everyone is required to attend."

"We'll leave later, then," said Tempest. "Forgive me, but I couldn't help but to notice your ring, sir. It's the same stone the foreigners wear, but you don't sound like them. I was curious how you knew the king. How long have you been in his service?"

She probably should have kept her curiosities to herself, but the guard didn't seem to mind her asking. Though, Patch seemed to mind a great deal. She could feel his eyes boring through her, even without looking.

"I joined him after he arrived, so I don't know him too well yet," the guard admitted.

"Is he a good king?" she asked. The more she could learn about the new king, the better. Patch slouched in his seat and shook his head. He couldn't do much to stop her without breaking character.

"The only thing I cared to learn before joining up with him was that he's a dangerous king," said the guard. "I chose to serve him because I value my life, not the quality of his rule. If you ask me, I think everyone should do the same."

"We'll take that into consideration. Thank you." She coiled the reins in her hands and leaned forward. "Do you know what'll happen to our titles? Will we have to abandon them as you have, or will the king allow us to keep our guilds?"

"As of now, it's a choice," he said. "But, I feel that in the end, we will all bear the bloodstone rings, or we ourselves will paint the stones in blood, if you get my meaning." He spoke with a grandeur that Tempest found humorous, but his point struck all the same. "I made my decision early. These two lads think I'm being paranoid, which is why they've kept the sapphire. They seem to like this new king and believe he'll allow us to keep our guilds and way of life. They ask, what king would force his people to leave everything they've ever known? No just king, that's for sure. But what's to say he's just?"

"I suppose we'll see," said Tempest. "Before my brother and I leave, may we ask you to advise us on one more bit? Could you direct us to the nearest inn?"

He laughed at the sudden change of topic. "Of course. Follow me." He spurred his palfrey and led them down the road to a battered inn. "This here is the piss-water inn. Or, at least that's what the small folk call it. No one can quite recall what its true name is. It's been changed too many times. Got its new name from the taste of the ale, though. I don't recommend you try it. It's not a pretty place, but it's a roof over your head."

"It'll serve for the night. I'd pay you a coin for gratitude, but we don't have the coin to spare."

"No coin needed. Consider it a favor to be paid back later. I'm certain we'll meet again."

"Thank you greatly, sir," said Tempest, though she hoped he was wrong about their reunion.

When the guard departed, Tempest and Patch dismounted and led the horses to the stables. The stable boy took the horses and tied them up. He couldn't have been more than ten years of age, but he handled the creatures well. "How long?" he asked.

"Just the night," said Patch.

At the sound of his voice, Tempest feigned surprise. "It's a miracle! The mute boy speaks!"

"I'm sorry, Tempest... we were so close, and something felt wrong. I didn't think we were going to make it out, so I panicked. Turns out I was right in my thinking. We're stuck."

"It's only a delay," said Tempest. "Besides, I've found us an inn. No better place to dig up information than here. We'll be out first thing in the morning. Maybe by then the rest of the snow will be melted, and we'll be able to make up for lost time."

Patch shrugged, then pushed the doors ajar for Tempest to walk through. A fire warmed the space from the back of the room, though the crowd and the ale did just as much, if not more than the fire could. The air was heavy and hot from the mass of people filtering through. Tempest disliked the feel of it.

From beside the fire, she could hear the soft telling of a tale about the Dark Mage that had ruled the land hundreds of years ago. The Mage had thrived in the practice of black magic and would kill relentlessly. Tempest had heard the story at feasts in her youth. It was an old tale, but children always loved it. Even now, a group of children sat around the singer with locked gazes, awe inspired by his words.

Tables were mostly grouped by guild. A table of Blacksmiths laughed boldly at a joke one of their members had told. Next to them was a table of Medics, celebrating the end of Odemus' reign. Soldiers occupied the table to the left of the Medics, sharing tales and memories of training. The remaining tables represented a mixture of guilds, all here as solitary wanderers.

Patch pointed to a woman who strolled between each of the tables, picking conversation with people she seemed to know. Seeing her made Tempest flush. The woman had bright red hair, a shade lighter than Tempest's own, and she stood as tall as most of the men. Most prominent about her, though, was the fact that she wore hardly anything but the iron shackles that were clamped to her wrists and ankles.

"That's Tanith," said Patch. "I met her a few years back. She knows the secrets of the city before anyone else ever does."

"Think she'd know anything about Kaburem?"

"I'm sure we'll find out if we listen long enough. Come on." He grabbed Tempest by the arm and led her to the table Tanith hovered beside.

There was an opening on the bench at the edge of the table, so Tempest and Patch filled it, unnoticed by all but one. "My, my," said Tanith. "Do my eyes deceive me, or is that Patch who's come to join us."

Patch bowed his head. "Pleasure to see you again, Tanith."

"The pleasure is mine," said Tanith. "You came just in time. We need some intelligence about." She gestured to the others at the table. "These fools think the new foreigners are gods."

"That is not what I said!" sputtered a burly Blacksmith near the center. "I only said they're blessed by a god. Witnesses say they can summon thunder from nothing but air."

"I assure you all, no god came with them," said Tanith. "I'm told they're a godless people. Their weapons are just louder than ours, is all."

"Have you already taken one to bed, Tanith?" asked a woman with a siam ring. "They've only just arrived."

"If there's anything I've learned in my profession, it's that all men have desires, no matter where they're from. These men were no different, and they came with coin and secrets to share."

"Did they, now?" asked the Blacksmith. "What secrets did they bring?"

"You know well enough that secrets come at a price," Tanith said with a sneer. "And they're certainly not shared in public places."

"You're no fun," said the Blacksmith with a swig of his ale, and the conversation moved to talk of the winter.

As Tanith passed, Patch held a coin behind his back for her to take. "Follow me," she whispered, and she plucked it from his grasp. "Bring the lady."

Patch waited for her to get well away before he stood to follow, so Tempest watched to see where she was going. Tanith grabbed a key from the inn-keeper, then turned and nodded before she vanished up the stairs. "Come on," said Tempest. "She's gotten a room."

Together, they stood and made their way to the innkeeper, taking a key of their own as they passed. "Upstairs, fifth door to your left," he said.

It was a thin stairwell with room enough for only one person at a time, so Tempest took the lead. At the top, Tanith waited. "This way," she said, leading them to the room her key belonged to. Once inside, she closed and bolted the door. "You'll want to sit for this one," she said, gesturing to a bench by the window.

Tempest took a seat on the bench, and Patch sat beside her. The wood of it was old, and it rocked beneath their weight. "What have you got?" Patch asked, breaking the silence that'd fallen over the room.

Tanith leaned against the wall and crossed her arms. "I'm afraid what I know won't stay secret for long. You know as much as I how people gossip. It's about today's ceremony. The new king plans to use it as a platform for a public execution."

"Whose?" Tempest asked.

"Some boy from the castle," said Tanith. "Charged for thievery, but the man I was with thinks the boy helped the princess escape. Her body wasn't found with her parents."

Tempest's heart sped in her chest, and the only thing she could hear were her slow and panicked breaths. She looked down, eyes fixated on the wooden beams beneath her. The boy Tanith had mentioned could only be Prince. In helping her, she'd condemned him.

"This man told you all this?" asked Patch. "It seems like something they'd want to keep quiet if it were true."

"Men will tell you anything when they're deep in their cups and persuaded by a woman," Tanith said. "I have reason to believe it's true. After all, the evidence of his claim is sitting right beside you."

"That's preposterous!" said Patch, but the lie in his words showed clear on his face.

"Who else knows?" Tempest asked. "How many people have paid for this secret?"

"None but you," said Tanith. "I only baited it so I could give you warning without suspicion. I knew if I was right, you'd not pass up a chance to hear it."

"Thank you," said Patch. "We'll heed the warning."

Tanith nodded. "Best get to your own room, now. They'll come calling for the ceremony soon."

Tempest reached for the ring that hung at her neck, feeling it's smooth curve beneath the cloth of her shirt. It comforted her to know it was there. With a deep breath, she stood and followed Patch back into the hall.

Their room was only a few paces down. Fifth door on the left, just as the innkeeper had promised. Patch unlocked it with the key and pressed open the creaking door. It was a spacious room with minimal furnishings, and at the center was a bed.

Tempest set her bag down and took a seat on the edge of the bed, tears brimming in her eyes. "They have Prince," she muttered. "We have to help him."

"We can't," said Patch.

He hadn't known Prince, but there was sorrow in his words. Whether it was for the squire or for her, Tempest didn't know. "It's my fault," she said. "I should have never asked him to get my things. They must have seen him do it."

"Likely so, but his capture is not your fault," Patch said, crouching down in front of her so that her eyes were forced to meet his. "When I spoke to him, he said he knew he was being watched. He knew they were closing in on him, Tempest, but he decided to do it anyway. One last service to the Royal House, he told me. Whether you'd asked him for it or not, he'd still be standing before the executioner today. That much, I'm sure of."

Tempest let out a choked sob and wiped the tears from her eyes. She hated to cry in front of people, but Patch seemed not to mind, and she could no longer hold it in. "Will you take me to the ceremony?" she asked. "He deserves to have a friend in the crowd."

"If I refused to take you, would you still go?"

"I would."

A soft chuckle rang through his chest. "Perhaps it's for the better. They'll be expecting you to hide. They won't be looking for you in the crowd. We should leave after, though."

"Should we not give it time? Leaving so soon might raise suspicion."

"Maybe, but as I see it, our best option is to continue our false journey to Vulcan before the guards change out and it's no longer believed."

Footsteps moved outside and a man pounded at the door. "Ceremony's starting," said the man, and his footsteps receded.

"We'll leave after, then," said Tempest, rubbing her swollen eyes. "Let's go."

~~~

Tempest and Patch joined the river of people in the streets. The stream of it flowed towards the square at the base of the temple. Children ran through the crowd, shoving through the tangle of legs to claim a viewing spot. Tempest had no idea how many people were here, but the numbers seemed endless.

Twelve massive statues stood guard around the square, each depicting one of the supreme gods. In the middle, an ivory platform stood erect, marking the center of the city. Behind it all loomed the temple of the graces where Tempest had been taken during her lesson only weeks before.

Half an hour passed before the whole city had made their way to the square. The sun beat down on them and warmed the clustered air, but the wind still wielded an icy touch that cooled Tempest in their waiting.

People stood packed together, pressed closer by the Kaburem guards, trying to get everyone in. Children were placed on the shoulders of their guardians for both the view, and to make room for more people. Once the yard was overflowing, the people filed into the buildings that surrounded the space, filling balconies, windows, and rooftops. Tempest was glad for the chaos of it all. She'd go easily unnoticed in a crowd of this size.

When the people were settled, a man stepped onto the platform and sounded a deep horn that echoed off the surrounding walls. A hush grew through the square, and a section of the crowd began to part. Tempest couldn't see the cause, but a few moments later, a young man stepped onto the platform, wielding a banner painted with the likes of a bone crown. Behind him came another, older man, who wore a black cloak with red streaks that pulsed like molten rock when he moved. On his head sat the bone crown the banner showed.

The new king, Tempest realized.

"Alyria," said the horn-blower in the strange accent of the foreigners. "May I introduce you to your new sovereign, King Lazareth."

The king stepped forward and nodded to his announcer. "It pleases me to stand before you all today, though I wish circumstances of my arrival had not been so dreary. I host this ceremony tonight in honor of the deceased Royal family. Bring them forward," he said, gesturing to a pack of soldiers who stood amongst the crowd.

They came forth at his directive, carrying three caskets with a white rose sitting on each. The caskets were set down and opened for the city to see. Tempest's father and mother occupied two of the boxes. The other held a girl of similar age and looks to Tempest. She wondered who the girl had been. Whoever it was, she hadn't deserved this.

"We give you this chance now to look upon the great King Neymar and his beloved family for the final time before they are put to rest."

Tempest's cheeks wetted with tears as she looked at her parents once more. She hadn't thought it possible to cry any more, but sorrow and rage lingered deep within her heart for both her family and the innocent girl they'd killed to keep the world from knowing of her escape.

"We came from a land quite far from here in hopes of making an alliance with your people," said the new king. "When we came, however, Neymar lay on his deathbed. It was his dying wish that I watch over both his family and kingdom upon his parting. Now, I am tragically left with only his kingdom.

"I will do my best to be as great a king as Neymar was," he said, then he paused, face twisting from a thought unspoken. "No, that's wrong. My goal is to be a better king than Neymar, but for me to do this, laws must be obeyed. Neymar may have let it slide, but under my rule, thievery will not be tolerated."

He gestured to a couple guards who'd arrived holding Prince by the arms. He'd been badly beaten, but he kept his head held high. "This boy stole something very valuable to me, and when I demanded its return, he tried to kill me. For this, he will pay with his life."

The king shoved Prince to his knees, and the boy spit at Lazareth's feet. "I stole the princess!" he shouted. "She's alive!"

Murmurs of doubt spread through the people. To unknowing eyes, it would seem impossible. The princess was clearly dead in the box before them, but Tempest stood as proof to his words. She tugged her hood down to hide her face, feeling oddly exposed.

"She will rise again, you'll see," said Prince, and the king pulled out a gun.

Tempest wanted to turn away, wanted to pretend none of it was real, but she couldn't. Prince had given everything up so she could live. The least she could do was give him the honor of seeing him die.

Bang!

The sound jolted through her heart, leaving in its wake an empty pit. Her whole body tremored with despair, but she kept her eyes forward, watching as Prince fell lifeless to the floor.

7

*T*empest felt a hand touch her back, urging her forward in a direction she didn't know. The crowd was moving too, shifting and dispersing. The king had gone, and with him, the guards and the caskets of her parents, but Prince remained, abandoned on the ground with no one to mourn his passing but her.

She wanted to run to his side, take him away and give him a proper burial, but all she could do was keep walking and pray she wasn't caught, pray he died with meaning. She looked back one last time before he vanished from her view, and she saw a Necromancer standing over him, guiding his soul to Odemus.

Once around the corner, Tempest sped her pace, eager to be away from it all. Patch stayed beside her, never parting until they reached the inn's stable. He called for the stable boy and asked him to bring their horses when the boy emerged from within the stalls.

"I thought you wanted the horses taken care of the whole night," the boy said.

"Plans have changed," said Patch, but the boy shook his head.

"I was told a night for the horses, and I expected a night's pay, so a night they will stay." He crossed his arms in stubborn defiance.

"We aren't staying the night," said Patch fists clenched by his side.

Tempest reached into her purse of coins and threw the boy the remaining coppers that Liz had given them. "That should suffice," she said, interrupting the brewing tensions.

The boy looked down at the coins, shifting them around in his hand as he pondered the offer, but eventually, he gave a nod and turned to retrieve their horses.

Tempest mounted hers with greater ease than the last time, and she dug her heels gently into the creature's side, spurring it into motion. Patch followed close behind her, eyes flitting nervously to the gatherings of people still wandering the streets.

To their luck, the same three guards manned the gate, and from what Tempest could tell, they were the only people in the area. "Back so soon?" the Kaburem man asked. "Almost as if you wanted to escape. You wouldn't happen to be this fugitive princess I've been warned about, would you?" His brow lifted in playful curiosity.

Patch drew a dagger from his hip and held it at the ready. Tempest wasn't sure what he intended to do with it, but his meaning was clear enough. They'd be getting through this gate, no matter what.

"Bad idea, boy," said the Kaburem guard, shaking his head as he pulled out his gun. The two other mounted guards drew their swords beside him.

Without hesitation Tempest pulled her gun out and aimed it at the Kaburem soldier, her meaning as clear as Patch's, but the Kaburem man laughed, clicking his tongue with amusement.

"Now where'd you get a pretty thing like that?" he asked. "Foolish child, if I wanted you dead, I would have already killed you." He chuckled and gave a wink, turning his gun to the man beside him. In turn, Tempest shifted hers to the other, mind scrambling to make sense of the situation.

The man she'd aimed towards lifted his blade. "You've been lawfully dethroned, Dasha," he said. "You're a fugitive of the king's. I cannot let you pass."

"I wasn't asking," she said, cocking her gun for emphasis. His loyalty was not with her. That much she knew to be fact.

He spurred his horse forward and swung his blade, but she pulled the trigger before it could land its marking. The man and blade fell from the horse, leaving only a small cut on Tempests arm. *Two.* She counted. Two had died by her hands. The amount that'd died for her was three times as many.

The other guard pleaded for his life at the end of the Kaburem soldier's barrel, but the soldier pulled his trigger anyway.

"You *killed* him!" Tempest yelled, half shocked, half furious.

"Aye, and you killed the other one," he said with a shrug, gathering the reins of the deceased guards' horses. "What's your meaning?"

"This one attacked." She jabbed a finger towards the guard the soldier had killed. "He yielded."

"Dead men can't share secrets."

"By that logic, perhaps I should kill you," said Tempest, turning her gun back to him.

"You'll find I may have value," he said, halting her in her action. "I'm well acquainted in the north. That, and I believe you owe me a favor."

"I'd hardly call it an even trade."

"Which city?" asked Patch

"Ah, finally we have someone who thinks rationally." He turned to face Patch. "I know a great deal of people in Aquius, and you know what that might bring."

"Ships," said Patch. "Let's go, then. We're on our way to Firethorne. You can ride with us till then."

Tempest lowered her gun, fury and helplessness clashing in her mind. She couldn't fathom why Patch trusted him so suddenly, but she supposed none of them had much of a choice. He'd forfeited his position in Kaburem to help them escape, and they were in dire need of assistance.

"I don't suppose you have any coin with you?" he asked, spinning his mount to take the lead.

"Not a sufficient amount," said Tempest, stroking the neck of the horse beneath her. The creatures hadn't taken kindly to the sounds of the guns.

"Pity. Looks like we're sleeping under the stars tonight. We'll sell these horses along the way."

~~~

They rode until the sunset, stopping only when the light was gone. There was a quietness to the forest that comforted Tempest. It sang with the sounds of animals but was untainted by the noises of men. Off the road a bit, they set camp, surrounded by nothing but trees. No one would find them here.

"What should I be calling the two of you?" the soldier asked. "If we're to travel together, we ought to know each other, aye?"

"My name's Patch," Patch said, and the soldier held out his hand in greeting.

"You can call me Tempest. What's your name?"

"I have the honor to be Adrian." He took a slight bow then sat on a rotting log, leaning forward to prepare a fire.

Tempest settled in a small clearing of snow, laying her cloak out to sleep upon. Patch laid opposite her, huddling close to the warm, glowing embers of Adrian's freshly lit fire. Tempest watched the sparks of the flame drift towards the stars, and behind the smoke she caught the eyes of their maker.

"Adrian?" she asked softly. Patch had closed his eyes to sleep, and she didn't want to disturb him. "Why did you help us?"

Adrian's smile gleamed in the light of the fire. "We'd gotten word of your escape the morning you arrived at the gates with that Vulcan tale," he said. "I figured it was you, but I didn't know for sure, and I didn't want anyone else to start guessing either.

"When you came again after the ceremony, that was all the proof I needed." He stuck a twig in the heart of the flame, then pulled it out, watching it flare red in the breeze. "I only joined Kaburem because I thought the Royal family was dead. There would be no recovering from that. It was safer to join the foreigners than to question them, so that's what I did. When you came up alive, it meant there was still hope.

"I follow the person who I think has the best chance of survival, and in the end, though it doesn't look like it now, I think that person is you."

~~~

By morning, a layer of frost coated their surroundings, waking Tempest with its frigid touch. The sun had barely risen, but Adrian was already up and preparing for the day's journey, humming a tune as he worked.

Tempest sat up, shedding the half-frozen blankets from her torso. Her body ached from the cold, and a chill set deep in her bones. She flexed her fingers, trying to get feeling back into them. The blood returned quickly, and an agonizing tingling sensation shot through her nerves.

"Mornin'," said Adrian, repeatedly poking at a rabbit roasting over a freshly made fire.

Tempest's stomach growled at the smell of the cooking meat. Hunger was a pain she'd not been accustomed to, and neither it seemed had Adrian. He poked at the rabbit again, and the roasting creature, having decided it'd suffered enough of his jabbing, fell off the spit and landed in the fire.

Adrian stood up with a frown on his face. "I do believe our breakfast has committed suicide," he said.

"And I believe you were the cause," said Tempest, though the prospect of the rabbit leaping into the flames to avoid torture did seem a bit more amusing. She had to admit, it made for a far more dramatic tale, at least.

"Ah, well." He shrugged and put out the flame. "Time to go."

Adrian walked towards Patch, grabbed the edge of the coat he lay on, and gave it a tug, dumping him flailing into a soft pile of snow. It took him a few moments to gather his bearings, but once he had, he grabbed a handful of snow and chucked it at the soldier. The ball shattered the second it left his hand, crumbling to the frost covered ground.

"Missed." Adrian laughed. "Get up, we're leaving."

"Have we got any food?" Patch asked, brushing the snow from his palms. "I'm starved."

"It sacrificed itself to the almighty fire god, Zalder, to prance and frolic through all eternity," said Adrian, raising his eyes to the heavens for dramatic effect.

Tempest collected what remained of it from the ash and offered it. "It's a bit charred, but it'll do. Someone insisted on playing with their food."

"Well, now you've gone and made it boring," said Adrian.

Within the hour, they were packed and moving forward. They stayed off the road for a time to ensure no Kaburem soldiers were on their trail. Adrian had promised them a shortcut through the woods to get to a road called the Vesuvian, which would then take them to the mountains of Firethorne. He claimed to have lived in an inn beside the road as a child, but according to him, it had gone up in flames many years ago.

It took half an hour to find the Vesuvian road. They'd hoped once they reached it, the going would be smoother and quicker, but Tempest had doubts. The winter goddess still had her fingers laced around parts of the land, and large chunks of the road remained shielded with ice.

Often times, the path would fade to nothingness, covered in rotting branches that'd fallen in the winter storms. At one point, they went half a league without seeing the road. Tempest had the mind to turn back to the city and take the main road instead, but she knew that was impossible. To turn back would be to die. Besides, Adrian kept promising a river would appear soon, and at that river, the road they were on would combine with another, more populated road. From then on, he assured the path would be better taken care of.

Sure enough, within the hour, they reached the promised river. A wooden bridge stretched across the water with a plaque on its side, naming it the Wooden Serpent. The bridge was made up of five arches, joined together by four cobblestone walls that protruded from the water, connecting each arch at its base. Lanterns hung from the sides of each arch to help guide night travelers. It was an old bridge with moss growing between the stones. Tempest enjoyed the look of it.

Adrian had been right about the two roads joining together at the river, but he'd been wrong about the improved quality. Snowmelt turned the road to muck, and the horses struggled through it.

Despite the complications, however, the going was made easier by newfound company. A small caravan joined them shortly after they passed the bridge, hailing from the main road. Their company consisted of two Merchants, man and wife, who sold food produce from the river villages, a Priest who wandered the land, teaching people of the gods, and a drunkard with a Kaburem ring they'd picked up in a tavern on his journey to spread word of the new king.

They were quite the odd band of travelers, and Tempest thought it'd make an interesting tale for the singers to tell one day, but in case no such things occurred, she recorded the events in her notebook to be recollected on a later date when all this faded into distant memory.

Patch bought some food from the Merchant's wagon while Tempest discussed the gods with the Priest, flipping through the pages of her book as they spoke. The Priest had a thick accent. He was from the southern farm-lands of Mirenor, renowned for its beauty. Behind them, Adrian rode with the drunken soldier, singing a song they'd heard in the taverns.

As the sun hit its peak, the caravan parted ways, heading west to the trade city, Laurus.

~~~

It took six days to reach Firethorne, and in that time, it had snowed twice. Once, a light dusting, the second time a decent storm. Tempest had woken that morning draped in a blanket of snow three fingers thick. By afternoon, it'd melted down to a mere portion of that. It was frigid and wet, but she couldn't help but to find a nostalgic joy in its beauty. She recalled the early winter mornings of her childhood when the snow was freshly fallen, untainted by footprints or the sun. It'd muffled out the sounds of the world and looked so pure and soft from her windowsill. This snow was much the same, but the safety and warmth of the castle lay leagues behind her.

Come evening of the second day, the mountain range Firethorne sat in became visible. The height of the mountains and the flatness of the road to get there made the city look deceivingly close, but it took most of another day to reach its slope. On the final night, the colorful lights of the north painted the sky.

Tempest sketched them in her book, in awe with their beauty. They made camp beneath those lights, setting a fire that contrasted the green wisps within the stars. She relished in the wonder of it all, wondering what adventures lay ahead. She could already see the shadows of dragons in the sky, which thrilled her to no end, but to her dismay, Adrian and Patch would make their separate ways in the morning, and Tempest would have to continue alone.

8

$\mathcal{M}$orning came quick to Tempest's disappointment. She wasn't quite ready to say goodbye to her last remaining friends. They'd had a long journey together, but Tempest knew it was nothing compared to what lay ahead.

"I hate to leave you alone," said Adrian, mounting his horse to leave. "But I doubt you'll be alone for long. You've got a kind heart, Tempest. People like that sort of thing."

Tempest took his hand in hers. "I'll be okay," she promised.

"I know you will," he said. "We'll meet again, I'm sure of it." Then he spurred his horse and was off, leaving Patch and Tempest behind. This time, she hoped he was right about their reunion.

"How long do you reckon it takes to get to Aquius?" she asked, turning to Patch, who sat packing his bag.

"I couldn't tell you," said Patch. "But it seems closer than Alyria on the map."

"Will you be all right, journeying back all alone?"

"I'll manage well enough." He stuffed the rest of the provisions in his pack, then buckled it shut, standing to bid her farewell.

"Will I ever see you again?"

"I hope so," he said. "Goodbye, Tempest." He gave a somber smile, then climbed onto his horse, riding off without any further words. It was a simple farewell. Tempest was glad for that. She'd have stopped him from leaving if given the chance.

With a sigh, she took the reins of her horse and began walking up the path to the city of dragons. The earth blackened as she neared it. Dark stone buildings towered over the walls, and dragons soared all around her. At the top, the ornate city gates stood tall, guarded by two massive stone dragons and a man and woman who stood at the base of either.

The woman approached with a dragon following in her steps. "What's a young girl like you doing traveling alone?" she asked, taking the reins from Tempest to help her inside.

"I wasn't alone a moment ago," said Tempest, looking back, "but my companions had other places to go."

"Have you got anyone within the city to go to?"

"No," Tempest admitted.

"What brings you here, then?"

"I've come from a village just outside of Eris." Eris was a city not too far from Alyria, so it seemed the easiest to claim. She knew a bit about it from books, and the Priest on the road had talked about it as well, reflecting on his training within the holy city. "My parents were killed by Winter's illness. Most of my village was, too, so I left."

It wasn't unheard of for entire villages to be wiped out by the winter goddess, so she hoped they would believe her. "I've always wanted to be a Dragon Keeper, so I figured I'd come here."

"This winter was a cruel one, for sure," said the woman. "I'm sorry for your village. I might be able to get you work at an inn if you need lodging, but you'll need to find your own after that."

As they neared the gates, the man pressed them open, nodding to his colleague when they passed. The view of the city upon entering left Tempest awe struck. Its buildings looked as if they'd risen straight from the mountains themselves.

The woman led Tempest through the streets, a smile touching her lips when she caught Tempest marveling at the oddities the city beheld. The towers were high, but the mountains were higher. A warm wind shifted through the lingering winter chill, and streams of molten rock snaked around buildings and into the mountains where the rock cracked open.

"Firethorne sits between three volcanoes," the woman said. "They've been asleep for as long as we know and show no signs of reawakening, but if they ever do, we'll bid farewell to our entire west coast. Studies speculate the blast would trigger the chain of volcanic mountains all the way down to the city of Vulcan. It's a dreary thought, but it's one we've come to accept. Have you ever read the book, *Midnight Dragon*?"

"No," said Tempest. She'd read many stories, but that one wasn't familiar.

"It's an old book, and only one copy remains known," said the woman. "It's about the land that crowned the first king. One of the volcanoes near the kingdom's center erupted. The king had advised his people to evacuate, saying he'd received a message from the god of fire himself that a great flame would level the city. When the volcano began showing signs of eruption, he pleaded with his people to leave, knowing that it was the start of the great flame.

"The people didn't listen. They laughed at the prospect. Their mistake cost them all their lives. Records told a horrific tale of day turning to night as the ashes rained down. The earth shook in fury, and buildings imploded from the shifting land. Only a few survived. We never heard of them again.

"Living here is a danger, but the dragons love the land, so the Keepers followed. The creatures can usually sense when a new crack will open in the earth. Perhaps they'll sense an eruption as well. Hopefully we won't take the signs lightly next time." She paused, pointing to a distant castle built from the side of the mountain. "That right there is the Dragon Keeper headquarters. Around here, it's known as The Claw."

It was a fitting name, Tempest thought. Its towers protruded from the earth like the talons of a giant beast. She was eager to explore it.

"This here is where you'll be staying," said the woman, gesturing towards an inn to their left. A small sign swayed above the door, naming the establishment, The Smokey Inn.

The woman handed a stable boy the reins to Tempest's horse, and he led it away. "I know the innkeeper here," she said, walking Tempest inside. "She'll set you up with a room if you work for it."

A bell chimed when they stepped through the threshold, and an elderly woman looked up from the desk. "Ah, Evelyn, who've you brought to me today?" She wiped her hands on a cloth and stepped out to greet them.

"My name is Tempest. I've come from a village near Eris."

"Her village was lost to Wynris," Evelyn filled in, and the innkeeper's face fell solemn.

"Poor child," said the innkeeper. "I've got room for her."

"Thank you," said Evelyn, then she left to return to her post, bidding Tempest luck.

"Now," said the innkeeper. "I take you in under my good graces, but if you want to stick around, I expect you to help me staff the place."

"Of course," said Tempest.

"How long are you expecting to be here?"

"Just until the month of Zalder, ma'am. That's when I enlist."

The innkeeper nodded, deep in some thought. "You intend to be a Dragon Keeper, do you?"

"I do," said Tempest.

"Good. Zalder takes kindly to the Dragon Keepers born in his month. He's the patron of the guild, you know." She grabbed a key from the wall and turned towards the hall. "Come along, now. I'll show you to your room."

Around the corner, they came to the tavern hall. Guests were scarce at this hour, but a few sat at the long tables for a meal or some ale. One man laid across the bench, passed out with a drink still in hand. "That's Markus," said the innkeeper, following Tempest's gaze. "He's regular around here. Spends most of his waking hours deep within his cups, but he's mostly harmless. He'll only talk your ear off with tales of absolute absurdity."

Tempest smiled, interested in hearing these supposed absurdities. "I look forward to meeting him," she said.

"He'll be waking soon. Should be on his ramblings by the time you're settled." The innkeeper opened a door and gestured for Tempest to follow. "Right this way."

Tempest followed her up a set of stairs and through a long, stone brick corridor. At the end of it was where they stopped. The innkeeper held out the key and nodded to the door. "This one'll be yours. You'll have the rest of the day to get settled. Find me in the foyer come morning, and I'll put you to work."

"Thank you," said Tempest as she took the key.

"I'll be in the tavern if you need anything," the innkeeper said, halfway down the hall before she finished.

Tempest inserted the key and twisted the lock, pressing open the door to her new room. It was smaller than the room that had been given to her and Patch in the Royal city, but there was only one of her, and she'd rarely be using it anyway. The room had no windows, lit only by the flickering of candlelight and a fire pit in the back. It had an earthy smell to it that comforted Tempest, and a bed sat in the corner, piled high with furs. Despite its unfamiliarity, it felt homely.

She placed her things beside the bed, taking a seat on its edge. Her fingers fumbled with the clasp that rested at the nape of her neck, and after multiple failed attempts, it came unlatched. She slid the amethyst ring off its chain and replaced her child's ring with that of the Royal House. It looked odd on her finger, like it didn't quite belong.

Etched on the side was the dragon her mother had had engraved to honor her time as a Dragon Keeper. Tempest wished she'd been told more about that part of her mother's life, but her mother rarely mentioned it. It'd seemed a painful subject for her after the death of her dragon, so Tempest had never pressed.

The smell of cooking food drifted from the kitchens, making Tempest's stomach twist. She'd not eaten since the night before, and hunger had set in. With a sigh, she returned the ring to its place at her neck and put the child's band back onto her finger.

Once out of her room, she could hear the small murmur of voices from below. They talked, laughed, and sang to the new day's arrival. Tempest walked down the stairs and joined them in their contentment, flagging down one of the serving girls to bring her some food.

Massive, candlelit chandeliers dangled from the rafters above, and between them, young dragons leapt from beam to beam. Markus, having woken, watched the creatures too. His eyes focused loosely on the dragons, though he appeared to almost be looking beyond them rather than at them. When he found what he'd been looking for, he took a swig from his cup and turned to face the man beside him.

"It was a black dragon with golden wings and purple eyes," he said. "Nothing like any I've seen around here. Severed on its right talon was a black snake with blood red eyes, and in the left, it held a crown of bones."

Tempest approached the table and sat across from Markus, trying her best not to disturb his telling. His words intrigued her already. No king but Lazareth had worn a crown of bones. She wondered how he'd known of it.

"The beast took off into the stormy night, and the crown shattered in its grip. The snake, just before it died, lashed out and sank its fangs into the dragon's underside. Both creatures fell into flames below."

"Did the dragon die?" Tempest asked, and Markus looked up, startled by her appearance.

"I don't know," he said.

"Don't listen to his ramblings, girl," said the man he'd told the story to. "They're meaningless, drunken dreams."

"They're not," Markus said, leaning close to Tempest so only she would hear. He reeked of spirits and a hint of vomit, but Tempest didn't pull away. She wanted to hear more.

"The snake showed up in my dreams last week and came back every night following," he said. "It would move through a bank of purple snow on its way to bite a weeping woman. I wasn't sure of the dream's meaning until this morning. When I woke, a man walked in and told a grievous tale from Alyria. This man had a ring on with the same colors as the snake. He told us of the king's illness and demise, and he told us of the queen's suicide. I knew then the dreams were visions. The purple snow signified a Royal death, and the weeping woman was the queen, but the snake bite... I haven't figured that part out yet."

"Perhaps it wasn't a suicide," said Tempest, knowing well what the dream had meant. "Maybe the snake poisoned her."

"Ah, a venomous bite, then." He nodded "That makes sense. Now, how about this new one. It's plain the snake will die, but when? By whose hands? Who is the black and gold dragon?"

Tempest shrugged. "I suppose we're in the proper place to find out." She gestured to the rafters where the dragons still played. "Plenty of dragons in these parts."

"True," said Markus, "but only one that'll kill the snake."

"Do all your dreams come true?" Tempest asked.

Markus shook his head. "Only the ones that repeat like this. It hasn't happened since I was a boy. Something big must be coming."

A chill ran through Tempest's spine at the thought. She knew she'd have a role in this, but she knew not when or how.

9

$\mathcal{T}$he evening faded much faster than Tempest had hoped. She spent most of her time talking to the tavern guests, learning, through them, the history of Firethorne and the scorched lands it was built upon. It was a thrilling history, and she was eager to explore what the city had to offer.

As promised, first thing in the morning, Tempest found the innkeeper in the foyer. "Are you ready to begin?" asked the woman, and Tempest nodded. "This way, then. You'll scrub the tables and floors until guests arrive. Once you've finished that, bring orders to the kitchens and run food to the dining hall. You'll find rags and buckets in that closet." She pointed to a door near the kitchen. "Fill the bucket at the well just down the street. Have you got any questions?"

"No," said Tempest, so the innkeeper left her alone to her tasks.

Tempest worked diligently, day in, and day out, scrubbing down the dining hall by morning and serving food and ale by night, losing herself to the easefulness of normalcy. She spent this time in vastly different ways than she'd spent it in Alyria, but the monotonous tasks brought a familiar comfort all the same. Her days were slow and uneventful, but her nights made up for some adventure. She heard many stories from the drunkards and traveling singers, and she recorded the ones she found most interesting into her notebook.

She spoke to a mixture of guilds, learning their stories, the places they came from, and how they ended up in the guild they chose. Some had followed the family trade through numerous generations. Others sought out new adventures for themselves. She found each of them fascinating.

Markus visited many times, telling the same tale of the dragon and the snake. The dream remained the same. Tempest wondered if it would ever change, and when it did, if it would change in favor of the dragon.

About two weeks into the job, a band of freshly trained Dragon Keeper recruits strayed in. There were five of them, and two of the five carried small, newborn dragons. One was colored a deep green, the other a sleek contrast of black and white.

Tempest approached the table. "What'll it be?" she asked the group, watching the baby dragons curiously prowl the table.

"Two flagons of ale to celebrate the hatching of our dragons!" one of the boys said. His companions clapped and hollered in support, and others in the tavern joined in their merriment, lifting their cups in salute to the new recruits.

The green dragon waddled towards Tempest. It belonged to the boy. She could tell by the way he watched its every move, seeming to enjoy its desire to explore, but worried that it might come to harm if it strayed too far. The dragon pressed its head against her hand, purring like a reptilian cat. She jerked her hand back, startled by its touch.

"Don't be afraid," said the boy. "He's quite harmless at the moment, and he seems to like you."

Tempest extended her arm, tracing her fingers down the turquoise stripe that lined the creature's back. Its muscles rippled beneath her touch, and it curled into a ball, settling into a quiet slumber.

"With the ale, could we get some water for Sparrow, here?" asked the boy, pointing to the young girl beside him. Her features were like his, but they were softer with youthfulness.

Sparrow crossed her arms and glared at the boy. "They let me tag along because I'm Mereb's sister," she said to Tempest, "but they won't let me drink because they think I'm too young." The child sighed, and the boy raised his hand, identifying himself as Mereb. "I don't understand why though... I mean my enlistment day isn't *that* far away. Surely, you can convince them to let me have some."

Tempest chuckled. It was plain the girl still had years before she was of age. "May I ask how old you are?"

Sparrow flushed and lowered her head. "Thirteen," she admitted.

"I fear I may have to agree with your friends on this one. Try again in five years."

"But, that's so far away!" said Sparrow.

Tempest lifted the child's chin. "Those five years will be over before you know it. Then you'll be celebrating your own enlistment."

"How do *you* know it'll go quick. You haven't even reached yours yet."

The child had a fire in her that Tempest liked. "I know because I was once five years away from *my* enlistment day, and now I'm only months away," she said. "Do you intend to take the emerald like your brother?"

"Yes!" Sparrow said confidently. "Both of our parents are Dragon Keepers as well. They've taught us everything there is to know about the guild."

"You're very lucky," said Tempest

The child puffed her chest with pride. "Will you take the emerald, too?" she asked. "Or will you join some other guild?"

"I intend to take the emerald if I can," said Tempest, hoping Kaburem wouldn't find her in the months between now and then. "Though, I was never taught much about it. Perhaps next time you come here you can teach me some things."

The child beamed at the idea, nodding her head in excitement.

"We won't be back for some time," said Mereb, "But I'm sure my parents would welcome you at our house if you wanted to stop by some days."

It was a generous offer, but Tempest declined. "I'm afraid I'm here most every day," she said.

"Surely, the innkeeper allows you a day off every once and a while," said Mereb. "Perhaps she'll give you the weekend if you ask."

"I suppose I can ask the one favor of her. I'd really love to get some training under my belt if it's not too much a bother."

"It's of no bother to us. We'd be glad to have you, truly." The older girl rolled her eyes, but she said nothing to dispute. "May I get your name?"

"Tempest." She was starting to get used to the name now. The longer she claimed it as her own, the more it seemed to fit.

"Welcome to the crew, Tempest," said a boy with black, spiked hair and sharp, blue eyes. "I'm Tyce."

"And I'm Zeke!" a third boy said, shaking Tempest's hand.

Gazes turned to the final member of their party, the older girl Tempest thought wasn't fond of her. She had hazel eyes that seemed to pierce through Tempest's soul, but with a sigh, she shook Tempest's hand. "I'm Theria," she said. "Care to bring us our drinks, or will we have to wait for the weekend to see those too?"

"I'm terribly sorry," said Tempest. "I'll bring those right out."

~~~

On the first morning of the weekend, Mereb and his friends showed up at the inn to lead Tempest to their house. She couldn't help but notice the absence of Theria in the welcoming party.

Upon gathering her things, Tempest followed the group through the city streets, stopping at a house near the walls. Two dragons lay in the yard, sleeping away the frosty morning, and a man and woman stood in the doorway, awaiting their arrival.

"Mum, Pa, meet Tempest!" said Sparrow as they neared the door.

Tempest bowed her head. "It's a pleasure to meet you," she said

"The pleasure is ours," said Sparrow's mother. "I'm Ari Paxton, and this is John."

John opened the door, welcoming her into their home. "Sparrow has been very excited about your coming," he said, and the girl blushed, ducking through the threshold.

"I'm glad I could come. It'll be nice to get to know more about the Dragon Keeper lifestyle before I join."

"Are you a first generation?" Ari asked, and Tempest shook her head.

"My mother was a Dragon Keeper, but she didn't talk much about it. Her dragon was killed shortly after I was born."

"What a wretched thing to do," said Ari. "I hope whoever killed the poor creature received proper punishment for their crime."

"He did," said Tempest, content in knowing it was true.

As her parents told it, the dragon had been killed on her first birthday during a feast of celebration. Her uncle had snuck into her room to secure his place as heir. The dragon died defending her, and the guards rushed in just as it collapsed.

For his crimes, her uncle was stripped of his title, chained, and shackled to a whaleboat with no oars. They sailed him out and dropped him far into the sea. His body was never found.

Tempest stepped into the house, spotting a table in the center of the room where Theria was feeding three baby dragons. She recognized the sea green one as Mereb's and the black and white one as Theria's own, but the third she hadn't seen yet. It had a scarlet body with silver spikes down its back, and silver lining traced the edge of its wings.

Tempest's eyes met Theria's. She had her brow raised. "What are you looking at?" the girl asked.

"The dragon," said Tempest. "Whose egg hatched?"

"Mine!" Tyce said, a bright smile showing from ear to ear. "He hatched yesterday morning!"

"I'm the last one," Zeke said, giving a solemn sigh and pointing to a beautiful stone-like egg on the countertop. It was black with bright streaks of red like the earth of Firethorne and Lazareth's coat.

"Come on!" Sparrow shouted, grabbing onto Tempest's hand and dragging her out a back door that emptied into a cave for the dragons. Past that, an archway opened into a small oasis of greenery they'd converted into an arena. A row of wooden swords and real swords alike lined a ridge in the rock, and at the end hung a rack of bows, their arrows in a pail beneath them. Five straw sentinels stood along the edge of the range, some grotesquely wounded.

"Combat is a part of training," said Sparrow. "They used to train for the sake of wars, but in times of peace, it's only a formality. There's an art to fighting with dragons, and it must not be lost."

"There's an art to fighting in general," said Tyce, overhearing Sparrow's words. "What say we give our guest a show. Zeke, care for a duel?"

It was a good match, thought Tempest. Tyce and Zeke had similar stature, making them nearly equal for the fight.

"That leaves me with Mereb!" Theria said, grinning as she skipped towards the swords.

"She'll purposefully lose," Sparrow whispered to Tempest. "She has a thing for Mereb and won't want to show him up."

"Winner takes on Tempest!" Zeke threw in.

Tempest opened her mouth to protest, but Sparrow stopped her with a touch. "Every new recruit comes in with some knowledge of fighting. Better to learn amongst friends than in the heat of training, don't you think?"

"I suppose," said Tempest, then quieter, "Now we have a theory to test. Which does Theria value more? Preserving Mereb's dignity or beating me?" Sparrow giggled and sat upright, eager to see the verdict.

The other three challengers followed Theria to the armory, and each emerged with a wooden sword.

Both pairs positioned themselves for a duel. The tops of their swords touched, and their stances widened. Theria was the first to move, striking at Mereb's hip. He twisted his arm, parrying the attack with ease. Mereb had seen what she wanted to do long before she did it. He rolled the blade, swinging it in an arc to disengage Theria's sword.

"You keep score on them. I'll score the boys. Each hit is a point. The victor of the match gets five," Sparrow directed.

The fight was vicious. Each time one would seem to be coming out victorious, the other would pull ahead. Mereb had twelve points, and Theria had seven when Zeke and Tyce had finished. Everyone was watching them. Mereb went for the fatal blow, quickly stabbing at her stomach, however his grip faltered for a split second when Theria's blade met his to stop it.

Theria saw the chance, slid her blade down, and caught Mereb's sword at the hilt. She flicked the sword up and yanked it from his fingers. It clattered on the rocky floor, echoing off the stone around them. She pressed the blunted tip to his heart, and silence fell over the group, broken suddenly by her laughter.

"I won!" She cackled, dropping the end of her sword and pointing it to Tempest. "Your turn, princess."

Tempest's gut twisted at the nickname, even though it was only meant as a jest. She stood, regardless, and grabbed one of the smaller, wooden swords.

"First step, get your stance, said Mereb, tapping his sword between her shins. "Spread your feet. Make sure you're balanced, and put your dominant foot forward."

Tempest stepped her left foot back, bending her knees a bit for more control.

"Angle the point of the sword to Theria's shoulder."

Tempest did as was directed, and Theria followed. The blades met in the middle.

"Where the blades touch is the weakest section of the sword. Just below it is the fuller," he said, pointing to the lower section of the blade. "This is the strongest section of your sword. It's what you'll want to use when defending. And, *this*," he started, touching the pad of his index finger to the blunted end of the blade, "is the point, used for stabbing and cutting."

Tempest nodded, and Mereb stepped away from the pair. "Go."

Theria spared no hesitation to attack. Her blade arced through the air and landed hard upon Tempest's shoulder. Pain shot through her arm, and she groaned, cursing under her breath as Theria reset the opening stance.

"Take it easy, Theria," said Mereb.

"How is she supposed to learn if I take it easy?" Theria asked, swinging down once again.

This time, Tempest knew where Theria meant to land the blow, so she lifted her sword to counter it. The maneuver succeeded and stopped the attack, but the impact of the blades colliding was a jarring sensation of its own that Tempest had not prepared for. She nearly lost her grip on the hilt, and would likely have dropped it had Theria not reset and waited.

With the next attempt, Tempest swung first. It seemed to surprise Theria. Elsewise, the blow would have never landed, but this one did, striking Theria right on the hip bone.

"Getting bold, now, are we?" asked Theria. "This ought to humble you." She stepped forward as Tempest swung and drove the tip of her sword hard into Tempest's diaphragm.

Tempest doubled over, sword falling from her hand as she coughed and gasped for air. The world spun around her, and her vision spotted with pain.

"By gods, Theria! What did you do that for?" Mereb asked, running to Tempest's aid. "Help me get her inside!"

An assortment of hands held her upright and guided her into the house. She could hardly feel the ground beneath her, and she couldn't really tell if her feet were even moving, but somehow, they got her to hobble far enough to find a seat in the kitchen.

"Here," said Theria, handing Tempest a flask of water. "You'll be bruised for a bit, but otherwise, you should be fine."

"I'll be the judge of that," said Ari, entering the room. "Get out, the lot of you."

10

empest's blurred vision focused on the kindly face that hovered before her. "How do you feel?" Ari asked.

"I've been worse," said Tempest with a chuckle that sent pain through her ribs. "Gods, she hit me hard, though."

"She's a bit impulsive with her emotions, but she'll not harm you more than this. May I see the injury?"

With care, Tempest untucked her blouse and lifted it for Ari to inspect. There was a large, red welt already formed just beneath her ribs, but outside of that, damage seemed slim.

Ari probed at the flesh, then nodded, satisfied. "There's been no internal injury," she said. "You'll be well bruised, as Theria said, but otherwise, you'll be all right."

"Thank you," said Tempest before taking a drink from the flask Theria had given her. The water ran cool down her hoarse throat, soothing as it passed.

"There are a few things I need to ask you, Tempest, if you're well enough to answer."

Tempest set the flask aside and nodded. "Go ahead."

"Where are you from?"

"A village just outside of Eris," said Tempest. "I fled after Wynris set in." She was determined to keep the lie as close to the truth as she could. That way, she wouldn't betray the story with future inaccuracies.

"Do you have any family? You mentioned your mother when you arrived."

"Only my mother and father," said Tempest, pushing away the pain in her heart, "but they're both dead now."

"I see," said Ari, holding out her hand. "You'll be wanting this back, I imagine."

Tempest looked down, finding her mother's ring in Ari's palm. "How?" she asked, heart pounding within her chest.

"You dropped it walking in. The chain it was on was broken when I picked it up. I'll get you a stronger one from my jewelry box, if you'd like."

"Does anyone else know?" Tempest asked. She trusted her new companions well enough, but not with this.

"No," said Ari. "I'm the only one. It'll stay that way as long as you wish. You can lie to everyone, including my husband, but Tempest, there can be no more lies to me."

Tempest nodded, slumping in her seat. "No more lies," she promised.

"Now, will you tell me the truth? How did you end up here? You're a long way from home."

"It's a rather long story at this point," said Tempest, "but it starts with Wynris. That much was true."

Ari took a seat and settled in, so Tempest began. She recounted everything, telling the story of her parents' deaths for the second time, and following it up with everything that'd happened since. She felt unburdened after telling it all, content in knowing she was no longer the only one present who carried the weight of the truth. Ari, on the other hand, appeared all the more distressed.

"I'll leave if you wish me to," said Tempest. "I don't want my being here to put your family in any kind of danger."

"Don't be ridiculous. Kaburem will never look for you here. We'll keep you safe; it's just a lot to take in." She turned and dug through the cabinets, emerging with a jar of arnica oil. "This will help the bruising when it forms. Go join the others, we'll be making supper soon."

"Thank you," Tempest said, taking the jar before leaving, head still reeling from their conversation. She didn't know whether to be terrified or thankful, so she settled on a bit of both.

"See, what did I say, she's fine," said Theria when Tempest stepped into the common room.

"Are you sure about that?" Sparrow asked, looking Tempest over. "You don't look well, Tempest."

"I'm all right," Tempest assured. "Just a bit out of sorts, is all."

"I've been there before," said Tyce, "You're not the first person Theria has hit with a dirty blow. You handled it well enough."

"There's no fair play in actual combat," said Theria. "Consider the hits a warning."

"You say, having experienced real combat, of course," said Sparrow with a giggle.

"As much as I hate to admit, she's right," said Tempest, thinking of her flight from Alyria. "When lives are on the line, etiquette is abandoned."

"Have you seen real combat?" Sparrow asked, eyes wide with curiosity.

"It wasn't a battle or anything of the sorts, but it was a fight with mutual intention to kill."

"Is that a common thing where you're from?" asked Mereb. "I've heard rumors that in some of the more remote parts of the land, they still use duels to sort out disagreements."

"It's not common," said Tempest. "Or, at least it wasn't until Kaburem came."

"That's the name of the foreigners, isn't it?" Sparrow asked. "Have you met them? What are they like?"

It was a simple question that Tempest should have been able to fabricate an answer to with ease, but her heart twisted at the thought of them. She fell silent, unable to respond, unable to do much anything but stare forward and focus on the present.

"It's bad, isn't it," said Mereb. "Their coming, I mean."

Tempest only nodded, not trusting her voice.

"You've seen them first hand." He was guessing now, but he was right. "You know what they're capable of."

"I do," she said, wishing she wasn't so easy to read. "But, you'll not hear that part of my story just yet."

Footsteps approached, and the group turned, finding Ari in the threshold. "Supper's ready," she said, saving Tempest from further questioning. They each rose, conversation forgotten, and made their way to the table. Ari handed Tempest a new chain for the ring as she passed.

Laid out on the dining table were two loaves of bread with a pork roast in the center. John distributed the meat once everyone had taken their seats. Tempest's mouth watered at the smell of it. She hadn't realized how hungry she was.

Once everyone was settled, she took a bite. The meat was tender, melting in her mouth with wonderful flavor. A silence hung over the room while everyone ate, one that trapped Tempest in her own thoughts, so she interrupted it. "How did all of you end up here?" she asked.

They looked at one another, waiting for someone to answer. John spoke first. "My wife and I met each other when we were young," he said. "My father was a Merchant; my mother was a Naval trader. A few years before my enlistment, we were in the rivers of the southern farmlands. A storm had come through, blocking our path back to sea with fallen trees. We were forced to stop for a few days. My parents ended up liking the village and decided to settle there until I enlisted."

"Was the village close to Mirenor?" Tempest asked. "I've heard it's a magnificent city."

"It wasn't, but I've been, and it is. I met Ari in the village. Her parents were both Medics, which is why she was able to help you earlier. They had taught her the ways of the trade, expecting her to follow the same path they had. I suppose I ruined that plan."

Ari smiled at that. "I'm thankful you did," she said

John took Ari's hand in his and continued. "She hadn't seen much outside of her little village and found excitement in the tales I told of dragons and their riders in the north, the elephant planes in the south, and the mountains in the west. She loved it all, but especially the dragons. Come our enlistment days, we both decided to become Dragon Keepers.

"The two of us settled here after we had our fair share of adventure, and we started a family. Years later, here we are. A son in the guild, and a household of his friends."

"Most of our parents live in cities and villages far away, so we stay with Mereb," said Zeke. "He's the only one with family in Firethorne."

"Where are the rest of your families?" Tempest asked.

Zeke answered first. "Mine are on a small island called Neptus in the Black Sea of the north," he said.

Tyce followed after. "My family lives in the grasslands south of Mirenor. They are the furthest from Firethorne. I have a younger brother there who is to enlist in a few years, and a baby sister who was born a couple months before I left."

"Your family isn't the furthest from here," Theria said. "Mine is."

"Where are they?" Tempest asked, though she already knew the answer from the look on Theria's face. She recognized that look. She'd seen it in her own reflection.

"They're with Xudor."

"As are mine," said Tempest in a hushed voice.

Ari took both their hands. "You're both welcome here at any time, no matter where your futures take you. Same to the rest of you," she said, looking at Zeke and Tyce, but they were too focused on the meal to pay the sentiment much mind. "Tempest, I meant to ask. Where have you been staying since you got here?"

"At the Smokey Inn. I work for the innkeeper to pay off the room."

"Would you want to stay here instead?" Ari asked. "I've talked to my husband about it, and he agreed it'd be a good idea. It would give you more time to learn about the guild."

Tempest thought on it. The offer was nearly perfect. She would no longer have to worry about keeping a roof over her head or affording a warm meal. She'd be able to train more and would be better protected. However, the inn provided her with valuable information about the events of the world through the people straying in and out during long travels. Perhaps, she thought, she could compromise. A plan was worked out by the end of the meal.

~~~

Tempest worked at the inn for four days each week and trained the other three. She gave up the room the innkeeper had given her and moved in with

Theria instead. There'd been minor disagreements in the arrangement, but these fell away with time.

Tempest kept the book of the gods on her nightstand, claiming it as a token from her home city. The rest of her belongings, she stored locked in a drawer, keeping the key hidden so no one would find what was inside.

Theria was inquisitive at first, eager to discover the secret contents in the drawer, but after numerous attempts at breaking in, she gave up, and the drawer was forgotten.

As the days passed, Tempest was taught more about the Dragon Keepers' history. On sunny days, she would spend her time in the practice field, training in the art of sword combat. She found it thrilling to learn. In the Royal House, it was not the queens place to fight, so Tempest had never been taught.

Sunny days were slim, though. Rhumir had taken the throne of the gods, washing away all signs of winter with his storms, turning the skies a seemingly permanent dark grey. On these days, when no one was around, Ari would discuss politics with Tempest in the study.

Word of the king traveled on the lips of many. Tempest sat with a woman once, who spoke of the state of the kingdom at one of the long tables in the inn. This woman had come by sea from the military city, Sylvos, and she had two young children that ran around the table, paying no heed to the conversation.

"The people in the west weren't as accepting to new rule as those who lived closer to the heart city," said the woman when Tempest sat down to listen to her words. "I suppose it's easier to dream of separation when you aren't neighbor to the capital."

Tempest twisted the child's band around her finger, pondering. "Did they manage to do it?" she asked.

The woman's brow raised in question. "Manage to do what? Separate?"

Tempest nodded.

"They did," she said. "Colonel Atheris made the announcement a couple weeks back. After constant demands from the people, he decided to take a stand against Kaburem, despite the guild leader's wishes. The king agreed to let them exist as an independent province to avoid shattering the peace. There were conditions with the agreement, though. Trades and soldiers are to remain under control of Kaburem. If broken, there will be war."

"Do you think the north will follow their lead?"

"They might, but I hope not," said the woman, her eyes falling to her children. "There's more security in following Kaburem than there is in challenging them. People can dream of independence, but it will someday come with a cost, and I have a family to look after. I can't afford to take such risks."

A whistle broke through the air, and Tempest's attention was brought to the innkeeper. She stood in the doorway to the kitchens with her hands on her hips. "Back to work, child," she said. "People are waiting."

Sure enough, a group of Naval officers had entered the inn. They sat at an empty table in the corner of the room.

Tempest made her way to the group, carrying a few plates piled high with food. From what she'd heard them talking about, they had come to discuss the new political structure with Sagua and the other guild leaders in the area.

Interrupting the flow of conversation in the hall, however, was a young man who stumbled through the door. Everyone turned to look at him. He had an olivine ring on his finger, and a single silver chevron was stitched onto the shoulder of his coat.

Rhumir's rains had soaked him to the bone. He stood in the doorway, shivering uncontrollably with a parchment crumpled and wet in his hand. He pried the folds of paper apart with difficulty, squinting at the smudged ink in an attempt to make sense of the letters on the page. Shaking his head, he gave up on reading it and closed the paper in his fist. "There's been a massacre," he announced, the sound of his words trembling as much as his hands. He shuddered with worrisome intensity, then he fell to his knees.

11

*W*hispers washed through the room, and a group of people helped the soldier to the hearth. Tempest ran to get him a bowl of hot stew, unsure what else to do. When she returned, the Naval officers she'd served a moment before had surrounded the young man.

They yelled obscenities and pushed him around, pestering the lad for answers he couldn't seem to give. A red mark lingered on the surface of the soldier's skin from a blow one of the officers had dealt him. He shrank into the corner, cowering away from their torments.

"*Enough!*" Tempest yelled, and the Naval officers glared at her but stepped back all the same. "Can't you see he's scared? Give him a moment to breathe." She crouched down to give the young soldier the bowl of soup she'd retrieved, and he guzzled it down. "Can you tell me what happened?" she asked when he'd relaxed.

The soldier wiped the rainwater from his brow and sat up, fixing his coat to look somewhat less battered. "I was in Laurus, meeting with two Army recruits who'd come from the south," he said, eyes flitting nervously to the officers who still stood by his side. "A fleet of Kaburem soldiers arrived that morning as well, sent from their homeland to regulate trade and bring more profit to the crown. They had the square surrounded, tracking all who entered and left.

"When they arrived, the Kaburem soldiers imposed a tax on all the goods being sold. They called it the freedom tax, saying it was the price the province had to pay for their freedom. There was no order from the crown. There was nothing that proved their demands. It was thievery and nothing more.

"Despite this, Merchants who refused to pay had their produce taken from them and were imprisoned, so people began to gather in protest at the center of the square. As the crowd grew, so did the number of Kaburem soldiers. They carried larger flintlocks than those that came in the first wave of invaders. These were longer, and they bore a thin blade at the end of the barrel.

"One of the Merchants decided he'd had enough of their demands. He was furious, and rightfully so. He grabbed a stone from the ground and threw it at one of the Kaburem soldiers. It struck the soldier in the head, and the riot began. Kaburem shot the Merchant, and at this, the crowd raged. They grabbed anything they could use to defend themselves, rocks, daggers, swords, and bricks.

"With the impending violence, Kaburem took arms. A section of them knelt, aiming their guns into the crowd. I left before the firing began, desperate to get the recruits to safety, but from what I'm told, there were no survivors. Upon my return to the main base in Sylvos, I was given this letter to deliver to Sagua."

One of the Naval officers snatched the parchment from the young soldier's hands. The letters had turned to watery blotches, erasing any message that had once been there. Everything but one word. Tempest saw it etched on the parchment over the man's shoulder. *Rebellion.*

The officers grabbed the soldier by the arms and pulled him to his feet, dragging him back into the rain. The doors flapped closed, and Tempest watched through the window as the men hurried towards The Claw.

She wanted with all her heart to follow them and learn more about the letter, but she knew she'd never make it far, and the stare of the innkeeper held her in place.

~~~

The days of Rhumir ended quickly, and the flowers of Ides rose from the soaked earth as the goddess claimed the throne for spring. The trees that blanketed the mountain began to bud and flower, some small leaves forming on the branches.

When the sky had cleared of the storm god's clouds, and the sun showed its face once more, Tempest discovered a group of convicts who approached the city with a Kaburem guard. She passed them numerous times in her daily chores, veering her course at times to see them. She was intrigued by their evolving project just beyond the wall. All through the week, they hammered wooden planks and metal beams into the ground, then one day, they were gone from view.

She hadn't a clue what the track was for, but the answer came at the end of Ides while she walked the streets near the Paxton's house. A great war horn tore through the air, and the ground shifted, pebbles jumping and rolling at her feet. She feared, for a moment, that the volcano had decided to rupture, but conversation from the city wall convinced her otherwise.

A child ran past her, skipping steps to join the sentries on the wall. The boy called for others to follow, pointing towards the track. He didn't seem worried, and neither did the city guard, so Tempest climbed to look.

She didn't entirely know what it was she looked at. It seemed a black beast made of metal that spewed smoke from its top like a dragon with no flame. Attached to its rear were massive wagons, carrying goods and the occasional

Kaburem passenger. She, amongst others, gasped as it passed, but a group of children down below found it a challenge rather than a marvel.

They chased after the final wagon, arms stretched forth to grab hold of it. The eldest was the first to succeed. His hand wrapped tightly around the bar. He stumbled a bit, but his grip held true, and he managed to pull himself on board. His group of pursuing friends all chanted and cheered, but their celebration drew to a sudden halt when a Kaburem soldier stepped through the back door, unamused by their childish game of bravery.

Down the track a bit, the black beast squealed to a stop, and the boy was removed. With a cuff to the head and a muffled verbal threat, the band of children fled with the eldest at their lead, ending the morning's excitement, so Tempest left to continue with the day's tasks.

Over time, she grew accustomed to the metal beast the Kaburem people called a train. She no longer stood in awe each time it passed, but she enjoyed the sight of it and would visit the wall often.

The dragons found amusement in the train, as well. Many of the creatures flew alongside it, gliding on the air current it caused. The Kaburem soldiers tried to stop the dragons from flocking towards it, but they gave in with time, realizing it a pointless endeavor.

On one particular day, in the midst of the month of the nature god, Fejun, Tempest joyously watched a young bird join the dragons, cavorting alongside the train. It flew with them, riding the wind with a freeing bliss, for the most part, undisturbed. That was until a moment later, when it vanished down the gullet of a crimson beast. Tempest gaped in horror and turned away to look instead at the valley where flowers bloomed and trees foliated into various shades of viridescent beauty.

At the base of the wall, a man stood on a box, ruining the tranquil view with shouts of despair. It hadn't been the first time this occurred, and she knew it wouldn't be the last. Every week, there was another grievance against some torment from a Kaburem soldier. Thievery, brawls, muggings, and unlawful raids were amongst the majority of complaints, but this one was different.

Rather than mere tangents of anger, this man spoke boldly of a revolution to come, urging the people to join together and stand up for themselves. His shouts summoned the attention of two passing Kaburem soldiers who approached the man with guns drawn.

"Inciting insurrection is a crime against the crown," said one, stepping forward. "Halt your proceedings immediately, or we will be forced to take action."

The man did not stop. Instead, he spoke louder, bringing in a larger crowd. Tempest turned to abandon the wall and the crowd that surged beneath it. She didn't want to see how this ended, but when she reached the edge of the gathering, the crack of a gun echoed through the air.

~~~

Fejun's time on the immortal throne passed with no further spoken grievances and was followed thereafter by the month of Zalder, carrying the world into the birth of summer.

Tempest rose early on the first morning of Zalder, sleep deprived and nervous. The excitement of her enlistment day had kept her awake long into the night.

The sun seeped through the window, and birds chirped outside, singing to the waking of the world. Theria still rested, so Tempest moved quietly. She inched her way off the bed and slowly opened the drawer that held her belongings, careful not to wake Theria as she did it.

She pulled out the notebook first, setting it gingerly in the small pack she was able to take with her to training. Next, she pulled out the dagger, smiling at the memory of it. After stowing the dagger away, she rolled up a collection of garments from the selection Liz had sent her with, and packed it in, hoping to hide the gun within the layers. Lastly, she pulled out the gun, setting it on a gown Ari had given her to be rolled up and concealed.

"Were you one of them?" Theria asked, startling Tempest.

"One of who?" she asked, trying to keep her voice calm. She hadn't noticed Theria awaken.

"Kaburem. That weapon is one of theirs, and you said you'd seen what they were capable of, but you refused to say anything else. Is it because you were one of them?"

Tempest almost laughed. She was equally amused and horrified that someone would think her to be like them. "No," she said. "I was never one of them."

"Then who are you?" Theria asked. "I've lived with you for months now. I have a right to know."

"Now isn't the time," said Tempest, "but I promise you'll hear my story eventually."

"I'd like it now, if it pleases you," Theria said, arms crossed in stubborn defiance. "There's nothing you could have possibly done to require such secrecy… Unless you're a fugitive. Are you a fugitive?"

"I'm not a criminal," said Tempest, "but I was witness to a crime. That's all I can tell you for now. Is that enough?"

Theria hadn't the time to respond before Ari walked in. "Are you ready to go?" the woman asked, and Tempest nodded, wrapping the gun up before stuffing it into the bag.

She rose to her feet once she was packed, and she gave one last glance to Theria. "You don't want to know the truth, trust me," she said, then she followed Ari out.

Tempest's makeshift family all waited in the common room to send her off, and Theria joined them shortly. Hugs and farewells were exchanged in short. There wasn't time for prolonged partings, and Tempest knew she'd see them again. Within a few minutes, she and Ari were on the road, walking towards The Claw.

The morning air was chilled, warmed by the fires beneath the earth's surface and the lava streams that snaked through the city. The sun barely peeked over the mountain tops, leaving long shadows to stretch over the land. Others meandered through the streets, preparing for their long days ahead. Amongst them was a girl with dark hair who joined Tempest on her journey to The Claw, her mother following close behind with tears welling in her eyes.

"It's so hard to see them go," she said to Ari.

"First one?" Ari asked, amused, and the woman nodded, wiping salty tears from her cheeks. "I was the same way when my son left to enlist."

The daughter rolled her eyes and turned her attention to Tempest, quickening her pace to avoid association with her mother. "Sorry about her. She's always had a flare for the dramatics." She looked back at the blubbering woman, and Tempest looked too, wondering how her own mother would have reacted to this day. "I'm Lyra, by the way," said the girl, pulling Tempest from the thought.

"Tempest." She held out her hand in greeting, and Lyra returned the gesture. "Are you from around here?"

"No, I'm from the plains out east. Locals come in a different way. Most of them have already met Sagua." She pointed to the guild leader who stood by the gates down the road some ways, giving Tempest a name to the face. What she didn't know was that Tempest had met Sagua before, too. "What about you?" she asked.

"Eris," said Tempest. The answer came with ease by this point. She could almost believe it was true.

"The holy city." Lyra's eyes fell unfocused, seeming to be envisioning some far off idea. "Is it as beautiful as people say it is?"

Tempest wasn't sure how to answer. She'd never actually been. "To a visitor I'd say it's stunning," she said, relying on vagueness to hide her lie. "But, to a girl who's lived there her entire life, it's suffocating. I needed to see more of the world."

"I can see that. I suppose any place can become boring if one stays there for too long."

The small remainder of the walk was near silent. The only thing heard was the soft rhythm of four pairs of footsteps treading on the rocky road.

Upon their arrival to The Claw's gate, Sagua stood at the entrance, and Zauryn lay at her side. One other recruit waited there as well. He was a Blacksmith's son. The father stood close, towering over the boy with a black diamond ring on his finger.

Eventually, others trickled in, one a boy whose father had the clear stone of the undecided. Separated ever so slightly from the group stood a mother and daughter pair. The mother had a jet ring on her finger, marking her a Necromancer. The daughter stood awkwardly beside her.

Tempest gestured to the daughter, drawing her closer to the group. The girl stepped forward, hesitantly, persuaded further by a nudge from her mother. "Go on," the Necromancer mouthed, and a smile crept onto the girl's face as she moved to stand by Tempest's side, Zauryn's gaze following her movement.

The dragon stood about five feet taller than Sagua, larger now than the last time Tempest had met him. He eyed her with odd curiosity, and she couldn't help but feel as though she was standing before a judge. She shifted under his gaze, nervous.

"It seems we've all arrived," said Sagua when no one else came. "Let's begin." She stepped forward and bowed to Ari. "Tell me, who do you bring to join the Dragon Keepers?"

"I bring you Tempest," said Ari, "Second generation of the guild."

"I welcome her into the guild," Sagua said, turning to face the next.

Tempest listened to each of their names. The Necromancer's daughter was called Cora, the brown haired boy whose father wore the clear ring was called Reuben, and the Blacksmith's son was called Niklaus. When each had been introduced, the parents were dismissed, and their training began.

"Welcome to The Claw," said Sagua once she was alone with the recruits. "Each of you have come to me as children in our society. In three months' time, you will leave here as men and women. It will not be an easy feat. You must prove yourself in intellect, skill, and bravery. Whenever you find yourself ready, join me inside."

Sagua stepped through the gates and sat cross legged on the ground, leaving Zauryn at the entrance to block their path. She watched intently, observing, calculating.

The other recruits glanced around nervously, but Tempest stepped forward, meeting the glower of the beast. Zauryn lowered his head at her next step, and let out a low, rumbling growl. Tempest continued forward despite it. He snapped at her, his jaws only inches away from her body, sparks forming in his throat, but she didn't budge.

Tempest's heart was racing, but she dared not show it. "Don't you remember me," she whispered, reaching towards the beast without ever breaking eye contact. Her fingers traced the underside of his snout, and she took another step forward. After a moment, Zauryn relaxed beneath her touch.

Sagua stood, confusion plastered to her face. "He knows you," she said, "and you know him... We've met before, but I never thought we'd meet again." A smile twisted her lips. "Come to receive a dragon after all, have you?"

Tempest stepped back, yanking her hand down to her side, afraid. Patch had warned her she'd be recognized by the guild leader. She should have listened.

"Have no fear, Tempest, remember what I told you about dragons and fear."

"They turn it into a game."

"That's right. You can't show fear with a dragon. They sense your weaknesses and use them against you.

"It's not the dragon that scares me," said Tempest, looking warily towards the guild leader.

"You shouldn't be afraid of anyone or anything, Tempest. We must never let people rule our lives with fear. Don't you ever forget that."

Tempest took a breath and relaxed. Sagua seemed not to have any desire to turn her in just yet. Stroking the underside of the beast again, Tempest looked into Zauryn's eyes, and a smile spread across her lips. Fear had driven her so far from home, but now, in the dragon's eyes, she found hope.

Zauryn bowed his head and allowed her to pass.

"Welcome to the guild. I'm honored to be your mentor," Sagua said, holding Tempest's hand. "Now tell me, what are you afraid of?"

"Nothing," Tempest answered, confident in the statement.

12

*S*agua welcomed the rest of the recruits into the guild as each found the courage to pass the dragon. When all were through, she addressed them as a group once more. "Eryn will take you to your barracks," she said. "He's likely just finished welcoming the local recruits, and now, it's time I meet them too. I look forward to seeing how each of you progress. Wait here, and don't stray far. Eryn will be here soon."

Sagua turned and left, but as she'd promised, in a few moments, a young man hurried towards the group, beads of sweat on his brow. He paused, catching his breath. "Sorry, I'm late. Please, follow me." He huffed and motioned them forward.

They walked through the streets, passing the massive domed building at the center of The Claw. Tempest could hear the screeches and growls of the many dragons contained inside it. The doorways looked thick and heavily strengthened, likely to protect both the dragons and the people. Two sentries stood at the doors, monitoring those who came and went.

Once past the two furthest talon-like towers, they were engulfed by a sea of trees. A few shops were scattered along the road that wound through the mountainous forest. One hosted a Merchant crafting saddles of all size for the riders of horses and dragons alike. Another hosted a Blacksmith who'd built an underground workshop, making use of the magma below.

The tree line came to an end abruptly, opening into a large field with buildings lining the edge. A portion of the field had been fenced off, and a small section of seats stood on either end, creating a miniature arena. Two people sparred in the center, fighting one another with sword and dagger. Only a few spectators sat scattered on the benches.

Behind the arena was a longer strip of land dedicated to target practice. Straw sentinels decorated in feathers and arrows stood guard at the end of it. One had caught fire and spread its burning disease to its nearby comrades.

A group of Fire Keepers worked to douse the flaming sentinels in water while someone ran and chased off the dragon that'd caused the damage. Two of the sentinels were reduced to ash by the end, and three more had scorch marks that still glowed red hot, threatening to catch fire again if the wind blew too hard.

The recruits were led into one of the buildings on the edge. A long corridor stretched before them with various doors on either side. A few doors opened to one person suites for the upper ranks, but the ranks lowered the further back they went, and the quality of room followed suit. The first housed two beds, the next housed three, and the final collection of rooms housed four. Each of these were reserved for officers. Tempest knew they'd see no such luxury as recruits.

They reached the dining hall at the end of the officer suites, passed that and arrived at a large room full of pallets. A wooden chest sat beside each for storage.

"You have until noon to report to the dining hall where you'll be introduced to your mentor," said Eryn before hesitantly departing, seemingly unsure whether he was allowed to leave the recruits alone or not.

Lyra moved towards the nearest pallet, but just as she was about to sit, Niklaus claimed it with his stuff, flopping down beside his bag. Lyra glared at him and raised her own bag to drop it on him.

"Don't!" Tempest blurted, grabbing Lyra's arm and dragging her to the next row of pallets. "Best not to pick fights you know can't be won."

"Who says I couldn't win?" said Lyra, glaring back towards Niklaus. "I'll not be pestered into submission by a boy who thinks himself a man." She spat at the foot of his bed and cursed.

"It's day one, Lyra," said Tempest. "Save your wrath for the training field. At least then you'll both have swords and Niklaus will stand a chance."

Niklaus' face twisted with rage, and he sat up, leaning with his elbows against his knees. "Niklaus is my father's name," he said. "If you intend to beat me on the field, you'll at least do me the honor of calling me Klaus instead."

"Klaus it is, then," said Lyra, setting her bag on the pallet between Tempest and the girl, Cora.

Tempest unloaded her things into her chest, keeping the weapons wrapped in clothing so they wouldn't be seen. At the bottom of her bag sat her notebook. She pulled it out and propped herself up against the wall. Unraveling the leather strap that held the notebook closed, she began to flip through the pages, watching her transformation from Dasha to Tempest occur. Her fingers lingered on the page with the first Dragon Keeper she'd seen drawn on it. She wondered where he was. Perhaps she'd see him on the grounds some day and get the chance to meet him.

She continued through the notebook until she reached a blank page, then she dug out a charcoal pencil and began to sketch a dragon flying in a storm with a crowned snake severed on its talon like Markus had dreamed. She wished drawing it would make it reality. If only it were that simple.

On the next page, she drew King Lazareth with his fiery cloak and crown of bones, standing over three caskets. In place of the innocent girl, she drew herself, eyes open with a dragon perched on the edge of the box. On the floor in front of her, Prince lay dead, a snake coiled around his neck.

"You came from Alyria?" a boy asked, startling her from her task. She didn't know how long he'd been standing there, but it was long enough to see her drawing. Tempest glanced up, eyes meeting his for just a moment. He had dark, almond shaped eyes, deep brown in color, that scanned the drawing with wary intrigue. "I don't recall the creatures, though," he said.

Tempest returned her focus to her drawing, grazing the dragon with her index finger, and she voiced the thought in her head. "I heard a man once, in a tavern near here, tell of a dream he had of a dragon killing a snake like this one." When she looked up again, his gaze was locked on her, and she could tell he understood what she'd implied.

She knew she shouldn't have been so free with such thoughts, and for a moment, she regretted speaking them, but the boy's lip twisted upward, a flash of curiosity gleaming in his eyes.

"You ought to be careful with those words. You don't want them reaching the ears of the wrong person."

"You aren't the wrong person, are you?"

That genuine, unguarded smile returned to his lips. "I'm not," he said, "but I can't vouch for everyone else in this room."

Tempest nodded, relieved. She shut the notebook and stuffed it in the chest, fastening the padlock to secure it. "What should I call you?" the boy asked, and Tempest gave him her pseudonym. "Nice to meet you, Tempest. I'm Cyrus," he said, bowing his head when she stood to meet him. He was taller than she was, and the top of her head only reached his chin.

The local recruits had arrived while she drew and were now unpacking their things, Cyrus amongst them. Once settled, they each introduced themselves. There was only one girl with them. Her name was Paris. She had a dark complexion like Cyrus' and icy blue eyes that were stunning to look upon. The other two boys were named Luke and Sage. At first glance, Tempest almost mistook them as brothers, but after a moment, their differences became clear.

"Were you in Alyria?" Tempest asked Cyrus, drawing his attention back to her. She found herself not wanting their conversation to end.

He nodded. "We were near the city when the announcement of the monarchy change came. My parents decided to veer our course to the capital to pay respect for the king and queen. My father had trained with the queen back when she was in these same barracks, learning to be a Dragon Keeper just like us. That was before Neymar took her to wife."

Joy sparked in Tempest's heart. It was a small burst of hope that she suppressed reluctantly. Maybe one day, she'd be able to talk to Cyrus' father about his adventures with her mother and learn what her life in this city was like, but it wouldn't be for some time. It was a curious thought to Tempest, though. If her father hadn't been Royalty, perhaps she'd have been raised here in Firethorne; perhaps she'd have met Cyrus sooner.

A bell chimed from the roof, signaling the recruits to report to the dining hall and severing her imaginings of alternate histories.

"Shall we go eat?" Cyrus asked, gesturing to the door.

Tempest nodded and followed the others to the dining hall where a small piece of meat was served with a potato and a cup of water to wash it down. Paris and Tempest were the first to claim their serving, so they found a table for the group. Klaus was the last to join. He walked up with his plate and wedged himself between Cora and Lyra, forcing everyone to move.

Tempest slid her plate, shifting down to make room for him, and Klaus smirked at Lyra, biting his lip in a horrid attempt of flirtation, a fire igniting behind his eyes. To this, Lyra turned her back and moved to the other side of the table, huffing when she sat back down. Tempest wondered if he'd mistaken the girl's earlier retaliations as a display of interest. If that was the case, she thought he couldn't have been more wrong.

Luke took the seat Lyra had abandoned, shaking his head and laughing. "Good try," he said, patting Klaus on the back sympathetically.

Klaus recoiled from his touch, and for a fleeting moment, Tempest thought she saw fear in his eyes, but he didn't let it reside for long. Instead, he replaced it with further flirtatious endeavors. He moved closer to Cora and draped his arm around her shoulders.

The girl kept her head down and her hands clasped, tension in every muscle, but a flush touched her cheeks. She didn't seem used to being the center of attention.

"Leave her alone," said Cyrus, taking a seat at Tempest's left side.

Klaus rolled his eyes, but he removed his arm from Cora nonetheless, slouching in his seat. "Aw, come off it, Cyrus, it was just a joke. Must you ruin the fun?"

Tempest glanced between the two boys, a realization dawning in her mind. Klaus had listened to Cyrus. He acted as though life's rules didn't apply to him, showing his power with fear and pestering, but he wasn't the strongest player in the room, and he seemed to know it.

"So," said Cyrus when Klaus' advances had been subdued. "What do you think tomorrow's training will consist of?"

Tempest perked up, eager for an excuse to change the course of the conversation. The others reacted similarly. His question spurred debate into motion, and when the discussion was well underway, Cyrus leaned close to her, startling her momentarily. She gave a sharp inhale, catching the scent of pine and field grass as he drew near. With his right brow raised in speculation, he whispered something into her ear.

"We were interrupted earlier, but I have a puzzle for you." He put up a confident façade, but Tempest noticed a slight hesitation in his voice. "I saw something else in that drawing of yours. There was a familiar girl lying in a casket, and a boy with very powerful dying words. You'll tell me about it later?"

Tempest froze, her eyes locked forward. She held her tongue, not trusting any words that might come out. Prince's voice echoed in her mind. *The princess is alive,* he'd said. When she gave no response, Cyrus sat upright, joining in on the conversation at hand, and Tempest knew her silence had answered his inquiry.

Lyra glanced towards her, confused by her sudden trance. "What's wrong?" she mouthed, but Tempest shook her head.

"Nothing," she replied, trying her best to rejoin the conversation, but the weight of Cyrus' words could not be ignored. She'd entered a mental game with him, both of them trying to figure out the other.

"Cypher," Reuben said. "I think I'll name it Cypher." They were discussing dragon names.

"You should name yours Shadow," Klaus suggested to Cora. "Or maybe Ghost, depending on its coloring."

"Kids used to call me Ghost when I was young. It was always meant as an insult when they said it."

"That's unfortunate. I quite like ghosts. They're always lingering about, ensuring no one is alone."

"You'll have to find one elsewhere," said an approaching man. "The title no longer belongs to her. She's not a ghost anymore. She's a dragon."

Tempest's eyes lingered on the scar that traced down the center of his right eye, distracted by the sight of it. She had to blink a few times to convince herself it wasn't a dream. He was the man in her drawing, the one from Alyria. "Welcome to The Claw," he said. "My name is Jax, and I'll be your mentor for the next three months."

Tempest's heart sped. She worried for a moment that he would know her, but the thought quickly faded. It was an irrational fear. There was no way he'd recognize her. Even if he had seen her all that time ago on the rooftops, he certainly wouldn't have known who she was. But, Cyrus did, and she didn't know what he intended to do about it just yet.

13

"Tempest!" said Cora, shaking the bed to wake her from her dreams.

"What?" asked Tempest with a groan, struggling to open her eyes. Her blurred vision gradually focused on the girl who sat perched on the edge of her bed.

She wanted to yell at Cora for waking her, but when she sat up, her eyes caught Jax, standing in the doorway, shouting commands. "Let's go!" he yelled.

"What time is it?" Lyra asked, pulling herself slowly from the bed, furs still pulled tightly around her shoulders for warmth.

"It's game time!" Jax said. "We've only got half the night left so get going!"

Tempest stumbled out of bed, throwing on a jacket before joining the procession of people in the hallway. Familiar faces surrounded her, but for everyone she knew, there were two more she didn't.

The strangers all had smiles on their faces, and excitement rippled through the hall. "Look alive! It's game day!" said a girl who walked beside her.

"What game?" Tempest asked with a yawn.

"Well I can't give it away, now can I?" She spoke with an energy far too high for Tempest's comprehension at this hour. "This is your first, isn't it? You can always tell the new folks from the veterans. Look around, all your peers are still asleep," she said, pointing to the others.

She was right. Through the gaps of the crowd, Tempest could see her fellow recruits staggering down the hall with sleepy eyes that seemed too heavy to keep open, their movements were slow and labored. She figured she looked a lot like them. She'd never been one to rise before the sun.

The girl didn't seem to mind. She continued rambling regardless. "Those who have done this before are wide awake. Most probably didn't even bother trying to sleep. There's no point in it." She reminded Tempest of Patch when they'd first met, energetic and spontaneous, moving too fast for anyone to keep up.

An officer propped open the doors, letting in the chilled night air, and the recruits proceeded through, bumping into each other as they filed into the night. Tempest lost the girl in the chaos of it all.

She pressed her way out, greeted by fresh air and darkness. Her eyes soon adjusted, and she saw orbs of light lining the stream of recruits. A Mage trainee stood behind each orb. Evidently, they'd come from the city, Hekatia, which wasn't far from Firethorne.

Everyone assembled into a small field in the woods, and the fire orbs followed. Sagua stood at the front of the crowd beside Vitani; guild leader of the Mages.

"Welcome new recruits, and welcome back to the rest," said Sagua. "As many of you know, this is a monthly tradition between our two guilds that began many years ago. It started when a group of recruits went out in the night to celebrate their coming of age through a friendly competition with our neighboring guild, the Mages. This competition became tradition between our two guilds and has evolved into the widely anticipated game we now call Lumin."

A cheer erupted from the recruits who had done this before, but the fresh recruits looked around in confusion, still trying to figure out what was happening.

"The rules," said the Mage guild leader, voice booming over the crowd, raising a hand to silence the uproar. "All must play fair or suffer repercussions. The first team to get the opponents Orbis to their base wins the game. There will be no use of weapons, only strategy. Apart from the guardian, no magic will be used either. Lastly, no harm is to come to any player or dragon during the game. Enjoy the night, and may the best team win." As she concluded, two dragons were led through the crowd.

The recruits were split into two teams, evenly distributed by guild and amount of training. Lyra, Cyrus, Sage, and Reuben were put on Tempest's team. The other half of the new recruits were put on the opposite. A captain and guardian were chosen for each team, and a dragon was unchained and taken to each base. Both captains were handed a parchment with their team's base location, and the two groups parted ways. A line of fire ignited down the center of the land and around the arena, creating the boundaries of each territory.

The captain sent groups of people out into the trees to cover as much land as possible, telling none the location of the base. That way, no one could slip up and give away their position. The light of the fire orbs slowly died out as more Mages branched out for defense.

"Everyone else will be offense," the captain said to those who remained in his procession. "You will pair up and scatter around the boundary line, but don't go where any of the opponents are. Our defense will take care of them.

"If you have an open shot at retrieving the Orbis, take it. Remember though, you must also get it back here. If you don't have a clear path, send one member to report back to me and we'll gather a convoy to surround and defeat them. All must report here for the convoy if you see three flashes in the air. One rule you must never forget. Don't get captured."

One of the dragons lay at the entrance of a large crevice in a wall of rock. A bright blue orb of fire hovered behind the beast, and the guardian and captain stood on either side. All who remained paired up Mage to Dragon Keeper, then left to find the central boundary line. Tempest and her partner settled beneath a tree, waiting for the game to begin.

The orbs of light each Mage carried could be seen through the foliage around them. Tempest climbed the tree they sat under, scouting for any color change in the opponent's land. She could see the distant line of fire that surrounded the arena and a red aura radiating over a formation of rocks near the edge. "I think I found their Orbis," Tempest whispered down to the Mage.

He climbed up beside her and looked into the direction she pointed. "Perfect," he said, jumping back down to the ground before helping her off the branch. The distant lights faded to nothing, leaving only the moon, stars, and the shimmer of the northern lights to light the way. A war horn echoed through the trees that sent an owl into panicked flight. "Showtime."

The Mage grinned, and a small wisp of blue light formed beside him. Tempest turned her head, curious if she had one as well. An identical wisp floated beside her. She reached for it, but her hand simply fell through it.

"How are we supposed to get to the other side?" she asked, pointing to the border of flames.

The Mage said nothing, just jumped through the fire. It parted as he crossed, forming back into a solid line when he landed. "Your turn."

"How do I know that wasn't some Mage trick?" she asked, skeptical.

"We're not allowed to use magic, remember?" he replied. "Jump."

Tempest closed her eyes and jumped through the flames. She felt the warmth engulf her, but her skin remained unburnt. The ground was suddenly beneath her, and she sighed in relief, thankful it had worked. When she opened her eyes, she was greeted by three faces, one was the Mage's smiling face, but the other two were strangers with red lights hovering beside them.

The Mage's smile dropped with Tempest's heart, but the two strangers ran past them, jumping to the opposite territory. The Mage fell to his knees in laughter. "You were so scared!"

"So were you," Tempest muttered.

"Come on," he said, standing back up and walking into the trees.

Wolves howled in the woods around them as the night creatures prowled, and an eerie silence hung in the air. Tempest heard the faint murmur of voices behind a cluster of trees, and she spotted red dots drifting between the branches. A team of defenders had perched atop the timber, waiting to pounce on any offense to stumble beneath them. The pair of them were about to fall prey to the trap.

Tempest grabbed the Mage by the arm before he could step into their view. A twig snapped below her feet when she shifted her weight, however, so the two ducked behind a bush, desperately trying to hide themselves and their tag lights from a few members of the group who dropped from the trees to inspect the sudden noise.

"You all heard that, right?" a boy asked.

"Maybe it's a wolf," one of the girl's said.

"Nah, we would have seen it by now if it was."

"Unless it's hunting us," another boy japed.

"Not funny," said the girl, smacking him on the shoulder.

The first boy shrugged. "Oh well, whoever, or whatever it was, it's bound to be gone by now. Let's go back."

The others agreed and reascended the tree, so Tempest and the Mage continued forward, arcing their path to avoid being seen by the group.

The red glow of the opponent's Orbis shimmered from its location, highlighting the trees with a warm glow. Guards became numerous in the area, leaving Tempest on high alert. Every sound made her muscles twitch with anticipation. It was a feeling of thrilled anxiety she hadn't felt since her childhood, when she'd hide from her magister in the dark crevices of the castle with a book clutched in hand, heart pounding in terrified delight, sure to give her position away.

Her heart beat similarly now as they neared the Orbis, dodging glances of nearby guards. It hovered in the center of a circular gathering of standing stones. There were twelve pillars of stone for the twelve supreme gods, each attached by horizontal slabs that lay on top. The dragon paced around the circle, scanning the area for intruders.

"Stay here. I'll report back to base," said the Mage. "If anyone else shows up, send them to join the convoy. I'll have the signal out as soon as possible."

Tempest nodded and lowered herself into a cage of roots that protruded from the base of a leaning tree. The roots arched and twisted above her, secluding her in an earthen cavity the size of a wolf's den. She concealed the holes with a combination of twigs, leaves, and mud, then silently watched through the spaces of her disguise, observing the number of people that walked past her, unnoticing.

The sound of breaking sticks and cracking leaves grew louder with the approach of a pair of recruits. Blue lights hovered at their sides, and when the two neared, she was able to identify one of the faces. "Cyrus!" she whispered urgently, and he stopped, looking around in confusion. "Cyrus!" she said again.

"Tempest?" he asked in the same hushed tone, searching the trees for the owner of the voice.

"Yes," she said.

"Where are you?"

"In the roots."

He looked down, startled. "Why?" he asked, crouching to hear better, and the Mage with him stood guard.

"Waiting for someone to show up. A convoy is gathering at base. I was left here to tell people until the signal was released."

As if on cue, three lights flashed in the sky above the blue team's jail, so Cyrus and the Mage left to join the convoy, leaving Tempest once again to a silence, broken only by the occasional sound of voices or the distant howl of a wolf. Crickets and ants were all she had as company.

A few moments later, the branches behind her snapped under the weight of a body, and a person dropped suddenly into her cage. "Klaus," said Tempest, backing away.

He had a sadistic grin plastered to his face, and his eyes glowed red from the tag light at his side. "Look what I've found! A storm in a cage." He stood crouched to the ground like an animal, blocking her only way out of the small cavity. "I reckon storms don't like being caged, do they? Maybe I should let you free." He shuffled to the side, leaving room for her to exit, but Tempest stood still, not trusting his offer. He gestured for her to hurry. "Come on, before I change my mind," he said.

Tempest stepped forward, and when Klaus made no move to stop her, she continued. However, just before she could pull herself out of the elaborate tangle of roots, he grabbed her by the waist and forced her to the ground. She gasped, back striking against the rocky surface.

Klaus' palms pressed together with his index fingers placed lightly against his lips as if in prayer. "But wait," he said, lowering his hands and crawling towards her. "According to Kaburem, freedom comes with a price."

Tempest reeled backwards on all fours, but the end of the cave came quick, and she had nowhere left to run. Her heart raced, and her thoughts scattered. There was nothing she could do. Klaus climbed over top of her and trailed his fingers over her skin, tracing the line of her jaw. "What shall my payment be?" he asked.

She couldn't bring herself to respond. His fingertips drew ice cold patterns down her chest. There was a look of rabid hunger in Klaus' eyes that made Tempest's soul shrivel. She didn't dare to look him in the eyes, but something stood as a beacon of light in her path. Sagua's words of bravery echoed in her mind.

"I'm not afraid," Tempest whispered to herself. Her thoughts were beginning to fight, but it was her soul that needed the most convincing.

"I'm sorry, I didn't catch that," Klaus said, wrapping his hand around her throat with an iron grip.

Tempest took a deep breath and swung. Her fist caught him just below his jaw with a blow that sent him stumbling back. He snarled in fury, glowing eyes seeming to be aflame.

"Fine!" he said, spitting a wad of blood at her feet. He then whistled, summoning his comrades. "I found a spider in the brush!" he shouted, hauling her out of the root cage by the arm.

They half guided, half dragged her to the jail. Klaus' grip was tight and unrelenting to her attempts of escape. Wrath still flooded his eyes. There would be no fleeing, so Tempest relaxed, following as best she could to refrain from further bruising.

Upon reaching their destination, she was thrown into another, much larger cage with twenty people locked inside. Cracked and crumbled stone lined its edges, and in the corner was a boarded entry point to what looked like an old mine. It seemed a sanctuary compared to the trap she had just escaped.

Some of the prisoners sat on benches. Others scattered the ground. The rest slouched against the walls. All of them looked down with somber defeat.

"Why so sad everyone?" she asked, trying to keep her mind from wandering back to the first cage.

"We've been captured, genius," said a boy. "We get to sit here for the rest of the game while everyone else has fun."

"Who says we have to stay here?" Tempest asked, seeing the possibilities in what lay around her. The new cage wasn't as secure as it seemed. It certainly provided more freedom than the roots.

"The locked and guarded gate," another responded.

"But!" said Tempest. "I don't see a roof, do you?"

The boy looked up and quickly dismissed the option. "How are we supposed to get over the walls? They're twice the size of any of us and impossible to climb."

"Impossible is not a word I know," Tempest decided, and after a thorough inspection of the space, she came to a conclusion. "We build," she said. "I need two people against the wall. The strongest ones in here." Two boys stepped up. "Stand face to face and create a pocket with your hands, then lift someone over."

They did as she directed and successfully got the smallest girl out. The first few escapees took some time, but the attempts became quicker and smoother the more they tried.

Eventually, the only people left in the jail were the two boys and Tempest. They sent Tempest over the wall, then the stronger of the two hoisted the other up. In turn, the one who'd escaped dangled over the edge and pulled his comrade over. Smiles returned to her teammates faces. "There's a convoy on its way to the enemy base, probably there by now. We'll meet them at the Orbis. Follow me," Tempest said, and the group slipped into the woods without the guards noticing their disappearance.

As she expected, the convoy had already arrived by the time they got to the opponent's base. "Welcome back," Cyrus said, approaching her as her people infiltrated the group. "Thought you'd gone and gotten yourself captured."

Her lip twitched into a slight smile. "It takes a lot more than that to stop me."

His eyes met hers with burning curiosity. "I know," he said, though it seemed he was no longer talking about her capture. He reached for her neckline, and her body tensed when his fingertips touched where Klaus' had been, lingering momentarily on her collarbone, but he wrapped his fingers around the small chain that hung there, and she relaxed, heart still beating fervently in her chest. It was not out of fear that her heart continued hammering, though. Rather, it was something different, something that sparked from the ghostly remnants of Cyrus' touch. "May I see?" he asked, words soft as the wind. With a quick glance around to ensure no one watched, Tempest nodded.

Cyrus carefully tugged at the chain, pulling the ring from where it hid. She had the urge to clutch it in her palm and hide her identity from this boy she hardly knew, but she resisted that urge and allowed the ring to be pulled from its safekeeping.

He let out his breath, and a smile touched his lips, thumb grazing over the amethyst stone. "So the executed boy spoke truly. The princess is alive." Tempest opened her mouth to protest the condemning words, but he held a finger to his lips. "I won't tell," he whispered, tucking the necklace back beneath her shirt. "I promise."

Promises were empty agreements until acted upon. Her father had taught her that, but there was unwavering sincerity in his words, and despite caution, she believed him.

The captain whistled, summoning the convoy into action. "Forward!" He shouted over the masses, and they emerged from the trees, completely encircling the red Orbis. The guards backed away, looking for a break in the wall of offense. They were about to close in on it when the Orbis suddenly began to flash.

The red team cheered, a newfound determination flooding through their ranks. They held strong, linked together to protect their Orbis.

"They have the blue Orbis!" someone in the crowd shouted, distressed by the flashing.

"Defense will take care of them," said the captain. "Our job is to get theirs. Hold your ground!"

A wave of wind barreled towards a line of blue that sent some of the offense tumbling backwards. The guardian held off one side of offense while the dragon took the other half, and the defenses of the red team fell back to assist the protecting of the Orbis. Everyone seemed occupied.

"Will the Orbis hurt me if I touch it?" Tempest asked the person nearest to her. They shook their head, so she gave one last look around to make sure her path was clear, calculating the chances of her success in her mind before taking off into the heat of the standoff. She broke through the walls of defense with ease. No one had paid her any attention. It was a foolish mission she'd embarked on. No one would have thought to watch for it.

Her hands touched the Orbis, and the guardian Mage turned her attention to the intruder. "You honestly thought that'd work?" she asked, and a wall of earth shot through the ground, closing Tempest into the circle the dragon and Mage stood in. Everyone else remained beyond the wall.

The guardian applauded; slow, rhythmic claps that bounced off the rock enclosure. "Oh, the joys of novices. See, the goal of this game is to go in stealthily and come out unnoticed. You, however, ran straight into a trap. Your captain had a faulty plan to use brute force to win this game. Strategy is the key to winning," she said, gesturing to the flashing Orbis in Tempest's hands.

Suddenly, it stopped flashing, wiping the grin off the Mage's face. "It seems your strategy is failing too," said Tempest. Using the time given from the Mage's hesitation, she ran to execute part two of her radical plan. Gusts of wind swirled around her, but she kept her footing and scaled the back of the dragon. It reared, aggravated by the sudden mounting, but she stroked its scales in hopes of calming it, urgently demanding it to fly and praying that it would listen.

The beast obeyed and lifted into the air with great flaps of its massive, leathery wings. The earthen walls crumbled around her, and the guardian watched in shock, but her peers erupted in cheer.

It was terrifying in the air, but peaceful at the same time. She'd dreamed of this moment all her life, but nothing could have prepared her for the immense bliss she felt soaring towards the clouds. The northern lights swam in the stars above, and the trees below were decorated with stars of their own, red and blue from the tag lights. The only sounds were the wind and the beating of the dragon's wings. Beneath the clouds, the air was thin and cold, warmed by the internal fire of the beast below her.

She relished in the fleeting moments of the flight, wishing she had time to prolong it, wishing she could harness this freedom and exist in it for all eternity, but she knew she couldn't. Her team awaited.

Eyes stared up at her in awe when she passed over the boundary line and lowered into her team's base. She landed swiftly in front of a girl who had taken the blue team's Orbis, and the girl froze in her tracks, backpedaling from the gusts of wind being thrown at her from the dragon's wings.

Upon landing, Tempest slid off the dragon's back and presented the red Orbis to the blue team's guardian.

After some time, Sagua emerged from the trees, followed shortly by the Mage guild leader. "Well done," said Sagua, and the Orbis' burned out, replaced by the Mage lights to help guide everyone back. Each were colored a radiant blue in honor of the winning team.

14

$\mathcal{T}$he recruits filed back into the barracks to rest before their morning lesson. Klaus dragged his feet, shuffling in with his head lowered, hand cupping the swollen portion of his bruised jaw.

"What happened to you?" Luke asked, taking in the damage to the boy's face. The muscles in Klaus' arms clenched suddenly, and his jaw set with irritation.

Tempest looked down at her hands. They stung from the blow she'd dealt him, and the impact had split the knuckle where her fist had struck his chin.

"Did you do that to him?" Cyrus asked from beside her, and she nodded, half ashamed and half proud of herself for standing her ground. "What did he do to deserve that?"

"He... um... well, he tried to bribe my way to freedom through unconventional methods," Tempest answered, and Cyrus' joking mood turned to fury. He didn't seem fond of the prospect of Klaus laying a hand on her. "He didn't get very far." She feigned a laugh and lifted her hand, trying to make light of the situation, but his brow furrowed, and his eyes darkened.

"It's not a joke, Tempest. I knew a boy like him in my youth. He's got a rabid determination about him that I fear may prove dangerous. He might not have succeeded with you, but what about the others?"

Sure enough, Klaus had his arm wrapped around Cora's shoulders, but she seemed not to mind it just yet, so Tempest let it be. There was no point picking a fight where one wasn't yet warranted.

The sconces dimmed in the hall, burning out with what tendrils remained of the night. Tempest lay in her bed and stared at the ceiling, hoping sleep would take her quickly. To her contentment, her body listened, and her mind went freely to the realm of dreams.

In them, however, she found no solace. A nightmare claimed her thoughts, in which she stood with her back flush against the earthen walls, surrounded by the cage of roots once more. Before her crouched the king instead of Klaus, and rather than the fiery glare and cruel intentions Klaus had had, the king held the barrel of a gun aimed to her head. His finger twitched over the lever.

"No," Tempest said, calm as if the mere word would stop him. The ground beneath the king caught fire. He stayed there, petrified and burning. His screams rang in her ears, carrying into her conscious mind. They mutated with reality, existing beyond the dream.

Tempest opened her eyes, suddenly alarmed. Everyone else had woken to the cries as well, and each of the recruits stared at the source of the commotion. Klaus sat upright with eyes wide open in terror, thrashing at the air and clawing at his already torn up shirt that exposed lashes down his back and brandings that had been burned into his skin. He was sweating profusely and screamed an agonized wail.

"What's happening to him?" Cora cried, standing over his bedside.

"It's a night terror," said Cyrus, voice level. "My sister used to get them when she was young." A sadness lurked in his eyes at the mention of her.

"How do we stop them?" Cora asked, voice quavering with panic.

"You don't," he said. "It'll stop on its own. We just have to wait."

The group watched in silence until Klaus lay still and fell back into a trance-like sleep. No one spoke of it in the morning, and the only acknowledgement of it happening were the worried glances thrown at him every time he turned away.

Jax arrived shortly after Tempest woke again. The others had risen as well, so he led them through the grounds to the castle and down a long hallway that emptied into a grand library. The ceiling was decorated with a beautiful artwork made of colored glass, shaped into an image of a man riding a dragon into battle. Candled chandeliers hung gloriously from the rafters, their flames flickering in a way that made the image above them ripple and move as though it were alive. Books on dragons and Firethorne populated the shelves alongside collections of scriptures written on the land's history. Tempest wished she could read every one of them. There were many titles here she hadn't seen in the capital, and the thought of new stories thrilled her.

A handwritten account sat at each seat of the long tables in the center of the room, each book titled, *The Great History of Elijah and Remus.* Tempest took a seat amongst the others, and Jax began the lesson.

"Please turn your books to page ninety-three," he said.

Tempest pulled the book towards her and pried it open with care. The pages were crisp and yellowed with age, and the ink blotched and faded. Written on the top of the page were six words. *The Origin of the Dragon Keepers.* Each page was carefully written. To have copied it so many times would have taken quite some time, thought Tempest.

"In the beginning of recorded history, dragons were considered monsters," said Jax. "They posed a great threat to human societies, burning down villages and raiding livestock. Tribes would often send their bravest warriors to compete in a game of hunting the beasts. The ones who killed the fiercest of dragons would become chieftains of their tribe. The noblest fighters decorated themselves with the skins of the creatures they slew." As he spoke, he carried an oil lamp to the corner of the room where he set it beside a large crate that hid in the shadows.

With great care, he opened the metallic clasp that held the crate tightly closed. Tempest inched forward in her seat, eager to see what lay within. Jax slipped on a pair of black, leather gloves, then reached into the crate. He eased his arms into it and emerged with a pile of folded armor made of crimson dragon scales. Resting on top of the armor was a helm crafted of the scales and bones of the beast that had been hunted.

The sight of the armor filled Tempest with an odd mix of dread and wonder. She could see in her mind an army of soldiers garbed in armor like this. Hundreds of dragon pelts crafted to create a suit for every warrior. They would have looked magnificently dangerous. But, in her mind, she also saw the hunt. Hundreds of innocent creatures had been mutilated and skinned for humanity's false sense of nobility. She shuddered at the thought of it.

"A few centuries later, killing dragons became sport. Empires were built around those most skilled at slaying the beasts, the best were named kings for their ability to protect the people from the fiery wrath of the dragons. They were seen as god-like men who had been given their ability to kill from the deities themselves." Jax set the armor back in its box with grace, then continued the lesson.

"One rose in the legends as the greatest dragon slayer in the realm. He was known by every man that saw him. They rallied behind him, and he created the largest empire in the history of man. In his later years, this king bore two sons, one of which became an even greater dragon hunter than the king himself. His name was Remus, and he was widely respected throughout the land. But, with this respect, he was also highly feared.

"Remus' younger brother was quite the opposite. The boy had been crippled all his years, said to never be able to walk a day in his life. He was pitied, and everyone knew the poor lad would never sit the throne. As the two boys aged, the older grew crueler and bolder, always trying to prove himself in the battle against the dragons. He had his father's legacy to uphold and was determined to keep the family name in the histories. It was often said that one day, the beasts would be the elder son's demise. Remus became power hungry and overcome with greed.

"The younger brother, Elijah, spent most of his time with the people, growing relationships with the commoners and learning from them. The rest of his time was spent in books."

A smile formed at the corner of Tempest's lips. These brothers reminded her a lot of what she'd been told of her own family. Remus was similar to her exiled uncle, hungry for power and brutal like his father before him. Elijah reflected more of her father. He'd been determined to learn and change the cruelty of the world he saw around him. She hoped her life would follow the path of Elijah and her father rather than the paths of the barbaric warriors.

"Elijah had a unique desire to know everything about the world he lived in," said Jax, "and in his studies one day, he found a collection of stories. They were ancient stories of people riding dragons like horses. The idea intrigued the young prince. Man on the backs of dragons... If he could manage to do it, he believed he'd no longer be known as the boy who couldn't walk. He'd become the man that could fly.

"Elijah left for the scorched lands that were said to be home to thousands of dragons. He had a small party consisting of himself and the man who functioned as his legs. No one else would back him. No one believed that man could tame a dragon, especially a man as crippled as the prince.

"The two spent weeks rounding up and rescuing dragon eggs from hunters. At the end, he had over a hundred. He settled down with his dragons just off the edge of the mountain range and wasn't seen again for years. Many believed the young prince had been killed at the city of dragons, which made the game of hunting the beasts all the more popular. They mourned the loss of their kindly prince and sought revenge on the monsters that'd killed him. Using this, Remus formed a guild of the greatest dragon hunters in the land to end the dragon species for good."

Tempest looked down at the page before her that recorded the history Jax recited. On it was a sketch of a man holding a sword and shield up in defiance while a dragon launched swirling flames his way. She wondered which had won. Did the hunter go down in burning glory, or did the dragon die at the end of the blade? It made her wonder, also, which would win now. Would it be the snake that claimed victory in the storm or, as Markus predicted, the dragon that held the snake's lifeless form?

"In this time frame, Elijah raised his company of dragons, training them and teaching himself how to ride. When the time was right, he flew to all the nearby villages with an army of dragons behind him. With this, he convinced the people of the power an army could have if they used the dragons instead of slaughtering them. Many stood behind the prince in his efforts, overjoyed with the news of his return. But without his knowledge, they spread rumor that Elijah had only come back to take the throne rights from his brother and was raising an army for a revolution. Hearing this information, Remus declared war against his brother and named Elijah a traitor.

"Elijah denied the accusations and refused to come to the capital to fight his brother, so Remus brought the fight to the scorched lands, giving Elijah the advantage. Despite Elijah's denial of the charges, the evidence was against him. Why else would he raise an army of dragons, and why would his followers say the revolution was true? Even if it wasn't what the young prince wanted, rebellion was what the people demanded.

"Remus gathered the largest army known to man and rode out to the scorched lands. Their father came along too, hoping to end this farce before it began, but he was killed on the journey. History says that Wynris caused his demise, but many believe that Remus had his father murdered before he could convince anyone not to fight. All records show that the elder prince was hungry for blood and willing to do anything to secure his position on the throne, even if it required killing his own kin."

A horn echoed through the halls, halting Jax in his lesson.

"That's all we have time for today. Get some food," he announced. "We'll continue with the war tomorrow."

Tempest rose to her feet and followed the others to the dining hall. The meal of the day was a warm stew with a small slice of bread to accompany it. She sat at the table with her peers, eager to have a taste of it. At the end of the table, however, she found distraction. Klaus appeared to be whispering something into Cora's ear, and she giggled, eyes wide and cheeks flushed. She covered her face, embarrassed when she caught Tempest looking.

"So, how did people like day one?" Sage asked, awkwardly trying to start conversation.

"It was dull," said Klaus without hesitation. "I came for dragons, not history lessons."

Tempest didn't see the issue with the histories. She found them to be fascinating tales, and she wished they had more time in each day to learn about them, but she didn't want to start any arguments, so she sat quiet and ate her food.

"You'll get to the dragons eventually," said Jax, having heard their conversation in his approach. He stopped at the end with the same confidence Tempest remembered from Alyria. "I didn't sign up for this guild to teach you history, but it's required for me to do so, and rightfully so. The history is just as important as the rest. As I'm sure you are aware, history has an odd habit of repeating itself. We learn it, and we study it to refrain from making the same mistakes again. Every recruit has learned these histories, and every future recruit will learn them too, therefore you will do the same."

Klaus nodded, humbled by the scolding, so Jax walked off to sit with the officers.

"Want to get out of here?" Cyrus asked, leaning in so only Tempest could hear.

She tilted her head, gaze turning to him, but he kept his eyes forward. Firelight flickered from his right side, casting soft shadows upon the sharp lines of his face. "Where to?" she asked. The others had planned to use the evening to practice sparring drills, but Tempest wasn't opposed to other suggestions.

"To add some more drawings to your collection," he said, holding out her notebook.

She smiled and took it from his hands. "Gladly," she said, then together, they stood and left the dining hall.

15

*T*he barrack doors swung closed behind them, and Cyrus led Tempest into the woods. "I found this place during Lumin," he said, a bashful grin twisting his lips. "It was beautiful and peaceful, so I thought perhaps I'd share it with you."

The woods looked different to Tempest in the daylight than they had during the night. They seemed more colorful—more alive.

Small animals scampered off at their approach, and the tree line soon broke into a meadow with a small pond in the corner. Leading to it was a thin stream that trickled through the forest. Thick vines draped between the trees that traced the edge of the meadow, ornamenting their surroundings with natural garland.

Cyrus latched onto one of these vines and laid across them. "Isn't it beautiful?" he asked, staring into the sky where a flock of birds flew through the clouds.

Tempest's gaze didn't follow his. Instead, it lingered on him. She found him a curious boy, sitting in a tree and finding wonders in the clouds. He looked as though he belonged here, silhouette framed by nature's beauty. She wished she was as calm as he appeared to be.

A nervousness formed in her gut as she watched him. Part of it spawned from knowing he was one of the few people left in the world who knew who she truly was, and she didn't yet know what he'd do with that knowledge, but part of it spawned from emotions foreign to her. Something in him told her that it was okay to trust him, and trust, to her, was terrifying.

His gaze fell to meet hers, and for a moment, she feared that he'd want to ask questions about her past now that they were alone, questions she wasn't ready to answer, but he simply said, "Look up. Tell me what you see."

She turned her gaze upward, relieved, and she watched the birds move, looking for something unique about them, but he didn't follow. His eyes remained focused on her, seeming to be searching for something quite the same.

There was nothing different between these birds and the other flocks that wandered the air, thought Tempest, but Cyrus had found something in them, and she was determined to find it too, so she continued to watch.

The longer she observed them, the more captivating they became. The birds moved together with effortless synchronicity, riding the wind in a dance only they knew. Tempest wished she could join them. Their wings beat and fluttered like her heart did, and in their dance, she began to hear a symphony. High strings as they climbed towards the clouds, a peaceful melody as they floated on the breeze.

As she watched their symphony of movement, she found other things joining it. The sway of the thin leaves of the weeping willow, the soft murmur of the pond rippling minuscule waves across its surface. All the while, her heart kept time.

Tempest looked to Cyrus, unable to explain what she'd seen. It was poetry, music, and dance all in one. When her eyes met with his, she noticed the symphony never faded. That feeling, that magic, it lingered in him.

A young bird distracted her from the moment, straying from the flock, clumsily lowering itself into the shallow edges of the pond. Tempest moved to follow it, and suddenly, something shifted in the waters, breaking through its calm surface and scaring the little bird into flight. Wet, deep-blue scales glimmered in the light as a dragon-like creature emerged from the pond, shooting small waves crashing against the rocks. The beast's eyes were calm and friendly, and down its spine traced lustrous gold plates that waved in the breeze.

"Cyrus!" Tempest called, hushed so as not to disturb the beast.

He jumped down from the hammock of vines and cautiously approached the pond. Tempest stepped back so he could take her place by the water. He reached out his hand and stroked its dripping scales, fearless.

Beams of amber sunlight broke through the foliage, painting his skin with shadow-flecked gold. His eyes reflected a similar hue, turning honey-colored in the light.

Like the dragon before him, he seemed, in this moment, to have been born of flame, containing a fragment of Zalder's divinity within. The dragon appeared to sense this too. It watched him inquisitively, listening to the words he whispered to it. Tempest couldn't hear what it was he said, but she knew it to be a prayer. He watched the creature with equal reverence and curiosity.

Cyrus met its gaze, not with the casualty man usually looked upon animals with, but rather with an expression that declared to anyone who watched, "We are equal." It was the same glimmer of existential fascination he'd pressed her to see in the birds only moments before.

"What is it?" Tempest asked, opening her notebook to sketch the creature. She hadn't heard of dragons inhabiting ponds before.

"It's a Nyoka," he answered. "A water serpent. They're very rare... I always thought they were mere legends." He flashed a bright smile towards Tempest, and she smiled too, content in the beauty of the moment. "According to the lore, they're omens of great fortune."

She held her pencil poised and drew the image before her, wishing it would last, but her hopes were shattered when the beast submerged once more into the waters. Tempest wondered what was down there, how deep the tunnels weaved, and where the beast had come from. She had an odd desire to follow it.

Cyrus touched the surface of the water where the creature had vanished. "Nyokas were my sister's favorite dragons," he said. "She'd read about them in books, and she used to tell me about them when I was a child. She was ten years my elder, and thus, she taught me a lot. What I remember most from those days, however, was the constant quest for adventure. We would follow streams and probe through lakes in an effort to find legendary creatures, though the main goal was always the Nyoka." A tinge of longing lurked in his voice. There was a sadness in his eyes again. It was the same look he'd given the last time he'd mentioned her.

"Did either of you ever find one?" Tempest asked, curious to learn more.

Cyrus shook his head, swallowing the emotions that threatened to spill from his eyes. "She got sick. Melancholia was what they called it. She didn't want me to know, so she started sending me off on my own. She'd convinced me that if we split up, we'd find the Nyoka faster. I would follow one stream; she would follow the other." He closed his eyes, distant from Tempest now, seemingly lost in the memory.

Tempest sat beside him, and he placed his hand on the ground, only a palm's breadth from hers. "Will you tell me about her?" she asked.

He didn't answer at first, but when his gaze met hers once more, he continued.

"There was one particular day, when I returned to the place we always met, I found a letter written by my sister," he said. "In it, she told me she'd finally found one of the mystical beasts. I was mad, at first, that she hadn't come to get me, but I kept reading regardless. She told me the creature had spoken to her and promised her a world under the sea. She'd been invited to join them in it. The Nyoka was magical, you see, and it could turn her into one of them. She said only her soul could make the transition, though, so her body would be left behind.

"At the end of the letter, she told me to take it to our parents. If I did, she promised to come and visit me one day to prove the world under the sea was real. I, being the naïve and hopeful child that I was, ran the letter to my parents, beaming from ear to ear."

Tempest's heart sank. She knew how this would end.

"My parents, when they read the letter, fled from the house to try to stop her. They understood what she truly meant to do. I waited by the door for their return, dreaming of the dragons under the sea and wondering how many adventures my sister would tell me about when she came back to visit.

"They returned a few hours later. It had started raining by then, and the water had smudged some of the ink on the letter they'd dropped. I picked it up to save the words as my father walked by, carrying my sister in his arms. She was soaked, dripping, and tinted blue like the water." Cyrus' voice stopped there and a tear fell from the corner of his eye.

"What was her name?" Tempest asked, wanting to help him carry the weight of the memory. She knew how hard it was to bear such loss alone.

"Zuri," he replied.

Tempest carefully opened her notebook to the page where she'd drawn the water dragon. Just below the sketch of the creature, she wrote the name of the girl who had joined the beasts, memorializing Cyrus' sister in the pages of her book. When she'd finished, she closed it softly and held it to her chest. "It never goes away, does it? The pain, I mean."

"It changes, and it fades a bit, but no. It never goes away." He took a deep breath, composing himself quite suddenly. "We mourn those lost to us, but they're never completely gone, not truly. They linger in the small phenomena of the world around us. They're found in the trees, in the flowers, in the animals, and in the moon. All these things stand as a constant reminder that life as a whole goes on. No matter how many are lost along the way, those we love remain eternal."

Tempest found it a comforting notion. She ran her fingers through the grass and smiled. She enjoyed being with him, sharing her burdens and bearing his. With him, she felt she could truly be herself. There were no secrets barricading their friendship, and he understood the magnitude of the fear and grief she held within her heart.

"Ready to go?" Cyrus asked, a reflection of Tempest's smile on his own face. She nodded and followed him out of the meadow, wishing they could have stayed longer.

~~~

All but two of the recruits were at the barracks when they returned. "Where have you been?" asked Reuben upon their arrival.

"Where's Klaus and Cora?" Cyrus asked, not giving Reuben an answer.

"They ran off some time after lunch," said Reuben. "They'll be back soon; the supper horn is about to sound."

Conversation ended there, and a waiting silence fell over the room. Tempest moved to sit on her pallet, and Cyrus walked towards his, giving a slight parting glance when Tempest left his side. She sat down and pulled out the book of the gods, flipping through its pages to pass the time. Her fingers traced over the letters written at the top of one page near the middle. *Xudor*, it read. A ribbon lay in the crease of the binding, marking the place she had left off with the Priest who'd accompanied her on her journey to Firethorne.

In the bottom corner of the page was a drawing of the god, sitting on his great throne in the underworld. He was half man and half corpse. A depiction of Odemus stood by his side, gesturing towards the gate that merged the mortal and spirit world. Two lions sat on either side of the threshold, guarding the boundary between realms. Tempest propped herself against the wall and began to read.

~~~

Her reading was interrupted by the return of Cora and Klaus just before the horn sounded. As the recruits filed out, Cora grabbed Tempest's arm and pulled her aside.

"Can I talk to you?" she asked, flitting nervous glances towards Cyrus, who watched from the edge of the room.

Tempest nodded and turned to the boy. "Tell the others I wanted to show Cora the Nyoka," she said. "We'll be there soon." Cyrus nodded and left to give the two some privacy.

"You saw a Nyoka?" Cora asked, amazement in her eyes.

"We did," said Tempest, showing her drawing of Cyrus with the beast.

Cora stood there for a moment, stunned. "So... " She smirked. "It's mutual, then?"

"What's mutual?"

"Oh, don't play the fool. Can't you tell he fancies you?"

Tempest felt suddenly abashed. "What makes you think that?"

Cora gestured to the notebook. "You don't see him running off to the woods with anyone else, do you?"

"No," said Tempest, glancing down to avoid Cora's eyes. She didn't know where her feelings stood with Cyrus just yet. He was greatly intriguing to her, but she wasn't certain there was more to it. The rushed beating of her heart seemed to think perhaps there was.

Even if it were true, she hardly had the liberty to explore those fancies with her future being so uncertain. "If we're going off that logic, I should ask the same about you and Klaus," she said in an effort to shift the focus of the conversation.

A flush crept to Cora's cheeks. "That's sort of what I wanted to talk to you about." Her mood shifted, and a shadow crossed her face. "I'm not supposed to tell anyone... He *told* me not to tell anyone... but Tempest, I have to, and well, you were the first person to show me any kindness here, so I know you'll understand."

"What did Klaus tell you?" His demanded secrecy had Tempest worried.

Cora seemed to read her fear. "He's not a bad person, Tempest. He's really not..."

"What happened?"

"Remember when he asked us to call him Klaus instead of his full name? He'd said Niklaus was his father's name." She paused. "Did you see the scars on his body during the night terror. I was right beside him, Tempest. There were so many." Cora's voice was distant.

"His father did that to him," she said. "His mother left him as a boy, and his father blamed him for it. He would come home drunk and beat Klaus. He even burned Klaus sometimes, branding him with whatever he could find..." Her words trailed. "You can't tell *anyone*!" she said, suddenly afraid.

"I won't," Tempest promised. "This conversation never happened."

"Thank you," said Cora with a breath, and the two of them made their way to the dining hall.

Cyrus looked over when Tempest sat down, silently asking if everything was all right. She nodded and joined in on the conversation.

"We've got a little wager on a tale Cyrus told us about your adventure this afternoon," Luke said.

"If your story matches what Cyrus says, then I win," said Sage. "So, tell us, what happened out in the woods?"

"Hmmm..." Tempest pondered aloud to make it seem as though she had to think on it. "Well, we found this beautiful meadow," she played.

"And?" Sage pressed, leaning forward to hear every detail.

Tempest shrugged. "The birds were stunning, but that was about it." It meant nothing to the others, but Cyrus' lip twitched upward.

"Ha!" said Luke, taking a few coins from Sage's hand.

"Oh wait!" Tempest exclaimed. "We also found something called a Nyoka."

Sage grinned and took the money back.

"What if she's lying?" asked Luke. "What if they planned this?"

"Maybe we did. Maybe we didn't. I suppose you'll never know," Cyrus teased.

Luke grumbled, but the conversation moved on. When they'd finished supper, the recruits all returned to the barracks for some time before settling down for the night. Sleep came easy for Tempest that night, and nothing came to haunt her dreams. She woke refreshed and grateful for the whole night's rest. Perhaps the Nyoka had been an omen of luck after all, she thought.

Eggs were served in the morning before the recruits made their way back to the library for their lesson.

Jax stood at the front of the room, nodding a greeting to the recruits when they entered. Once everyone was seated, he jumped right back into the story.

"As we left off yesterday, Remus took his men north to the scorched lands, determined to quell his brother's rebellion. The size of Remus' army made travel slow, so word reached Elijah of their approach long before the army arrived."

"Elijah spent that time gathering strength. He took his army of dragons to more distant lands, flying over the villages, hoping to rally the people. If you turn to page one hundred and four, you'll see an account of one of Elijah's flights written by a villager." He paused, waiting for the students to open their books and read the tale. Tempest looked to the words on the page, losing herself to the memories the pen strokes preserved.

~~~

The feast of Aborh was fast approaching. Everyone worked in a chaotic swarm, laboring in the fields to prepare for the great harvest. The sun beat down on our backs, drenching our clothes in sweat. My skin turned sensitive to the touch and reddened the longer we stood under its rays.

Despite the conditions, there was an energy amongst the people. The feast of Aborh was a great celebration to our small village, and the excitement was spreading... but something felt odd. Something felt different.

I left the field and joined the party in the forest that was collecting wood for the fires, desperate for the shading of the leaves. Dread settled in my heart, however, when a massive shadow fell upon the earth, and dozens of screams echoed through the air. I looked towards the sky to see what was causing the pandemonium, only to see hundreds of leathery wings and glimmering scaled bodies.

My stomach dropped at the sight. Our celebration was about to turn into a slaughter. Every instinct told me to run, but my mind was stubborn. Not many people had ever seen a gathering of dragons so large.

One of the dragons circled above, watching the flock below. It was the largest of the dragons and was colored a void-like black with purple patterns on the wings and spine.

"It's the prince!" A woman shouted, pointing to the circling beast. I could see it now. On the shoulders of the dragon was the silhouette of a man. Everyone had heard tales of the prince and his dragon army, but none of the stories gave the sight justice. It was beautiful, magnificent, and terrifying.

The prince looked strong and almost godly on the dragon.

~~~

"The prince's flights demonstrated a power previously unknown, and a fire grew inside the people's hearts that burned brightly. They all desired to join the fight," Jax began again.

"When Remus arrived, his men were worn and exhausted. They were in no condition for battle. Elijah met with his brother in private to discuss terms of peace. He wanted no blood to be shed. Remus refused these offers of peace and returned to his people, telling them that he'd desperately tried to get his brother to agree to civility and grant their father's dying wish, but that Elijah had denied his offer and sought war instead, determined to take the throne from his brother.

"The following day, the campaign began, and after three months of fighting, Remus met his demise. The land lay scorched and painted red with blood, and the air reeked of death. Elijah's dragon set fire to his brother's horse as Remus charged at the lead of his army. All hope left the soldiers when they watched their king burn, and shortly after, fell from his horse in death.

"Elijah was given the crown, and the people were told the truth about the old king's intentions of war. He taught the people how to tame the dragons as he had, and he established the guild of the Dragon Keepers. The Dragon Hunters were abolished by law, and those who refused to give up the trade were given to the fires of Zalder to appease the god and keep the chain of volcanoes from erupting. This offering has kept them at bay ever since."

Tempest closed the book with a soft thump, thoughts still lost in the world the words had told of. Prince had given her a book about the Dragon Hunters back in Alyria. She'd been horrified at the thought of the guild, but it comforted her to know its members had been punished. Elijah had delivered retribution for all the slaughtered creatures, protecting the innocent as any good king should do.

16

$\mathcal{A}$ soft breeze stirred the humid morning air, and birds chirped to the coming of the new day. Jax stalked past the line of half-asleep recruits and stood before the doors of the armory. Two men guarded its entrance.

"Today, we will begin combat training," he said. "It is an important skill to carry with you, and it must be continuously cultivated. Every two days, I will present you with an introductory lesson in the wielding of various weapons. We will begin with the sword, as that will be your most common companion. Next, we will train with the bow. After that, you will have two days to train with a weapon of your choice. On the last day of the week, a mock battle will be hosted in the woods. Teams will be decided by skill level shown over the next few days.

"If you would, please follow me." He stepped into the armory. "Choosing a sword is a more difficult task than some would presume. You must make sure it fits you. Does it balance right? Does it feel like a mere extension of your arm, or is it too heavy? Knowing your blade can mean the difference between living or dying."

Inside the armory, weapons lined the walls. On one side hung an array of blunted swords, daggers, and knives. On the opposite, the wall was covered in an assortment of bows and arrow stuffed quivers. In the back were the lesser used weapons such as spears, tridents, hammers, and axes.

Tempest selected one of the swords that matched the size of the one she'd fought Theria with. It was metallic, and therefore heavier, but otherwise felt much the same. She widened her stance and pointed the tip of the blade to the shoulder of an imaginary person. Steel met hers, and Jax took position opposite her.

"You've dueled before?" he asked. "But, combat is not a duel." He whistled for the guards, and the two men fell in behind her. "You're surrounded. What do you do now?"

Tempest tapped the point of her blade to his chest. "Kill the leader, I suppose. But that's what you're supposed to teach me."

Jax made a guttural noise. "That'd work, but you'd likely die for it."

"Perhaps it'd be a risk worth taking," said Tempest, and Jax dismissed the guards.

Off to the side, Tempest watched Cyrus approach one of the swords and carefully take it from its stand. He clasped his hand around the hilt and moved his arm in circles, testing the weight of the blade, then he gave a curt nod and slid it into its scabbard, latching it to his hip. It suited him well, she thought.

When everyone held a proper sword, Jax led them back to the field, positioning them in a circle before standing in the middle. "Tempest, come to center," he said, motioning her forward. "Everyone else, scatter around her." The remainder of the group walked aimlessly around her until Jax held up his hand to stop them. "Without looking, tell me who stands behind you."

Tempest blinked, trying to remember who had passed. Only Paris, Reuben, and Lyra stood in view, which left too many options. She shook her head, giving up.

"Hi," Cyrus whispered, stepping close enough for his presence to be felt. It was tranquil, unyielding, and undeniably alluring. She grinned and spun to face him.

"You'd be dead," Jax said, turning slightly to address the rest of the recruits. "The most important thing in combat is to know your surroundings and use them to your advantage."

Tempest ducked down and grabbed a rock from the ground. With swift precision, she launched it towards Jax, but he caught it with ease. "Next rule," he said, tossing the rock with amusement. "Never let your opponent read you. Never let them see what you plan to do."

"Wouldn't have been able to catch that if it had been a bullet," Tempest muttered. She heard steel draw behind her and quickly turned, preparing to block the oncoming blow.

"Hold," said Jax, halting Cyrus' attack. With a quick glance, he checked her stance, then pushed her lightly, knocking her off balance. "Always keep your feet apart. As soon as you put your feet together, you lose your grounding and can easily be pushed off your center."

Tempest stepped her feet apart and raised the blade again. "Attack at will," Jax said.

Reuben and Cora came at her first, swinging from opposite sides. She dropped to the ground, grabbed a handful of dirt, and threw it into the face of the nearest opponent. Reuben stumbled, temporarily blinded by the raining dirt. Tempest used this opportunity to take him out. She swiped her legs underneath him and knocked him to the ground. He groaned, back striking the solid earth beneath him.

Cora's blade arced with speed, but she had hesitated, not wanting to do any harm, so Tempest dodged the blow with ease and rolled behind her, lifting the blade to touch it to her back.

Cyrus and Lyra applauded, but they stopped when Klaus joined the fight, swinging his sword up to push Tempest's away from Cora. He came at her with rapid, heavy blows, backing her into the tree line. Cyrus stepped forward to help, but he was stopped by Jax's arm. "I want to see how she does."

Tempest's heart raced as Klaus advanced, backing her into a trap. Behind her lay an expanse of trees and roots. Perhaps that wasn't such a bad thing though, Tempest thought. She was smaller and quicker than Klaus was and would be able to weave through the obstacles faster.

Tempest darted into the tree line and waited for him to approach. As he neared, she quickly scaled a tree and swung off the branch to land behind him. He whirled around to block her oncoming attacks, and she tried to mimic his tactic of beating the opponent back into a trap with hard, rapid blows, but he didn't budge. She tired quickly of these efforts, and with one last jarring blow, she lost her grip on the sword. It clattered noisily to the rocky ground.

Jax nodded, approving. "Next pair," he said, pointing to Lyra and Sage. "To the field."

~~~

The recruits sparred for the remainder of the day, stopping only for small breaks. By the end, Tempest was exhausted, sore, and well beaten, but no rest was given.

The following day, they were paired up against each other for a competition to find the best swordsman in the group. Tempest's first match was with Cora, who, with her wits about her, put up a strong fight. Despite this, Tempest came out victorious.

She praised Cora for her skill, then turned her attention to a new pair, sparring a short distance away. Cyrus and Paris danced around each other, each uniquely skilled, but Cyrus, even exhausted after his last duel, was stronger.

The fight took longer than Tempest expected. Paris was quick and played on Cyrus' weaknesses. In the end, however, Cyrus proclaimed victory. He was given a moment to breathe before his next battle with Reuben.

For the next duel, Tempest found herself once again fighting Klaus. They each stood ready in the dueling stance, waiting for Jax to give the starting command. A whistle shot through the air and steel collided. Klaus wasted no time to start this duel. She lifted her blade, blocking his attack. Her arm reverberated with the impact, but Klaus swung again. There was no time to let her arm recover. She parried and bolted, running around him and jabbing at him when she found an opening in his guard.

Klaus quickly grew annoyed with her play. His blade swooped down behind her and knocked out her knees. She fell to the ground and rolled in attempt to regain composure. As she went to stand, the tip of Klaus' blade pressed to her throat, ending the duel.

Jax clapped. "That would have been an excellent maneuver if it'd been executed properly. You must always be prepared to defend yourself."

Cyrus and Reuben still sparred when Tempest sat to catch her breath. She watched them, studying each of their movements. Beads of sweat dripped down Reuben's face, and his cheeks were flushed with exhaustion, but Cyrus looked like he could go on for hours. He seemed well practiced in the art of the sword. His muscles were leanly toned, and his movements were precise. It looked almost choreographic. Eventually, Reuben yielded, dropped his sword, and raised his arms in surrender.

With a prideful grin, Cyrus sat on the bench beside Tempest and guzzled down a cup of water from a basin that'd been delivered earlier in the day. It had gone warm long ago, but no one minded in this heat. Both Cyrus and Klaus were given a moment's break before facing each other for the final victor.

A short distance away, Tempest watched Klaus approach Cora with a single white rose in his hands. He seemed to have picked it from a bush near the armory. With chivalrous regality, he offered it to the girl.

"A ghost flower for my ghost," he said, and she took it from his grasp.

"Don't you remember," said Cora with a flush. "According to Jax, I'm a dragon, not a ghost."

"Not until there's an emerald ring on your finger," he said, raising her hand to his lips. "May I have the favor of the fairest maiden in the land before I leave for battle?" Klaus asked, mocking the old stories of great heroes fighting for the favor of their ladies. Tempest found the scene amusing. She'd have never thought Klaus to be an old romantic.

Cora giggled and her cheeks flushed an even brighter red. "Of course."

Jax approached the center of one of the fields, drawing the attention of all the recruits. "Final round!" he announced. "Cyrus and Klaus." The two boys stood and made their way to the center, and Cora joined Tempest on the bench.

Klaus' cold composure returned, and he positioned himself for the duel. Tempest wondered who would win. They were both equal in strength, so Klaus' previous tactic of brute force wouldn't work. It would be a game of deception and strategy. As to who was better at that, she didn't know.

"Ready?" Jax asked, and together, the boys nodded.

A whistle split the silence, and the two stood, watching each other, waiting for the other to make a move. Klaus swung first, but it was too slow. Cyrus easily parried, quickly pulling back to strike. He landed a blow on Klaus' shoulder.

Klaus snarled like a beast, furious that Cyrus had been able to reach him. The two circled each other like wolves, striking random blows to test the opponent. Klaus resorted to his former strategy, growing impatient with the dance. He attacked hard and fast, pushing Cyrus into a corner.

Tempest sighed, saddened by Klaus' apparent looming victory, but something caught her eye. Cyrus was grinning. He wanted this to happen, she realized. He knew this would happen.

Klaus was confident in his victory at this point and became careless with his attacks. He exposed himself for a split second, and Cyrus charged, forcing his opponent stumbling back, caught unaware. He flicked his sword just beneath Klaus' hilt and ripped the blade from his grasp.

Klaus sat stunned on the ground, and the tip of Cyrus' blade touched his chest. "Victory," said Jax, pleased with the fight. "Tomorrow we begin with bows. Come ready to work, and put the swords back in the armory before you go. I'll see you all in the morning." And with that, he turned and left.

Cyrus held out his hand to help Klaus back to his feet, but the offer was rejected. Klaus smacked Cyrus' hand away and stood on his own.

"That was rude, Klaus. He was just trying to help," said Cora, walking up to the pair.

"I'm sorry," said Klaus, wrath crossing like a shadow behind his eyes, "did you just scold me?"

Cora froze, confused by his sudden anger. "I didn't mean to—"

Luke pulled Klaus aside in an effort to sever the brewing tensions. "Let's get back to the barracks," he said, starting down the path to the buildings.

Tempest followed close behind, moving to walk beside Cyrus. "Nice fight," she whispered, and he smiled and mouthed a thanks.

Upon returning, Cora curled up in the corner of her bed, staring at nothing, so Tempest joined her, looking at the others in a silent bid for a moment of privacy.

Luke set a hand on Klaus' shoulder. "Can I talk to you outside?" he asked, and Klaus stood to follow, throwing an apologetic glance towards Cora as he left. It comforted Tempest to know that he at least understood he'd hurt her.

"I didn't mean to upset him," Cora said when Klaus had left, turning slowly to look at Tempest.

"I know," said Tempest. "And so does he. His adrenaline was high from the fight, and losing shamed him, especially losing in front of the girl he's trying to impress. It doesn't excuse his anger, but perhaps you can find it in your heart to forgive him."

Cora didn't give a verbal answer, just sat there in silence and nodded.

A few moments later there came a rasp at the door. "May we come in?" Luke asked from outside.

Tempest looked one last time to Cora before answering. "Yes," she said, and the door inched open.

Luke walked in, followed by Klaus, whose head hung low. Tempest stood and joined the others outside, and Klaus approached Cora.

"I'm sorry," he whispered. "I shouldn't have snapped like that."

The door clicked shut behind them, leaving Klaus and Cora to settle things.

~~~

Come morning, the recruits were led to a separate section of the combat training field than they'd been before. This area was populated with the straw sentinels Tempest had seen her first day. Those that had been burned down by the dragon had been replaced with new ones that were already decorated with arrows.

A collection of bows lay in the grass for the recruits to choose from. They'd been brought from the armory and set out to save time. Tempest picked one up with a decent draw weight and nocked an arrow, holding the bow to the side.

Jax whacked at it with a stick and glared at her. "Always load towards the ground. Never point the arrow at a peer. Remember, these can kill."

Tempest lowered the bow, waiting for the rest to choose. When each recruit had one, they were led to the range of sentinels. A line of stones marked the standing point for the range. "Unless you wish to be shot, don't cross this line until all quivers are empty and all arrows have stopped flying. You will watch me perform the steps first, then you will try it yourself.

"Step one, stance," he said, demonstrating. "Your feet should be shoulder width apart and perpendicular to your target. Step two, nock your arrow. The three feathers should rest on top. Third step, draw. The arm holding the bow should be almost fully extended but with a slight curve so the string doesn't rub your arm raw.

"For the hand drawing the string, your index finger should be above the arrow, your middle and ring finger should be below it. When you draw, your hand should pull to your chin. Breathe in when drawing, and exhale when you release." He aimed and released the arrow. There was a small twang of the bow string and the wisp of the arrow cutting through the air. Before Tempest could blink, the arrow had wedged itself into the heart of the sentinel.

His accuracy was deadly and precise, but he showed no pride in his shot. He simply turned to the rest of them and waited for them to begin. Tempest drew first and aimed it at one of the sentinels. She exhaled and let go of the string, watching the arrow fly. To her despair, it sailed over the sentinel, landing somewhere in the brush behind.

"Congratulations, you killed the grass," said Cyrus behind her, but Tempest found no amusement in it.

"I'd like to see you try," she said, stepping aside.

Cyrus shrugged and gave it a shot, sticking an arrow in the sentinel's shoulder. "At least I hit the target," he teased.

Tempest nocked another arrow, hoping to redeem herself, but a twang behind her halted her motion, and an arrow sailed past and struck the target with a lethal shot. Looking back, she found Cora, grinning with deep satisfaction.

Once all arrows had been fired, the recruits gathered them up and started again.

The day grew old, and the sun began to set. Tempest's fingers ached and her arms were heavy. They had taken breaks throughout the day and were given an hour for lunch mid-day, but exhaustion still seeped through her bones.

When the sun touched the mountains, the recruits returned the bows and headed back to the barracks for supper.

~~~

Cora won the tournament the next day, placing Reuben in second and Klaus in third. The conversation at the dining hall that night consisted of banter over which weapons certain people would be good at using for training the next two days. At this talk, Tempest was reminded of the two weapons she'd brought with her.

She snuck off to her pallet when she was confident no one would pay her any mind for it, then she dug through her chest to find the weapons she sought. She carefully unraveled the dagger from its rags and set it on the floor before her. It'd been a while since she'd held the blade in her hands, and she figured she'd do well to train with it.

The gun, however, took precedence. That was the weapon she'd need to know most about if she ever hoped to rise against Kaburem. She picked it up and slowly unraveled it. Looking at the gun, she could hear the deafening cracks it made when the bullets sprung free. She closed her eyes, remembering.

Each thunderous crack held a memory lodged in the deep corner of her mind. One for the Necromancer. One for the Medic. Both had died together to give her time to run. One for the guard that stood in her way. One for each searing wound that had torn through her skin. And lastly, one for Prince. That one rang the loudest in her mind.

She placed the gun carefully into her bag, and the sound of footsteps echoed down the hall behind her. "What are you doing in here?" Cyrus asked. "You disappeared and never came back."

"I was making sure I still had the weapons I wanted to train with," she said.

"Is that one of them?" He pointed to the dagger still laying displayed on the floor.

Tempest nodded and lifted it for Cyrus to see.

"It's a pretty blade. Where'd you get it?"

"The Blacksmith guild leader gave it to me a while back."

That day seemed like a lifetime ago. She wrapped the blade back up and slid it in her bag beside the gun to take in the morning. Soon after, the other recruits filed into the room and settled down for the night.

Morning came quickly, and with it, another day in the training field. The others browsed the armory for any weapons they wished to try, but Tempest stood off to the side, she'd brought both the gun and dagger with her. Once all had come to their decisions, they gathered outside. Klaus had grabbed an axe, Cora had a crossbow, Cyrus took a trident, Luke a spear, and the others held a variation of daggers and throwing knives.

"Where's your weapon?" Jax asked upon seeing her empty handed. Tempest patted her bag in response.

Each recruit was sent off to the station that best fit their weapon. Tempest followed Cora to the archery range. "You can go first," said Cora, wrangling with the crossbow. "I want to wait for Jax with this one."

Tempest nodded and reached into her bag. Her fingers found the shape of the wrapped gun and pulled the object out. Corner by corner, she unraveled the weapon, suddenly nervous. She placed the cloth back in her bag and inspected the gun in her hands. The last time she'd used it, she'd killed someone with it.

Cora's mouth fell open at the sight of it. "How did you get one of those?" she asked, worry and fascination warping her features.

"It was given to me by a boy who was murdered by the new king," said Tempest, trailing her forefinger down the side of the barrel until it reached the trigger. "I have a mind to learn how to properly use it."

Cora stepped back, and Tempest loaded and primed the weapon, cocked the hammer, and lifted it to her target. With a deep, shaky breath, she pulled the trigger. It hit the sentinel in the chest with a thunderous crack. In her mind, she saw not the mutilated body of the straw man, but rather the collapsing form of a fatally wounded king.

Everyone in sight had stopped what they were doing, and all eyes locked on her, Jax's burned with fear. He stormed towards her and grabbed her wrist, yanking the gun from her hands. He swiftly disabled it and dragged her towards The Claw. "You better pray no one heard that," he said, eyes flitting to the people on the path as though every one of them planned to do him harm.

17

*J*ax sat in the corner of the room with his arms crossed. His eyes bore through Tempest, who sat in a chair opposite of Sagua. The guild leader had her elbows propped up on the desk between them, resting her chin on her thumbs. "There's been a new law implemented in the kingdom of Alyria," she said, taking the gun from Jax's grasp. "All use of firelocks by any civilian who is not a member of Kaburem is strictly prohibited. We didn't feel the need to announce this information to our recruits because we didn't expect any of you to have one, let alone to use one, but it seems we've underestimated your stupidity."

Her voice carried an icy bitterness that hurt Tempest more than the scolding. "Why in Zalder's name would you, one, bring a gun inside these walls, and two, draw attention to yourself by firing it? You're supposed to be hiding, not advertising your location," said Sagua.

Jax's face twisted at the last sentence.

"I know," Tempest admitted. "If I'd known about the law, I wouldn't have brought it out. But, it's a weapon... one that very few people on this land have mastered the use of. I simply wanted to learn." She looked down at her hands, nervous but feeling bold. "I keep it on me because there is nowhere else it'd be safe. By having it with me, I will always know there is one less gun for Kaburem, and one more for Alyria." She paused a moment before continuing, eyes meeting once more with Sagua's. "We cannot hope to revolt with swords and arrows. We need these firelocks."

Jax shifted to the edge of his seat, a choked noise sounding from his throat. "She speaks of treason! A child has no right to talk in this way! Who does she think she is?" He stood abruptly, chair falling with a clattering echo that bounced off the stone walls.

Sagua lifted her hand to quiet his worries. "I appreciate your concern, but oddly enough, I think this particular child does have that right," she said with a slight smirk. "Jax, meet Dasha; daughter of the late King Neymar. You'll keep this knowledge in this room, I hope."

Jax's lips moved as though he wished to protest further, but disbelief kept him silent. He gave a nod and recovered his fallen chair, taking a seat in it once again.

Tempest eyed him warily. She wasn't confident that Jax would protect her name. His only motivation to do so would be out of respect for his commander. She prayed that was enough.

Sagua passed the gun back to Jax who held it with unstable hands. He was a part of this now, Tempest realized, and that made him a traitor to the crown, just like them.

"Despite the girl's mistake, she makes a valid point," said Sagua. "We can never face Kaburem without the use of guns. Jax, you'll start up a collection of firelocks in the mountains. Gather anything you can get your hands on. We may need it in time. Tempest, you're dismissed."

Tempest bowed her head and rose to depart. "May I ask you something before I leave?" she said, and Sagua gestured for her to continue. "Why did Kaburem ban guns?"

Sagua smiled, a spark of excitement in her eyes. "Because an uprising is brewing," she said, then she stood. "Jax, please escort Tempest back to her lessons, and speak no word of what's been discussed in this room."

Jax bowed, then guided Tempest back to the field, hiding the gun away before anyone caught him with it.

Tempest was greeted at the field by confused glances from her peers, but all left the matter alone for the moment. The day expired soon thereafter, and the horn for supper rang through the air. It wasn't until after the meal that someone finally confronted her.

Cyrus pulled her out into the meadow when the time allowed, walking silently beside her until they were well away from any stray ears. He stopped once they reached the meadow where only the trees would hear them. "What compelled you to use one of Kaburem's weapons?" he asked, terror in his eyes. "Are you trying to get caught?"

"Of course not!" said Tempest, arms crossed. "Prince gave me the gun so I could protect myself from Kaburem. I've only ever used it once, and I wanted to train with it further on something not made of flesh."

"Prince? Was that the boy... on the night of the ceremony..." Cyrus paused, struggling to find the right words.

"The boy Lazareth killed? Yes, he was."

"I'm sorry, Tempest," he said, features softening with an exhaled breath. "Will you at least promise not to do it again… at least until you're somewhere safe?"

"Don't worry, Sagua already gave me this speech." She knew his lecturing was out of compassion, but she didn't care to hear it again. It was rash what she'd done, and she knew it, but she'd gladly do it again.

"Did she take the gun? I didn't see you return with it."

"She did. Kaburem has banned the use of firelocks by all Alyrian citizens."

"She's not going to turn you in, is she?"

"No, actually," Tempest said. "She's using it to start an armory. If she wanted to turn me in, she would have done so my first day here. She's known who I was since the start, and she seems to be on my side."

Cyrus gnawed on his lower lip and began to pace. "You said Kaburem banned guns..." he muttered, stopping to look once more at her. "There has to be a reason behind that right? Someone must have turned the guns on Kaburem." His brow lifted, and he rolled his weight to the balls of his feet, leaning slightly forward in anticipation. "Did Sagua say anything about that?"

He seemed significantly more eager to face what lay ahead than Tempest was. Sagua had confirmed the rebellion Tempest longed to bring to the land, but dreaming of it was one thing; experiencing it was another. There was a storm coming, and she knew its rain would be made of blood. "She only said one thing before I left. She said an uprising was brewing."

Cyrus' eyes widened, dark with the same terror Tempest felt. "So it's started... I'd heard rumors. Prince succeeded, then. They're fighting for you."

"They're not fighting for me, they're fighting for their freedom," she corrected.

"But,"—He held up a finger to stop her from arguing—"they couldn't do that without something to stand for. People must be beginning to believe the dying words of your friend." Cyrus lifted Tempest's chin so she would meet his gaze, but she sighed and looked away, turning her back to him.

"You don't know that," she whispered. "Besides, all the good it's doing right now is ruining my chances of a future rebellion. It's too soon. The nation isn't ready for war yet. I'm not ready for war yet"

"It will be, and so will you. I promise you that. For now, it's giving the people hope, and that's more than enough." He grabbed her hand to turn her back towards him.

"What if you're wrong?" she asked. That fear she'd vowed to leave behind crept into her words, but she didn't mind, not with him.

"Then you start that spark of hope when you believe it's time to do so," he answered.

"What if it's never time? What if they don't stand with me? There are too many what-ifs."

"Then stop asking them," he advised. "None of them can be answered yet, so just wait it out. For the time being, all we need to worry about is getting back to the barracks before the sun's gone. Everything else can wait."

Tempest looked up to the setting sun and the stars that faded into view, speckling the night sky. It was a stunning image with the trees and mountains casting long shadows on the ground, shadows that marched to reign the night. It was a peaceful view that eased her troubled heart. She took a breath and followed him back to the barracks, arriving just before the sun disappeared behind the horizon.

~~~

Tempest spent the next day training with the various usages of her dagger. At the end, teams for the mock battle were divided. Klaus and Cyrus were deemed team captains, and despite Tempest's hopes, she was placed on Klaus' team.

Come morning, they followed Jax into the patch of woods where Lumin had taken place and were soon sent to a set location where they were to wait for further instruction. Tempest leaned against the trunk of a nearby tree, listening to her teammates banter over possible strategies.

"We should surround them," Cora suggested, but Klaus shook his head.

"We don't have the numbers for that. If they're spread out, there's no way we could get all the way around them."

"What if we're defense? Then none of that matters," said Luke.

"If we're defense, we need to find higher ground," Paris added.

The sound of approaching footsteps silenced the conversation, and a man stepped into view, holding a carefully folded sheet of paper. He handed Klaus the parchment and quietly submerged back into the sea of greenery. Klaus pried the folds open, catching a separate sheet that fell from the other. He handed the smaller parchment to Cora and began reading the letter to the team.

"Inside this letter you will find a map," Klaus began, pausing to look at Cora who worked at unfolding the map in her hands. "On the map is a marking of where intelligence has recently spotted an enemy camp. Your task is to take this camp in order to aid in the advancements of the King's Army."

Cora turned the map towards the others, pointing to a small circle drawn just west of a stream that traced through the woods.

"We'll follow the stream north, then turn west until we reach the camp," Klaus said, tracing the path with his index finger. "If you look here, there seems to be an elevation dip in the land. We can keep the hill to our left. That way, we'll be able to stay our course west. Keep your eyes up, there might be enemies on the hilltops."

Cora turned the map back towards her. "They'll expect us to come that way," she said. "We need to take a different route and come at them from behind. Look, their camp is positioned in a bowl of land. If they're smart, they'll use that as an advantage and be guarding the rim, waiting for us to walk into a trap in the center of the bowl. We'll be doing just that if we come in from the east."

"That depends on what's on top of that hill. If it's too thick of foliage to fight on, then they might be using it as protection on their back and sides. They'll have all their focus on the opening, so we'll have to hit hard, but if we back them into the corner, we can easily take them." It was the same tactic he used in sparring. Trap the enemy with force. Cora was right. No matter the field, that wouldn't work against Cyrus. "That's just my opinion, though. I suppose I ought to step down and let you lead if you wish. You seem to think you're better at this than I am."

Tempest stepped forward, leaving the brace of the tree. "Brute force doesn't always work. What if we send our swordsmen down the stream to follow your pathway, then send the archers around to take the hill. If they're in the bowl, then we'll have them cornered with the possibility of taking them from above as well. If they're on top of the hill, while they focus on our swordsmen, the archers will come from behind and take them out." She hoped to find a neutral ground in the suggestion, but Klaus shook his head, growing angry with their continuous violation of his command.

"No," he said. "This is my charge, so we'll do it my way. Am I clear?" No one dared to challenge him further. "Everyone meet me by the stream," said Klaus. "I have to take care of something before we begin."

Tempest and the other recruits started towards the stream, but Klaus grabbed Cora's arm before she could get far. "Not you," he said, voice barely above a whisper. "We have something to discuss."

Tempest slid behind a tree to watch undetected. The way he'd spoken to Cora made her uneasy. His tone had been cold and unforgiving, and she knew what that meant from people like Klaus.

"Never question me like that again, do you hear?" he asked when the others were a distance away. His grip on Cora's arm held tight, keeping her from escaping, but she had other methods of defiance.

"Yes sir!" she said with a sloppy grin and a halfhearted salute.

From her hiding place, Tempest watched, waiting to ensure Cora's safety. He grabbed her other wrist, wrath in his eyes. "Do not mock me." His voice was calm, yet stern, and it demanded to be listened to.

He raised his hand, and Cora cowered, bracing herself for an expected blow. This had happened before, Tempest realized. Cora had been ready for it.

"You two coming?" she asked, casually strolling into their view, unsure what she was doing, just trying to keep Klaus from hurting Cora. He released his hold on her and dropped his other hand. Tempest acted as if she saw none of it. It seemed the safest option for all involved. "We do have a battle to fight, you know."

Klaus stalked past her without a word, and Cora followed suit, fumbling at the base of her sleeve and pulling it down to conceal the red fingerprints that snaked around her wrist.

"Are you okay?" Tempest asked when Klaus was well ahead. Cora gave a silent nod in response, but Tempest knew it was a lie. She'd have to talk to her about this at a later time.

They joined the other recruits by the stream and slowly made their way north to attack their opponents, turning west when they reached the bend in the stream that marked the latitude of the enemy base.

No one spoke. They simply marched forth, keeping the sun behind them and the hills to their left. When they reached the bowl, Cora stopped the procession, looking around in confusion.

"It's right here," she muttered. "The map says it's here." She pointed to the spot on the map to prove her proclamation.

"Where are they?" Paris asked, glancing about with the nervousness that came with expected surprise.

"Here," said Cyrus, emerging from the brush, covered in leaves to conceal himself. He held a bow in his hands, and he had a padded arrow trained on Klaus.

Tempest drew her sword, and Cyrus let fly the arrow, killing their commander. She charged, swinging the blunted blade at Cyrus, who frantically tried to nock another arrow. When his attempt failed, he turned the arrow upwards to stab her, but she twisted out of the way and struck him in the stomach, knocking him to the ground, breathless.

"I'm sorry," said Tempest as he doubled over and accepted his defeat in a fit of laughter. After a quick glance to ensure he was okay, she took command of her small company. "Everyone face outwards, backs together. Protect each other like your lives depend on it."

They stood there in a small circle, silently waiting for the rest of Cyrus's team to appear. Tempest was about to give up and tell them to move and look elsewhere when the leaves above them began to rustle. Her archers aimed for the skies, searching for something to shoot, but nothing could be seen through the thick foliage.

Suddenly, arrows began to rain from above, taking out Tempest and the remainder of her team, marking the end of the battle and their final day of field combat training.

The dead stood up, brushed the dirt off their clothes, and joined the others on their way back to the barracks. Cyrus' team celebrated their victory and praised Klaus' team for their bravery after the loss of their leader, even though Tempest had killed their leader too.

"Perhaps you've learned something today, Klaus?" Luke asked.

He was answered by a silent glare. Tempest couldn't help but to smile. She was glad someone had the courage to call out the foolishness of Klaus' plan.

"What *should* Klaus have learned today?" Cyrus said when it was clear no answer would come from his opponent.

Luke perked up at the response, happily answering the question for Klaus. "What this man fails to understand is," he paused, glancing towards Cora and Tempest, "that the women are always right."

Laughter erupted from everyone but the subject of the jape, and they retired to the bedchamber early, exhausted from the day's adventure.

Once most had fallen asleep, Tempest rose to her feet, looking at Cora expectantly. The girl gave a nervous, flitting glance towards Klaus' sleeping form, then stood to join her.

"Where are you going?" Cyrus asked in a hushed voice so as not to wake the others.

"I'm not feeling well and wanted some fresh air," said Tempest. "Cora didn't want me going alone, so she offered to come with me."

"Want me to come too?" he asked, sitting up, but Tempest shook her head and gestured towards Klaus.

"If he wakes, tell him where we've gone and that we'll be back shortly."

Cyrus nodded and lay back down as Tempest pressed open the doors and stepped into the hall, leading Cora to the meadow she and Cyrus often visited.

"What did you want to say to me?" Cora asked once they'd arrived, feigning ignorance.

"Klaus," said Tempest, not wanting to waste time dancing around the matter at hand.

"It was nothing," Cora promised, the falsehood of her statement apparent on her face. She wasn't a very skilled liar.

"Prove it to me, then. Roll up your sleeves."

"Why?" she asked, rubbing her arms nervously like one trying to warm themselves on a cold winter night.

"To prove to me that Klaus isn't hurting you."

Cora closed her eyes, tears welling within them, and she looked down, shamed. "I can't prove that," she said, slowly rolling up her sleeves to reveal her arms. Even in the darkness, Tempest could see the bruises that decorated them. "He cares about me, Tempest, he truly does. I deserved these, every one of them. He tells me not to do things, and I do them anyway. I shouldn't be so stubborn." She seemed to be trying to convince not only Tempest, but herself as well. "I deserved it," she said once more.

"No one deserves this, Cora. Especially not you."

Cora shuddered, and everything that'd been holding her together suddenly crumbled. She let out a choked sob and wrapped her arms tight around herself. "Why does he do it?" she asked. "I know he cares about me, so why does he hurt me? He knows what it's like to be hurt, so why would he ever do it to someone else? Why would he do it to someone he cared about?"

Tempest thought for a moment. "Perhaps it's all he knows... Maybe people who are mistreated when they're younger grow up to act the same because that's how they learned to love." She pulled Cora into a soft embrace. "It gives him no excuse for what he's done, but it might just give you an explanation behind his actions. Perhaps this lifestyle has been ingrained into him, and unfortunately, you will never be able to force it away."

"What do I do?" Her eyes pleading for a simple answer, but Tempest had none to give.

"I wish I could give you a definitive answer, one that'd solve everything, but there isn't one. Perhaps, though, I can give you some sort of guidance." She sat in a bed of grass and waited for Cora to join her. "You've given him time and time again to prove himself. He's out of chances. Tell him that what he does to you is something you won't tolerate… You have to mean it, Cora. Tell him that if he can't treat you the way you deserve to be treated, then you'll leave. And if he doesn't change, you must follow through."

"I don't want to leave him," she said. "He's a good person. It's just buried under a lot of bad, and I want to help him out of it."

Tempest looked into Cora's eyes, contemplating the words in her throat. "There's an old story my father used to read to me about two larks fresh from the nest," she said. "May I tell it to you?"

Cora nodded, wiping tears from her eyes, so Tempest began to recite it.

"Once, there was a lark," she said, "who upon emerging from the thicket of twigs, immediately took flight, singing songs of silver, leaving behind another. The other lark looked on with longing, for when it spread its wings, it could not seem to fly."

Cora settled against a tree to listen to the tale.

" 'Why can't I fly?' asked the grounded lark, and the singing lark replied,

" 'Flight is powered by the song. You cannot fly without it.' At this, the grounded lark began to sing, but still it could not fly. 'Your song has no heart!' the singing lark cried. 'Don't worry. It will come with time. Until then, you'll need help.'

"The singing lark left the grounded lark and returned with an eagle." Tempest paused for a moment and glanced to the side. She could almost see her father reciting the words beside her, and it took everything in her willpower to keep herself from breaking under the weight of the memory. When she could trust her voice again, she continued.

" 'Will you teach me how to fly?' the grounded lark asked to the eagle, and the eagle agreed to do so.

" 'Spread your wings,' said the eagle to the lark,"—Tempest spread her arms like the wings of a bird—"and so the lark obeyed. 'Flight lies in the size of the wing, for the wings mirror the bravery in one's heart,' the eagle explained. 'Your wings are much too small. I cannot help you, but I may know someone who can.' The eagle then left and returned with a flying squirrel." She enacted each part of the story like her father had always done for her.

"The lark was doubtful but tried once more. 'Will you teach me how to fly?' asked the lark, and the squirrel looked at the lark with pity and agreed to do so.

" 'What my friends have failed to teach you is that flight is only made possible when you trust the wind. Take a leap of faith, arms outstretched, and the wind will catch you,' said the squirrel to the lark, and so the lark obeyed.

"It leapt into the air and spread its wings. For a moment, there was freedom, but soon the lark realized that this was not flight. It was merely gliding. The lark, saddened by this knowledge, landed upon a branch only a short distance from where it had started." Tempest lifted her hand, reaching for a goal that was impossible to touch. This part had always made her sad when she was a child.

" 'I have watched many birds learn to fly from these branches,' came the voice of the tree. 'And you, my dear flightless lark, are going about it in all the wrong ways.' The lark listened, intrigued. 'Each of your friends are correct. You need heart, bravery, and trust to fly, but they are missing the most important thing,' said the tree. 'Flight comes from the roots of the soul. Only you can find it. Look within and find the thing that makes you fly,' said the tree to the lark, and so the lark obeyed."

"Did the lark ever manage to fly?" asked Cora, hope bubbling in her words.

Tempest looked to the clouds. "The story never said, but I think it did fly, and I think Klaus might do the same if you let him. You can help him like the creatures helped the lark, but in the end, he must find happiness for himself."

18

$\mathcal{T}$he recruits stood before the gates of the domed building, waiting for the gatekeeper to open it. Iron creaked as the first portcullis lifted, opening the way for their entry. Jax motioned them forward, stopping before the second portcullis until the first closed behind them.

Once through both gates, they came to a small tunnel that sliced through the dome's thick walls. Tempest's footsteps bounced off the stone, echoing through the hall that led to the third and final gate. In the opening of this one hung massive metal chains that'd been charred by dragon flame.

The group weaved through the chains and entered the small world within the dome. Walls of rock towered over them, populated with the beasts of the sky. An emerald dragon turned its head, looking down at them with curiosity. It clawed its way towards the group, sending small chunks of rock tumbling down the wall. Its scales glinted blue from the giant orbs of light that hovered in the air around the room.

Jax reached out his hand and stroked the beast before him, and Tempest realized she'd seen it before, wrapped around Jax's shoulders so long ago. It now stood nearly eye to eye with him. He tossed the creature a chunk of meat, and it charred the meal with a short burst of flame before snapping its jaws around it. The emerald beast curled up on the cold floor and gnawed contently on the strip of meat it'd been given.

Jax walked past it and into a small opening carved into the wall with a torch on either side. It was a thin crevice, just wide enough for Jax to slide in sideways. They followed and entered a stairwell that spiraled down further into the mountain. Hidden in small notches of the wall were candles to light their path.

The rock parted in the wall beside them, revealing a cavern pooled with lava. The only thing protecting people from falling in was a thin, rusted chain. With care, Tempest continued down the long stairwell, soon reaching the end where an iron door opened to a warm room of shelves, padded with cloth, feathers, and straw. Rested atop the shelves were row after row of dragon eggs, each magnificently colored in an array of patterns.

They continued past these shelves and into another hall. At the door of this new hall, there hung more chains, these smaller than the last. Tempest brushed the chains to the side and was greeted by the chirps and squeaks of baby dragons.

"Welcome to the nursery," Jax said once everyone had made their way inside. Two of the young dragons played with each other, leaping and gliding through the air, nipping when the other got close. A small red one approached the group, tilting its head when Jax neared a box in the corner of the cavern. He reached inside and wrapped his fingers around a rodent that squealed and thrashed in his grip.

The noises attracted every dragon in the room, and a determined hunger burned behind their eyes. "No matter how domestic a dragon becomes, it will always have an innate desire to hunt," said Jax, placing the rat on the floor.

The tiny creature sprinted in frenzied flight, fleeing from the dragons that dove towards it from all sides. Its cries were ear piercing and made Tempest squirm. "When they age, the most important thing to do is make sure they know you are not the prey," Jax said when one of the dragons scooped up the rat and took it to a corner of the room to eat, snapping and growling at any that tried to challenge him for the food.

Jax picked up one of the younger dragons that'd been scared off by the one with the rat, and it curled its tail around his arm, nuzzling its head into his shoulder. He handed the small beast a chunk of meat. "When your dragon hatches, it is important that you be one of the first people it sees. It's harder to tame them when that initial bond isn't formed."

He handed the dragon to a beaming Cyrus and gave each recruit a handful of already cooked meat to feed to the small creature. It sniffed curiously at Tempest's hand when she approached with the meat, quickly sinking its teeth into the flesh before tossing it in the air and engulfing the chunk. The dragon purred contently and looked around at the others, smelling the meat in their hands.

Tempest heard something scrape at the rock above, and when she looked up, a small head peeked into view, hanging just above Cora. She was just about to say something when this dragon snatched the meat from Cora's hand. The thief flew back to its corner and lay atop the rat bones it had left. "Oh, come on," Cora said. "Was the rat not enough? You had to take this from the poor guy too?"

"He's clever," Jax said.

"And rude."

The other dragons had caught on to the fact food was being distributed, and the clump of recruits was soon surrounded by small, hungry beasts. They worked with the baby dragons for some time, feeding them and learning how to train and care for them.

To Tempest's surprise, the creatures were quite social, but they seemed also to be content with the simplicity of company, not demanding anything further than that. They were gentle and elegant in their movements, evolved so perfectly for hunting. Tempest wondered what it'd be like to see a grown beast seek and capture its prey. The poor hunted creature wouldn't stand a chance.

Evidently, the dragons preferred to use their talons and teeth for killing, hunting like hawks but with much larger prey. They ate significant amounts of food in a day but for the most part, could fend for themselves when in an open, forested environment. They preferred to nest high in tree tops and mountains where they'd go mostly undisturbed, and when it came time to mate, they'd do so for life.

The day's work came to an end just before supper, so the recruits were dismissed and sent straight to the dining hall.

Cyrus sat beside Tempest at the table with a parchment in one hand and a charcoal pencil in the other. Sketched on the parchment was a basic map of the land used for Lumin. "I've devised the perfect plan for the games in a few days," he said with giddiness, holding the map out for Tempest to see.

"What if we're on different teams?" Tempest asked, hiding the plans from view with her palms.

"Then I hope you don't use them against me." He flashed a grin and gave a wink, but Tempest shook her head, laughing.

"If my team wins, I don't want it to be because we were told enemy plans. That won't happen very often in the real world."

Cyrus frowned and stuffed the paper into his pocket, standing up to get a tray of food, but he turned once more after a few steps. "Are you positive?" he asked, walking backwards. "I could be a spy."

A smile tugged at Tempest's lip. "Yes! Now watch where you're going!"

Cyrus spun around seconds before colliding with Klaus, who carried a tray of food precariously balanced. He feigned a smile and ducked away, rushing off to get his own food.

Klaus sat grudgingly on the opposite side of the table, deliberately ignoring Cora, who sat at Tempest's side. Tension weighed heavy between them and drew confused looks from those around. Tempest had seen them less and less together since the mock battle, but now they wouldn't even look at each other.

"What's with them?" Cyrus asked Tempest when he'd returned, whispering into her ear so Cora wouldn't hear. She shook her head in response, just as confused as he was.

When Cora stood to take her dishes to the kitchen washroom, Tempest followed close behind, seeking answers. Once secluded behind closed doors, she stopped Cora and pulled her to the side.

"What happened?" Tempest asked, hushed so as not to draw attention.

Cora glanced towards the door, then sighed. "He stopped me on the way here and asked me why I'd been avoiding him. I told him I'd been avoiding a conversation, so we talked, and I told him everything I'd told you. He knows now how his actions hurt me, but instead of promising better, he's stopped talking to me entirely."

"I'm sorry to hear that," Tempest said. "But, give it time. Maybe someday soon, Klaus will find his wings and return to you."

Cora gave a halfhearted smile. "Or he'll fly away," she said.

"And if he does, you must let him. Oftentimes, things happen for a reason, just never for the reason we expect them to."

Cora gnawed on her bottom lip, seemingly deep in some thought, then she nodded an acceptance to Tempest's words, and the two returned to the table where they waited for the rest to finish eating.

~~~

The following days continued similarly. The recruits worked in the nursery through the morning, then they studied the dragons in the dome through the late noon hours, learning how to deal with the different personalities each creature had. Tempest enjoyed the company of the young dragons. Each beast had unique curiosities about the world. They were like small stories wrapped in scales.

On the third day, one of the eggs began to hatch while they trained. Its owner stood in the room, impatiently waiting for it to enter the world. Luke had been the first to notice the cracking egg. They all stood back, allowing the owner to be the first to interact with the newborn dragon. A small coat of slime covered the beast, and bits of the egg still clung to its body when it stumbled from its casing, stretching its wings for the first time, and hanging them low to let them dry. A small plume of smoke trailed from its jaws as it yawned, then it tilted its head, taking in the new world it'd joined.

As the week went on, an energy began to brew in the halls. It was a building excitement for the upcoming game of Lumin. Tempest and her peers sat in the barracks wide awake the night before the game, waiting impatiently for the night to age and the games to begin.

A scream echoed through the hallway from the wing of the new recruits, turning excitement to panic. "*Fire!*" the voice cried, and sure enough, Tempest could see traces of smoke filtering into the room, a soft red glow radiating from behind the door.

The recruits frantically gathered their important belongings and fled the room. Reuben threw open the door, guiding the others out and into the smoke filled hall, but Tempest didn't follow. She sat instead on the floor, fumbling with the lock on her chest.

"Tempest! Come on!" Cyrus shouted over the roaring of the flames.

With a yank, the lock came undone, and she ripped the chest open, snatching the dagger and the notebook out before standing to leave. At this point, the room had filled with smoke.

As Tempest ran, the notebook slipped from her hands, landing with a soft thud on the wooden floor. She turned to retrieve it but was stopped by Cyrus' grip on her arm. "Leave it," he said, dragging her from the room. "Your life is more important than the book." Tempest reluctantly followed.

The beams groaned under the flames that engulfed them, spreading with lightning speed. The hall was packed and slow moving. Coughing echoed off the walls, and Tempest clawed at her throat, desperate for a cool sip of water to soothe the burning. Her breaths grew shorter the more she inhaled, and sweat dripped down her body like small streams in the heat of the surrounding flames.

"Stay calm, and stay low!" Jax shouted from the door. The other trainers stood at alternate doors, aiding the flow of bodies.

Tempest and Cyrus finally managed to make their way outside, the night air a welcome change to the suffocating heat inside, but the air was oddly cold, thought Tempest. It should have been much warmer with the raging fire behind them. She turned to figure out where the warmth had gone and found the building glowing from the red flames licking at the wood, but there was no longer any heat to them. She looked around, noticing another oddity. No Fire Keepers were present. They should have been there trying to contain the flames before everything burned down.

A group of Mages caught her eye, and standing amongst them was Sagua, watching the recruits to see how well they handled the situation. The Mages all stood eerily motionless with their eyes rolled back into their heads, controlling the flame that burned inside.

Once the last person had evacuated the building, every trace of the flames disappeared, along with any bit of evidence that the fire had ever even been there. Sagua nodded, and the Mages returned to normal. She strode to a small tree stump, using it as a pedestal.

"Fire," she began, "is a very common and dangerous consequence that comes with dragons." A murmur washed over the crowd once people realized it had all been a ploy. "We must learn how to deal with it safely and quickly, which is why we perform this exercise every three months. It tests your efficiency and ability to work as one to safely evacuate."

The rest of the Mage recruits filed into view, surrounding them with their small orbs of light hovering above their hands.

"Welcome new recruits, and welcome back to the rest," Sagua began, reciting her introduction speech to Lumin.

19

empest's team strolled through the woods, searching for the location of their base. She began to recognize the places around her from her first time playing the game. They passed the cage of roots she'd hid in while awaiting the convoy, and the old mine she'd escaped from stood fortified to her left.

A dragon waited for them at the base, laying in a field of ash with a single dead tree standing in the center. Hovering above the tree was the red Orbis. "What happened here?" Tempest asked to anyone who would listen, looking down at the charred earth that encircled the tree.

"Legend has it that Zalder landed here when he created the scorched lands eons ago," a girl replied. Tempest turned to face her. It was the team captain with the guardian standing at her side. "They say the first dragon was created here. When it died, Zalder brought its body back and turned it into this tree. It was always one of my favorite stories growing up. To think the very first dragon's soul lives within these branches. It's an ancient tree with history etched in its very roots. If you look close enough, you can see the patterns of flames carved into it by the Mages who immortalized it. Come, have a look for yourself." She guided Tempest to the tree.

Looking at its base, Tempest could see the flame-like patterns the captain had mentioned. They seemed to come alive under the red glint of the Orbis hovering overhead. "Can I trust you to defend it?" the captain asked.

Tempest nodded, silently admiring the work of art that traced through the bark on the tree. The carvings sparked a memory that'd been lodged in the hidden shadows of her past. It was an image sketched in a book back in Alyria. She'd read it long ago. In the book, it was said that time was written in this tree. Past, present, and future. It knew it all, and sometimes, when the fire god thought someone worthy, it would share, delivering visions through the eyes of dragons.

"Good," the captain said, turning to the remainder of the group.

She walked through the ranks, tapping various people on the shoulder as she went. "Those of you I've picked will be offense. Everyone else will be defense. I want all of you to spread out as much as possible, but keep each other in your sight lines. We must not leave any holes for the enemy to weasel their way through. I'll lead the offensive charge, and you," She turned, pointing to Tempest, "will help the guardian protect the tree."

At her directive, everyone split apart, heading in whichever direction they were told to go. Tempest stood beside the guardian, patiently waiting for the game to begin. Eventually, the war horn sounded through the trees, and the Mage orbs faded away, replaced by the small tag lights that hovered at every player's side.

"It begins," said the guardian. "Unfortunately, you can't do much in regards to defending the tree, but what you can do is be an extra set of eyes. Holler if you see the enemy."

Tempest paced back and forth. She'd been honored to stand with the guardian, but she hadn't anticipated the extensive waiting. No one came. She supposed that was a good thing. It meant their defense was doing its job. Either that, or the opponent's offense was terrible. Cyrus was on that team though, and he'd claimed to have the perfect plan. Perhaps making them wait an eternity was a part of it. Maybe they were all lurking in the shadows, waiting for the perfect opportunity to strike.

She sighed and cleared her mind of thoughts and worries. She had no intention of being useless, so she focused instead on possibility. In order to reach the Orbis, her opponent would have to climb Zalder's tree. If she watched the tree, there'd be no way someone would go undetected. However, by the time she saw them, it'd likely be too late. She turned back to the tree line, analyzing the options her enemy faced.

To the right, the trees were spread thin. It would be easier to navigate through that section but harder to move undetected. Recalling the words said to her by the guardian she met the first time she played the game, Tempest locked her gaze on the thick brush to the left. Stealth would be easier from there.

She heard the soft rumble of thunder in the distance and could see grey clouds rolling in. After a few moments, she felt a cool drop of water land on her skin and watched it as gravity pulled it to the ground, leaving a cold trail down the side of her arm.

"It seems Rhumir has returned for the harvest," said the guardian, looking to the sky with disdain as the drops became more copious. Lightning flashed across the sky, illuminating their surroundings for a split second, then giving it back to darkness

Visibility worsened as the rain thickened, and it soaked her to the bone. Tempest could only see about ten feet in front of her, but through the rain, she heard the faint sound of footsteps cracking the sticks and leaves that covered the forest floor, muffled but distinctly there.

"We have company," Tempest said, and a blue light emerged beside a shadow from the line of trees.

A flash of lightning revealed the boy, and the guardian hit him with a blast of wind that sent him reeling for the trees. Two more took his place, so the guardian crouched to the ground, compelling the roots below to ensnare the pursuers, wrapping around their ankles like snakes. Tempest watched, mouth agape. It was a marvel what the Mages could do.

The dragon's snarl turned her attention to their exposed side where a line of Mages and Dragon Keepers alike closed in on them. The dragon growled and snapped at the ones who were more fearful, but it and Tempest were the only ones standing against the many. The Mage was still preoccupied by the strays coming from the opposite side.

A short ring of fire erupted around the protectors and the tree, separating them from the enemy for a just a moment before the blue team got the courage to enter. Before long, Tempest and the guardian were surrounded—odds overwhelmingly against them. Tempest grabbed at one of the recruits, trying to be of some minor assistance, but her target charged past her, followed quickly by the rest of their group. The blue team sprinted towards the tree, belting a war cry.

Two from the onslaught made it up the first few branches when the tree shuddered and seemed to come alive. It shook its branches like a dog trying to dry water from its fur. Tempest turned to the guardian, watching him control its limbs. The climbers fell to the ground, whipped from the tree with no remorse.

A third boy took up the attempt, clinging stubbornly to the flailing branches. Their peers watched in curiosity, wondering if he would make it. He reached the halfway point when Tempest decided he had gone far enough. She ran to the tree, looking for the best path up, hoping the Mage could distinguish her from the others in his magic using state.

When she found one, she grabbed hold of the lowest branch, and a tremor shot through it, one not made by the guardian Mage. Tempest's eyes rolled back into her head, thunder cracked above, and her vision went black.

~~~

Pain shot through Tempest's head as light poured into her eyes. Everything seemed so bright, and it was all distorted. Colors looked abstract to the point where she couldn't quite place a name to the shades she was seeing. Without her control, her view shifted to something far below. Talons clutched the wood beams beneath her, and down on the floor moved shapes resembling bodies. For a moment, she thought perhaps the book had been right about the legend of the tree, but doubt still lingered in the back of her mind. She hadn't been the only one to touch it, and none of the others had fallen.

Whether it was the god of fire guiding her sight or something unrelated, she knew what she was seeing was real. She recognized the place now. It was the utterance made in the corner of the room that made her sure of it. "Another ale!" called Markus from the table.

"This is your last one," said the innkeeper. "If you want to die, kindly do it outside please. I've just cleaned the floors."

Markus tapped nervously at the wood, glancing about the room as if the kegs of alcohol behind the counter planned to murder him. Tempest wondered what had set him off. She remembered the dreams he told her quite vividly and was terrified that one had finally spooked him.

"The snake… jaw wide open… tear drops of blood… it's coming." The words were barely mumbled, but somehow, Tempest caught every one of them. He looked up suddenly, eyes meeting with those that Tempest looked through. "It's coming," he repeated.

The crack of thunder rumbled through the tavern, and the room shook from the strike of lighting that had caused it. A disgruntled squeak came from the creature Tempest seemed to be following. It scurried to another post, compromising Tempest's view of the storyteller.

Through the door burst a group of men, guns resting in their blood-stone clad hands. The innkeeper shoved her way out of the kitchen. "What is the meaning of this madness?" she demanded, waving her arms in frustration at the men with the guns. "We're a peaceful inn; we don't need no trouble here."

"We're not looking for trouble, ma'am," said a guard just barely in view. "We're looking for a man that goes by the name Markus."

Tempest heard the slam of a cup on the wooden table, and a bench squealed against the floor. "That'd be me," Markus announced, stepping into view. He had sobered up immensely. Tempest supposed facing death had a way of doing that.

"Word has reached the king that you tell tales of treason, sir," the soldier said, walking towards Markus.

"I tell of my dreams, sir. A red snake killing a weeping woman in the purple snow. A dragon holding a dead snake in its talons. That same snake coming to kill me." Markus reached down and picked up his drink, guzzling the rest before letting it clatter to the floor. "Do you,"—He stumbled forward, jabbing a finger towards the soldier—"mean to tell me that you associate the king with such a creature of chaos?"

He stood tall now, hands on his hips in a stance of defiance. "Because if you do… well, then I suppose I do speak treason," Markus admitted. "But if you do as my dreams say you do, and you kill me in the name of the snake, then perhaps the last of the dreams will also come to fruition." He looked the soldier dead in the eye. "I will die today, but the king may die tomorrow." Markus reached into his pocket and pulled out a square of cloth. Tempest could hardly see it as it rippled and waved in his hands, but on it, she saw a black and gold dragon clutching the limp body of a snake. "Long live the king."

The sound of squelching flesh broke the silence that followed, and a thin blade stuck out from his chest. His face contorted, and he fell to the ground, bathing in a pool of his blood. Without so much as a second glance, the soldier tossed a bag of coins to the man behind Markus. "Thank you for your service to the crown," he said. "Now, it seems we have a murderous dragon to find."

Wings carried Tempest away from the scene, and the beating of them morphed into the sound of her own heart.

~~~

Thunder ripped through the air, and Tempest's eyes flew open. To her surprise, Cyrus sat beside the pallet she lay in with his head resting on his arms. His eyes were closed, and he breathed deeply, a slight smile curving his lips as he slept. Tempest sat up slowly and took in her surroundings. Several pallets lay in two rows on either side of the room, most were empty, but a few held the sick and injured. Recalling the reason she was here, the memories of her unconscious dreaming suddenly flooded her mind. "Markus... " she mumbled. "They killed Markus."

Cyrus stirred in his sleep, slowly waking to the sound of her voice. "Tempest!" he shouted, covering his mouth and looking down nervously. "What happened?"

"They killed Markus," she replied, and he looked at her, confused.

"What do you mean? Who's Markus?"

"He was a drunkard at the inn I worked for when I first arrived in Firethorne. He had these strange dreams that always stood for something. One of them predicted the death of my parents. I told you of him once before when you saw me drawing in my notebook. He was the man who gave me the metaphor of the snake and the dragon." Cyrus nodded, recalling the image. "They killed him... Kaburem killed him... and now they're coming."

"Coming here? How do you know?"

"I watched it happen in my dream. It wasn't like most dreams, though. It felt real, like I was watching through the eyes of someone else, or some*thing* else. Kaburem came to the inn and murdered him, but he told them about the dragon before they did. They're going to find me, Cyrus."

"Do they think you're the dragon?"

"Do you?" Tempest asked, and he nodded, lips pressed together in thought.

"They won't find you. I promise you that. All of us will stand by your side. We'll protect you."

"We can't tell the others. Protection or not, the less people who know the better."

Cyrus paused, fidgeting nervously with his thumbs. "Tempest... they already know."

Tempest's eyes widened, and her heart sped with terror. "How?"

"You know how I told you to leave the notebook behind when you dropped it in the fire?"

Tempest nodded, dreading whatever was to follow.

"Due to its falsity, nothing actually burned, which left your notebook intact." He paused. "Klaus found it after the game. By the time I got in, everyone had huddled around the book. They saw something they shouldn't have, Tempest. They saw the drawing of your father..." He swallowed.

"They saw the drawing of King Neymar dying in the castle. They saw the drawing of you in a casket beside your parents. They saw too much."

With these words, Cyrus placed her notebook carefully on the edge of the bed, and Tempest reached to grab it. She felt utterly exposed by this newfound knowledge, and she was angry too. Not only had her identity been so suddenly revealed, but so too had her memories. It was as though her friends had perused through the deepest corridors of her thoughts unbidden, carrying torches as they went.

"How much did you see?" she asked, hoping Cyrus hadn't joined in their gawking.

"Only the two drawings, and one of which I'd already seen the day we met." A slight grin twisted his lips. "You really ought to be more careful with that thing, leaving it around with all those secrets inside."

"That so?" she asked, meeting his playful stare. "Was it not you who made me leave it behind?"

"In my defense, it was supposed to go up in flames. I was simply trying to prevent you from doing the same." He leaned back in his seat, eyeing her curiously. "Why risk your life for it anyway? Surely, some of it could be recreated if need be?"

"Perhaps," said Tempest. "But, it'd never quite be the same." She lifted the book and flipped through the first few pages. "It was the last lesson my father gave to me. He sent me into the city and told me to notate what I learned from the people. Even after everything, I've kept it up. I know he'd want me to keep going."

"Is that Jax?" Cyrus asked, pointing to the man sketched on the page she'd turned to.

"It is. He was at a butcher's shop near where I sat one day, buying meat for his dragon. I had no idea who he was at the time. He merely intrigued me. It's curious how people's paths cross before they ever meet, isn't it?"

"Like us at the ceremony. I wonder how near each other we were."

"Only the gods know," Tempest replied, flipping to the page that held the memory of that dreadful day.

"I know the dragon is meant to kill the snake," said Cyrus, looking at the creatures she'd added to the scene, "but is there more to their story?"

"There is." She turned a page back and flipped the notebook for Cyrus to see the image of Markus' dream she'd drawn upon it. As he took the book in his hands, she retold the series of events as best she could. At the end, Cyrus' face twisted with horror.

"You've never mentioned that the snake might kill the dragon too. A bit of an important detail, don't you think?"

"Not if the snake dies with it."

Cyrus let out his breath and shook his head. "Then I pray we're all wrong about who this dragon is."

"And if we're not?"

"If we're not, then it is a good day to have brought you this." He reached into the inner pocket of his coat and pulled out a folded piece of parchment. Contained within was a wisp-like, red-orange flower that'd been pressed flat.

"It's called Zalder's Flame," he said. "It grows here in the northern mountains, and it only blooms during Zalder's reign. My mother presses them between book pages to preserve them. She believes that as long as Zalder's Flames are protected, the god will watch over our family. And now, perhaps he'll watch over you."

Cyrus handed the flower to Tempest, and she placed it with care into the back of her notebook where it could safely remain.

20

"*Y*ou're free to go," the Medic said, taking the tag off Tempest's pallet. She sat up, relieved. Cyrus had been forced to leave for training an hour before, leaving her with nothing to do and no one to talk to. She slowly rose to her feet, dizzied by the blood that rushed from her head.

The Medic led her from the infirmary and pointed down the hall and towards the exit that would take her to the dome. When she arrived, Jax was sitting atop the shoulders of a dragon, and the others watched, listening to him speak about the tricks of riding. He paused when Tempest stepped into view. "Welcome back," he said, and everyone turned to meet her.

"Took you long enough," said Cyrus with a nudge and a smile.

He appeared to be the only recruit who thought kindly of her return, however. None of the others would look her in the eye.

Jax ignored all this and continued his lesson. "This position on the dragon's back is the most stable position for a rider to be in." Tempest couldn't focus on the words he said. She felt eyes on her back and heard the faint sound of the other recruits whispering. Jax jumped from his saddle, noticing the whispers too. "Is there something that needs to be discussed before we continue?"

Cora mumbled under her breath.

"What was that?" Jax asked with one brow raised.

Cora turned to Tempest and asked, "Is it true?"

"Is what true?" She already knew what Cora meant, but she'd hoped the conversation wouldn't occur until later.

"Are you who Klaus thinks you are? Are you the princess?"

"No," Tempest replied. "I'm an orphan who, like you, will take the emerald." It was nothing but the truth.

Cyrus leaned forward to speak to her privately. "They already know, Tempest," he whispered. "They'll find their own proof if you don't give them any. You ought to quell their curiosities before their digging betrays you. Show them the ring."

Tempest gave a nervous, flitting glance to the faces around her, then her eyes locked with Cyrus' and she sighed, reaching around the nape of her neck to unclasp the chain. He held out his hand, and she set the ring in his palm.

"An orphan that had once been in line for the amethyst," he said, revealing the ring to the others. "You have no need to hide from us, Dasha."

His last words were softly spoken, and she knew he spoke truly, but she still tensed at the sound of her former name.

"Dasha died long ago," she said with sad sincerity. "Who I was before doesn't matter anymore." She grabbed her necklace from Cyrus' fingers and returned it to its place, tucked away where no one would see. "Not while Lazareth sits the throne. I'm Tempest, the orphan from Eris, or I'm dead." She turned to face Jax. "Now, if it pleases you, I'd like to learn how to fly."

The others fell silent, so Jax moved to continue with the lesson, a hint of amusement in his eyes. "For the safety of everyone in this guild, you all will keep Tempest's identity a secret. Anyone who breaks this will answer to Sagua. Follow me," he said, shooing the dragon away.

Tempest walked at the back of the group, watching the dragons that sat perched on the walls of rock around them. The rocky cliffs seemed closer today, as though at any moment, they'd fold and entrap her. At the center of the dome, there lay a field of stone with ten dragons chained to the ground. A leather saddle rested on the shoulders of each.

Jax approached the nearest dragon and carefully removed the chain from its neck. "Lyra, this one's yours," he said, motioning the girl forward. She walked up to the beast, never breaking eye contact, so the dragon lowered its wing and stretched it to the ground, allowing her an easier path up. Jax stroked its neck and watched Lyra ascend. Her name is Vera," he told her, moving on to the next dragon. "Reuben!" he called.

The ninth dragon was given to Tempest. Its scales were a charcoal color much like that of storm clouds. "This one's name is Zephyr," he said. Tempest latched onto the scales of the dragon's neck and pulled herself onto its back, using the wing as leverage.

Jax unlatched the chain of the final dragon and led it to the front of the group. He climbed into the saddle, then leaned forward, bracing himself against its neck. "Up," he commanded. The dragon lowered its head and launched itself forward, sprinting a few steps before flapping its massive wings to gain altitude. A gust of wind rolled over the recruits as the dragon took to the air.

Tempest lurched in her seat when her dragon made course to follow. She quickly wrapped her fingers around its scales and clung to the beast, hoping she wouldn't fall. The sound of ten dragons ascending into the sky beat like drums against the air. Tempest's adrenaline skyrocketed with the altitude, and the dragons fell into formation behind Jax.

He turned in his saddle to face them. "Well done," he shouted over the noise of the wings. "Tomorrow we'll get into the *real* flying. For now, though, I suggest you hold on tight." He smirked, grabbed the back of his saddle, and the dragons dove down.

Tempest tightened her grip, squeezing the saddle with her legs. Her stomach churned with the plummet. It seemed far too quick a dive to recover from, but Zephyr veered upward at the last second, slowing himself for a gentle landing. The sudden force crushed Tempest as if trying to flatten her, and it dizzied her to no end.

The landing was soft, and Zephyr lowered his wing once more to let Tempest off. She jumped from the saddle, glad to be on solid ground again. This flight had not been nearly as peaceful as her first.

"Welcome to the fun part of training," Jax said, walking past the nauseated recruits. "You'll meet in the dining hall in two hours for the feast. We'll start here again tomorrow." He tipped his hat, then walked from the dome without looking back.

"That. Was. Amazing," said Luke with a grin, but he seemed the only one who thought so. Cora stood against the nearest rock wall, retching up her breakfast. She appeared to be the one with the most disagreement to Luke's joy.

"Come on, let's get cleaned up," said Lyra, guiding Cora to the door. The rest followed close behind and made their way to the barracks.

Cyrus fell in beside Tempest, hand grazing slightly against hers. "I'm sorry if I crossed a line earlier," he said, voice hushed.

Tempest looked up and met his worried eyes. "It's okay," she said. "I've just gotten so used to hiding."

"Trying to be the next king, Cyrus?" Klaus asked from behind them, and Cyrus' muscles tensed, but his lips twisted into a smile.

"Just because you couldn't keep a girl happy doesn't mean you have to attack me for trying," he said, and heat rose to Tempest's cheeks.

"They could kill us all for this knowledge, and you boys want to crack jokes," Cora muttered through gritted teeth. She'd recovered a bit from the aftermath of the dive.

"Better to laugh in the face of death than to cower," said Luke. "Lighten up."

"Besides," Cyrus pitched in. "How many people can say they know Royalty?"

"*Exiled* Royalty," Cora said.

"Makes it all the more interesting, don't you think?"

"Are you all going to keep talking about me without including me in the conversation?" asked Tempest.

"No," Cyrus decided for the group, opening the barrack door for all to enter. "Let's get ready for the feast, shall we?"

Tempest grabbed a dress from her chest and headed to the bath house. It was a green dress, vibrant like the forest. Ari had given it to her with a few other garments just before training. It was one of her favorites. The color mirrored her eyes. She stripped down from her clothes and slid into one of the baths that steamed from the fires underground. The water was soothing to her aching muscles, and all she wanted to do was get lost in its warmth.

Cora and Lyra slipped into adjacent pools, cleaning the grime from their bodies. "So," said Lyra, leaning against the wall that separated Tempest's water from hers. "Have you ever even been to Eris?"

Tempest couldn't help but to laugh. She remembered telling Lyra about the holy city when she first met the girl. "No," she said. "I haven't, but I've met the guild leader if that counts for anything."

Lyra giggled and sent a wave of water towards Tempest. "You *lied* to me! How dare you!"

"Has anything you've said been true?" Cora asked, silencing the laughter that echoed in the room.

Tempest shuddered. Despite the warm water, Cora's words had felt like ice. "The only things I've ever kept secret were my name and my history. Everything besides that has been me… I'm still me."

The statement seemed to ease Cora a bit, and Tempest hoped her friend would someday forgive.

When silence returned to the room, Paris popped her head through the doorway. "Can one of you help me with my dress?" she asked.

Lyra pulled herself from the water and wrapped herself in a towel, following Paris into the other room, and Cora rose to join them.

It wasn't long before Tempest was alone again. She preferred it this way. She sat soaking in the water for a while, using up all the time she had to relax. "We're heading out," Lyra said to Tempest when the three girls approached the exit.

"All right, see you in a bit," Tempest replied, and she closed her eyes and rested her head on the ledge of the pool.

After some time passed, footsteps approached once more. "Lyra?" Tempest asked, listening to the rhythm of the steps. They were heavy and moved with a different gate than Lyra's. Cold fingers clamped over her mouth, and a strong arm wrapped around her throat.

"Shhh," Klaus whispered in her ear. She clawed at his hand, struggling against his iron grip. "Word has it there's a group of Kaburem soldiers who arrived at The Claw this morning. They're looking for a girl with looks like yours. Someone is bound to turn you in eventually, so it might as well be me, don't you think? You've got quite the pretty price on your head." He tightened the muscles in his arm, slowly closing off her windpipe.

Tempest dug her nails into his skin and sank her teeth into the palm of his hand, tasting his blood in her mouth. He ripped his hand away, hissing in pain, to which she used as an opportunity to scream, praying that someone would hear her.

Klaus slammed his palm into the back of her head and pushed her underwater. Air burst from her lungs, and her throat became raw. She grew light headed quickly, energy exhausted from her attempts of fighting. She was on the verge of fainting when the grip on her head suddenly fell away. She shot out of the water, gasping for air and clinging to the edge of the pool, cowering from the place the threat had once been.

From her vantage point, she could see that Cyrus had Klaus pinned to the wall, one hand just above Klaus' sternum, twisted around the cloth of his shirt, the other hand clamped around the boy's throat with an unyielding grip. "Never lay a hand on her again," he said, chest heaving with angered breaths. If he could, Tempest believed he would have set Klaus on fire with his gaze. "If you so much as come within an arm's length of her, I swear to the gods, I will kill you."

"What in the world is going on—" Lyra shrieked, sprinting to Tempest's shivering figure. She helped Tempest out of the pool and wrapped a thin towel around her.

Blood flowed from Klaus' nose from a blow Cyrus had dealt him, and a dark bruise began to form around his eye. Cyrus showed no mercy for it. With one final swing and a push, Klaus was out the door. Cyrus turned to Tempest and gave her a quick once over. "Are you okay?" he asked, worry burning in his eyes.

She nodded in return, not trusting herself to speak without losing her composure. She refused to let them see her terror.

At her confirmation, Cyrus left the room to allow her some privacy. She focused on getting ready with Lyra's help, swallowing the tears that threatened to spill.

"I came back to bring you this," Lyra said, holding up a small vial of dye. "Sagua gave it to me. There's rumor going around that Kaburem is here. From what I could gather, they're looking for a girl with auburn hair, not for one with black. They don't know your face, just a list of characteristics to look for. A change in hair color should protect you," she said. "Do you want me to put it in?"

Tempest nodded, tucking her knees to her chest, and with a brush, Lyra lathered the dye into her hair. The motion of it comforted her. It reminded her of her youth when her mother would dress her hair for special occasions, singing songs of dragons as she worked.

"We'll keep you safe, Tempest," Lyra promised when she'd finished with the dye.

Once the color had settled, and her hair had dried, Lyra helped her style it for the feast. It was a simple twist, secured with a braid. At Lyra's approval, she slipped into her gown, completing the look.

Cyrus waited for them in the hallway, garbed in a black frock coat. Gold thread had been embroidered down the edges and around the cuffs in an intricate pattern. Upon seeing their approach, a smile touched his lips. "May I just say, the two of you look stunning," he said.

"Why thank you, Cyrus," Lyra replied, skipping down the hall to the feast.

Tempest's lip twisted upward in a bashful grin, and Cyrus extended his hand. "I do believe you've enchanted me," he said. "May I escort m'lady to the feast?"

She hesitated a moment but soon returned the gesture. "You may."

He bowed his head and turned, guiding her towards the entrance of the dining hall. Music washed over them upon their entry, resonating from a small band in the corner of the room. It seemed like half the city was here. Tempest had never seen the place so full.

She scanned the crowd, wondering if Mereb and his family had come, but her breath caught when her eyes locked with a commanding Kaburem soldier for what felt a moment too long. The whole group of men she'd seen in her dream stood in a line along the back wall, searching the room. She froze, panicked.

A hand touched her shoulder, startling her from her paralysis. "Relax," Cyrus whispered to her, and she exhaled, relieved that it had only been him. "You're too tense. They'll see you if you don't calm down."

She nodded and turned away from the soldiers, focusing instead on him.

"Cyrus!" called a child from behind them.

He spun at the sound of his name and was greeted by a young boy who couldn't have been more than five years of age. Cyrus crouched down, welcoming the boy in an embrace, and a man and woman followed behind. "Who's this?" the boy asked, looking to Tempest.

Cyrus stood and straightened out his coat. "Mother, Father," he said, nodding to each in greeting. "Kai, this is Tempest."

"Is she your inamorata?" Kai asked in a whisper that was much too loud, fumbling with the final word, which he seemed to have only recently discovered. Tempest's cheeks reddened at the question, but it went unanswered as Cyrus whisked the boy into the air.

"Why don't you go introduce yourself to the rest of my friends," Cyrus suggested, setting the child down and pointing him towards the table where the others sat. Kai nodded and ran over to them.

"Nice to meet you, Tempest," Cyrus' mother said, bringing her attention back to them.

"The pleasure is mine," she replied.

Cyrus' father looked at her with a strange expression on his face. "Forgive me," he said, "but, have we met before? You seem oddly familiar."

Tempest shook her head. "Not that I'm aware of, sir," she answered. "But perhaps you knew my mother." Cyrus had told her as much when they first met. "I hear the two of you trained together."

His face lit up, eager to hear more. "What was her name? I may remember her."

"If it's all right with you, sir, I'd like to talk to you about her when there are less ears to hear it. Your family can come too."

Recognition flared in his eyes, and he nodded, then the four of them joined the other recruits at the table. Luke and Paris' families had come as well.

"Where's Klaus?" Cora asked when they sat down.

"He won't be joining us," Cyrus replied through gritted teeth, and Tempest shuddered at the thought of seeing him again.

Kai ran around the table and sat beside her, his chin barely tall enough to reach above the edge. "Tempest?" he asked, and she looked at him, waiting for him to finish his question. "I-I was wondering... if... if I could have a dance with you," the boy said.

"Why, of course you can, but first we need to eat. If you eat all your food, we can dance," she promised, and Kai smiled, satisfied with the deal.

"Better watch out, Cyrus. If your brother keeps this up, he might one day be your king," said Luke.

"Is that so?" Cyrus asked, ruffling Kai's hair. "Perhaps I ought to learn a thing or two from him." He flashed a grin, then turned to watch the doorway where the feast was being brought in.

The smell of food filled the room, making Tempest's mouth water. Tray after tray of meats, breads, greens, and fruits were carried out and set on the tables. Sagua stepped into the center of the room and raised her hand to silence everyone.

"We hold this feast in honor of Aborh for providing us with an excellent year of harvest," she announced, and the room erupted in cheers. "Here's to hoping for many more to follow." Sagua walked back to the dais where the high-ranking officers sat in a line, watching the feast below.

The meat melted in Tempest's mouth. She wanted to try all the food at once. A bite of bread here, a taste of sweets there. She ate until her stomach felt like it would burst, then she washed it down with a sip of water and set her silverware carefully flipped upside down on her plate.

Kai tugged on her gown a moment later. "I finished my food!" he said, showing off his empty plate to prove it.

"Then I suppose it's time to dance, isn't it?" Tempest replied.

Kai nodded and jumped off the bench, nearly sprinting to the dance space. Tempest followed close behind, taking her place amongst the others who'd been summoned by the quickened pace of the band's tune. She took the young lad's hands in hers and guided him through the steps. He was much too short to do any of it properly, but Kai had no notion of what was wrong and what was right. All he cared about was the fun of it.

Tempest tried at first to teach him the correct motions, determined to set order to the boy's cavorting, but Kai ardently refused to listen, and soon, she gave up, abandoning the traditional movement for whatever Kai desired.

Watching him, she recalled her own dancing lessons as a child. She'd had a similar spirit to Kai, and she'd driven her magister mad with the additional moves she added to each dance. With age, she became more refined and eventually agreed to learn the proper methods.

Many celebrations had been hosted in the castle throughout her years, and the feast of Aborh had always been her favorite. Each year, come the time of harvest, they'd bedeck the halls in lavish décor, and the whole city joined in celebration. This was a humble comparison, but the energy felt much the same.

A smile tugged at Tempest's lips, and she gave way to the joy in her heart, but Kai's features scrunched in frustration. "I hate fancy clothes. They're too long and heavy," he said, fumbling with the cuffs of his coat.

"I think it looks wonderful on you. You look like a little prince," said Tempest, pulling up his sleeves.

"You think so?" he asked, eyes brightening at the prospect, and Tempest nodded. "Thanks."

Shortly thereafter, their dance was interrupted by the commanding Kaburem officer. The man tapped Kai on the shoulder, and the boy turned to meet him. "May I have a dance with the young lady?" he asked, and Kai backed away, lowering his gaze from the cold stare of the soldier.

"I-I guess so..." said Kai.

"Go tell your brother that your date's been stolen," Tempest said to the boy. Kai nodded and ran back to the table.

"Stolen is a bit harsh. I only mean to borrow," the soldier said, slipping into the motions of the dance. The music had slowed, and thus, so too had their movement.

Tempest's heart beat with vigor in her chest, and she was certain it would give away the terror lodged deep in her soul, but the Kaburem soldier seemed not to notice. "I hope you'll forgive my intrusion," he said, throwing a glance over her shoulder to ensure he had the right step. "You seemed to be having quite a lot of fun with the boy, but I couldn't resist a dance of my own."

"You've picked it up quite well," said Tempest, diverting her panic to light conversation. "Are the dances of your land similar to ours?"

"Ours are more reserved, but otherwise, the differences are remarkably slim." He watched her inquisitively as they circled around each other. "You're quite good at this yourself. May I be so bold as to ask your name?"

"It's Tempest." She responded quickly, knowing a moment's hesitation would be her end.

"An intriguing name. Where are you from, Tempest?"

"Eris," she said. "The holy city."

"That's a long journey, is it not? What brought you all this way?"

"I've always had a love for dragons," she admitted.

"Ah," said the soldier. "They're quite dangerous creatures. We have none in our homeland, but we'd heard stories before we came. I must say, the stories did them no justice. It is no wonder your people once hunted them."

From behind the soldier, Cyrus approached, putting an end to their conversation. "May I take a turn with the lady?" he asked, and the soldier bowed his head and left. The other soldiers joined their leader, and he whispered something to each of them. Tempest watched, reading his lips.

"It's not her, search the building," he said, and at that, the Kaburem soldiers departed.

"You're shaking," said Cyrus, wrapping his arm around her waist and taking her right hand in his left. "Breathe, Tempest."

She let out a ragged breath and looked him in the eyes, not daring to look back. "What if they find Klaus? He'll surely give me away."

"We'll ensure his silence," said Cyrus.

"Should we tell Sagua?"

Cyrus shook his head. "It'd draw too much attention, but I think I have an idea." As the coda of the song faded into silence, he drew her hand to his lips and bowed. "Come with me."

He led her through the crowd and out into the night air, drawing the attention of a group of harlots and seducers who awaited business after the feast. Some wore shackles on their wrists and ankles, much like Tanith had, but otherwise, they wore little to no clothes.

"We need a service for a friend," Cyrus said, holding out a few coins.

"Male, female, or both?" A woman asked, sauntering towards them.

"Female," Cyrus replied.

"What about Cora?" Tempest asked, unsure this was a good idea. "What will she think of this?"

"If he truly cares for her, he'll deny the woman, and this will all be a waste, but something tells me he won't," Cyrus said, then he turned to face the woman. "Tell him Cyrus sent you. A night with you for a night of silence."

The woman scooped the coins out of his hand. "Where can I find him?"

21

wigs snapped beneath Tempest's feet. She walked through the woods beside Cyrus' father, and the rest of his family followed close behind, the rhythm of their steps joining hers.

"You're a lot like your mother," he said. "The more I watched you, the more I saw it. You have her smile and her heart. Both showed when you danced with Kai. She was stubborn, too. She had a fire in her, and your father had one to match.

"The prince, Neymar, came to Firethorne years ago. He was visiting the major cities of the nation, 'studying the world' as he called it. After his enlistment day, he came to realize how poorly his parents had ruled. Neymar decided to go on a crusade of sorts. He was determined that the answer to the nation's problems lay within its people. He brought his younger brother along with him, hoping to teach him the proper way to rule, but as I'm sure you know, that mission failed, and the young prince grew corrupt.

"When he arrived in Firethorne, a great feast was held in his honor. That's when he met your mother. She and I were training at the time, and she intrigued him. Every time she entered the room, the prince's gaze fell to her, captivated by that spark inside her."

Cyrus glanced to Tempest at these words, and she wondered if he saw the same thing in her. The thought made her both happy and somber. As Cora had predicted weeks before, Tempest found herself growing fond of Cyrus, and he'd made it clear that the feeling was mutual, but he deserved someone better, thought Tempest. He deserved someone whose future was promised.

"Neymar stayed in Firethorne for a month to be with her," Cyrus' father continued. "After she received her emerald ring, he asked her to come with him back to Alyria. She agreed, and the next time I saw her, she lay in a casket beside her family, displayed before the city. I never suspected that one of you still lived." He paused, then turned to face Tempest entirely. "Can I ask you something?"

Tempest nodded. "Anything."

"How did she die?" Tempest figured he'd never gotten closure for the loss of his friend. Perhaps this conversation was helping him as much as it was helping her.

"Poison," she replied. "My father was ill; everyone knew it. He'd been claimed by the gods, but Kaburem was lurking in the shadows, waiting for the perfect moment to strike. That moment came the morning my father passed. She was grieving and I just sat in silence, unable to do anything. The guards came in—I thought they were there to help, but they had already switched sides. A squire boy who'd come along with them warned me of what was to follow. I didn't understand until I saw my mother dead. He helped me escape. Same with the Necromancer and Medic charged to look after my father. All of them died for it." Her voice caught on the words, and tears brimmed in her eyes.

She felt Cyrus' fingers touch hers, and a nervousness shot through her gut, but she didn't object. Instead, she found herself latching onto his hand for comfort.

"Are they still looking for you?" Cyrus' mother asked, glancing to their connected hands. "I saw a soldier come up to you when you were with Kai. Do they know you're here?" The woman kept a wary eye on the boy who ran around, swinging a stick like a sword.

"They've speculated. But, with the help of a couple people here, I've gone unnoticed thus far."

"And if they are to catch you, what then?" she asked. "What will that mean for Cyrus?"

Cyrus shifted, seemingly discomforted by the question, but Tempest found it a rational fear. The woman had already lost one child, and now her second was aiming down a doomed path. Tempest pulled her hand from Cyrus' in resignation. She knew it could never work between them. The risk was too high.

"It means death, Mother," Cyrus said, watching Tempest as she stepped away.

"Are you ready to face that?" his father asked.

"Yes." There was no hesitation in his response.

"Good." Cyrus' father placed a hand on his son's shoulder. "Stand for what you believe in, and bow to no one, even if it's death at the door."

Cyrus smiled. "Yes, sir."

It was a blessing Cyrus' father had given them, Tempest realized, one that permitted them to be together if they wanted. Her heart fluttered at the prospect. "Thank you for meeting with me," she said to the family once they stepped beyond the tree line. "It was nice to hear a bit more about my history."

Cyrus' father bowed his head. "The thanks is mine to give," he said. "I wish you luck in the trials that await you."

After a few exchanged courtesies, Cyrus' family left to return home, and Tempest and Cyrus made their way back to the barracks. Before they entered, however, Cyrus gently grabbed her arm and stopped her. "Can we talk about this for a moment,"—He gestured to the space between them—"about us?"

Us, thought Tempest. Could she dare to entertain the idea of it? He'd admitted only moments before that he was willing to face death to stand by her side, but she had not the courage to let him do it.

"Is it a step too far? I'll back away if that's what you want."

"No," said Tempest, a bit faster than she'd intended. She closed her eyes and took a breath. "I want this—I want you... believe me, I do."

"Then why hesitate? Why push me away?"

"Because it's dangerous to love in a world with so much loss," she said, and Cyrus' composure softened.

He looked at her with a knowing stare and said, "Perhaps it is a risk worth taking." He pressed his hand to the door to open it, then turned to say one last thing before entering. "If there is something you want, seize it, and never let it slip away. You can't protect yourself from loss, so love wholeheartedly, without fear." With this, he gave a slight smile, then stepped inside, holding the door open for Tempest to follow.

The rest of the recruits waited outside the door to the room. Cora sat curled up in Lyra's arms, her cheeks stained with tears. "Don't go in. Klaus is... busy," said Cora. Tempest's heart sank at the sight of the girl's pain. She had done this to her.

"The blame is mine," Cyrus said, reading the guilt on Tempest's face. "I'm sorry it had to happen this way. There was no other option."

"Why?"

"He tried to kill Tempest. He tried to drown her in the bath after training today." Lyra nodded, confirming Cyrus' words. "I'm sorry you had to be hurt in the process, but I couldn't risk Klaus getting to the Kaburem soldiers at the feast. At least now you know where his heart truly lies."

The door opened, and the woman staggered out with her lips curled into a malicious grin. She paused and looked at Cora. "Sorry, sweetheart," she said halfheartedly before continuing down the hall.

Cyrus stepped through the doors first, ensuring it was clear to enter. The others followed soon after.

"Thanks for the gift," Klaus sneered. "You managed to keep me quiet tonight, but I can't promise that I'll make it another day... Unless you want to give me another gift, of course." He placed a hand on Tempest's shoulder, and she tensed under his touch, revulsion coiling through her body.

Cyrus grabbed him by the shoulders and threw him to the side. "I told you not to touch her!" he seethed, only receiving laughter in return.

"I wish you understood just how fun it is to piss you off. We should get some rest; don't you think? Can't be tired for training now, can we? Shall we continue this later?"

Cyrus turned away, not giving an answer, and the recruits settled down for the night.

~~~

With morning came further flight training. Each day brought more difficult, more elaborate methods of flying, and by the third day, Jax had them riding in a standing position. It was much harder than he made it seem. At the end of the flight, Tempest's legs could hardly hold her own weight.

The following week brought dragon mounted combat training, and on the final day of this training, the dragons awaited them in the field with blunted swords lying on the ground beside each. "Today is the last day of flight training, so naturally, it's time for a contest," said Jax. "If you're hit with a fatal blow, you'll join me on the ground. The last person in the air wins."

Tempest grabbed the sword that lay beside Zephyr and mounted the dragon. He lunged forward, taking to the air. The others followed her into the sky, circling each other, waiting for the game to begin. Jax lifted his fingers to his lips, and a whistle shot through the air.

Everything became a frantic mess of scales and steel as dragons interlocked in battle. Tempest sat perched atop Zephyr's shoulders, taking in her surroundings. Off in the distance, Reuben and Luke charged at each other as if engaging in a joust. Cora and Paris teamed up against Lyra, who, in turn, was targeting Cyrus. Lyra quickly lost, fighting a battle on three fronts. As Lyra returned to the ground, her three killers turned on each other. It was now every man for themselves. Tempest looked around, trying to find Klaus amidst the fighting.

A shadow fell over her, and talons crashed into Zephyr's side, knocking the dragon off balance. Tempest clung to the beast as it rolled, and Klaus hovered before her, lounging on the back of his red beast. "I'll be back for you," he said, diving down towards Paris and Cyrus.

Cora and Reuben had joined Lyra on the ground. Tempest left Klaus to tend to the two he pursued. The less people in the air, the better. Perhaps one of them would take Klaus down for her.

Out of the corner of her eye, she spotted Luke barreling towards her, so she shot up, taking the battle to the clouds above where she and her dragon could hide. The green scales of Luke's dragon made him easy to find. She saw him circling below, spinning around in search of her. When he turned his back to her, Zephyr, with Tempest's urging, folded his wings and dove towards Luke.

She leapt from Zephyr's back, and landed upon Luke's dragon, praying her plan would work. She swung her blade, tapping Luke on the small of his back, and talons wrapped around her. But, they were red talons that didn't belong to the dragon meant to catch her. Within seconds, she was free falling, slamming hard onto Zephyr's back. Pain shot through her body at the impact.

Klaus swung down from his dragon's back, landing in front of Tempest. "Told you I'd be back," he said, and Tempest clambered to her feet, lifting her sword in front of her, preparing to fight. Klaus was clumsier on the backs of dragons than she was. He had not the advantage of stable footing behind him. That'd count for something, at least.

Klaus shook his head and tutted at her. "You don't really think that sword will save you, do you?"

She watched him, waiting for him to take another step. He didn't have his sword with him, so she stood a chance if she could knock him off balance. Klaus shifted his weight, and Tempest swung, but he caught the blade in the palm of his hand and ripped it from her grasp. He lifted it, and Tempest ducked, fearful that he actually meant to kill her.

He made no move to hit her with it, though. Instead, he opened his hand and let the blade fall to the ground far below. "We won't be needing that," he said, backing Tempest to the dragon's neck. She intended to drop down and urge Zephyr into a roll that'd dump Klaus from his back, but she had not the time to enact such plans.

Klaus grabbed her wrist and pulled her close so that her back pressed to his body. Like snakes, his arms wrapped around hers, preventing her from fighting back. The cold touch of a blade skimmed over her throat, burning as it left its mark. "Cyrus isn't here to save you now," he said, watching the small stream of hot blood trail down her neck from where the blade broke skin. "But, as much as I'd like to, I can't just kill you." He lowered the blade. "Not when there's time to enjoy this."

Klaus tangled his fingers into her hair and tilted her head to expose her neck. She shuddered, feeling his hot, ragged breath hit her skin, and his hand traced the lines of her body. In a final effort of escape, she threw her head back, shattering Klaus' nose. He howled in pain and backed away from her. This was her chance. She dropped down and swiped at his legs with her foot. His knees buckled, and he stumbled, losing his footing on the beast.

Klaus' eyes bore into hers with a fiery mix of fear and hatred, and he slipped off Zephyr, lashing out at anything he could get his hands on. His fingers grazed the saddle but he was too slow. Tempest watched in equal horror and relief as Klaus plummeted to the ground.

Cora's gut-wrenching scream rang in Tempest's ears from far below, and she flew away, unable to confront what she'd done. She glanced back down at the others who all stood around his body. Cora sobbed in Lyra's arms, and Jax crouched down beside him, checking the boy for a pulse. Tempest turned and left the field behind her, landing in the small meadow she and Cyrus shared. It was the only place that felt safe.

Tempest paced back and forth, her mind a war zone. One part hoped Klaus was dead so he could never hurt anyone again. Another part shamed her for thinking such things. Her internal battle was interrupted by the sound of beating wings. She hid beneath the branches of a tree, not ready to talk to anyone. The dragon landed beside Zephyr. It was Cyrus' dragon.

"Tempest?" he asked. "I know you're here. Don't try to hide from me." He dropped down from the dragon's shoulders, looking around for her. "He's not dead..." Cyrus paused, waiting for a response that never came. "I don't know if that's a good thing or a bad thing, but he's not dead... at least not yet. They took him to the infirmary. He was still breathing at the time, though not all that well. The others are with him. We should probably join them."

"I can't go back there," she replied, drawing his attention to the trees. "It's my fault." She stepped into the clearing, and rage filled Cyrus' eyes, his gaze falling upon the thin wound that traced the center of her throat.

"I'll kill him myself if he was the cause of that," he said, brushing his finger lightly over the cut.

Tempest backed away and shook her head. "Klaus is in the gods' judgement now. They decide whether he lives or dies, not you."

Cyrus' eyes glazed over. "What happened up there?" he asked, so Tempest slowly retold the events. He was silent for a while, and when she finished, he looked her in the eyes and said, "I hope the gods judge him harshly." He then climbed back onto his dragon and flew off, leaving Tempest alone in the silence.

She sat down, weaving her fingers through the blades of grass, listening to her surroundings. She heard the soft murmur of the pond and the rustling of leaves dancing in the wind. Things were peaceful here. Everything was so simple. She wished there had been birds in the sky as a reminder of the bygone moment of wonder she and Cyrus had shared in these trees, but the sky was empty.

Tempest took a deep breath and rose to her feet, saying farewell to simplicity, saying goodbye to the calm that'd come before the storm. She pulled herself onto Zephyr's shoulders and returned the dragon to the dome, making her way to the infirmary.

None of the recruits were there when she arrived. She assumed they'd all gone to supper. The wood beneath her feet creaked with each step she made towards Klaus' pallet. He seemed at peace, chest rising and falling with each struggled breath.

Footsteps came up behind her, and she turned to greet the woman who approached. "He's fallen into a comatose state," said the Medic. "It's like a sleep, but one that most normally don't wake from. There's a possibility he'll return, but his chances are slim."

Tempest nodded, taking one last look before turning to leave, repeating Cyrus' words in her mind. *I hope the gods judge him harshly.*

22

*T*empest stared at the coordinates in her hand, eyes flitting back and forth between the numbers and the map the Mage held beside it. She frowned, struggling to think of a plan under the pressure of nearly a hundred eyes that awaited her direction. Cyrus had been given command, but he'd passed it over to her. She really wished he hadn't. Her mind wasn't focused on the game. "Cyrus!" she called, and he turned at the sound of his name. "Do you still have that strategy you told me about, or did you use it in the last game?"

"I have it. They wouldn't listen to me. Do you want to see it?"

"I need something, and I need it fast. What do you have?"

"Deception," he said with a grin, eager to finally put his plan into action. "The only person allowed to use magic is the guardian, but the rules don't specify where. We can find a location that's suitable and have the guardian project a false Orbis. We put the bulk of our defense around the fake, and shroud the real one as best we can. Around the real Orbis, we put two broad rings about thirty paces away from each other. That way, if the first ring is breached, a second one will catch the ones that made it through.

"As for offense, we only send three. They will scout for the enemy Orbis. Once it's found, the guardian will return to the real Orbis and everyone who was protecting the decoy will split into two groups to flank the enemy." He gestured to the map, providing a visual to his directives.

"All right. Those who wish to be offense, stand with Cyrus. Those who wish to be defense, stand with the guardian. Those who wish to run, come with me," she announced.

Everyone separated into their groups and were moved according to need. Instructions were given, and soon, all were in place.

Tempest stood beside the guardian, waiting for the game to begin. He braced himself against the formation of rock they'd chosen for the decoy and prepared to create the replica.

His eyes rolled back into his head as he channeled the needed magic. It was somewhat terrifying to watch, but Tempest had gotten used to it. She looked to the top of the rock tower, watching a blue orb begin to form.

Shortly after, the tag lights appeared, and the game started. Her team stood in waiting, hoping for either an enemy to attack the decoy or for one of the runners to return with intelligence. Tempest stared up into the sky, watching the stars and wondering if Cyrus' rings had been breached or if the enemy had fallen for the trap.

A rustling of leaves caught her attention, and a red light shot through the branches. "They're here!" she shouted, and chaos erupted. Dozens of people burst from the branches and all bolted for the decoy Orbis. Most were captured quickly, but a few made it through the defense. Tempest watched as one of them scaled the rocks. The girl was determined, her gaze never falling from the Orbis, not even breaking to look for the guardian.

"Wait!" she heard Luke shout from the crowd, and the girl stopped to turn to her captain just before she reached the Orbis. "They've tricked us." He laughed with pure amusement. "A dragon also guards the Orbis. Where is it? And look at the guardian. It's magic." The Mage blinked, and the false Orbis disappeared.

Everyone from Luke's team turned to look at their captain, trying to figure out what to do next, but they were trapped. All who hadn't already been captured were soon detained, including Luke. They marched the offenders in a mass procession towards the jail. On the journey, a boy burst through the line. He was one of the runners sent to find the enemy Orbis.

"We found it!" he said, sprinting towards Tempest. "It's in the springs!"

Tempest paused, looking to Luke's captured team. "Leave them!" she shouted. "Defense, fall back to the Orbis, Offense, come with me!"

It was a race now. Luke collected his people as the blue team scattered, and Tempest ran at the lead of her offense, dragging the guardian with her. Their feet thundered over the ground like a stampede. It was a thrilling sensation, to charge at the head of such a large group.

As they neared the line of fire that separated the lands, the guardian turned and ran back towards their actual Orbis, glancing side to side to be sure no one had followed. Tempest leapt over the flames with the remainder of her group. The stragglers were caught by Luke's defense, but the pack continued with the runner at the lead.

Tempest sped her pace, catching up with the runner. "Are we close?" she asked, and the runner nodded, unable to speak through the deep breaths he took. "B team, follow me!" she called, veering to the right with half the group.

The glowing of the enemy Orbis colored the trees around them in a red hue. Tempest's B team lined up shoulder to shoulder and prepared to close around the enemy, waiting silently for the command to move.

A whistle broke through the silence from a member of A team, and they began the double envelopment. There weren't many people defending the Orbis. Most had gone to assist Luke's offense when word had arrived of their capture. Tempest approached the small cave of rock that hosted the red Orbis. A thin stream of water spilled from the top, falling like a door to the opening of the cave.

The guardian Mage emerged from the falls, and a ripple shot through the water as rock from the stream bed lifted into the air, flying towards Tempest and her people. She ducked down and rolled away, dodging all the stones but one that landed between her shoulder blades, knocking her down to all fours.

Tempest staggered to her feet and picked up one of the rocks. The Mage rolled her eyes. Both knew her attempts to fight back were pointless. Tempest didn't need to fight though, all she needed was the Mage's attention.

The runner inched towards the Orbis, his eyes flitting between the Mage and the dragon that paced before the line of offense. His foot caught a loose stone on top of the falls, and all eyes locked on him when the rock clattered down to the stream below, making a soft popping noise as it broke the water's surface.

In the short moment that everyone froze, waiting to see what would happen, the Orbis began to flash. Luke had gotten to theirs. The runner snatched the red Orbis and bolted into the tree line, and Tempest tackled the guardian, trying to buy him more time.

"Follow him!" she shouted. "I don't want to see that thing back in this spot. Protect it!"

Her company scattered, and Tempest stayed, waiting until her team was well into the woods before she let the Mage up. "I wasn't going to chase them," the Mage grumbled, brushing the dirt from her clothes.

Tempest shrugged and sat on a stone. "Better not to risk it," she said, and she picked up a small stick from the ground to pass the remaining time. As she dragged it across the dirt, shapes began to form.

"What're you drawing?" the Mage asked, sitting beside her.

"A skull," she replied, working out the details.

"What's on its head? A crown?" The Mage pointed to the poorly sketched crown. It was difficult to draw in dirt. The shape never stayed.

Tempest nodded. "A crown of bones."

"I heard once that King Lazareth wears a crown like that. Does the skull belong to him?"

"Perhaps," said Tempest, though she thought perhaps it belonged to her. With a sigh, she wiped the drawing from the dirt, and a few seconds later, the tag lights faded from their sides.

"Moment of truth," the Mage said, holding her palm towards the sky. A small blue light formed a few inches above it. "Congratulations," she said, standing to brush the dirt from her clothes. She held out her other hand, helping Tempest to her feet, then the two made their way to the field. The girl joined the line of Mages who lit the way, and Tempest followed the Dragon Keeper recruits back to the barracks.

"Has there been any word about Klaus?" Tempest asked when Cyrus came up beside her.

He shook his head. "Not tonight, but the last I heard, it wasn't looking good."

"You never told us about what happened, Tempest," said Lyra. It was true. Every time one of them had asked, she'd promised she'd tell them later. She hadn't been ready to face it yet, but she supposed it was later now. "Did you..." Lyra thought for a moment. "Was it on purpose?"

"No," said Tempest. "I'd never... He tried to kill me again. He had a blade... a real one."

"Is that how you got that scar?" Luke asked.

Tempest nodded. "He planned to torture me," she said. "But then he fell... I didn't mean for him to fall."

"It wasn't your fault, Tempest. You can't blame yourself for this," Cyrus said.

Tempest wanted to believe him, but she couldn't bring herself to do so just yet. Upon their return to the barracks, she lay curled in her pallet, eager for the night to shroud her worries in darkness.

"Are you tired?" Cyrus asked.

"Aren't you?" she mumbled, propping herself up on her elbows.

"Very," he replied, but he sat on the edge of his pallet and leaned forward as if ready to get up at any moment, and he stared at his hands, fidgeting with his thumbs in thought.

"Want to take a walk?" Tempest asked, sitting the rest of the way up.

"I don't want to keep you awake."

Tempest stood. "We only have an hour anyway. Besides, we have more lectures tomorrow, I won't need to be alert. Come on." She gestured for him to join her, so he followed her out the door and back into the woods. "What's on your mind?"

He stopped and leaned against a tree. "The final month of training," he said, turning his head to look at Tempest, dark eyes glittering in the light of the moon. "Have you given any thought to where you might go after this or what you might do?"

"Do you want to hear what I want to do or what I will do?"

"Both."

Tempest took a deep breath before answering. It felt odd to put her desires into words. "What I want with all my heart is to stay here," she said. "I want to live the rest of my days as a Dragon Keeper and build a home here in Firethorne—to build a family... I never wanted to be a Royal when I was young."

Cyrus pondered this, fumbling with a twig that dangled from the tree and danced in the soft summer breeze. "Do you want it now?"

She shook her head. "I want justice and peace, but no. I have no interest in the crown."

"You see, then, why you must take it?"

"I do." She hadn't quite known it until those words slipped from her mouth, but now her path seemed clear. "My talk with your father gave me an idea. I was thinking I might follow my own father's footsteps and go on a crusade... of sorts, travel the lands and get to know the people. Maybe I'd manage to get a few of them to rally behind my cause while I'm at it." It all seemed like ideas of a distant future, but she knew the time for it to come to pass drew near. This knowledge formed like a pit in her chest, uncertain and dreadful. "What about you? Where will you go?"

Cyrus looked at her for a moment before responding. She didn't like the way he watched. It felt like he was preparing to say goodbye. "I plan to stay here and go through the ranks. Sagua thinks I could succeed amongst the officers."

This statement made the pit in her chest twist. She didn't want to face what lay ahead alone. "Must we part so soon?"

"Only for a short while if the gods are good." He reached forward and took her hand. "I'll wait for you if you wait for me."

Tempest hesitated in her response. This was a promise of being reunited, one she wasn't certain could be kept. "I'll wait," she decided. "Perhaps when we find each other again, we can give that thing called us a try."

"Perhaps so."

Morning bells chimed above The Claw's towers, summoning them to the lecture hall. Its song welcomed the start of the new day, though, to Tempest's distress, it was one that brought them closer to their separate ways, and suddenly, time was moving too fast. She didn't want to leave him, but she knew she'd need to, so she relished in the moment and enjoyed the feeling of having him beside her as they made their way to the hall in silence.

They were the first to reach the room. The others were most likely still crawling from their beds, drowsy from the minimal amount of sleep they'd gotten. Tempest could feel her own exhaustion setting in. The adrenaline rush of the night had faded, leaving her with nothing but the desire to sleep. She dropped into one of the seats, resting her chin on her arms, too tired to hold her head up.

When all had arrived, Jax rose to his feet and hung a long scroll of parchment on the wall. On it was a list of the Dragon Keeper rankings. Each title had a small emblem beside it, all except the last. The title at the very bottom read *Enlisted*. It was the rank the majority of the Dragon Keeper population stayed in. Most received their emerald rings and the dragon they were charged to protect, and they moved on, settling down in some city or village to someday start a family or whatever they wished to do after training.

Others, like Cyrus, would stay behind in the barracks to become an officer and make their way through the ranks. These people would be consultants to the military or mentors for the next batch of recruits. Sometimes, they'd even be advisers to the Royal House.

At the very top of the list was the guild leader. Beside it was the silhouette of a dragon with its wings outstretched. Sagua would occasionally wear this emblem on a patch on her shoulder.

Every guild leader had an emblem. The symbol of the Royal House was a gold crown. The Merchants had a coin, the Farmers a bushel of wheat, and the Necromancers a head of a lion split one half black, the other half white. It had once been a requirement to wear the guild's emblem if one succeeded in the ranks, but the tradition had long died out.

The door creaked open and a pair of footsteps silenced Jax's lecture. Tempest looked up to see who had entered. It was Sagua, standing a few steps into the room with a Necromancer at her side.

Tempest blinked, staring at the pair in disbelief. Their coming could only mean one thing.

"I'm sorry to interrupt, but I have some regretful news to deliver," Sagua said, glancing apologetically to the class of recruits. "Klaus is dead."

Tempest's heart sank. All at once she wished she could take back her words, wished she hadn't asked the gods to judge him so harshly. She questioned whether everything he'd done to her was worth death, but at the same time, she was thankful. She hated the fact of it, but she couldn't help but to feel somewhat free. She didn't have to live in fear of him anymore.

Her guilt returned as the weight of the room settled over her. There was a heavy silence that hung over the occupants, each digesting the words Sagua had spoken. The faint sounds of Cora's sobs were the only thing that broke the silence. No one could speak. No one could move. Everyone just sat there, confused.

"The service will be held in three days' time to enable the family time to travel," Sagua said, then she bowed her head in solidarity and silently left the room.

Jax looked to each of their faces. "You may be dismissed," he said. "We'll continue the lesson later."

Tempest stood and walked out of the room, tears welling in her eyes. She pushed open the doors and left, not strong enough to look back.

23

*C*yrus laced his fingers through Tempest's, giving her hand a soft squeeze as a tear rolled down her cheek. "Three," she said, looking mournfully down at Klaus' body. He'd been dressed in formal wear, and an emerald ring had been placed on his finger. Cyrus looked at her, confused by the number she'd given. "Three people dead by my hands... How many more will follow before the end of this? How many people will either die for or because of me?"

"More than you want," he answered truthfully "Many lives will be lost in this fight, and their deaths will never be easy." His features were composed, but a fire raged within. "I've received letters from my parents. It's getting bad out there, Tempest. People are going to fight, even if you don't join the cause." He whispered the words into her ear, wary of the numerous people around them that could be listening. The only ears that seemed to hear were those of the corpse laid before them.

Klaus had been doused in oils before they placed him on the pedestal, but he'd been dead near four days, and the signs of Odemus' grasp were beginning to show.

One of the Necromancers approached from behind, holding a single lit candle. He touched the burning wick to eleven other candles that lay in a neat circle around the pedestal Klaus rested on, setting the twelfth in the gap that completed it. He whispered a short prayer, then departed into the halls of Firethorne's temple.

Cyrus and Tempest backed away from the display to allow others to view. The room was dark, lit only by the candles and a small window that let in the sun's natural light. It illuminated the deceased in a beam of amber that caressed the boy like the hand of a god. Not much was required to light the room. It was a cramped space, no larger than her bed chamber had been back in Alyria. They didn't need much space, though. Not many people had come.

Sorrow filled Tempest, as she realized just how alone Klaus had been in this world. Cora was all he'd really had, and Tempest had helped take even that from him. The recruits were the only ones that visited. Them and his mother, who'd come earlier, weeping over her son's body, and cursing the gods for taking him.

'His mother left him as a boy, and his father blamed him for it,' Tempest recalled Cora saying. She wondered how well this woman even knew the broken and

battered boy who lay on the pedestal. Tempest turned, seeking Cora in the midst of the others. She found her sitting on a bench in the far corner of the room.

In the soft light, Cora's features looked hard, seeming as though they were chiseled from stone. Her eyes had dried the previous morning. At this point, she looked cold and hollow. She hadn't eaten in over a day, and she wouldn't speak either. It worried Tempest to no end.

Tempest tried to pull her friend from the darkness that enshrouded her on many occasions, but it was in vain. Cora's skin had grown so pale, and her eyes so distant, it was difficult to find any life in her features. She looked like a ghost, guarding the body from afar. In this act, Tempest saw that, despite everything, Cora had loved him.

On the other hand, Klaus looked like the boy Cora claimed to adore in this calm and eternal sleep. He looked like the boy who had softened in her presence, the boy who'd told her the secrets of his dark childhood, the boy who, despite the front he put on, had fallen in love with her. Tempest had never seen that side of Klaus, but from the stories Cora had told her, she imagined the tranquility of death to resemble it well.

She watched as Cora looked down at her wrists and traced the fading bruises that decorated them. Those, thought Tempest, would likely be the last things she would remember from him. Even after the bruises disappeared, they would always remain in memory. Klaus may have managed to love, but he failed to show it. Cora seemed to think the same. She stood and left the temple without a word.

Her gaze met with Tempest's before she walked out the door, so Tempest followed, hand slipping from Cyrus'. She looked up, silently bidding him not to come.

They walked down the stone path for a while without a spoken word. Tempest began to wonder if Cora knew she'd followed when the girl finally stopped and turned to confront her. The same hollow look burned in her eyes that'd been there back at the temple.

"Did you do it?" she asked. The question caught Tempest off guard. "Did you kill him? We saw him leap onto your dragon, then a sword fell from the sky. We thought that was the end. One of you had been disarmed and the game was over... that's when Klaus fell. Did you do it?"

Tempest paused, trying to think of a way to answer. "I did," she admitted, and Cora's gaze fell to the ground, the tears returning to her eyes. "He disarmed me and threw the blade over the edge. I wish that had been the end, but Klaus was no longer playing the game. He trapped me in his arms and put a dagger to my throat. It was supposed to be me on that pedestal today.

"He could have killed me with ease, but he didn't. He said he wanted to make it fun. I don't know what he intended to do next, but I'm glad I never have to find out. As soon as he removed the knife from my throat, I pushed him, trying to get free of his grasp, but he lost his footing. I'm sorry, Cora."

Cora's lips pressed together in a thin line, and she nodded, taking in the story. She didn't speak for another week, and when she did, it was only to voice her forgiveness.

~~~

One morning, Tempest woke with a crumpled sheet of parchment in her hands. She pried the folds open and lit a candle to read the words that'd been written. Her heart skipped a beat as she read them.

Tempest, addressed the words.

If you wake, and I am gone, don't attempt to find me. I will be deep in the woods by then, and the way will be unsafe.

She dropped the note onto the bed and threw on a cloak, sprinting into the night air. The world was still asleep, but the sky seemed so alive with its glittering stars and the ghostly green glow of the northern lights. A full moon hung amongst the stars, lighting her way to the woods where wolves howled. They raised their voices in a song that sent chills through her spine and made the hair on her arms stand.

The trees swallowed her in their shadows, the foliage blocking much of the light the sky provided. Her heart raced in fear of both the night creatures that stalked unseen around her and fear that she had been too late.

Her throat dried, and her lungs grew weary, but she continued searching. As the sun began to show its face just over the mountains, she heard a muffled cry. Beneath the branches of a fallen tree, she found Cora sitting in the mud. She sighed, relieved, and crouched down before her friend.

Somber, water-brimmed eyes met Tempest's. "I'm sorry," said Cora. She pulled her knees to her chest, and wiped the tears from her eyes. "Why did you follow me? I told you not to come."

"I came to help you," Tempest replied.

"Did you come to help me run or to help me return?"

Tempest sat beside the girl and leaned against the tree trunk. She knew the answer she wanted to give, but her mouth spoke another. "Whichever you want me to do," she said. "But before you decide, tell me why you want to leave, and let me tell you why I want you to stay."

The sounds of birds joined the night's chorus, singing the creatures of the moon to sleep. Light crept through the leaves, painting pretty shadows on the ground. Tempest traced them with her finger while she waited for Cora to speak.

Her response was soft, and Tempest could barely hear it over the wind, but from Cora's lips, she caught the words. "He won't leave me alone," she whispered. "It's like he's still here… taunting me… blaming me. I didn't summon him. I don't even know how to… but he won't go away."

Tempest thought back to Alyria where the dead seemed to follow her. In her dreams, they appeared the most. Though, for Cora, she figured it was different. "Unfortunately, death doesn't need summoned for the dead to come haunting."

"Every time I see his empty bed. Every time I see a white rose. Every time I close my eyes, he's there. Why won't he move on? Why can't *I* move on?" Cora's fists clenched and tears spilled from her eyes.

There was nothing that Tempest could do to ease Cora's pain, but the least she could do was try. She fished through blades of grass until her fingers found her goal. With care, she plucked a winged seed off the ground. "Do you know what this is?" she asked.

Cora blinked away the tears and looked hard at the seed. "A samara," she replied.

"Right," said Tempest. "The tree it came from sheds its seeds in autumn when most trees begin their slumber. Do you know why it does this?"

"No," Cora answered, reaching out to hold the pod.

Tempest placed the seed into Cora's hand, then continued. "It drops its seeds in autumn because it does not fear the ice. It knows that when the month of Jukion comes and goes, and the year begins again, that Izasel will return one day, and the sun will gift its seed life. It is in this trust that time continues that new beginnings are born. Time will move forward, and Klaus' section of it will fade like the tree that birthed this seed. In this new time, you will find hope, and you will find growth." She pointed to Cora's heart as she said the next words. "All you have to do is trust the strength of the seed."

Cora's fingers wrapped gently around the fragile casing of the seed, and she planted it into the dirt. "The seed will grow, and so will I," she decided, standing to brush the dirt from her clothes.

Tempest stood to join her. "We're almost done. Just hold strong for a little bit longer."

A smile touched Cora's lips, and she thanked Tempest for her words. "Do you know the way back?" she asked.

"I do. Are you coming?"

Cora looked up at the twisting branches of the tree as the breeze set more of its seeds into flight. "Yes."

~~~

That little bit longer Tempest had promised seemed to take an eternity with the excitement and nervousness of graduation that loomed ahead, but finally, the day came, and the recruits filed into The Claw. Tempest's fingers clasped around the thin chain on her neck that held her mother's amethyst ring. In another life perhaps she would have received her own version of this ring today, but that life was long behind her. Instead, she would take the emerald as her mother had done many years before.

A murmur washed through the room when the recruits paraded in, taking their seats in the front row of the assembly hall. Tempest glanced back at the many faces who waited for the ceremony to begin. Amongst them was Lyra's mother, whose eyes were glazed over with tears of joy. Tempest had never seen that woman without tears in her eyes. Lyra must have taken after her father. She was nowhere near as emotional as her mother.

In the corner sat Cora's mother, waiting silently in isolation away from the other families. Tempest's gaze moved to Cyrus' family where she spotted Kai, holding a small wooden dragon, and a young girl watching him at his play. It was Sparrow, Tempest realized, and her eyes lit up with joy. Beside the children sat both of Cyrus' parents, who conversed with John and Ari Paxton. To her disappointment, Mereb and his friends were nowhere in sight.

Many other faces populated the hall, but only a few she recognized. They were all parents and family members of the other recruits.

The room fell silent when Sagua entered, and Tempest turned her attention to the stage that'd been set for the ceremony. Jax stood in the back, waiting for his turn to speak.

"Thank you all for coming today and joining us in celebration as we send these young men and women off to claim their place in our society," said Sagua. "We'll begin with the rings."

Jax stepped forward and gestured to the first person in line. "Luke," he called. Luke stood and ascended the stairway up to the stage. The crowd of parents applauded as he was given an emerald ring to replace the child's band on his finger. He bowed his head and hurried off the stage to rejoin the others, grinning and flashing his new ring when he sat.

"Tempest," said Jax when Luke had settled in his seat. She stood and walked to his side. He placed a small box that held the emerald ring in her hand, and she accepted it graciously, giving a slight bow before exiting to return to her friends.

"Wait," a voice whispered from the shadowed corner of the room. Tempest turned to meet Sagua who held something in her hands. She pulled back a corner of the cloth it was wrapped in, revealing the barrel of the gun. "You may need this sooner than I'd like. Good luck, Tempest," she said, handing the weapon over.

Tempest thanked her and returned to her seat. She felt Cyrus shift and lean closer to her. "What's that?" he asked in a whisper.

Tempest pulled back the corner, giving Cyrus a small glimpse before covering it back up to hide it in the folds of her dress. He nodded and stood when his name was called. Tempest opened the box in her hands and pulled the child's band from her finger, slipping the emerald on in its place.

At the end of the ceremony, Sagua reclaimed center stage and motioned for them to stand. Together, they rose and followed Sagua to the nursery to claim their dragons. Tempest scanned the rows of eggs, looking for one that stood out to her. Her eye fell to one on the bottom shelf. It was a deep black with small accents of gold. She reached out and held the egg in her hands. "This one," she said to herself. The choice was more instinct than thought.

When everyone had made their decision, they found their way to the dining hall to be reunited with their families. Sparrow ran up to Tempest with a smile broad on her face and wrapped her arms around Tempest, so she set her things down on a nearby table and greeted the child. "You've grown taller!" she exclaimed. Sparrow now stood eye level with her.

The girl beamed at the prospect. "You think so? Mother says I'll be as tall as Mereb someday."

"You'll pass me up soon enough. Where is Mereb anyhow?"

"He and Theria stayed home to watch the dragons," she said, leaning in to whisper something in Tempest's ear. "But, if you ask me, I think he only offered it so he could be alone with her." She smirked, giving Tempest a quick wink before Ari approached. Tempest covered her mouth, trying desperately not to laugh.

"What are you two murmuring about?" asked the girl's mother.

"Nothing," Sparrow said sharply, then she turned and skipped towards Kai, looking back at them with innocent eyes.

Ari shook her head and laughed. "I've got quite the troublemaker with that one. It seems she's grown quite attached to that little lad over there. Perhaps I can send her off to them when I can't handle her," she said, watching Sparrow reenact an epic tale about one of the great dragon riders, using Kai's wooden beast as a prop. "Would you like to come with us back to the house? I'm sure Mereb and Theria would be glad to see you again. The others have gone back to their homes, so the house has been quite quiet."

Tempest smiled. "That's very generous. It'd be nice to settle down somewhere for a bit, but I can't stay long. Could I stay until the dragon hatches? It'll be easier to travel once it's born."

"You can stay as long as you need." Ari's gaze shifted to look behind Tempest.

"May I?" Cyrus asked, putting an end to their conversation. Ari nodded and left to join her husband and daughter with Cyrus' family.

The two of them walked side by side in a comfortable silence for a while, until Cyrus finally spoke up. "My parents agreed to let me stay and join the officers."

"I hope I can visit soon," said Tempest with a halfhearted smile. She wasn't ready to say goodbye yet. The chance that she would never see him again filled her with dread.

"What's the first stop on this crusade of yours?" he asked. Tempest was glad for the question. It provided them with at least a little more time together before they parted ways.

"The Paxtons are taking me in again until the dragon hatches. After that, I think I might go to the city of Mortem. The month of Xudor will be nearing then." She had no need to say more. Cyrus nodded in understanding. It had been something she'd been thinking about the last weeks of training. If she managed to get to the city, there was a chance for her to speak to her parents again.

"How long do you reckon it'll be before our paths cross again?"

"Likely a few months," she said. "But it could be longer..." She didn't want to think about time or distance right then, not while they were still together.

He stopped suddenly and turned to look her in the eyes. His index finger touched her chin, and before she could make sense of his actions, his lips were pressed to hers. His kiss was soft, caring, and gentle, but he held her strong, grip betraying the desperation in his heart.

Tempest responded equally, heart pounding in her chest. A flush crept to her cheeks when their lips drew apart. "Forgive me, but if the time was going to be so long, I couldn't risk you going and forgetting me," he said.

Her lips curved into a sheepish grin. "I'd quite like to do that again someday," she replied, reaching forward to touch him one last time, but she pulled back her hand when she spotted Sparrow out of the corner of her eye with her mouth agape, nudging her mother, who had watched it all.

24

$\mathcal{A}$ ri pushed open the door to allow the others inside. Sparrow was the first to enter, shoving past the rest. "Guess who's here!" she shouted, looking around for her brother. Mereb stepped into the room with his dragon in his arms. Soon the beast would be too large to hold.

"Tempest!" he said. "You came back!"

Theria's bitter cold eyes stared at her from beside him. Tempest figured the girl shared none of the joy expressed by the others in her return. "Only until my dragon hatches, then I'll be out of your hair," she promised.

Mereb's face lit up, seeming to have forgotten the dragon egg. "Right! You can put that over here," he said, gesturing to the makeshift nest the other dragons had hatched in. Tempest set the egg inside, then leaned against the countertop, taking in the state of the room. It was quiet without the bustle of people moving through the halls. She missed the chaos that once reigned here.

"So," said Sparrow, inching towards Tempest. "What was it like? Did you get to ride a dragon?"

"Of course she did. Every recruit has to," Theria replied.

"But I didn't ask you, now did I?" said Sparrow, placing her hands on her hips in a gesture that made her look much like her mother.

"We should celebrate!" said Mereb, standing between them. He had a wearisome look upon his face that pleaded for peace between his sister and Theria. "Why don't we go to the inn where we can all discuss Tempest's training over a drink."

"I think that's a great idea," Tempest said, hoping a drink would douse Theria's anger long enough to hold a proper conversation, but Theria rebutted.

"You can go without me," she said, crossing her arms. "It's not safe out there anymore."

Mereb placed a hand on her shoulder, coaxing agreement with a soft touch. "Come on, Ther, just one night. Please... do it for me," he begged.

There was a moment's silence as the girl made up her mind, but soon, Theria sighed and dropped her arms. "Fine."

Ari spun at this decision and shook her head. "No one is going anywhere tonight. It's far too late, and you've only just arrived," she said. There was authority in her voice that would go unquestioned. "Let's at least get you settled before you run off again. There's a room just down the hall."

Disappointment rose in Tempest's heart. She'd looked forward to catching up with the others, but perhaps it was best for them to wait till morning. Exhaustion tugged at every fiber of her being, and she wanted little more than to rest.

Cracked boards groaned beneath her feet as she followed Ari down the walkway, and the click of the door locked them in isolation. Tempest placed her bag in the corner of the room, then she turned to thank her host, but Ari had her ear pressed to the door. When the hall was clear, she looked up, gaze meeting Tempest's.

"The city was asleep during our journey from The Claw. You weren't able to see what it's like." Her words were softly spoken, and they filled Tempest with dread. "No matter what you see tomorrow, keep your head low, and stick to your own business."

Tempest nodded, pulling the gun from her dress to hide it in the drawer. "I'll be careful," she promised.

"I trust you won't be taking that," Ari said, pointing a finger towards the cloth wrapped weapon.

"It'll stay here, but this," Tempest said, pulling the dagger from her bag before setting it beside the gun, "will be coming with me."

"Good," said Ari, and she opened the door. "Get some rest."

She closed the door behind her, and Tempest was left alone. It had been a while since she'd had privacy like this. The silence was unnerving, and it left too much time for thought. She found her mind wandering to places she could not control. At the forefront of those thoughts was Cyrus. This was the first of many nights they'd spend apart. Tempest touched her lips where his had met hers, and she smiled. She knew they'd see each other again someday, no matter how many things stood in their way.

With her hand against the wooden planks, she pressed open the shutters that covered the window. Outside hung the moon, and inside poured the fresh mountain air. Her eyes focused upon a cluster of stars that formed her favorite constellation. It was the smaller of the twin bears written in old mythology. She could sometimes see it from her room in Alyria. At a certain point in the night, the moon would fall upon its head, and it would carry the moon on its snout. When Tempest was a child, her father would tell her stories about the small bear catching the moon. He'd always had a tale to tell. She wondered if when she saw him again, he'd have another.

Tempest closed the window, taking one last breath of the night air before returning to the dark shadows of the room. She pulled her dress up over her head and laid it down on a wooden chest. The air was still cold, and bumps rose on her skin, but she smoothed them out with the palms of her hands. She then curled beneath the warm fur blankets and lost herself to sleep.

When morning came, Tempest woke to the comforting smell of cooking food. Voices murmured in the main room, and the sounds of conversation drifted to her door. She shuffled out of bed and let the furs fall to the ground, sifting through her clothes to find a dress for the day. She settled with a silky gown the color of ash. It slipped over her head with ease, and beneath the flowing folds of the bottom, she strapped the dragon hilted dagger to her thigh.

After a few jumps and stretches to ensure the blade was secure, Tempest made her way into the hall. Around the table sat most of the household, eating what looked to be a type of porridge. Sparrow leapt to her feet and offered to pour Tempest a bowl. She kindly accepted, taking a seat beside Ari at the table.

"So," said John when Sparrow set the bowl of porridge down. "What comes next for you, Tempest?"

The room fell silent, and each of the tenants waited for her response. She quickly took a bite, forcing herself to swallow the steaming cereal as she pondered over a response. Settling for a morsel of truth, she said, "I'm going to Mortem."

"To see your parents?" asked John.

Tempest nodded. "I need to talk to them… at least once more. They were taken so fast."

He gave a sad smile. "I pray you know the risk. People like us rarely make it in, and it's a long journey."

Tempest couldn't help but wonder if he'd tried before. "I intend to take the train," she said. "It'll be much faster, and if I don't make it inside, I'll turn course to Mirenor. There are things there that I must do."

"Well, then I wish you luck." He scraped the last of the porridge from his bowl, then took it to the kitchen to scrub it down. As he left, Mereb and Theria entered.

Conversation was small, and the time passed slowly, but Tempest was fine with that. For once, there was no need to rush. Sparrow thought otherwise, however. She cleaned bowls as they emptied and practically shoved everyone out the door, leading the charge to the inn. Ari and John stood in the door, waving farewell while the rest followed Sparrow down the dirt path that lead to the road.

The city was emptier than Tempest remembered it being. Most of the people she saw were Kaburem soldiers who patrolled the grounds. A few citizens also scattered through the streets, garbed in tattered rags, begging for food or coin, but otherwise, the city remained quite quiet.

Tempest walked beside Sparrow through the winding mountain roads, taking in its broken remains. So much had changed in the three months she'd been gone.

As the Smokey Inn came into view, a painted stone protruding from the ground captured her attention. On it were the words, *Join the Rebellion.* They were written in scraggily handwriting over and over again. A torn Kaburem flag hung over the top of it, failing to conceal the words beneath. Tempest pressed her hand to the cracked graffiti, wondering how many people stood behind those words.

"Kaburem is causing havoc in the cities," Mereb said, walking up beside her. "Tensions are rising, and the people are standing up. But it's a worthless cause. They don't stand a chance."

"I wouldn't say it's completely worthless," Tempest said, and Mereb looked at her, confused. "They're a cruel and dangerous people, Mereb. Someone has to stand up to them."

"Quiet, the both of you!" Theria shouted, pushing open the door to the inn. "Unless you want to end up like that drunkard they killed here."

Tempest frowned at the reminder. "Markus... his name was Markus."

"Ah, the child returns as a woman grown," said the innkeeper from the doorway. "I suppose congratulations are in order. Have a seat, a server will be right with you."

Their group made their way into the dining hall, taking their seats at one of the long tables. Despite the large number of guests in the hall, it seemed emptier without Markus in the corner, rambling about his dreams.

A boy slightly younger than Sparrow came to the table. He lingered around for a short while, awkwardly waiting for an order of drinks. "Three cups of ale and a cup of water for the girl," Mereb said, and the boy scampered off to the kitchens.

"So, what all have I missed?" Tempest asked, filling the silence that followed the lad's departure. "Clearly, there's been a lot."

Mereb thought for a moment before responding. "Mirenor and the southern farm towns around it took a stand against Kaburem, threatening to separate themselves and their services from the nation if Kaburem soldiers continued to harass the Merchants. There were riots almost nightly. Soldiers were sent in to quell the protests, and a decree was sent out, declaring a death penalty to anyone who spoke against the crown.

"Colonel Atheris, was the first to test that theory. The people of the western province demanded full independence and threatened to overthrow him if he didn't do the same. He gave an announcement to the public that he denied King Lazareth's claims and was shot on sight.

"The province Colonel Atheris once ruled has since collapsed on itself, and its people have turned on each other for power. Half its citizens want to keep up with the rebellion, but the other half are yielding to Kaburem in fear. Many have started to leave their guilds, trading their rings for the bloodstone to ensure their family's safety."

Adrian was right, Tempest thought to herself, recalling his fears of forced submission.

The lad returned with their drinks and set one in front of Tempest. "It won't work," she said, taking a swig of the alcohol. She had never tasted ale before. It was bitter, and it burned as it rolled down her throat, setting her insides on fire. She coughed, shocked by the taste.

Mereb waited for her to build on her statement, so Tempest continued once she'd recovered. "People can't be ruled by fear," she said. "They're going to rebel." A second swig went down smoother, and she was able to keep the strong liquid down.

"Must we talk about such dreary things?" Theria interjected, setting her cup brusquely onto the table. "We should be celebrating little victories like your graduation and Mereb and I's relationship."

"Tempest doesn't care about your relationship, Theria," Sparrow said. "You don't have to worry about her taking Mereb from you. She's already got a man. I saw it with my own eyes. His name is Cyrus, and he has the most adorable little brother."

"All right, Sparrow, that's enough," said Tempest, embarrassment rising red in her cheeks. "They don't need all the details."

"I beg to differ," Mereb said, taking a sip of his ale. "Enough of politics. Tell me more about this Cyrus fellow."

Tempest opened her mouth to protest, but a woman's cry ripped through the air from outside, silencing all conversation within the room. Tempest leapt to her feet and ran for the door, Mereb hot on her heels. "Tempest, wait!" he called, reaching out to stop her, but he was too late. Tempest had already stepped through the door.

She froze, shocked by the scene that lay before her. A man and a boy stood shackled against the wall of a butcher's shop down the street. In front of them was a woman on her hands and knees, weeping and begging a soldier for mercy. He paid no mind to her pleading, simply pointed the barrel of his gun to the boy who still had the band of a child wrapped around his finger.

"Please, not my son. I beg of you; he's just a boy," the woman wailed. The boy stared into the barrel with defiance. No fear in his eyes.

Bang

Tempest's heart stopped, and the woman screamed, watching her son fall lifeless to the ground. The blood spilled slowly, and time slowed with it.

Bang

Down went the husband, and the woman collapsed. Tears joined the blood in the street, painting despair into the stone. The woman shook with muffled sobs, and Tempest ran to help her.

Bang

A scream tore from Tempest's throat. It was not one of fear, but rather one built of rage. "You monster!" she yelled, running at the Kaburem soldier, drawing the dagger from her side.

"Don't try me, girl. I've got more bullets in this thing, and I won't hesitate to use them," he said, and he aimed the gun to her chest, putting a stop to her advance. "I'm no monster. I just do what I'm told, and I was told to weed out the treason. These folks here spoke of rebellion. Had to make a spectacle out of them to show the other folks what happens when you try to organize a mutiny."

Hands grasped her shoulders and turned her away from the soldier. "Come on, let's go home," Mereb whispered.

Tempest could hardly see past the tears that brimmed in her eyes, but she let his grasp guide her away, turning back to look at the dead one last time, vowing to remember them. She watched a Kaburem soldier drag the bodies into the butcher's shop and light the building on fire. "Let it burn," said the man who'd executed the family. "Make sure no one stops it."

~~~

Rhumir looked down on the city and pitied, for on the night of the fire, the god let down a torrent of rain, putting out the flames before they consumed more than three of the surrounding buildings. However, the devastation did not end there.

A mere few days after, Kaburem raided every home in the city on the charge of speculated contraband. The search party broke through the doors of the Paxton's house at early light one morning, flinging open cabinets and drawers, dumping their contents onto the floors. The Paxtons had heard of the raids before Kaburem reached them, and a plan had been set into motion a few nights prior.

Tempest scurried from her bed when she heard them enter, strapping the dagger to her person before covering herself with a loose gown. She locked her belongings in the drawer and slipped the key beneath the cloth strap that held the dagger.

The soldiers' footsteps were heavy, and she could track their location as they moved throughout the house. Her heart beat like a war drum in her chest when they neared. Shouts and screams echoed through the hall, and their footsteps pounded towards her.

Three men burst through the entrance, immediately ravaging the state of the room. They dug through the closet and disheveled the mattress, tearing apart whatever they could. When one came to the locked drawer, he turned to Tempest and demanded the key.

"I don't have it," she said with feigned confidence.

The man's brow raised, doubtful. "Search her," he said, and the other two obeyed. They grabbed her by the arms with a grip that left her skin bruised, and their hands wandered to every crevice of her body. She held back the urge to wretch as they probed.

"What's this?" asked the one to her right, and his fingers wrapped around the hilt of her blade. He pulled it out carefully and inspected it with great interest. "Looks valuable, doesn't it? I think I shall keep it."

The first man tangled his fingers into the fabric of her dress. "Got anything else hiding under there?" he asked.

Tempest shook her head, and the others laughed. "I'll bet you do," said the one with the dagger. With careful precision, he tore open her dress, then began to undo the strings of his breeches.

She stared forward, fists clenched, trembling, unable to do much of anything but determined to try at least something to break free. A fourth set of footsteps approached the door, and Tempest dreaded the worst, but through the entry came a woman. She was garbed in the soldier's gear, and atop her head, she wore a tricorne hat. "While valuables are fun to collect, they are not what we've come to take," she said. "Give the girl whatever it is you stole, and get your hands off her."

They backed away with no questions asked, and the man who'd taken the dagger quickly recovered his modesty, then set the blade aside. Their commander draped a blanket over Tempest's shoulders and apologized. When she left, Tempest curled into the corner of the room, shaking beneath the blanket's warmth.

~~~

It was another three weeks before her dragon began to hatch. She was in the main room when it started to wiggle and crack. Her gut flooded with a mixture of nerves and excitement at the sound of it. She jumped up and ran to the egg, watching in awe as the beast pried its way into the world. The shell fell away, leaving a small black dragon with gold leathery wings that dripped with leftover albumen from the egg. Gold spikes trailed down the center of its back to its tail.

Tempest stroked the beast, and it purred beneath her touch. *'It was a black dragon with golden wings and purple eyes.'* She remembered Markus' words with a smile.

"The King's bane is born," Tempest whispered to herself, and a rare type of fear festered in her soul. If Markus was right, the birth of this beast meant the birth of a war, and she was the only one alive who knew it was coming. "Gods be good," she prayed.

"Does this mean you're leaving us?" Sparrow asked, tears welling in her eyes. Tempest turned to face the child, realizing a crowd had gathered behind her.

"There are things I must do, little bird, but I promise I'll visit when I'm done," Tempest said, holding the girl in her arms.

Ari stepped forward, eying the pair with fondness. "Tempest," she said, and Tempest looked up. "A dragon must have a name."

Tempest had no need to think of one. She'd known it long ago. "His name is Neymar," she said, and Ari smiled at her decision, but the others looked puzzled.

"After the dead king?" Sparrow asked, face twisted in confusion.

Tempest chuckled. "He was more than just a king to me, little bird. He was my father."

She pulled the amethyst ring from under her garments, and the confused looks morphed into disbelief. Mereb's eyes widened, and his jaw slightly dropped. "You mean... I'm sorry about what I said earlier, Tempest... about how the rebellion was a worthless cause. I didn't know."

"You were right," she replied, silencing him before he could continue any further. "They have no chance at winning with an opposing force like Kaburem, especially with how divided they are, but how can I stand by when people are dying fighting for the same thing I am? How can I watch quietly while my home is destroyed?"

"We didn't ask to join your fight. We could die for this," Theria said, hands trembling. "We could all be lined up and shot like that family by the inn."

"None of you are going to die," said Tempest. "The only people outside this room who know who and where I am are those who have protected me time and time again. The only way you'll get caught is if someone here betrays us. Understood?"

The others nodded. There was nothing else they could do. The damage was already done. "Good," she said, cradling the small beast in her arms. A heavy silence loomed over the household, disturbed only by the faint sound of whispers. Tempest could barely hear any of it, but she didn't care. Even if the words were about her, there seemed little else that mattered more in this moment than the creature she held. In its dark eyes, she found hope amidst the chaos.

"Are you ready to go?" asked Ari, stepping away from John, whose lips pressed together in bewildered contemplation.

Tempest looked around at the faces of her friends one last time, then nodded. "Yes."

The others parted down the center, allowing her a pathway to the door. She felt like she was walking the gallows, each step beating a song of impending doom. Eyes watched her every move. She wondered what they saw now that they knew her history. Was it the same fear that coiled within her? Was it fascination? There was no telling from their hollow stares.

"No," said Sparrow, stepping in front of Tempest before she could reach the door. "You don't get to say that and walk away like it's okay... like it doesn't change everything."

"My words change nothing," Tempest said. She was tired of people thinking they did. "Everything you've known me as was real. Every experience was authentic. I could be shot tomorrow and only a handful of people would know who I was. Of that handful, only a few would weep. I could be killed, and the world would move on as if it never occurred. Telling you my history won't change that."

"Now that we know, we can help," Sparrow said, glancing about the room.

Tempest gave a smile, but a sorrow lurked within. "You have helped me in more ways than you'll ever know. For now, you must stay far away from whatever is coming. There are storms brewing that will not end quietly."

"Then we can help create the noise." There was infinite determination in her little heart.

"All I ask is for you to stay alive," Tempest said.

Ari handed Tempest her bag, then turned to her daughter. "That means staying quiet," she said, placing her hands upon her hips.

Sparrow nodded, biting her lip to seal away any further retaliation she may have wished to voice. "Goodbye, Tempest," she said.

"I'll see you again," Tempest promised, then she followed Ari into the streets with her dragon curled around her shoulders.

It had been a while since she'd seen the giant metal beast, and it still left her in awe. Steam billowed from it as it squealed to a stop in the station three hours after they'd arrived, blowing its great horn.

"Before you leave," said Ari when Tempest stood. "Can I offer you some advice?"

Tempest settled her pack onto her shoulder and waited, curious to hear what the woman had to say.

"Dragons fly best above the clouds, where the air is light and the world is endless," Ari said. "Below the clouds, there are many obstacles that must be faced. When you reach them, do not be afraid. You have wings, and the enemy does not. You can fly above them."

The doors swung open, and Tempest gave Ari one last hug. "Thank you," she said before climbing into the small mobile room. She took a seat on one of the benches and looked out at the crowd of people below. She spotted Ari in the masses, waving farewell to Tempest as the train pulled away from the station.

25

A map hung framed at the front of the train car, showing the path of the track. It started in the city of Aquius and curved down the center of the land with stops in the major cities.

To the east, plains stretched as far as the eye could see, and occasionally, Tempest would spot a herd of aurochs grazing on its massive grass sea. To the west, the mountain range stood tall, reaching even higher than the clouds.

There were only around twenty others in the car with Tempest. She wondered what had brought each of them here. A Kaburem soldier paced up and down the aisle, monitoring the passengers on board. He had the accent of the Kaburem natives. Tempest often tried to envision what it was like on their land. She imagined it to be cold and grey. Warm lands would never produce a people so harsh.

A young, mousy haired girl sat in the seat across from her, gaping at the dragon that slept on Tempest's shoulders. The girl tugged on the sleeve of her father's coat, whispering something in his ear. He replied with a smile, and the girl scooted closer to the aisle.

"Excuse me, are you a Dragon Keeper?" the child asked, inching further off the edge of her seat, trying to get a good view of the dragon. Tempest nodded and plucked the small beast off her shoulders, setting him down in the empty space on the seat. The girl reached out hesitantly, then quickly pulled her hand back, thinking better of her actions.

"Go ahead," Tempest said, and the child reached out once more.

Neymar curled into a ball and fell asleep, comforted by the caress of the child. "Does it have a name?" she asked.

Tempest thought for a moment, then said, "He's named after one of the great kings of the past." She didn't dare speak the name around unknowing ears. "Do you have a name?"

The girl giggled at the question. "Of course, I do!" she exclaimed.

"Well, what is it, then?"

"Lennox," she said, curling her lips into a smile. "What's your name?"

"My name's Tempest. Did you come from Aquius?" she asked, seeing the Naval ring on the man's finger.

Lennox nodded. "We usually sail to Alyria when we go. It's faster and easier than traveling by horse. Now that this train is here, father agreed to go by land. I've always wanted to see the country and visit the other cities."

"Is it everything you imagined it would be?" Tempest asked.

"The train ride gets a little boring sometimes, but Firethorne was exciting to see, even though we didn't stay long. Not many Dragon Keepers go north to the Naval city, so I rarely get to see a dragon unless there's some in Alyria when we visit." She looked down contently at the beast.

"Do you go to Alyria often?" Tempest asked. She enjoyed talking to the child. It made the long ride a bit less lonely.

"Mhmm, Father does business there a lot, and sometimes he takes me with him. Have you ever been?"

"I grew up there."

"Oh! So you're visiting your family?"

"Yes, but not in Alyria. They rest with Xudor now."

Lennox frowned. "I'm sorry to hear that," she whispered, lowering her eyes, afraid she'd upset Tempest.

Tempest tried to smile for the girl's sake. "Don't be sorry," she said. "Just learn something from me, okay?" The child nodded. "Don't forget to tell your loved ones that you love them."

~~~

It was a day's train ride to Alyria, which was far easier than the week on horseback it'd taken to get to Firethorne all those months ago. The time flew with Lennox to keep her company, though she did miss her strange band of companions from before. She missed the grandiose tales of Adrian's fancy, and she missed Patch with his hopes and dreams and fears. Tempest wished she could get off at Alyria and wander the streets of her city once more. Possibly, she'd even find Patch, and the world would seem normal again for just a moment, but there were other things that had to come first.

To distract herself from longings that'd go unfulfilled, Tempest pulled out her notebook and began to sketch the girl who sat beside her, petting Neymar while he slept. There was an infinite supply of innocence between the pair.

As the sun set over the mountains in the west, turning the sky a blazing red-orange, Alyria came into view. It stood tall compared to the small villages they'd seen all day. Tempest could see the tips of the castle towers she'd grown up in just outside the city walls. The memories of that place tugged at her heart. She wanted nothing but to run through those gates and never leave again, but what she wanted was no longer there. She had to go to Mortem. That was where her parents would be. Tempest smiled at the thought of seeing them again.

Lennox bid Tempest farewell once the train came to a stop, and she got off to join the commotion of the city. Tempest would miss the child during the next leg of the trip.

The soldier that'd been walking the hall made his way to the front of the car and turned to face the remaining passengers. "The train will be departing in one hour," he announced, stepping off the car to talk with another soldier outside.

Kaburem patrols ambled down every path Tempest could see. In the streets they outnumbered the citizens. She watched the interaction of the two soldiers with curiosity, wondering what they were discussing. The men shook hands, and one motioned for a troop that stood waiting a short distance away. At once, the group turned and marched towards the train, filing into the car two at a time.

Tempest looked up at the man who led the troop. He stood now beside her. "Up, girl, off the train. My men need your seat."

A few of the men snickered at his demand.

"But—" she began to protest.

"But nothing. Go on, off the train."

With reluctance, Tempest gathered her things and stood up, cradling her dragon in her arms. The men parted to allow her through, sneering and throwing jibes at her as she passed.

Tempest descended the stairs and looked around for a second option. One of the livestock cars had its doors pried open, waiting for the animals to be loaded in. She glanced about hesitantly, then slipped into the empty car and hid behind a pile of straw.

A man stepped into view shortly after and led three horses into the car. One was black as night, another a warm auburn color, and the third was brown with white speckles.

A gust of wind blew through the thin gaps between the wood panels that made up the walls, carrying the scent of Tempest and her dragon to the horses. The black one reared with a terrified cry, a wild fear in its eyes. The other two whickered nervously at the sudden commotion, and the man cursed, ducking away from the spooked horses. He jumped out and slammed the door shut.

With the caretaker gone, Tempest relaxed, slumping down beside the straw bales. She whispered softly to the horses and stepped warily into their view, trying not to frighten them again. Eventually, the beasts calmed down, and the train lurched forward.

As it picked up speed, Tempest watched the giant shadows of the mountains that loomed in the distance outside. The ride was long and uncomfortable, and the car reeked of manure, but despite conditions, she soon succumbed to the lure of sleep.

She woke with a start, roused from rest by the soft cries of her dragon. He had grown hungry on the journey, and so had she. Neither had eaten since the ride to Alyria. Neymar paced before her, looking hungrily at the horses in the car, likely frustrated that they were too big for him to take down. He spun and stalked to the corner of the car, pouncing before returning with a rat in his jaws.

Finally, sometime midafternoon, the train came to a stop. When the door slid open, Tempest bolted out, bumping into the woman that'd opened them. "Sorry!" she shouted, scampering towards the city gates with Neymar in her hands, fleeing before she could get into trouble.

At the gates, a Necromancer stood guard with a Kaburem woman at his side. "State your business," the Necromancer said when Tempest neared the entrance.

"I've come to visit the House of Xudor," she replied.

"Ah, best be warned, not many make it into the House, you may not get a chance to visit the deceased." Despite the warning he ushered her inside.

It was a desolate city with hardly any life within it. Standing tall in its center was the House of Xudor. It was much grander than she'd imagined it to be. The building was massive and embellished with silver accents that glimmered in the sun. Tempest was eager to get a closer look at it, but that would have to wait until morning. For the time being, she needed to find food and a place to stay.

She walked through the streets in search of someplace decent. Everywhere she went there were Necromancers. They worked diligently to merge the mortal and immortal realms.

After some time, Tempest came upon a small, rundown tavern, wedged between two other buildings. A bell chimed when she entered, and a woman sitting in the corner perked up, excited to have another customer. "Dining is right down the hall," she directed, pointing towards the noise that flowed from food filled tables. "Will you be needing a room tonight?"

"Yes ma'am," Tempest replied.

"Come back here when you're ready for one. We don't have many so it's likely you'll not be alone."

Tempest thanked the woman and walked through the short hall that led downstairs to the tavern. The wood of the walls was old and cracked, looking as if at any moment the whole thing would collapse. In the center of the room, there stretched two long tables, split by a wood beam that braced the rafters. Along the sides were smaller tables for the lone travelers

Tempest took a seat at one of the smaller tables nearest to the dormant fireplace at the end of the hall. The long tables were filled with Necromancers, and a few Kaburem men scattered between them, but otherwise, the tavern population was scarce.

A serving girl approached the table, looking cautiously at the dragon that prowled its surface. "Would you like some food or a drink?" the child asked.

"Both, please," Tempest replied, watching the girl hurry away. She returned moments later with a plate of meat and a cup of mead. Tempest thanked the girl with a few coins she'd gotten from Ari before she left, and she ripped a chunk of meat off for her dragon before digging into it herself. It was tough and overcooked, and she wasn't entirely sure what animal it had come from, but it was a meal all the same.

As she fed a piece to Neymar, someone entered the room. His heavy footsteps echoed in the silence that followed his arrival. Something was different and strange about him. The way he carried himself looked inhuman. He moved with too much grace and precision, and he was garbed in a long black cloak with a hood that concealed his face.

The Necromancers shifted in their seats and murmured to themselves. All of them had stopped what they were doing to look at this stranger. Their gazes followed him as he strode over to Tempest's table and took a seat. She was about to question him, but he lifted his gaze to hers. Her breath caught when the black hood fell to unveil the face of Prince. He looked at her with white eyes and pale skin that seemed almost transparent. The last time she'd seen him, he lay dead at Lazareth's feet.

A million thoughts raced through her head, and she opened her mouth to voice them, but he raised his hand to silence her before she could utter a word.

"Sepora wishes to have an audience with you," he said, then he stood and walked from the room.

Tempest collected her things, snatched Neymar from the table's edge, and hurried after him. She had to quicken her pace to keep up with his seemingly effortless speed, and they made their way down the long, barren path to the temple. The two of them soon arrived at the entrance. People had already begun to crowd its massive, black-marbled walls. Great stone pillars stood along the front of the House, decorated in glyphs that told the many tales of the underworld.

The crowd parted when Prince walked through, all looking at him with equal terror and curiosity. Some glared at Tempest with pure envy as she approached the large brass doors.

She paid no mind to them, however. Her eyes fixated on the two stone lions that guarded the entrance. One black, one white, representing the gatekeepers of the underworld. Lux and Noct.

A Kaburem man came running up behind them, flailing his arms to get their attention. "Wait!" he called. "You aren't permitted to go in there!"

Prince turned to the man and stared down at him with dead white eyes, saying nothing.

The Kaburem soldier muttered a prayer beneath his breath to a god Tempest didn't know. She wondered if the name belonged to a god at all. Tanith had said Kaburem was a godless people, but she supposed fear turned all men into believers, and she had never seen a man so horrified. "On your way, then," he stammered, backing away, tripping over the leg of one of the lions in his urgency. Prince turned away from the man and pressed open the ornate doors.

Great, candle-lit chandeliers hung from the ceiling, lighting up the massive black and white hall. As they entered the room, letting the doors close behind them, Tempest was greeted by two living lions that matched the pair outside, one black, one white. She froze when they neared. She'd never seen a lion before, but she'd read stories about them in her old library. Lions were a common sight in the deserts south of Mirenor and had been notorious for taking out entire villages.

"Have no fear, m'lady, they won't hurt you," a woman assured, walking towards them. "Welcome, Dasha, we've been waiting for you."

"You have?" she asked. It was odd to hear her name so casually spoken. At this point, it felt as though it hardly belonged to her.

"Yes. We've been keeping tabs on you. Special request from your father," she said with a smile. "Thank you, Prince, for bringing her to us."

Prince bowed his head and turned to retreat.

"No!" Tempest shouted, drawing his attention back to her. Her cheeks flushed, and she froze, unsure of what she'd intended to do. "Please don't go yet. I have so much I want to say."

"We'll have time to talk some other day, but a storm is coming, Tempest. Prepare for it well," he said, then he walked away.

"Follow me," said the woman, guiding her towards Sepora's office. Tempest followed, but her eyes remained on her retreating friend until he vanished into the maze of halls.

The guild leader waited for her, sitting behind a desk cluttered with letters and books. She sat up, setting the letter she'd been reading down on the desk. "It's good to see you again, Dasha." She smiled, white eyes meeting Tempest's. The first time they'd met, the paleness of her eyes had made Tempest uncomfortable, but here, they seemed to belong. "I see you finally got that dragon you wanted."

Tempest's lips curled into a smile as she looked down at the beast in her arms. "Yes ma'am,"

"I figured I would find you here someday. I had my officers watch for you in hopes of getting to you before Kaburem did. I'm pleased to know they succeeded. Have a seat." She gestured towards an empty chair in front of the desk, and Tempest pulled it out to sit.

"As you may have noticed by now, there's talk of a war going around, and I'd like to decide which side I'm on sooner than later. I figure you intend to be a player in all this, correct?"

"I do."

"In that case, I wish I could have brought you here to tell you that you have my full support, but my first duty is to my people. I need to know if you're a worthy cause. I need to know if you're even half the leader your father was.

"Tomorrow I'd like to sit through your meeting with your parents to see if I can make my judgement. I pray you don't fail me, Dasha. I did quite like your father, and I hope he taught you well," she said.

Excitement bubbled within Tempest's chest, mixed together with a concoction of doubt and fear. She hadn't expected this. "Yes ma'am," she said. "I'd be honored to have you accompany me. I pray that I don't disappoint. Your support would be of great help to my cause."

Sepora lifted a hand to quiet Tempest's nervous ramblings. "Meet me here at first light. Issakar will show you to a room."

She motioned to one of the men that stood guard at the door, and the one Tempest presumed to be Issakar moved forward to guide her to a bedchamber in the upper levels of the temple. The soldier wore black armor with a white lion engraved on his shoulder. An ornate helm rested upon his head, shielding his eyes. He walked silently, never even giving her a second glance.

After wandering through what seemed every possible turn, Issakar finally stopped. He reached out and pulled open one of the doors. Tempest turned and thanked him, but he gave no response, just simply walked away.

"No use in talking to his lot," said a voice from a few doors down. The woman it had come from stood watching in the threshold. "You won't ever get an answer. You see, nothing's underneath that armor of his but the flesh and bones of a reanimated corpse."

"Who are you?" Tempest asked.

"Just a visitor, much like you," she replied. "My name's Seraphine. It's very nice to meet you. Not many people come over here anymore and it gets awfully lonely." She held out her hand in greeting.

"I'm Tempest." When her hand touched Seraphine's, it passed right through. Tempest ripped her arm back in shock, confused.

"Sorry, sometimes I forget myself... And, I already know who you are. I'm Sepora's sister, and therefore, I know everything, even the things she tries to keep from me."

"Sepora has a sister?"

"I suppose *had* is the more proper word to use. I died many years ago."

"How?" Tempest asked. She'd seen corpses and momentary resurrection in her brief time in this city, but seeing a ghost was odd to her. She'd heard it was rare for a spirit to remain in this world.

"Wynris marked Sepora for death when she'd just passed her enlistment," Seraphine said. "I did everything in my power to save her. I even went beyond my power... but Sepora still died. People warned me not to, but I brought her back, and for that, Odemus took me. Xudor trapped me here, and I've remained here ever since... But that's not why I've come to talk to you."

Tempest leaned against the wall and asked, "Then why have you come? Do you know something I don't?"

"I know my sister," Seraphine said. "She is strong minded, and once she decides what she thinks of you, there will be no changing her opinion. When you meet with your parents tomorrow, come prepared with a plan of action. Be bold in the way you present it. There will be no room for hesitation." She looked down the hall at some distant thought. "I pray you succeed," she said. "I don't much like this new King Lazareth."

As the footsteps of another visitor approached, Seraphine faded to a golden dust and vanished into the air.

26

$\mathcal{A}$ rasp at the door roused Tempest from her slumber. She quickly leapt from the bed, threw on a white, silken dress, and draped her bag over her shoulder. Neymar remained asleep on a small pile of cloth in the corner of the room. She rushed to the beast and picked him up.

With another rasp at the door, Tempest hurried to open it. Issakar stood waiting behind it like stone, unmoving until she had exited the room. Silently, the two made their way to Sepora's office. The guild leader dismissed the lifeless sentinel and took up the tour, guiding Tempest deep into the shrine where few ever ventured.

The descent seemed eternal. The deeper they went, the longer it seemed to go. Sepora turned into a gloomy tunnel that stretched into the darkness. Doors lined the walls, branching off into smaller tunnels. With the amount there were, Tempest figured a person could navigate the entire city from them if they knew the tunnels well enough.

Sepora followed her gaze and smiled. "These tunnels were used in the old wars when the Dark Mage ruled the land. They were made to be elaborate in order to prevent the Mage from finding the realm of the dead. Only a select few knew how to navigate them, and he killed them all. When the Dark Mage's reign ended, we sent cartographers through them and relearned their secrets. Now they function as hidden roads that'll take you almost anywhere."

Tempest traced a hand over the bumps of the stone wall, letting the air flow through her fingers when the wall parted for another tunnel. "I spoke to Seraphine last night," she said, dropping her arm to cradle the small beast she carried.

Sepora stopped abruptly and turned to face her. For a moment, Tempest anticipated a scolding, but the guild leader simply lifted a brow and asked, "What did you learn?"

There were many things she'd learned in the brief conversation with the ghost, but only one thing kept her mind turning. "The cost of resurrection," she said. "It made me wonder; is a part of you still dead?"

Sepora turned and continued down the tunnel. "Yes," she said.

"Is that why your eyes are white like the dead you bring back?" Tempest asked, thinking of Prince.

"It is. I see everything they see. Energies, souls, death. It's beneficial in many ways, but it is also a great weight to bear."

"If it wanted to, could a soul brought back during Xudor remain in this realm like you did?"

Sepora shook her head. "No," she said. "The process is different. Most of their entity is rooted in the underworld, whereas mine is rooted here. They are living on borrowed time. My time is stolen. That is why the price was so great. You cannot steal from a god and expect no reparations."

"How does this resurrection work?" Tempest pointed down the tunnel to wherever it was they were going. "How do you borrow from a god?" There seemed to be infinite rules when it came to dealing with the dead, and Tempest found each fascinating.

"With these." Sepora rolled up her sleeves to reveal a set of symbols permanently etched into her forearm with black ink.

Tempest moved closer, studying the shapes of each. "What do they mean?"

"Unity," Sepora said, tracing them with her thumb. "When Xudor takes the throne, the veil between worlds thins. These symbols allow us to connect to the other side." She paused a moment, and reached out to touch the dragon that slept coiled in Tempest's arms. "Just as you are tethered to Zalder through your dragon, we are tethered to the gods of death. These symbols bind us to the realm of the deceased. Through them, we are connected to the souls we raise, and when each soul is returned to their body, we are burdened with the weight they carried upon their death. It is an exhausting feat that only the most advanced can perform."

"What determines the weight of a soul?" Tempest asked. She was fearful that the guild leader would soon tire of her questions, but Sepora just smiled and answered.

"When a human dies, their soul is met with a challenge. They stand before the twin lions at the gates of the underworld, and their soul is judged by each. Noct favors the heavy hearted. They are the souls plagued with sorrows upon their death. They are the souls that were taken prematurely. Their missions thus went unfulfilled. Noct guides them through the underworld shrouded in a darkness that only they can find their way out of. If the soul fails to find light in the emptiness, it is devoured.

"Lux on the other hand, favors those who found utmost meaning in their lives. Be it small and simple or elaborate and world altering, these are the souls that reached their deaths content with what they'd accomplished. They are the souls who knew their end was coming."

Tempest walked silently for a moment, contemplating a question that soon slipped from her lips. "Which lions favored my parents?" She knew her father had prepared for death well, but her mother was taken so abruptly. She feared that Noct had been the one to greet the late queen.

"Contrary to expectation, it was your mother who found peace upon dying," said Sepora. "She followed Lux contently into the underworld. She grieved and longed to say farewell, but she trusted the course of her destiny. She trusted you in accomplishing what she could not."

"And my father?" asked Tempest, pausing to look at the guild leader.

Sepora gave a somber smile. "He had much that he still wished to do. Noct greeted him upon his arrival and led him to the darkness. Your father prevailed in finding light, however, and he was reunited with your mother."

Tempest nodded and continued forward. They crossed through many doors before the maze of pathways came to an end in a dark chasm, lit only by a few scattered torches, glowing with a pale blue flame. Sepora took one of the torches from the wall and carried it to an altar in the center of the cave.

She touched the flame to the edge of the altar, and a ring of fire engulfed it. It burned blue like the torch, casting shadows of a moon-like pallor throughout the room. Upon hanging the torch back on the wall, she muttered a quick prayer over the altar, then she lifted her gaze to Tempest. "Do you have anything that belonged to either of them? It'll make this process easier."

Tempest touched the ring that hung at her throat. She didn't want to give it away. Even if it was for just a moment, to part with it seemed wrong. "It won't be damaged," Sepora assured, holding out her hand to receive the object Tempest hid. With great hesitation, she pulled the ring out and placed it into Sepora's palm.

The flames lifted higher as Sepora waved the ring through them. She uttered a second prayer and buried the ring in a bowl of sand that rested at the center of the altar. "Hold out your palm," she directed, pulling a bone-crafted blade out of the leather sheath that hung at her neck.

Tempest shifted Neymar to her left arm and held out her right. Her heart beat viciously as the knife drew near, and with careful precision, Sepora traced a thin line across her palm. The line bubbled red with blood.

When a sufficient amount had dripped into the altar, Sepora wrapped Tempest's hand in a cloth that reeked of alcohol. It burned when it touched the wound, but Tempest didn't flinch. She was determined to show nothing but strength.

Sepora lifted the bowl and carried it to the edge of the cave where symbols were carved into the rock that matched the designs on her arm. She carefully tipped the bowl, pouring its contents onto the floor into two separate piles. Tempest stepped closer, curious to see the process but fearful all the same.

Once the bowl was emptied, Sepora returned it to the altar. "Are you ready?" she asked.

Tempest nodded. "How does it work?" She was slowly gaining courage, her previous fears morphing into the excitement of reuniting with her parents.

"Come here," said Sepora, motioning her forward. Tempest joined her by the piles of sand. "Press your palm to the symbol closest to you." Tempest obeyed. "It is the symbol of life," Sepora explained, placing her palm to the opposing symbol. "This is the symbol of death. Together, they are strongest." She pointed to the piles of sand. "From dust we are born, and to dust we return. Those piles are where your parents will make their crossing. Are you certain you are ready?"

"Yes." There was no hesitation. Fear had subsided, and hope burned bright in Tempest's heart.

"Good," said Sepora. "Let's begin." The torches flickered out. Darkness consumed it all, leaving Tempest with thoughts of dread. Bumps rose on her skin, and a chill shot through her spine. The hair on her arms stood erect. Everything went cold.

From the darkness emerged two silhouettes, and when the torchlight returned, Tempest saw their faces. Her heart shattered, yet felt whole all at once. Despite the white eyes of death, their faces felt like home.

"Dasha," said her father in a breath. That name had terrified Tempest for months, but hearing it from his lips transported her heart back to the days when it meant love instead of death. Tears brimmed in her eyes, but she refused to let them spill.

Her mother reached out a hand, clasping Tempest's in her own. "This belongs to you now," she said with a smile, placing her old ring into Tempest's palm.

Tempest pulled her mother into a gentle embrace, careful not to disturb the beast in her grasp. "I'll make you proud," she promised.

"I know you will." Her mother broke away slowly from the hug, looking to the creature that woke from its slumber. "It seems we have a lot to catch up on."

"We do, indeed," said her father, holding out his hand expectantly. "Show me, what have you learned?"

Tempest set the dragon upon her shoulders and dug frantically through her bag. She felt the soft edge of her leather bound notebook and pulled it from the bag, turning to the accounts of her journey leaving Alyria. She handed the book to her father, who inspected each page thoroughly. Upon the first page was a tale of Patch and the Medic, Liz. She owed everything to those two individuals. Tempest relived the words as her father read them.

"This boy, Patch," her father said, looking up from the page. "You spoke of him after your first lesson in the city. Did he know who you were?"

Tempest nodded. "He knew who I was long before we met. He'd seen me with you in the city years ago."

"If you ever meet him again, tell him I am grateful." He flipped the page, continuing through the records of Tempest's life as a fugitive. When he came upon the writings from Firethorne, he paused on the drawing of Markus' dream. "The dragon and the snake. What do they mean?"

"It was a vision told to me by a seer named Markus when I first arrived at Firethorne. He'd had dreams of Mother's poisoning. When it was enacted, the dream changed to an image of this. I'm led to believe that the dragon in his vision is the same creature that's laying on my shoulders. Either that, or the dragon is me."

"What of the snake?"

"We hoped for it to be the new king," she admitted.

Sepora stepped forward, lifting a hand to interrupt. "I met Markus quite recently," she said. "He was still muttering about this vision when he crossed through to the underworld. What are your thoughts on how it ended?"

Tempest shifted nervously. She'd nearly forgotten that Sepora was there. She supposed this was the first test. "Markus said that in the vision, the captured snake bit the dragon and poisoned the beast. The dragon then killed the snake and fell into a pit of fire. It wasn't clear if the dragon survived."

"What if it doesn't?" asked Sepora.

"Then it dies, but the king does too."

"What happens next? This is not a revenge journey, it is rebellion. Who puts forth the next ruler if you are the dragon?"

"I intend for an advisor to take my place, one who I trust fervently."

Sepora shook her head. "Intentions do not win wars, and you have no advisors just yet. Who is next in line?"

"Patch," she said. It wasn't a decision that required much thought. "He grew up in the streets and knows what people want and need. He knows secrets told in alleyways, and he knows the stories of everyone he meets."

Sepora nodded approvingly. "What will you do to learn what Patch knows?"

"I will study as he has, and like my father did before me. When I leave here, I will go south to Mirenor. From there I will circle the land until I reach Alyria. As I go, I will bring together rebellious groups. I know they've begun to form. We saw propaganda for them in Firethorne. Though, if I want any of them to follow me, I'm going to need men. They need reason to believe I'm a cause worth supporting, which brings me to a request." She paused a moment, then mustered the courage to ask. "Is it possible to raise a battalion of soldiers like Issakar?"

Sepora pondered the proposal for a moment. "It'd take some effort… but I suppose…" She looked up with a mischievous grin. "An army of the dead. Quite a terrifying thought, isn't it? We'll discuss this later." Sepora gestured back to Tempest's father. He'd turned the page and didn't seem thrilled about what was drawn upon it.

"How do you know this man?" he asked. There was no joy in the tone of his voice.

Tempest looked to the drawing. It was the one she'd made of Lazareth standing over her family's coffins in the courtyard of the temple. "He's the new king. Do you know him?" she asked. His concern made her uneasy.

"I knew him once, long ago. I never expected that he still lived."

Tempest couldn't tell what was going through his mind. He seemed scared, enraged, and at peace all at once. "What do you know about him?" she asked. If he had insight to a weakness or strength of the new king, she wanted to know it.

"His desire for kingship has always been calamitous. He is dangerous, but he is also rash. You must outwit him." After a long final glance at the sketch, he turned to the next page where the drawing of the Nyoka waited to be seen. His features relaxed as his thoughts distanced from the last drawing. "You wrote Zuri at the bottom of this page. Is that the name of the dragon or the boy?"

"Zuri is the dragon," she explained, remembering the meadow in Firethorne that had borne so many memories. "The boy is named Cyrus."

"What did you learn from him?" her father asked.

A blush crept to her cheeks. "Love, I think," she said.

Her mother's brow lifted with intrigue and from her mouth came a sound of bewilderment. "Oh?" she asked. She'd been quiet for so long. Tempest couldn't help but laugh at what had sparked her interest.

A smile of amusement touched her father's lips, and he turned to the final page. On it was a drawing of Lennox from the train ride to Alyria. "What did you learn from her?" he asked.

"The tranquility of innocence," she replied.

Her father nodded and handed the book back to Tempest. "You've done well," he said. "Do you have something to write with? I have one last lesson to give."

Tempest sifted through the contents of her bag, pulling out the charcoal pencil she kept paired with the notebook. She turned to a blank page and held the utensil poised above the paper. When she was ready, he began to tell the lesson.

"These are words I discovered in an ancient book found in the heart of Eris," he said. "When the darkest night tries to lead you astray, become the phoenix who rises from the ashes and teaches the lambs to shed their skins. From the hearts of these lambs, lions will be born, and darkness will be eradicated."

Tempest scrawled each letter carefully into the book, trying to make sense of the words they formed. "You'll come to understand them as your journey progresses," said her father.

"And you'll come to understand this as well," her mother said, pointing to the ring that hung once again at Tempest's neck. "It will teach you extraordinary things."

Tempest clutched the ring in her hand and said, "I look forward to it."

"You won't be wanting to stay much longer," said Sepora. She looked to be growing weary. "Kaburem will be searching for you here."

Tempest knew the guild leader was right, but she didn't want to leave her parents just yet. Her heart longed to keep their company.

"We'll see each other again," her father promised. "Do you remember the story of the flightless lark?"

Tempest nodded. "Of course."

"Listen to its lessons of bravery, heart, and trust, but don't forget to also look within," said her father. "You will find your wings, and you will accomplish anything you desire. Go now. The world is waiting."

A tear rolled down Tempest's cheek, caressing her skin with a cold, damp touch, but a smile found her lips. "I'll tell you all about it when we meet again."

"Until then, goodbye," her father said, voice as soft as a breeze.

"Goodbye," Tempest replied, holding the notebook close to her chest, latching onto the lessons it held.

Sepora touched the symbol of death on the wall, and the torches flared. Tempest's parents crumbled back into the dust piles they'd been resurrected through, leaving the room in an unnerving silence. The sand settled onto the floor, and Sepora scooped it up with the altar bowl. Upon returning it to the center of the altar, she turned to meet Tempest's gaze. "You've collected many lessons over the past year, it seems."

"There are still more to learn," said Tempest, flipping through the empty pages that yet remained.

"And when you've learned all that you can, what then?" asked Sepora.

"The day I stop learning will be the day I die. When that day comes, the lessons I've learned will be passed down for someone else to pick up and continue."

Sepora doused the flames on the altar and lifted a torch from the wall. "You'll gift them a book of lessons from other people, but what will you contribute to it?"

The blue flame of the torch kneeled before the breeze that flowed through it as Sepora walked to the exit of the tunnel. "The answer I give now will be different than the one I'll give when Odemus claims me. I haven't learned nearly enough," said Tempest, following Sepora through the threshold.

"If he were to take you at this moment, what would your lesson be?"

Tempest thought back to memories of the past, recalling all who had helped her get to where she was. The list was long, and she remembered each name fondly. "I suppose it'd be a lesson in loneliness," she said. "No matter what tribulations lay ahead, it is important to remember that we are not alone in facing them."

"Good," said Sepora. "I can have your troops by nightfall. You'll want to leave shortly after that. Use the tunnels to make your escape. The Necromancer I leave in command of the soldiers will help you navigate out. Upon your exit, you'll be met with fifty horses to aid your travels. Meet me in the atrium at sundown. I'll have everything prepared."

"Thank you," Tempest said as they came to the end of the tunnels. "I'll see you then." She plucked Neymar from her shoulders and set him down to walk beside her.

The halls had grown busier since morning, but she managed to slice through the crowds without interruption. Once she reached her room, she gathered what little possessions she had and prepared for the journey. It was going to be a long one. When she was confident nothing was left behind, she found her way to the dining hall, hoping for a warm meal before departure.

Fires burned in the common room, filling the air with warmth and the smell of cooking food. The atmosphere felt like home, and she could almost trick her mind into believing that it was. The events of the day were the closest she'd ever come to returning to those nostalgic days. She filled a plate with foods of vast variety and found a seat beside the hearth. Neymar curled up on the corner of the table, slumbering away the hours.

As the sun sank below the horizon, Tempest watched its fiery tendrils fade from a long balcony that stretched around the temple. A massive crowd still surged below as people pressed inward, trying to make it inside.

When the last of the sun's rays disappeared, Tempest turned away from the ledge and headed back into the temple. Neymar padded close behind, his small legs moving double time to keep up.

Necromancers bustled around the halls, preparing for another day of Xudor's reign. Tempest scooped the beast off the ground and draped him over her shoulders before he got lost in the chaos of it all. Her footsteps echoed off the stone steps as she started towards the atrium, where the beginnings of her army were waiting.

Hundreds of curious eyes turned to greet her when she stepped into view. Sepora met her at the entrance with an older woman at her side. This woman's eyes were worn and tired, her hands wrinkled with age, and her black hair was speckled with silver strands. She bowed her head in greeting. "It's an honor to meet you, m'lady. My name is Tegan. I'm in command of this regiment, but nothing will be done without your consent."

Tempest smiled and thanked the woman, slowly walking through the ranks of her new soldiers. The living were a mix of men and women of a wide range of ages. She approached the one that appeared the youngest. The girl stood with shoulders hunched, and her eyes watched nothing but the floor. "What brought you here tonight?" asked Tempest. "Was it an order or your own self desire?"

"All of us are here voluntarily, m'lady," she said, lifting her chin ever so slightly. "I'm here because Kaburem killed my parents."

"As am I," said Tempest. "What did they die for?"

The girl stood tall, fury in her eyes. "A loaf of bread," she said with a bitter tongue. "Order of the crown."

"And you?" asked Tempest, turning to the man beside her. "What brought you here?"

The man smiled, recalling some memory in his mind. "I've just fathered a child," he said. "And this is not the world I want her to grow up in. Your father demanded peace throughout the land. If there's a chance for that peace to return, I have no right to deny it. Sepora trusts you, and thus, so do I."

"I won't fail you," Tempest said, bowing her head to her new troops. "Kaburem will pay for what they've done to us." She left the ranks of the living and walked amongst the thousand undead. They stood like statues in polished black armor with the white lion head on their breastplate.

Her nose wrinkled as the stench of death washed over her. "It will fade in time," Tegan assured. "Many of these soldiers are fresh from the grave. When they are reanimated, the decaying process sort of pauses in a way, so the smell eventually fades. Unfortunately, the worst of it will be while we're all traveling in close quarters."

The two returned to the front of the regiment where Sepora stood waiting. Tempest bid the guild leader farewell, thanking her one last time before leading the soldiers down into the dark tunnels with Tegan by her side.

The air was thick and musty. It wasn't long before the smell of the dead became unbearable. Its reeking led many to wretch, only making matters worse. The journey through the tunnels was long and agonizing. What would have taken the lone traveler an hour at most took them half the night.

Tegan dug through the small rucksack she had packed and pulled out a beautifully crafted violin. She plucked at the strings a bit and adjusted the knobs accordingly until the instrument was in tune. Once satisfied with the sound, she placed it under her chin and lifted the bow, dragging the strands of horsehair across the strings as she started an uplifting tune to raise the spirits of the living.

A voice from the back began to sing an old song Tempest had never heard. More voices rose and picked up the tune, and soon the entire tunnel was alive with music. The rhythm of the dead marching kept metronome for the tune as the living sang.

Tempest walked in silence, listening to the lyrics. It was a song about a young lad who had stumbled accidentally into the realm of Xudor. He lived his entire life trapped down there, finally emerging after near fifty years. When he arrived back into the mortal world, he found everything just as he left it. His friends hadn't aged a day, for in the mortal world a day had not yet passed. They all laughed at the old man their friend had become, and never again did man enter the realm of the dead.

The sun was near rising by the time they made it out of the tunnels, and just as Sepora had promised, there waited fifty horses. Some bore wagons full of provisions for the journey. She dispersed them amongst the ranks and mounted one of the horses at the forefront of the party, leading the beginnings of her army south.

27

$\mathcal{A}$ fortnight passed in their travels to the south, and the land grew perilous as they neared the river. Alongside its bank was a small village of thatch-roofed houses, charred and collapsed in a state of morbid display, with a murder of crows circling above. It was all quite eerie. The wind whispered through the rubble, voices of the land's memory carried by its gusts. Tempest held up a hand to halt her company's procession. "Something's happened here," she said, turning to Tegan for confirmation.

The Necromancer nodded. "Odemus has been here."

Tempest's tan palfrey flicked its tail and trotted nervously in place, sensing the sinister ambiance that lingered in the air. "Is he gone?" she asked, stroking the beast beneath her. The gesture was as much a comfort to her as it was to the creature. The silence here was deeply unsettling.

"Only for a short while," said Tegan. "Some souls remain."

"Are any of them alive?"

Tegan closed her eyes and touched the symbols on her arm, spending a moment searching for death. "There are a few still alive."

"Find them," said Tempest, spurring her horse forward, "and gather any provisions you see on the way."

A small, crumbled gate greeted them at the entrance, but there was no one left to man it. Tempest ducked her head and rode beneath it, followed by the living members of her company. "Spread out and search every home," she instructed. "We'll not be leaving until we find survivors."

Half the Necromancers split off to set a ring of dead around the village, protecting them from any unwanted visitors. The other half scattered through the rubble, joining Tempest in her search for any signs of life.

At the forefront of a small group, she pressed open the door to a house that remained mostly intact. There were footprints in the dirt, but she couldn't place their age. With careful steps, Tempest probed through the space. There were no humans present, but a few rats had taken to the leftover food, bellies full and bulging.

"There's nothing here, let's continue," she said, closing the cabinet before following the others outside.

"Nothing over here," said a Necromancer from across the path.

"Keep going," Tempest ordered, desperation setting in. Whoever remained in this desolate village would likely be in urgent need of help. She followed the path to the left and entered the next house. Only the scaffolding remained of this one. Ash coated the floor, and the wooden frame was streaked with soot. She ran her finger through the black substance, wondering what horrors had occurred here.

"M'lady!" shouted a Necromancer, barreling through the threshold. He bent over and huffed, face softening with relief. "There are survivors by the well."

Tempest's heart leapt with the news. "Continue searching," she told the others, then she followed the Necromancer to the well. As promised, huddled in a somewhat standing hovel, there were six individuals. At their center was a little boy who looked only four years of age. He was a sickly pale, and burn marks covered his skin. The woman Tempest presumed to be his mother held the child in her arms.

"Help him," the mother pleaded, mournful gaze locking with Tempest's. She had a jet ring upon her finger, and her eyes were hollow.

Tempest approached the woman and the boy, laying a hand on the latter. "Is there a Medic amongst you?" she asked, touching the child's brow. It burned hot with fever.

"The only Medic died last week," said a man on the edge of the circle. "We'd hoped you'd have one, but it appears you've only brought death."

"Death is strong here. It is the only reason we found you," said Tegan, entering with a crate of fruits.

"Feed the boy first," said Tempest, leaving the room briefly to retrieve a collection of herbs. As she approached the wagons, she scanned the crates for anything that looked familiar from the days she'd seen the Medic treat her father. A different illness plagued the boy, but some of the symptoms were similar.

"Can I help you with anything?" asked a young lad with a heavy accent. His features closely resembled those of the sickly boy. Tempest startled at his words. She hadn't noticed his arrival.

"Are you his brother?" she asked, recovering her senses.

The boy nodded. "Can you save him?"

Tempest pondered this a moment, grabbing what little herbs she could recall and some meat for a stew. "I'm going to try," she promised, handing the boy a pot. "Take that to the house and fill it with water from the well. Set a fire beneath it and wait for it to boil."

When she'd gathered sufficient materials, she returned to the house and dumped the herbs and food into the pot. The young boy lit the wood beneath it, and when the flames rose, he scurried back, sitting in the safety of shadows. His hands trembled, but he held a guise of bravery upon his face.

As the stew cooked, one of the Necromancers walked up with a pile of finely shredded, white bark in his hands. "This will help," he said, offering the shreds to Tempest. "My father was a Medic."

Tempest took the shreds with a motion of gratitude and dumped them into the stew, thanking the man for his assistance. Once boiling, she found a loose cloth and dipped it into the remaining water that'd been drawn from the well. When it was fully soaked, she took it to the child and lay it across his brow. His mother sat close by his side, whispering prayers to an assortment of gods.

With the initial chaos of their arrival quelled, the room settled in waiting, Tempest returned to the stew, taking a seat beside one of the villagers. He was the oldest of the group they'd found, but from looking at him, Tempest figured he was no older than her parents had been. A jonquil ring rested on his finger, and he watched the room protectively. "Are you their leader?" Tempest asked.

The man's lip twisted slightly upward. "I am. My name's Benjamin. What's yours?"

"Tempest," she replied. "What happened here?"

"Kaburem," said Benjamin simply. "A man came into the village one day, searching for rumored seeds of rebellion. None of us had any information to give, but he wouldn't leave empty handed. He insisted that something was amiss in this little village, but there was no proof. In attempt to dig up a false truth, he turned to the children. He held a gun to their heads, and they pleaded innocence, but the man refuted their claims. Jensen,"—He pointed a finger to a young man by the door—"came upon the scene and attacked the Kaburem man. It ended bloody.

"We buried the man with his gun in the field, hoping that would be the end of it. For a month, nothing happened, but then a patrol came through. They raided our crops and found the grave. We woke that night to the burning. They captured a few and killed many. We are all that remain."

"My condolences," Tempest said, lowering her head in solidarity. "I pray we can help in avenging those you've lost."

"For now, your helping the ones we haven't lost is enough," Benjamin said, looking to the boy on the floor.

Tempest's heart twisted. If Kaburem discovered she'd been here, she knew Benjamin would regret those words. "I'm afraid our being here will only bring more trouble to you," she said, scooping out a bowl of stew for the boy and handing it to the village leader.

Benjamin carried the bowl to the child and carefully assisted his consumption of it. "We have no intention of staying here. We'd have left days ago had we been able to. Perhaps once the lad recovers, we'll follow your lot for a while," he said, setting the emptied bowl on the floor. "We have nothing left here."

A draft of wind slipped through the gaps in the hovel wall, sending the fire dancing to its will. The orange arcs flicked and leaned but stayed safely within the pit. "You won't want to follow long with where we're going. It won't be safe."

Benjamin lifted his head, curious. "Where, may I ask, is that?"

"To war," said Tempest.

A grim look settled on his face, but a different voice spoke up in response. "Can we go, Benjamin?" asked the older child. "Oh, please, can we go? I want to fight!" He held his hands clasped together, and he begged on one knee.

"What's your name?" Tempest asked the boy.

"Felix," he said with a proud smile.

"Well, Sir Felix, stand tall. A warrior does not beg. Your brother needs you strong. Go, be with him."

The boy stood, motions stiff like a wooden soldier, and he bowed before departing to help his brother. "We'll go," said Benjamin when he returned to his seat. "We're not much for fighters, but we'll help where we can. There may not have been rebellion in our hearts before, but now… there's not a soul here who doesn't hate Kaburem."

"I'd be honored to stand beside you."

A fit of coughing burst from the lungs of the sickly child, and the bodies in the room shifted, murmuring words of worry. The Necromancer who'd offered the shreds of bark to Tempest moved to stand by her side. He leaned in close and whispered into her ear. "M'lady," he said. "May I have a moment with you?"

Eyes watched them from across the room. They were deep brown eyes that belonged to the man Benjamin had told her about earlier. Jensen tugged at his sleeves and paced back and forth, gaze boldly locked on Tempest and the Necromancer. "If you'll excuse me, Benjamin. I'll be back shortly," she said, dropping her gaze from Jensen.

He bowed his head and lifted his hand in dismissal. "Of course."

With a silent audience, Tempest followed the Necromancer out into the night air. "Is this about the child?" she asked when the door closed behind them.

The Necromancer nodded. "He won't make it through the night. We're wasting our efforts."

Tempest's heart grew heavy at the thought of losing the boy, but deep down, she knew it was coming. "Are you certain?" she asked, letting the spark of hope burn for just a moment longer.

"Yes," said the Necromancer. "Death is nearing. All of us can feel it."

Their conversation cut short as the door pressed open once more. From its threshold came Jensen with two bowls of stew. "Forgive my intrusion," he said. "The stew was nearly gone, and I noticed you hadn't eaten yet." He held out the bowls and offered them to Tempest and the Necromancer.

Tempest thanked Jensen and took the stew from his hands. Its warmth seeped through the bowl and into her palms. She found contentment in its heat. It was a brief moment of comfort in a situation that seemed destined for despair. "Set up camp," she said to the Necromancer. "We'll wait it out."

"Yes, m'lady." He bowed his head and departed, leaving Tempest alone with Jensen.

"You're too young to be a m'lady," he said, leaning against the wall of the house. "How'd you, a freshly trained Dragon Keeper, end up in charge of a troop of Necromancers?"

"There's a lot to that story, I'm afraid."

"Well, how did it begin?" he asked.

Her fingers found the ring that hung tucked beneath the cloth of her garments, and she slowly tugged it out. "With a silent murder in the pre-dawn hours," she said, watching as the ring swung through the air of its newfound freedom.

The breath caught in Jensen's throat, and a curse left his lips in a whisper. "You're the heir?" he asked, scanning Tempest's features as though she were suddenly a new person.

"I *was* the heir," she corrected. "Now, I'm just a rebel."

A smile touched his lips. "First rebel with an army, though."

"It's not very large yet," she said, looking to the silhouettes that moved in the sunset. "But, it's a start."

"Felix tells me we'll be joining you."

She tried to read what he thought of that, but his face revealed nothing. "Only those who wish to. The rest are free to do as they please."

"I doubt anyone here will deny a chance to strike back at Kaburem," said Jensen, and he lifted his forearm, displaying a deep cut that traced its length, inflamed and grotesquely scarred.

"Did they do that to you?" Tempest asked.

Jensen nodded. "With the blade on the tip of his gun."

The thought made the hairs on her arm stand, and she shuddered, discomfort aided by the cool breath of the approaching night that fell upon her skin. "Shall we return to the others inside?" she asked.

"Certainly." Jensen opened the door, and the warmth from the fire that still burned within the house engulfed Tempest in a blissful heat. She huddled close to it, holding her palms to the flame. She was the only one to go near it. The rest stood warily distant.

When she had sufficiently warmed herself, she returned to her seat beside Benjamin, who narrated an old story to an assortment of ears. At the forefront of the group was Felix.

The stories lasted through sunset and well into the night. Tempest's eyes grew heavy, but she refused to sleep. She focused instead on the giggles of the young child who lay on his death bed. Marco, she'd learned, was his name. He'd recovered some as the hours passed, but the ailment still latched on with a fierce stubbornness.

Each time Benjamin would finish a tale, young Marco would request another, and the village leader obliged. Tempest heard stories of heroes and villains of every kind. Some lived in fictional lands where magic and gods did not exist. Others lived in the world she knew, but years and years ago. One followed a man who lived on a cloud that drifted between worlds unknown. That story had been her favorite. It seemed to have been Marco's as well. He laughed boldly in the silence of the night, bringing a smile to all who occupied the room.

"Another one!" said Marco with a yawn.

"Another one," Benjamin agreed. "This one about a young lark who wants to fly."

Tempest looked up at the words, heart swelling with a longing of her youth. She wondered if it would be the same story her father always told. The boy laid back, staring into the rafters as the story began.

Word for word, it played out just as she remembered it. The lark met first with its fellow lark and learned a lesson of heart. Then, it met the eagle and learned a lesson of bravery. It was here that Marco closed his eyes to rest. The lark failed to fly, so it met next with the squirrel, learning a lesson of trust.

Marco's breaths slowed to a state of deep sleep during this section, but Benjamin continued the tale. It would be the last one the child would hear, and everyone in the room seemed to know it. A tear rolled down his mother's cheek, and she clutched his hand tightly in hers.

Benjamin recited the final scene where the lark met with the tree. There, it learned a lesson of internal belief, and it tried once more to fly. In a soft whisper, he uttered the last words, and as he spoke them, the breath expelled from young Marco's lungs.

A wail of despair burst from the throat of his mother, but Tempest did not mourn. In this child, she found the lark, and she knew that he would fly, silver wings glimmering in sunlight as he sang a song of divinity. His mother whispered a prayer for the soul, and the house fell to a silence that was only interrupted come morning.

~~~

They buried the child at the base of a tree and carved a bird into its bark. Beneath the bird, they wrote his name. Felix lay a flower at the foot of the grave and shrouded his grief worn face in the folds of his mother's dress. She held him close, comforting the last of her kin. "We must go now," she told the boy, crouching to meet his eyes. "Will you be strong?"

Felix sniffled but gave a nod, swallowing the remainder of his tears. He picked up the small sack of his belongings and turned to face Tempest, who stood off to the side, watching with a few of her Necromancers.

"Are you ready?" she asked, looking to the faces of the remaining villagers.

"Yes," answered Benjamin.

Together, they loaded crates of supplies and tools from the village into the wagons. The dead were marched into a formation at the rear of their company, and the living trod at the front. With the sun to their left flank, they continued forward, leaving the desolate village behind.

As they progressed, the trees thickened, and the way grew treacherous where roots surfaced and tangled in the rocks. In these places, they were forced to lead the horses by foot. It was a slow progression through the woods, but Tempest was content with the presence of the trees. They blocked out the sun which beat down in a wrathful heat. Moist air clung uncomfortably to her skin, but it carried a lush scent of nature that kept her mind calm.

The tree line halted and opened into a clearing that harbored the next village. Tempest looked forward to meeting new people, and she hoped they'd not suffered like the last group. To her disappointment, however, none of these villagers had courage enough to meet either her or the army of the dead. Windows closed with iron latches, and all who wandered the streets abandoned them, hiding in the shadows where no one would find them.

A group of children sprinted down the dirt path and into an unkempt inn. Only one allowed curiosity to overcome fear. A young girl peered from the window, watching wide-eyed as their convoy passed.

Tempest found no hospitality in this village or the next. Each turned a blind and fearful eye. She began to worry that none would allow her an extended presence, but hope arose as they neared the rivers that enclosed Mirenor. A village in the planes welcomed her with weapons drawn.

28

*B*illowing in the breeze was a white cloth held high for all to see. Tempest clutched it between her fingers, waving it to and fro. The villagers allowed their approach but kept their weapons drawn. Behind them stood a windmill as tall as the giants of old mythology. At Tempest's chest, the woman at the forefront of the villagers aimed a crossbow. "What do you want from us?" she asked.

Tempest dismounted from her horse and lay her weapons on the ground, draping the white cloth over them. "A break from our travels is all."

"Who are you?" asked the village leader.

"My name is Tempest," she said. "I'm a Dragon Keeper and the commander of this company." The woman's eyes squinted with skepticism, but she listened. "This here is Tegan," said Tempest, gesturing to the woman beside her. "She's in command of the Necromancers and the dead."

The woman scanned the gathering. "Who are you loyal to?"

"The king, of course," said Tempest. "Though, not the one who's currently living."

This seemed to be the answer the woman was looking for. She lowered her crossbow and ordered the rest to do the same. "I'm Nikita," she said. "Welcome to Isigodi. You'll be wanting drinks, I imagine."

"That would be nice," said Tempest.

The dead were set to guard the roads, and the living flocked to the tavern. Tempest stopped for a moment by the wagon Felix rode in. The child was feeding Neymar some spare scraps of meat from a stag the hunters had killed a few days prior. "Hello," he said when she lifted the flap. "Are we stopping?"

"We are. A kind woman has offered us reception. I'm going to let Neymar roam a bit. You're welcome to come too."

Felix pondered the idea, stroking the scales on Neymar's back. "Do they have biscuits?" he asked.

"Likely so," said Tempest.

For the first time since they'd left his village, Felix smiled. "I'll come," he said, scooting out of the wagon. Tempest placed Neymar onto her shoulders and followed the boy down the road.

They passed an assortment of shops on their way to the tavern, filled with vibrant woven textiles, rare jewelry, and figurines carved of wood. One of these figures caught Felix's eyes, and the boy strayed to look at it. His fingers grazed over the wooden elephant on the shelf. Tempest had never seen one before, but from its long tusks and its rotund body, she recognized the beast from the descriptions she'd read in her books.

"Do you like it?" asked the shopkeeper.

Felix nodded. "Is it for sale?" he asked, fishing through his pocket. "I've got coin." As he said the words, he pulled out a handful of coppers and counted each in his palm.

The coppers weren't enough for the figurine, but the shopkeeper paid no mind. "It's yours now. Do you have a name for it?"

Felix smiled as he gave his answer. "Marco," he said definitively. The shopkeeper whittled the letters into the elephant's leg and traded the creature for the few coppers Felix could provide.

"Come on, now," said Tempest. "Your mother will be waiting for you." He walked quickly beside her, clutching the elephant in his hand.

Upon their arrival at the tavern, Felix rushed into the crowd to find his mother. There was hardly room to move, but Tempest managed to make her way to the bar. "What will it be for you?" asked the tavern keeper.

"Nothing, yet," Tempest said, sitting on a stool. She placed Neymar on the countertop and let him wander. In the corner of the room, she saw Tegan. The Necromancer had struck up a tune beside a man with an animal skin drum, who beat out a rhythm that invited the body to dance.

A few of the local villagers circled around them and moved to the beat. It was a dance Tempest had never seen before. They cavorted around the drum, contracting, flexing, and isolating at every joint. With the crescendos of the song, they leaped to great heights. Watching them made her heart soar.

At the end of the tune, the room erupted with applause, and the performers stood to bow. Tegan dragged her bow across the strings and a melancholic melody took to the air. All who could hear fell silent, listening to the soulful cries of her song.

"Tell us a story," said Felix at the center of the room. His eyes were fixated on the man beside him.

"I suppose a story is overdue," said Benjamin, sitting on the edge of the table. "It's almost been a week since the last."

Tempest wondered how many stories Benjamin had recited in his years. He'd told so many to Marco. She couldn't fathom there being many more, but the words he spoke were fresh to her ears. They seemed new to the others as well. Everyone leaned forward to hear.

"In a time that was not so long ago, there was a peaceful people who called themselves the Umoja tribe," said Benjamin as the musicians played. "During the month of autumn, they busied themselves in the fields, planting oats for the winter harvest.

"One day, they came to find a beast standing in the field with bones protruding from its head like horns. It sowed disruption throughout the village until it came to a child. When it discovered this child, it stopped, seeking a truth that could not be found in the wrathful eyes of the beast. There was a wisdom in this child called peace, and it was a wisdom the beast could not grasp. The beast became fearful of this realization, so it reared its head and attacked the child."

Felix gasped, holding his elephant tight to his heart. "Did the child survive?" he asked.

"Yes," said Benjamin. "The child ran, and from the trees came a warrior of the Umoja tribe. The warrior took on the beast, courage in his heart, but the beast would not be defeated without struggle. Claws as sharp as a blade tore through the warrior's arm."

It was at this moment Tempest realized she knew this story after all. The warrior was Jensen, and the beast was the Kaburem soldier he had slain. Buried under fantastical elements, Benjamin was telling the tale of how their village fell.

"Crippled as he was, the warrior still managed to kill the beast," said Benjamin. "But, you see, these beasts were protected by the god of chaos, and when this beast died, the god sent more.

"The warrior saw this coming, so he buried the beast in the field, hoping to deter the creatures' path. When autumn came and went, he thought himself and the tribe to be safe, but one dreadful night, chaos' creatures found him."

The beat of the drum sped with the beat of Tempest's heart. She knew how this story ended, but she still had hope for a pleasant conclusion. Perhaps the Umoja people had survived where the villagers had not.

"An entire herd of the beasts stampeded through the tribe lands, spreading great wings of fire that consumed everything in their path. By morning, the beasts were gone, but the memory of them remained in the destruction they left behind.

"Only six lived to see the sunrise. Huddled in a hut that could hardly stand on its own was the Chief, the Spirit Guide, the Warrior, the Huntress, the Magical Child, and the Young Dreamer. The Magical Child had been struck by the fiery wings of the beast, and his life slowly faded.

"On the last day of his life, the four winds, called the Vindar, sent a blessing. It was a storm that whispered words of war. The five remaining Umoja tribesmen followed the storm in its pursuit of the beasts, and thus, the great war began."

"Did they win the war?" asked Felix.

Benjamin leaned close to the boy, meeting him at eye level. "The battle has yet to come, Young Dreamer," he said. "I'll tell you when it's over."

The song of the violin faded with the end of the tale, leaving the drummer to carry the atmosphere. Nikita sat on the stool beside Tempest, holding two cups of ale. She set one in front of Tempest and leaned against the bar. "If there's any truth to his words, I imagine you're in need of soldiers," she said.

Tempest took a sip of the ale and nodded. "That, I am."

"I'll post a roster," said Nikita. "Recruit as you please."

The room fell silent as Tempest stood upon her stool and lifted her cup. "A toast," she said. "To the Umoja Chief."

Benjamin bowed his head and lifted his cup in return. "A toast to the Vindarian storm."

A cheer left the lips of all who were present, and conversation returned to fill the hall. Tempest sat down, swallowing a swig of ale. When she set the cup onto the wooden countertop, Neymar scurried towards her and rubbed his head against her palm.

"There's a man I think you'd do well with meeting," said Nikita. "His name is Cedric. He runs an elephant sanctuary just down the river. They're powerful creatures, and he may have reason to help you."

"Are they tamed?" Tempest asked. In the stories she'd read of elephants, they were uncontrollable beasts.

"As tame as a wild creature can be," said Nikita, stealing a glance towards the small dragon that wandered the counter.

Tempest thought on the idea for a moment. "I'd want to go in a smaller group," she said. "Would your village be able to quarter my people while I'm gone?"

Nikita nodded. "Whatever you need."

Across the room, Tempest spotted Tegan. She'd stowed away her violin and now played a game of stones with Felix at a table. "Then it seems I have plans to attend to," said Tempest, and she set her emptied cup on the counter.

She scooped Neymar into her arms and approached Tegan, putting a stop to the game. "I'll only be a moment," Tegan promised the lad. "M'lady." She stood and greeted Tempest with a bow of her head. "How may I be of service?"

"I've received information that may benefit our cause," said Tempest. "I need to speak with you and Benjamin. Do you know where he went?"

Tegan pointed to the door. "Said he wanted some air."

"Let's join him, shall we?"

The Necromancer gestured forward, and Tempest led the way.

Benjamin turned to meet them as Tempest pressed the door open. "Is something happening?" he asked.

"Nothing to be fearful of," Tempest assured. "There is a man who runs an elephant sanctuary down the river. Nikita has suggested a meeting with him."

Tegan's eyes widened. "Do you intend to use the elephants in battle?"

"Only if he permits me to," said Tempest. "I'll need representation and protection when I go. Do I have leave to take a few of your men?"

Benjamin answered first. "Jensen will be the most useful to you. I'll ask him to go. When will you be leaving?"

"First thing in the morning," said Tempest, glancing to the setting sun.

"I'll send two of my Necromancers with the dead they charge. That'll be twenty dead to keep you safe," said Tegan.

"While I'm gone, I'd like the two of you to use the time to recruit some of the villagers," Tempest said. "Nikita has offered to post a roster. See to it that she and her people are rewarded for their assistance. We'll set up camp tonight."

"Yes, m'lady." Tegan bowed her head. "If that's all, may I return to Felix?"

A smile touched Tempest's lips. "That's all. I'll see you two in the morning."

~~~

The smell of fresh baked bread drew Tempest from her slumber. It had been a deep rest, and she was reluctant to wake from it, but the scent of the food lured her from the furs that kept her comfortable. She slipped into her green gown. The edges had begun to fray, and the fabric was torn in a number of places, but the emerald color remained true. It was one of the last remaining of the garments given to her. The rest were tattered or lost in travel.

She left Neymar to sleep in the corner and walked into the hall. Wood creaked beneath her feet as she made her way out of the bed chamber, and the heads of those at the table below turned to greet her. There were three children of various ages who she had yet to meet. They each stood when she approached, and they stared at her with equal wonder and curiosity. Tempest imagined that visitors were uncommon in this area.

"Good morning, Tempest," said Nikita, entering with a loaf of what looked to be cornbread. "Have a seat. I've just finished cooking." She set the loaf at the center of the table and divided it accordingly. "Did you sleep well?"

Tempest bowed her head to the others and took a seat. "I did," she replied. "I can't thank you enough for the help you've given me."

"It has been my pleasure," Nikita said. "I can't join the fight, but if I can help it, I will gladly do so." She scooped up a portion of the bread and placed it on Tempest's plate. When everyone had been served, she sat down and began to eat.

Silence filled the time as Tempest savored each bite. It was sweet and tasted a great deal better than the salted meats she'd consumed thus far on the journey. A squeak of fear from one of Nikita's daughters drew her attention away from the food. "Pardon me, mum, but there's a dragon behind you," the child said.

Tempest turned to find Neymar perched on the rail that looked over the room, bobbing his head up and down, preparing for flight. "Watch your heads!" said Tempest, and she stood to catch the beast. His wings spread and caught the air when he leaped. The flight was smooth, but the landing lacked precision. Neymar swooped over her head and crashed into a desk in the corner of the room. "I'm terribly sorry," she said, chasing after the creature.

He flapped his wings to regain balance and chirped when he saw her approach. "You'll get better at that," she told the dragon. "But let's not practice right now." She scooped Neymar into her arms and placed him onto her shoulder.

"It seems he's eager to go," Nikita said, picking up the rolled paper he'd crashed into. "He's landed on the map I had drawn out for you." She carried it over to the table and shifted the dishes to make room for it.

Tempest watched with interest. The map appeared to stretch a day's travel in all directions. At the center was Isigodi. Tempest traced her finger down the river towards the eastern coast, stopping when she reached a small sketch of an elephant tusk. "Only a few hours away, then?" she asked.

"Longer upon return if you have elephants with you," said Nikita. "I'll be sending you with one of my men. He's worked with Cedric before, so he'll be able to make introductions. He should be here any moment." She rolled up the map and handed it to Tempest.

"I'll get my things."

There wasn't much to gather. All of her possessions fit in the bag she'd carried since Alyria. She checked the state of the room, then closed the door behind her. The man Nikita had promised waited in the main room when she returned. He bowed his head and extended his palm. "Pleased to meet you," he said. "My name's Emil."

"The pleasure is mine," Tempest replied, shaking his hand. "The others will be meeting us at the tavern. Are you ready to go?"

"I am," he said.

Tempest turned to Nikita. "I'll see you when we return."

"Until then, stay safe."

Emil opened the door and followed Tempest to the tavern. As planned, Jensen waited beside two Necromancers at the doorway. On either side stood a line of the dead. "M'lady," the Necromancers greeted.

"Callum and Ivy, I presume?"

They both had sharp features and brilliant eyes. "We've collected horses and provisions for the journey," said Ivy, gesturing to the creatures that'd been tied to a post across the road. Beside them waited a small wagon. "It's not much, but the journey shouldn't be long."

"It isn't," said Emil. "If all fares well, we should make it by the sun's peak."

Tempest untied one of the horses and climbed onto it's back. "Let's get going, then." She spurred the horse forward, and the others scrambled to follow. When she turned back again, they had fallen in behind her with the wagon.

Emil cantered up beside her, looking out at the stretch of land before them that led straight to the horizon. There seemed endless possibility in what lay ahead. Tempest took in the view. It was peaceful here. Hardly a sound was made to be carried by the wind. The land was flat in all directions, and it was only blocked by the scatter of strangely shaped trees. "Have you ever been this far south?" Emil asked.

A chuckle arose from Tempest's chest. "Is it obvious that I haven't?"

"Those who see it daily often forget to see its beauty," said Emil. "It's nice to find someone who still feels its magic."

Shadows danced beneath the sun as the wind whispered through the tall grass, and Tempest understood his word choice. Pulsing deep beneath the ground, where the tree roots strive to grow, she imagined a great pool of magical energy. Each of the plants and the animals that ate them radiated with this energy. Perhaps, she thought, this was the energy harnessed by the Mages.

"Have you been here a long time?" Tempest asked. She'd sensed love in his voice. It was a type of love that one only gives to the land they call home. However, it was also layered with a tenor of longing. She knew that he'd included himself in the list of those who'd forgotten.

Emil stroked the neck of his horse, and looked up to the boundless sky. "I've been here all my life," he said.

"Do you want to see more?" she asked. The magic here was not limited to the south. A similar kind lingered in the north, tapped into by the trees and the mountains. Cyrus had taught her to see it.

"By gods, yes." He laughed. "If you manage to convince Cedric to join you, I'll likely follow the elephants."

"Nikita told me you'd worked with him before," Tempest said. "She believed I stood a chance in rallying them to my cause. Do you?"

Emil hesitated before answering, so Tempest knew the answer would not be hopeful. "If I may speak frankly," he began. "No, not at all."

Tempest nodded, gnawing on her lower lip. "But it's worth trying?"

"It most certainly is," said Emil.

Behind them, Callum cursed as wood cracked, and the wagon tipped. Tempest stayed her horse and dismounted to assist. "What happened?" she asked, stroking the distressed horse that'd been carrying the load.

"The wheel broke. It should be an easy fix, though. I just need a few moments and some hands."

"The time is yours," said Tempest.

They propped up the wagon, and Callum set to work with Jensen by his side. On a small boulder across the path, Ivy sat cross legged and closed her eyes. One by one, as she whispered incantations, the dead formed a protective circle around them. Tempest sat beside her.

When the ring was complete, Ivy's eyes opened and met with Tempest's. "You're curious," she said. "You want to know how it all works."

"I do."

A smile curved Ivy's lips. "I've seen the look before. Most aren't pleased with the answer."

It was likely an unpleasant one, and Tempest knew that. She'd had to frequently remind herself that beneath the shiny black armor, there was merely a corpse. She imagined the process of raising and controlling it to be grotesque.

"The brain is quite malleable," said Ivy. "Therefore, after death, when the body has no soul to guard it, the system can be manipulated... or for lack of a better term, enslaved." She paused. "The bodies we raise must be fresh to their graves. Otherwise, we cannot control them."

The dead stood like statues, no remnants of humanity left inside them. Tempest found herself wondering who they had been in life. She hoped they'd been remembered. "Once risen," she said. "How do you puppet them?"

Ivy touched the symbols on her arm and whispered a phrase. The soldier closest to them turned and bowed. "Simple actions are given by commands. Walk. March. Ride. Run. Stand. Beyond those, however, the process is far more hands on."

Her eyes rolled back into her head, leaving only white to show, and the dead lunged towards each other. Metal clashed with metal, and guttural noises burst from their throats. The way they fought looked like a dance. Their movements were precise, quick, and fatal. They locked each other in a grip worthy of death, then stopped. Ivy's eyes opened, and the soldiers returned to their posts. Beads of sweat glittered on her brow. "To make the dead move in such a way is an exhausting game of mind and endurance," she said, taking a deep breath.

"Well the next time you play it, be sure to give a warning," said Emil who sat fallen in the dirt. He brushed off his clothes and stood. "Nearly made my heart stop."

"You'll get used to it," Callum assured, spinning the new wheel on its boxing. "Wagon's ready."

29

$\mathcal{J}$ ust off the river bank, small, humble shacks populated the land. A trodden dirt path linked them all together. Wind rolled like waves over the tall grass, carrying with it a pungent scent. Tempest smelled the sanctuary long before she saw it. It reeked of manure, straw, and something only the horses could smell. They whickered nervously between each other.

A man approached at a distance. Tempest assumed him to be Cedric. They met him halfway and dismounted their horses. On his hand was the ring of a Farmer. He stood a great deal taller than her, and his skin had been darkened by the sun. Twigs ornamented his hair, but everything else about him was clean and collected. "Emil," he said, bowing his head in greeting. "It's good to see you again. We could have used you in recent months."

Emil's gaze shifted to the sanctuary. "Nikita told me what's been happening. I wish I could have come sooner, but times have been unfavorable."

For the first time since their arrival, Cedric acknowledged Tempest and the others. "Are they here to change that?" he asked.

"I'd like to try," said Tempest, stepping forward to introduce herself. "I think perhaps we can help each other."

"Hm," he said, turning upon his heels. "Come with me."

A massive iron latch held shut the gate, and behind tall wooden posts, the sound of elephants roared through the air. It was a cacophony of noise that, under different circumstances, would have terrified Tempest. She stepped through the gate and followed Cedric into the sanctuary. Emil walked beside her, a content look on his face.

"You love these creatures, don't you?" said Tempest.

Emil nodded. "I do. In each of these buildings, there's an injured or orphaned elephant. We become their lifeline. It's a symbiotic relationship. There's untainted wisdom in these beasts, and if you spend enough time with them, they tend to share it."

Through windows and cracked walls, she could see inside a few of the buildings. The first elephant she saw was as tall as the man caring for it. Tempest watched it, intrigued. She assumed the beast had reached its largest size, but Cedric assured that it would grow. Tempest doubted the statement. She couldn't imagine it'd grow much further. The way it was shaped, it'd surely topple over if it were taller.

"Oh, no," said Cedric when she voiced her fear. "Elephants are resilient animals. They refuse to fall."

In the next hut, there stood a short mass of muscle, and it stumbled about clumsily, crashing into its caretaker as it attempted to play. "What happens when they recover?" Tempest asked, watching the young creature amble around the room.

"We relocate them to the southern edge of the sanctuary where they can rehabilitate in a social environment," said Cedric. "Once we're confident they can survive on their own, we release them."

That idea saddened Tempest. She imagined a great connection was made between the caretakers and the beasts. "Do you ever see them again?" she asked, daring to hope.

"Yes," said Cedric. "Quite often. They know it's safe here, so they frequently return. We send patrols through the land each week to track the elephants that live outside the sanctuary. Many of the herds are under constant protection and monitoring."

Tempest's brow furrowed. "Protection?" she asked. "From what? They're so large. I figure the only thing capable of threatening them would be a dragon."

"There's a far more dangerous beast than a dragon," he said. "And their steel forged claws have recently evolved into bullets."

"But guns are forbidden…" she said, twisting the thought in her mind until a realization dawned on her. "Unless the king is ordering the hunt."

Cedric nodded, confirming her dreadful suspicion. "He's taken a liking to ivory. It's a regal material for erecting statues of himself. Any poacher who brings in sufficient ivory to the king's sculptor is rewarded lavishly." He climbed a few crates that sat against the fence and turned to her entourage. "Follow me," he instructed, leaping to the other side.

Emil was the first to follow him over, and Tempest the next. After a few moments, the others had joined. One by one, the dead landed on the ground beside them. When all were present, they rounded the corner.

A curse left her lips as they came to their destination. No more than twenty paces beyond the wall, a full grown elephant lay mutilated and slaughtered in a pool of its own blood. The tusks had been ripped off, and its body had been pierced infinitely by lead bullets. "We woke this morning to his terrified cries. He came for safety when the poachers descended. From what we've gathered from the body, the chase lasted days. He made it to our gates, and he died upon arrival. It took eighty-seven bullets," said Cedric.

The thought made Tempest's heart ache. She could almost see the beast in its final moments, pleading for aid and fleeing from its pursuers.

"To kill an elephant this close to the sanctuary… they're getting bold. They know we don't have the power to stop them."

"But I do," said Tempest.

"I figured as much," Cedric said. "Otherwise, Nikita would have never sent you." He sat on a boulder that protruded from the ground and looked down at the fallen giant. "What will it cost?"

A lump formed in Tempest's throat, and her heart desperately tried to suppress the words. "Something terrible," she admitted. "We're marching to war."

A laugh erupted from his lungs. "In exchange for protection, you want them to fight… That's not protection, it's organized murder." He shook his head. "No. I can't do that to them."

Emil stepped forward, placing a hand on Cedric's shoulder. "They'll all die if you stay," he said. "You know it as well as I. Is it not better to give them a fighting chance?"

"Give me time," said Cedric, holding his head in his palms. "I need to think this through."

Tempest looked to her people, then turned back to Cedric. "Three days," she said. "We're camped at Isigodi. If we don't see you by the fourth morning, we'll know your decision."

Cedric nodded. "If I don't see you again, I wish you luck."

"And I wish the same to you," she said, hoping beyond anything that no matter what occurred, he and his creatures survived.

~~~

Three days passed, and the fourth morning came with no sign of Cedric or the elephants. "Do you want to wait longer?" Tegan asked.

"No," said Tempest. "Strike the tents and gather the men. It's time we start heading north." She'd expected this, but it still saddened her. A part of her had hoped they'd come.

Tegan bowed her head. "Yes, m'lady."

With one last glance to the horizon, Tempest departed, meeting her new militia members in the tavern. The murmur of voices faded to silence as all gazes shifted to her. "Good morning," she greeted, counting the faces in the room. There were more than she'd anticipated. Close to a hundred people waited crammed in the confines of the tavern. "Each of us have our own reasons for being here today, but one goal unites us all. It is an end to the terror of the new king's reign." Murmurs of support joined the sound of banging cups. "None of you know much about me, but I hope to earn your trust," she said. "We've waited as long as we can, and it seems Cedric will not be joining the cause. We'll be leaving in an hour. You may use the remaining time to prepare for the journey. Meet at the gates before the hour passes."

As the others dispersed, Tempest leaned against the wall and snagged a cup of ale from the serving boy. She took a long gulp and closed her eyes, praying for a successful journey. Through the wall, she heard a great rumble, and the wood beneath her feet began to shake. "Is that a quake?" Tempest asked, stopping the serving boy as he walked by.

"No, mum," he said, eyes wide with terror. "That's the sound of elephants."

Tempest dropped her cup onto the nearest table and sprinted out the door. A crowd gathered as the sound grew louder, so she stood upon a fence post, trying to catch a glimpse of the approaching herd. Their silhouettes marched elegantly in the sunrise, trunks swaying side to side, and the small shadows of humans sat mounted on their backs.

Intermixed between the great beasts were the youth. They linked together tail to trunk and marched to the outskirts of the village. Tempest met them there. "Cedric," she greeted. "I didn't expect to see you."

The bull Cedric rode crouched, and he dismounted. "I didn't expect to come," he admitted. "But another attack came the night you left. They killed a bull within our walls, and we couldn't do anything to stop them."

Tempest looked behind the beast before her, counting the elephants that followed. Behind a few of them were massive carts piled high with greens and vegetables for the animals. "Is this the entire sanctuary?"

Cedric nodded. "Only those who couldn't make the trip were left behind," he said. "Some of the volunteers stayed back to guard over them. They're young and less attractive to the poachers, so they should be safe. The rest are here. Every elephant under our care, whether it lived on the sanctuary or not, was rallied together. All I ask is that the young and injured are not used in battle. They deserve nothing but humanity and care."

The trunk of Cedric's beast grazed against her arm, so she placed her palm against it. "Agreed," she said, looking into the creature's eyes. Emil had spoken of a wisdom inside them, and in this moment, she believed she caught a glimpse of it. "We'll be leaving shortly. Do as you need, but be ready to go at the top of the hour."

A tug on her dress pulled her attention from Cedric to Felix who stood behind her with a handful of biscuits. "Excuse me, mum," he said, chewing the biscuit in his mouth. "Your dragon is getting restless. I think he's hungry."

Tempest chuckled. "He probably got jealous of all your treats. Come on, let's get him fed."

With a smile, Felix followed, biting into his biscuit every few steps. Nikita had given him a sack of them for the road, but Tempest doubted they'd last long enough. The boy had an endless appetite for the treats.

When they neared Neymar's wagon, the dragon launched into the air, flapping clumsily as he barreled towards Tempest. She caught him in her arms and placed him on her shoulder. "Let's get you to the butcher, shall we?"

The beast hummed in agreement.

"Good morning," said the butcher as they neared. He was one of the new militia men from Isigodi. "How can I help you?"

Tempest bowed her head and returned the greeting, then said, "Have you got any unsalted venison?"

The man nodded, searching through his stock in the wagon. "It's different than the kind you have up north, but it's still venison." He pulled out a strip of the meat and held it out to Tempest. She traded it for a coin, then fed the piece to Neymar. He was getting larger by the day, and she looked forward to the time he'd be able to hunt for himself.

As they walked back to the wagon, Tempest spotted a woman she'd not yet met. This woman was young and bore strong features. Her eyes were a deep brown. On her finger, she wore the ring of a Blacksmith. The ringed hand stretched forward in greeting. "My name's Jada; Blacksmith and seamstress. I'd like to offer my service to you if you'll allow it."

"In terms of armor and clothes?" Tempest asked, taking the seamstress' hand.

"Or armor woven clothes," she offered. "I'll show you my work if you wish."

Tempest shook her head. "I trust your work is beautiful, but I'm afraid I don't have much to offer in the form of funds." What little coin she had needed to go places other than fancy gowns.

"Worry not. Fabric is easy to come by if you know where to find it. You want to be Queen, yes?"

"I do," said Tempest, clutching the ring that hung hidden by her throat.

"Then you ought to look like one," Jada said, gesturing to the holes and scuffs that scattered Tempest's dress. "All I want is to help you."

Tempest ran her fingers through the folds of the emerald gown. It'd come a long way, but it was old and tarnished. "Find me when we start to the north, and we'll discuss."

Jada bowed her head and departed, leaving Tempest alone with Felix once more. She helped the boy climb into the wagon and plopped the creature down beside him. "Are you ready to see the north?" she asked.

Felix nodded vigorously. "Are there as many dragons as the stories say?" he asked, stroking Neymar's back.

"There are more," said Tempest.

Felix's mother joined him in the wagon, and he split his biscuit in half, handing her the other piece. The woman took it with thanks, and Tempest left them to themselves.

With one last lap around her growing regiment, she ensured everyone was ready to continue. Her last stop was with the elephants. She found Cedric feeding the beast he'd been riding. "Have you ever heard the legend of the ancient elephant lords?" he asked as she passed.

Tempest stopped, turning to face the man. "I have not," she said.

Cedric passed a pack to Emil, who strapped provisions onto the elephant's back. "Elephants spend the majority of their lives standing up. They are quite heavy creatures, and their weight makes it difficult for them to rise if they lay down. But, the old legends say they weren't always like this.

"When humanity began to make its claim upon the land, Fejun, god of the beasts, made an agreement with the elephant and mammoth lords of the age. They gathered together in the ancient plains, and there, they changed their shape. They grew taller, heavier, and thick of skin, perhaps to demonstrate their great power and wisdom to the small, wrathful creatures called man. However, those who work with elephants know a different tale.

"You see, when the elephants stand and trod onward in their herds, through both good days and dark days, they show a celebration of life. In this simple act, they teach us that life can never die as long as we keep standing, as long as we keep moving. No matter how many eras pass, if we stand up for it, life will never vanish, and if life can never die, then neither can we.

"But we never learned. We killed them off to the point of near extinction, and we forced them to fall, but they kept their honor, and they never gave up." He linked the elephants together, and with a tap on the leg, his elephant knelt, allowing him to climb onto its shoulders. "And so, the elephants march," he said, smiling down at her.

"As do we," Tempest replied, and the beast stood tall again. She took one last look at the column of elephants, then returned to the front of the convoy.

30

*F*or three weeks they'd been on the road, and in each village they came across, people began to flock. Word of her army was spreading, and many wished to join.

The days grew short, and the nights grew colder as they entered the month of Ammos. Zalder's last breaths of flame faded from the world, making room for Wynris to blanket the land in ice once more.

"We'll make camp outside the nearing township. I'll send out a group of hunters to restock our food supplies while the regiment rests," Tempest said, then she turned to Tegan. "I need you to take command over the camp when things are settled. I'd like to visit the town and see what we can gather."

Tegan frowned at that. "You're not going alone, I hope."

"No," Tempest assured. "I'll bring Cedric with me."

Tegan was visibly hesitant about the decision but accepted nonetheless.

~~~

As the distant outline of towers peaked over the hills, Tempest brought the regiment to a halt. Tents were erected, and fires were made to warm the camp before nightfall. Tempest waited beside a hearth inside the main tent, watching the smoke billow towards the clouds through an opening at the top that revealed a blooded sky as the sun sank behind the horizon.

"M'lady," came Tegan's voice from behind the door.

"Come in," said Tempest.

The flap lifted, and Tegan walked in with ten hunters close behind. She thanked Tegan for retrieving them, and the woman bowed her head, dipping back through the door to return to the ranks of Necromancers.

Tempest motioned the group forward, lifting Neymar from the oak table he lay on to make room for the rough map one of her militia men had drawn for her. Hunters circled around the table, quietly awaiting direction. Each had come from one of the villages they'd encountered throughout the journey.

They were divided into pairs and given a small range of land to cover in their hunt. When each was satisfied with their assignment, Tempest thanked them and opened the flap to let them out, but a young girl who must have been near Felix's age gasped when the tent flap flew open, sending her scampering backwards. Her feet tangled, and she tripped, landing on her sit bones with a huff.

"Ava!" one of the men in her band of hunters shouted as the others slipped out. He'd been one of the militia that joined her just outside of Isigodi. "I told you to stay by our tent."

"I'm sorry, Father. I just got curious," said the girl, lowering her head to avoid his gaze.

"I must apologize for her actions, I assure it won't happen again," the father said, lifting the girl to her feet.

"It's of no worry to me. As the girl said, she was just curious." Tempest crouched before the child, meeting her eyes. "The world needs curious people like you to do great things," she said, then stood to address the father. "Do you mind if I borrow her for a moment? I have a mission of sorts to fulfill, and she seems like just the person to do it,"

The girl's face lit up with joy at the potential adventure and she looked up at her father expectantly.

He patted her head and nodded. "Do as she says."

"Thank you." Tempest turned her attention to the child. "Do you know the man who rides the elephants?" Ava nodded. "His name is Cedric, and I need him to meet me here. Could you tell him to come?"

Again, the girl nodded. "Yes, mum."

"I have one other request for you," said Tempest before the girl could run off. "I need you to deliver a letter to Tegan, who leads the Necromancers." She handed Ava a folded sheet of parchment that contained Tegan's orders to take command over the camp while she and Cedric were away. "You can read it if you'd like, though I'm afraid it's quite boring."

"I only know a few words, mum, so I couldn't read it if I tried." The girl giggled, then scurried off to complete her mission.

"Does she have someone to watch over her while you're out hunting?" Tempest asked as the father turned to walk away.

"No, but she's used to being on her own. I made frequent hunting trips back in our village," he replied.

"Very well. If you'd like, she's welcome to my quarters while you're gone. I could use a helping hand around here."

"It'd be an honor," he said, bowing his head before departing.

Tempest returned to her seat beside the hearth. By this point the sky was purple, and the stars began to wake, shining glamorously above. The flames in the hearth had nearly died out when Cedric stepped in and interrupted the silence. "You sent for me?" he asked, standing near the entrance of the tent with his hands clasped.

"I did," said Tempest, rising to her feet. "I want to go to this town." She pointed to the small symbol on the map. "Would you care to join me?"

There'd been a tension between them since his arrival. Tempest figured it accompanied the dilemma of whether or not bringing the elephants was the right choice. She wished she knew the answer so she could ease both of their hearts, but for now, all she could do was ask for trust.

"I'd be happy to," he said with formality. "When do you want to leave?"

Tempest looked at the glow of the embers that remained in the hearth. They wouldn't last much longer. "Would now work for you?"

"Now is just fine," Cedric agreed, holding out his arm to escort Tempest out. She threw on the old, familiar black cloak she'd once worn wandering the streets of Alyria, then stuffed her notebook and pencil into her small pack and graciously took Cedric's arm.

As the two walked out, the undead guards that stood at the threshold moved to follow, but Tempest motioned them away. "Keep the dead here and await Tegan's arrival," Tempest said to the Necromancer who controlled them. "She and a young girl named Ava are the only ones permitted in my quarters until I return." The guards swiftly returned to their posts, standing unwavering like stone.

"Shall we?" Cedric asked, gesturing to the path ahead. Tempest nodded, and they made their way through the crowd. The people parted, murmuring courtesies as they passed. Tempest remembered when Jax had walked through the crowd in Alyria and drawn a similar reaction. It was a strange thought. So much had happened since then.

The walk was long once they broke from the tents, but the view from the road was tranquil. Large trees loomed overhead, swallowing them in their shadows, and jagged rocks protruded from the dirt like knives. A small stream ran through the trees, rushing downhill with ice cold water that attracted many creatures. It amazed Tempest how quickly the land had shifted from sea-like planes to a rocky forest. As her feet began to tire, they came to a faint dirt and gravel path that led to the town.

A young man sat sharpening his sword beneath a cobblestone wall held upright with dark wooden beams. He leapt to his feet when Tempest and Cedric approached, and his foot knocked into a small pile of firewood that'd been stacked near his roasting spit, sending it tumbling about. They'd taken him by surprise. He cursed, tripping over one of the logs before regaining composure. "Who are you?" he asked, trying to sound more forceful than he looked. In his hands, he held the freshly sharpened sword, poised and ready.

Tempest pitied the lad and had no intention of scaring him, so she kept their identity and intention silent. Instead, she decided to enact the role of a commoner. She wanted him to feel empowered, not threatened. "Just travelers, sir, looking for a roof and fire for the night. Is there an inn here where we may stay?"

He looked warily between them. "If you give me your names and occupations, there might be. These are strange times and precautions are in order. I hope you understand."

"Absolutely. My name is Tempest, and this here is Cedric. I'm a Dragon Keeper, and he's a Farmer. I met him while doing business in the south. He wished to see the scorched lands, so we're heading north. It's been a mighty long journey, so you can imagine when we found this little town, we were quite ecstatic. I do hope you let us through, sir." Tempest accented the title once more to add a little more persuasion.

"Yes, ma'am, right this way," he said, pointing down the pathway into the dimly lit town. "You'll make the second turn to the right where you'll see a small, run-down inn called Smith's. It isn't fancy, but it's a bed, roof, and food if you've got the penny."

Tempest thanked the guard, and they followed the directions to the inn. She quite enjoyed the look of this town. The buildings were tall with sharp, plated roofs. They were made of dark wood and cracked stone. It felt old and full of history.

Inside the inn, the musty air made it difficult to breathe, and a strange energy buzzed through the people, an energy as wild as the flames that burned in the fire pit, warming the small tavern. She could see it in the eyes of onlookers, and she could hear it in the whispering voices. It was that energy expressed in fits of passion. The same energy she'd felt with Cyrus, that perfect mix of excitement and fear.

Everyone's focus remained preoccupied with whatever events were brewing in the center of the room, which made their entry go unnoticed. Tempest was glad for that. She took Cedric's arm and dragged him to a table in the corner where they wouldn't draw much attention.

A young man climbed onto the center table, kicking the empty plates and cups out of the way. "Word on the street says the fight is getting close, my friends. A revolution is coming!" he boasted, and his friends raised a chorus of shouts and cheers in support of the envisioned revolution.

"Sit down, Marius," said a man in the corner, pushing his way through the crowd. He was an older man. His hands were worn, and his face had aged quite poorly. "You can't defeat Kaburem. Not with your small gatherings of youth. It'll only end in blood. It's impossible to win a war against fire when all you have are swords, bows, and farm tools."

Marius never doubted. "You forget, old sir, but we have fire too!" he said giddily, leaping from the table. He took the hand of a man seated on the bench, displaying an emerald ring for all to see. "We have a dragon in our midst."

The skeptic laughed. "Congratulations, you have a single dragon. Kaburem should be terrified."

"Two dragons," Tempest corrected, lifting her ring for all to see. "Two dragons and many more to come, along with a battalion of the risen dead, a company of Necromancers, a horde of elephants, and a regiment of militia soldiers." She dared not say exact numbers while Kaburem could be listening.

The room went silent, and everyone's gaze fell to the strangers in the corner. "And who are you?" the skeptic asked, approaching the table where they sat.

"Tempest, don't," Cedric quietly pleaded.

"A traveler," said Tempest, easing Cedric's worries. "A traveler who has seen this army with my own eyes. They're not terribly far from your gates this very moment."

A murmur arose from the crowd, silenced by a hand that was lifted into the air. "How do we know you're telling the truth?" he asked.

"You're welcome to go see it for yourself, but otherwise, you'll have to trust my word."

The man scoffed and rolled his eyes, pacing ever so slightly as he looked at his peers. "Trust is difficult to come by these days."

Tempest shrugged and sat back down. When all had returned to normal, she sent Cedric to retrieve Marius for her. The boy approached warily, sitting across from her.

Though he stayed composed, Tempest could see the curiosity burning in his eyes. "Is it true?" he asked, fidgeting nervously with his thumbs. "Have you really seen it? The army I mean." His eyes gleamed with excitement, and Tempest nodded, feeding the joy within him.

"I'd like to show it to you if I can, but as that man said, trust is a rarity. I need to know who I can call a friend. Can you help me?" she asked.

Marius thought for a moment, grueling over a dilemma in his mind before finally agreeing. "There's a meeting tonight in an abandoned temple down the road," he said in a hushed voice, glancing around to ensure no one was listening. "A group of us are trying to connect with other village militias to get this rebellion moving. Are you staying here tonight? I can come and get you on my way... only if you'd like, of course... but before I do, may I ask what your name is?"

It was Tempest's turn to scan the surroundings for ears that may be listening on. When she was satisfied no one was paying attention to their small corner, she replied with, "Tempest. Or at least that's what people call me. I went by a much different name growing up... My name was Dasha, daughter of the late King Neymar."

Marius' eyes widened in equal shock and horror. His jaw fell open, and his eyes scattered in confusion. "But, you're dead," he muttered.

Tempest looked down at her hands, then back to Marius' petrified face. "Do I look dead?" she asked.

"No, m'lady," said Marius. "I meant no offense."

Tempest dismissed him with a wave. "As you can see, I'm very much alive." She placed her dagger against her forearm, preparing to drag it across her skin. "Do you need proof? The dead don't bleed."

Marius' face went pale. "No, m'lady. I trust you."

"Good," said Tempest. "The army I spoke of is as real as I am, and it's waiting only an hour's walk from here. Let me speak to your people tonight, and perhaps come morning, you'll join me."

"Yes, m'lady," he said. "I'll call for you three hours before the sun rises."

Tempest stood and stowed away her dagger. "I look forward to the meeting," she said, then she left with Cedric following close behind. As she looked back to check on Marius, one of his friends sat next to him, a boy with shaggy black hair and magnificent green eyes. He looked a bit like Patch, thought Tempest. The friend placed a hand on Marius' shoulder, offering him a swig of ale. It was the last thing she saw before they rounded the corner and approached the innkeeper for a room.

"I don't intend to question tactics," said Cedric when they reached the closed confines of the bed chamber. "But why did you give the boy a false identity?"

Tempest unclasped the chain that held her mother's ring and handed it to Cedric. "There was nothing false about it," she said.

The same pale complexion of shock washed over his face like it did whenever anyone learned her true identity, but he recovered quickly. "Why keep it a secret?" he asked, returning the ring to Tempest.

"I don't, anymore" she said. "I tell anyone who asks, but I find it better if it can be avoided. The problem is, people rarely trust me until they know who I am, but certain circumstances have allowed me to keep quiet. Loyalty should be earned by things other than a name when possible."

"A respectable mindset," said Cedric as he grabbed a pillow and lay it on the floor. "Will you tell the townspeople?"

She clasped the chain around her neck and tucked the ring beneath her clothes. "If it's necessary," she said, then turned to hang her cloak beside the door. "You're welcome to take the bed."

Cedric smiled but declined. "I don't mind the floor," he said. "I've spent many nights sleeping in odd places at the sanctuary. This won't be much different."

Tempest handed him one of the fur blankets, then sat on the edge of the bed. "Good night," she said, and she curled beneath the remaining furs and blew out the candle.

~~~

As promised, in the late hours of the night, Tempest heard a light rasp at the door. She slipped from beneath the warm blankets and padded towards the door, shaking Cedric's shoulder ever so slightly to wake him as she passed. Marius stood in the threshold, waiting for the pair to collect themselves before heading into the cold night air.

The moon was merely a small sliver in the sky, and the stars were blocked by clouds. Tempest could hardly see anything beyond shadows and silhouettes, but Marius was quick with his steps. She figured he'd made the journey many times. "This way," he said as he ducked through a small alleyway and waved them forward.

Tempest pressed her palms to the stone walls that enclosed the alley and followed the sound of his voice. The alley opened into a small plot of grass that lined the back end of the temple. She could see its spiked roof beneath dimly lit clouds.

Marius slid through a small door concealed by the ragged bushes that grew along the wall. Tempest followed close behind, pausing a moment to allow her eyes time to adjust to the warm glowing light of the room.

The conversing voices within the temple came to an abrupt halt as the door swung closed behind Cedric. There were whispers now and harsh gazes that burned through their guide.

"You're an even greater fool than I thought, Marius. Even after the last time, you still brought strangers to us!" said a woman Tempest could not yet see. The room they'd entered was small and overcrowded, filled with rusted crates and far too many people. Bodies shifted, making room for the woman to wiggle her way to the front. She was middle-aged with hollowed eyes and greying hair, and on her finger was the olivine crystal of the Alyrian Army.

"Last time was a mistake. It won't happen again. These two won't betray us. Not like the others," Marius promised, but the confidence faltered in his eyes when he looked towards Tempest.

"What makes them different than the last ones? They weren't going to betray us either, but look where that got us," said the woman.

"The girl said she was Neymar's daughter... that the rumors are true. The army is outside right this moment."

Tempest shifted awkwardly as they discussed her loyalties before her face. She hoped they'd come to an agreement soon, otherwise, she'd have to step in.

The woman's mouth opened again, and she fired back a rebuttal. "You trust too much, my boy. You must learn that words are empty. Where is your proof? Have you seen the army with your own eyes?"

Marius lowered his head in shame, fidgeting with the sleeve of his coat. He didn't need to answer; his silence had already done so.

Tempest shook her head and sighed. "You want proof?" she asked. "I have proof." She reached for the thin chain that hung at her neck and carefully pulled it out, displaying it so the woman could see the amethyst stone that rested in its metallic hold. In a sudden burst, the room erupted once more with the vibrant murmur of voices.

She refastened the ring, then stood on the nearest table, lifting her hand to silence the others. Their voices sputtered out. "Marius tells me you're meeting to unite the local rebellions. Is that true?" she asked.

"It is," said the woman.

"That's my goal as well. I'd like to work together if we can. Some of you heard me speak at the inn. What I said about the army was all true, and it's growing every day. It'll take time, but if we stand together, we'll stand a chance. We must face Kaburem with a united front, or we must not face Kaburem at all."

The woman crossed her arms and leaned against the wall. "What makes you think you can defeat them? Have you got any war experience?"

"No," said Tempest. "But I imagine you do. That's why they've made you their leader, isn't it? Come with me. Advise me. I cannot do this alone."

"You most certainly can't," said the woman. "And neither can we." She approached Tempest and held out her hand. "My name's Clio. It's a pleasure to be in your service."

31

edric and Tempest passed the remainder of the night in their room at the inn. Sleep was a worthless cause, however. Tempest tossed and turned in her rest, plagued by thoughts of battles to come. This war was approaching fast, and she wasn't sure she was ready to face the cost.

As the morning sun seeped through the crevices of cracked wood, she rose from the small bed. It'd been a rough surface to sleep on, but it was a bed nonetheless, and for that, Tempest was thankful.

Cedric, seated presently in the windowsill, turned to the sound of her movement and smiled. "Mornin'," he said, hushed so as not to disturb the quiet.

"Good morning," Tempest replied, crossing the room to sit with him. There was no conversation between them beyond the simple greeting, but Tempest was content in the silence. It was a calming contrast to the fears that swirled in her mind.

Within the hour, Marius showed up, knocking gently on their door. When Tempest opened it, she found him standing with a plate of honey coated crackers. "I'm afraid it isn't much," he said, handing Tempest the plate, "but I thought you might want some food before the journey.

"It's more than we require," she replied, thanking Marius for his hospitality. The honey was soothing to her throat, and it tasted sweet on her tongue. When there was nothing left but crumbs, they gathered their few belongings and left.

All who wished to accompany the rebel army congregated outside the old temple. The area looked vastly different in the daylight than it had in the shadows of the night. Green moss coated the stones, and a thin layer of frost glittered under the sun. They arrived at the camp shortly after mid-day when the sun was just reaching its peak.

Tegan waited for them at the edge of it. "Welcome back," she said as they neared. "I have favorable news. One of the hunting parties returned this morning with ample game. We won't be wanting for food any time soon, but we'll need to keep collecting if we want to make it through the winter. Especially with how fast our ranks are growing."

Several other small matters arose as they made their way to the heart of the camp. The first discussion was of a militia woman who'd fallen ill but looked to be recovering fast. She'd been placed in an isolated tent and watched over by a Medic. Tempest approved of the handling and waited for the next topic. "The elephants have grown restless in Cedric's absence, but the rest of the sanctuary volunteers have kept matters contained." She turned to Cedric then and said, "I'm sure they'll be happy to see you back."

His face lit up, and he rushed off to join them. Nothing else of importance had occurred in their absence, so Tegan fell in with the ranks of Necromancers and dead, leaving Tempest alone with the new militia. All of them watched their surroundings with curious, yet wary expressions. Marius' face showed no terror, however. There was nothing but excitement in his eyes. Tempest wondered how she would have felt if she'd come to this army an outsider. She couldn't say whether or not the oddities of elephants and dead would have terrified or fascinated her. Even having organized this gathering, a bit of both emotions filled her heart.

When they reached the militia tents, Tempest stopped and turned to the new members of her party. "You're welcome to set up anywhere here," she said. "My tent is just down the path if you need anything. We'll continue north in a couple days. Rest while you can; the road is long."

Tempest parted ways with the townspeople and headed towards her tent. She took a deep breath and ducked beneath the flap. On the other side waited an impatient Neymar. He sprinted about, chirping with excitement. Tempest picked the dragon up and set him on the table, settling into the chair beside it. It was silent in the tent, which she was grateful for. There was hardly ever a moment where nothing was happening.

Tempest unraveled one of the maps and lay it across the table at the center of the tent. This map was larger than the others, but the scale was much smaller. On it was a rough sketching of the entire continent, and at the top right corner, it was signed by a member of her militia.

Near the center, she placed a stone, marking the area they were camped in. They were a few day's distance from any major city. Tempest traced her finger over the land to the west. It'd tried to separate itself from Kaburem's reign, and at one point may have proven an excellent ally, but Mereb had told her of its collapse. Though perhaps, she thought, there were people who still wanted to fight.

Tempest rolled up the parchment and carried it out of the tent. "Where's Clio?" she asked to the nearest person.

"Third tent to the right," said the woman.

"Thank you." She walked to the tent, greeting Clio's followers as they cleared a path for Tempest to enter.

"What have you got?" asked Clio, looking to the scroll in Tempest's hand.

"A map," she said, and she rolled it out on the floor. "What do you know of the state of the land in this area?" she asked, pointing to the region formerly ruled by Colonel Atheris.

Clio crouched down to look at the map. "I'm afraid my information may be outdated, but the last I heard, Kaburem reclaimed most of it," she said. "The Army's city, Sylvos, was the first to resubmit. King Lazareth offered them training and fed them lies of glory and grandeur. Their guild leader, who never wanted to separate in the first place, accepted submission readily."

"What of the trade city?" asked Tempest.

Clio sat cross legged on the floor, looking at the city with curiosity. "Thousands of rebels had begun to gather there," she said. "We were in contact with them for a while, but nothing has been heard in over a month."

"What are the odds the rebels still stand?"

"Slim," Clio admitted. "But there's a chance."

"A chance is all I need," said Tempest. "Would any of your people know how to find them?"

Clio hesitated before answering, and a flicker of doubt crossed her eyes. "Marius," she said. "He's the one who connected us to them."

"Do you think he's capable of rallying them to the fight?"

Clio nodded. "He's apt to rash decisions, but you'll never meet a boy with more passion than he has."

This was a fact Tempest already knew, even after only just meeting Marius. "It's decided, then. Would you like to tell him, or should I?"

With a shrug, Clio said, "He'll take it better from you."

Tempest rolled up the map and stuffed it into the inner pocket of her cloak, then nodded. "Thank you," she said. "I'm sure we'll speak again soon."

"Certainly," said Clio.

Tempest left Clio's tent and found Marius sitting around a fire near a wagon with a few others from his town. She sat beside him, grabbed a cup, and filled it with ale.

"M'lady," he greeted with a bow of his head. "Is there something you need?"

She took a sip before responding. "I've just spoken to your commander," she said. "You've been recommended for a job."

Marius leaned forward, doubt in his eyes. "Clio recommended me? Impossible."

Those sitting beside him began to laugh. "Are you certain you heard her correctly?" asked the girl to his left. She nudged Marius in the ribs playfully, and a flush rose to his cheeks.

"It involves the rebel groups in Laurus," Tempest said. "I was told you might know how to find them."

Marius set his cup down and clasped his hands together. "They vanished a month ago," he said.

"But you know where they were before they disappeared?"

"I do," said Marius, then his voice lowered. "But trying to find them now would be suicide. There's a reason they went quiet."

"This whole thing will be suicide if we don't get proper support," Tempest admitted. "I'll send you with ample protection. If you find them, it could shift the balance of the war. It's too great a chance to pass up."

Marius shifted and fumbled with his hands. His eyes met with the girl's beside him, and he nodded. "I'll do it," he agreed.

"And I'll go with him," said the girl. "Someone's got to make sure he doesn't screw anything up."

A chuckle lifted from Marius' chest, and he took the girl's hand between his. "What would you have us do once we get there?" he asked.

Tempest drained the rest of her cup, then set it down. "I'll have a letter for you to deliver on my behalf," she said, rising to her feet. "Give it to the leader of the rebel group. I'll be waiting here at first light with everything you'll need for the journey."

"Yes, m'lady," said Marius, bowing his head as Tempest departed.

The sun began to sink towards the horizon, marking the decline of the day, but Tempest still had much to do. She hurried back to her tent and lit a candle, setting it down on the table. She found a handful of papers and laid them across the wooden surface. The words she wrote would need to be chosen with care. If these pages were to be lost, she needed to ensure it wouldn't put her army in harm's way.

An old book surfaced in her memory. It was a tale of a war from generations ago. The book itself, while being an epic novel, was also an encrypted document filled with battle plans. She had not the time to write her own book, but perhaps she could use the one she already had.

From her bag, she pulled out the well-traveled book of the gods. Each page had been marked with a number, and each line had been labeled as well. With those numbers, and the mental ones she placed over each word, Tempest began to write. Page, line, word, repeat. It was a long process that stretched deep into the night, but when the stars were out, and the moon hung high, she signed the bottom of the page and sealed it shut with a wax crown. Inside was an in depth description of who she was, the army she had gathered, and their destination.

Tempest took a deep breath and stuffed the letter into the book. With one order of business complete, it was on to the next. She hid the book under the furs on her bed and left to seek the Necromancers that'd accompanied her to the sanctuary. Callum and Ivy sat playing dice by the light of a fire with a few others. Jensen sat with them too. "Just the people I wanted to see," said Tempest, sitting on the bench beside them.

"Have you got another adventure for us, m'lady?" asked Ivy as she tossed the dice.

"That I do," Tempest said. "But this time I will not be joining."

Jensen nodded, scooped up the dice, and said, "Where to?"

"Laurus." She paused, looking to see their expressions. Jensen seemed hesitant, but the others were less fearful. "One of the townspeople, Marius, knows of a large rebel force in the area. I need you all to accompany him on his journey to find them. Are you willing to go?"

Callum and Ivy nodded, but Jensen held his tongue. He closed his fingers around the dice and placed them into Tempest's hand. "Have you ever played?" he asked.

Tempest shook her head, inspecting the small, marbled objects with dots speckled on each face. They were beautifully crafted and smooth. "How does it work?"

"Highest number wins the round. It's a game of absolute chance," said Jensen. "Just like this journey west. Occasionally, however, the gods look favorably upon a player and gift them with success. Roll."

With a swift swoop of the hand, Tempest rolled the dice, and each of them landed on the side with six dots. Jensen smiled. "I'll go," he said.

Tempest bowed her head and stood. "Meet me in the militia quarters at first light."

Upon her return to the tent, she found Ava waiting at the table. The child startled her. "Where have you been all day?" Tempest asked, sitting across from the girl.

Ava stroked Neymars scales and smiled. "A boy named Felix came by, asking about your dragon," said Ava. "The guards wouldn't let him in, so I went with him to play." A yawn escaped her lips, and she slumped into the back of her chair. "I didn't expect to be gone so long."

"I'm sure you didn't." Tempest chuckled. "Are you still awake enough to practice your letters? I have to write a message to Tegan."

Ava nodded with a bright smile on her face. "Yes!" she said, snatching a pencil from the edge of the table.

Tempest lay a paper before Ava and told the child which words and letters to write. The handwriting was crooked and shaky, but she knew Tegan wouldn't mind. Inside the letter she'd recapitulated all the conversations she'd had in the day. She told of the plan to go to Laurus, and the list of those who'd agreed to go. At the bottom, Ava signed both of their names. Tempest folded it carefully and handed it to the girl. "Well done," she said. "Deliver this to Tegan, then come back and get some rest."

"Yes, mum," Ava said, scurrying off to complete her task.

The light in the room faded as Tempest extinguished the candles. She left one by the entrance for Ava's return, then dressed for the night. Beneath the furs, she found the book she'd left hidden there. Tempest placed it under her pillow and curled into the warm comforts of her bed.

Morning came far quicker than Tempest desired, and the sounds of the rising camp flooded through the thin, cloth walls of her tent. She stood from the furs and found a gown to wear for the day. It was a pale dress, and it fit loosely. On the collar it'd been ornamented with silver plates that, when piled together, looked a bit like scales. It was the first dress fashioned by the seamstress, Jada.

In the corner of the tent, Ava lay in her bed, still fast asleep. Tempest grabbed the book of the gods and slipped out into the air, careful not to disturb the sleeping child. Neymar followed close behind, so she picked the beast up and set him on her shoulders.

"Good morning, m'lady," said Marius when she approached. "We're ready."

Tempest met eyes with each of those who stood before her, then nodded. "This is your mission," she said, holding up the letter for all to see. "And this is how it's read." She lifted the book next. "Both of these objects should never be carried by the same person. The only time they should ever be united is the moment they are delivered to the leader of the rebels. Am I understood?"

Marius nodded, taking the letter from her hand. He stuffed it carefully into the pocket of his coat and mounted his horse. Tempest then passed the book to Callum. "Place this with one of the dead," she said.

Callum took it and slipped it into a pouch carried by one of the dead he commanded. "Is that all?" he asked.

"That's all," said Tempest. "I bid you all a safe journey. Instructions of a rendezvous are in the letter. I'll see you soon."

"Goodbye, m'lady," said Marius, and he spurred his horse forward.

Their silhouettes marched into the distance, fading out of Tempest's line of sight. Twenty dead and five living. She prayed for their safe return.

With a sigh, she turned away and headed back to her tent. Most of the camp remained asleep, so the air held a temporary notion of silence. Only the birds interrupted it. It was a peaceful morning, and she dared not disturb it, but Ava had other plans. The girl burst from the tent just before Tempest reached it.

"Good morning, m'lady," she said as she scuttled past.

"Good morning," said Tempest. "Where are you going?"

Ava only stopped a moment to respond. "I promised Felix I'd meet him when I woke," she said, turning on her heels to continue towards the boy's tent.

"Who's Felix?" asked a voice from the trees. It was a voice that halted all of Ava's plans.

"Father!" she yelled, arms outstretched as she ran towards the tree line.

He stepped forward to greet her and lifted the child into the air, a great smile plastered on his face. "I hope you behaved while I was away, young lady," her father said, setting her back on the ground.

Ava giggled, skipping around him. "I did, Father, I promise."

"I'll let Tempest be the judge of that," he replied.

"Ava did very well," Tempest assured, walking with the newly arrived hunters to the butchers tent to have the meat skinned and prepared for the journey that lay ahead.

~~~

Her people were given one last night of rest before it was time to continue on. The dead with their Necromancer commanders fell in behind the growing militia, and behind them marched the elephants.

Dawn turned to dusk, and the cycle repeated until finally, the Mage city, Hekatia, crept into view. On the outskirts, Tempest brought her army to a halt. Galloping steps approached from within thick trees that concealed her people, and from those trees, two men from her cavalry emerged. "There's a Kaburem patrol not far from here," said one. "What will you have us do with them?"

"How many are there?" Tempest asked.

"Somewhere around twenty soldiers," the other scout said.

"It'd be an easy capture," said Clio who rode up beside them. "But it's best not to provoke when we don't need to."

Tempest nodded. "Take a group and lead them astray. Keep them occupied and far away from our camp. Can you do that?"

"Piss off a couple Kaburem soldiers?" asked the first scout. "Consider it done."

"What's the plan while they're off doing that?" Clio asked.

Tempest dismounted her horse and grabbed it by the reins. "Have you ever been inside the Mage's tower?"

"I have not," said Clio, joining Tempest on the ground.

"Neither have I," said Tempest. "Tonight, that changes."

"How do you intend to get in?"

There was a moment's pause as Tempest pondered her answer. They certainly wouldn't be admitted entry to the city as rebel soldiers. "We'll need a Merchant and a supply wagon."

A laugh burst from Clio's lungs. "Will we be the goods?"

"We will," said Tempest.

"I'll go find a Merchant, then."

Tempest took the horses to the camp stables, then she set off to find the others. She needed reputable companions on this small journey. Tegan was the first she found. The Necromancer sat on the ledge of a wagon filled with textiles from the southern villages. "M'lady," she greeted, rising to her feet. "Do you want us to make camp?"

"I do," said Tempest, "But I'll need you elsewhere this time. I want to go to the tower and talk to Vitani. Will you come with me?"

"Of course, m'lady," said Tegan. "Should I come alone, or should I bring the dead?"

Tempest scanned the ranks of corpses, then looked back to Tegan. "Bring the dead."

With Tegan's command, ten of them stepped forward. The motion sent a chill through Tempest's spine, but Tegan smiled, brushing her thumb over the symbols on her arm. "At your lead," she said, gesturing forward.

They met Clio with the Merchant on the edge of camp. The man with the burgundy ring extended his hand in greeting. "My name's Jyles," he said. "I sell herbs, medicinal and… otherwise."

"Oh," said Tempest, shaking his hand. She supposed there were many uses for herbs, and medicine was likely the least common. Perfume, food, magic, but also poison. From the way he spoke, she figured the latter was his specialty. "Do you think you can get us inside?"

The Merchant bowed his head. "When you deal in matters such as the ones I partake, smuggling becomes a simple task."

He was awfully free with his crimes, thought Tempest. "Why are you telling me this?" she asked.

His answer came quick. "Ensurance, my dear," he said, helping her into the wagon. "When you smuggle for a queen, the crime of it is washed away."

Tempest sat on a small crate filled with shreds of yew. "I'm no queen," she said.

"Not yet." He gave a smile, then dropped the flap and tied it shut.

The wagon lurched forward, pitching from one side to the other as it rolled over the rocks and divots of the road. Across from her, the dead sat motionless, staring straight ahead. Voices from outside the cart filled the silence that hung within, but all Tempest could concentrate on was the slow rhythm of her breathing.

With a gentle command from the Merchant, the horses stayed their progression, and the wagon stopped. "Name and business," said a man.

Jyles responded earnestly. "My name is Jyles," he said. "I'm a Merchant. Here to trade some herbs. There's a great market with you Mages, is there not?"

There was a brief pause before an answer was given, and the seconds elongated with terror. Tempest's heart seemed to stop when the voice of the guard broke through the silence. "Right on in," he said.

Without hesitation, Jyles spurred forth the wagon, and Tempest let out the breath she'd been holding. They rode through the small city, turning down unfamiliar streets. Tempest closed her eyes and pressed her ear to the cloth wall of the wagon. She could hear horses whickering and chatter between people. Children laughed, and dogs barked. She wondered what it all looked like.

The noise died down as they turned into an alley, and soon, the only sound left was the rumble of the wagon's wheels and the soft clopping of the horse's hooves. They drew to a stop, and Jyles whistled to signal safety.

Tempest was the first to climb out. She'd been closest to the door. Jyles rolled up the flap and reached out his hand to help her down. She took the offer with gratitude and jumped to the ground. When her feet landed, her eyes met with those of a Kaburem soldier who stood near twenty paces away. Poised in his grip was a gun.

"Who are you?" asked the soldier.

There was nothing she could say that wouldn't spark suspicion. Tegan and Clio had joined her, and with them came the dead. "There's no need for weapons, sir," she said, stepping closer to the man. "We intend no harm."

"You're her, aren't you?" The weapon clicked, and he held it steady. "You're the one they say is leading the rebellion."

"Put the gun down," Tegan demanded, but the soldier refused.

Instead, he fired. Time seemed to slow as the bullet barreled towards Tempest, but it struck the flesh of another. With inhuman speed, one of the dead had jumped in front of her. The bullet lodged somewhere deep within the corpse's chest.

Tempest's legs went weak, and her hands trembled, but a rage burned within her heart. "Seize him," she ordered, and the dead followed through.

The soldier flailed and cursed, pleading for mercy as the dead dragged him to the wagon. Jyles stepped out with a cup full of liquid and forced it to the soldier's lips. "This'll contain him while you're gone," he said, pouring the liquid into the soldier's mouth. Tempest wasn't sure what it was, but she wasn't certain she wanted to find out. The soldier's body fell limp within seconds. "He won't be like this for long, so make this quick."

Tempest and Clio helped him lift the body into the wagon. "Get out of here for a bit," said Tempest. "People will be curious about the gunshot. They'll come looking."

Jyles bowed and jumped onto the wagon, urging the horses forward. As he sped off, Tempest turned to Tegan, whose eyes were white and brow ornamented with beads of sweat. "Thank you," said Tempest, and the Necromancer's eyes returned to normal. "I owe you my life."

"Let's not make it a habit," said Tegan.

"Agreed." Tempest took a breath to recompose herself, then proceeded down the alleyway towards the tower gates. The rest of her party followed close behind.

A Mage officer stood with his arms crossed beneath iron teeth that sat bared at the peak of the archway. Vines crept through cracked stone and drooped to create a veil in the doorway, hiding the tower within granite clad walls. "Only Mages are permitted beyond this point," the officer said.

"Perhaps you can make an exception," said Tempest, pulling her mother's amethyst ring out for the man to see.

"Dear gods." He made a warding gesture over his heart. "This is impossible."

Tempest stowed away the necklace and made eye contact with the Mage. "I assure you, sir, it's possible. Now, I'd greatly appreciate it if you'd let us inside before someone else tries to kill us."

A look of hesitation crossed his face, but he obliged. "Follow me." He brushed aside the vine barricade and stepped through, holding the pathway open for Tempest and her gathering.

On the other side of the threshold, they came to a deep canyon that dipped far beneath the ledge of land they stood on. In its center, piercing the clouds above, was the Mage tower. Great bridges crossed the canyon depths and formed an elaborate system of pathways to it.

They crossed the main bridge, drawing curious eyes as they walked, but Tempest couldn't focus on the stares. Her eyes locked with awe upon the tower. It was much taller than she'd ever expected, and it pulsed with inexplicable energy.

The portcullis opened when they neared, revealing a beautiful haven within. With massive branching limbs, a floating tree stretched throughout the atrium. The leaves were made of blue flame, and water poured from its roots. Tempest recognized it from the book of sigils. This was the emblem of the guild. She reached out her hand and ran her fingers through the flowing water that cascaded to a dark, unknown abyss below.

"Magic," said the officer that had guided them, "is pulled predominantly from nature. Where the soul lacks in power, nature provides. Through it, we can control nearly everything. Though unfortunately, humanity has strayed quite far from its natural roots, so the connection has all but vanished. Only those heavily trained can tap into it." He flashed his ring in the fire's glow to highlight his proficiency. "Now, we can't control minds or anything of the likes, but perception can be manipulated." A smile curved his lip, and the mist from the waterfall spread to consume the air. Around them, reality seemed to alter.

Tempest stepped forward, and when she did, it was no longer stone beneath her feet but rather thick grass laced with flowers. Tall red trees towered over her in all directions, but in the base of one of them, an archway formed. Through it came Vitani. "Welcome to Galdramir," said the guild leader.

The mist dissipated at her arrival, and with it went the illusion of the forest. Tempest's voice caught in her throat as reality rushed back to her, so she resorted to a bow for greeting.

"Come with me," said Vitani, lifting Tempest's shoulders to an upright position. "We have much to discuss."

Tempest and the others followed Vitani to a secluded room within the tower. It wasn't until the door closed behind them that Vitani turned to face them. "There have been rumors of your revival," she said. "I didn't believe them until today."

The statement confused Tempest. She'd heard many folks who'd believed her to be dead, but none had spoken of revival. "I've come to request assistance," she said.

"And I brought you here to do the same," said Vitani. "So, how was it done?" Her attention shifted to Tegan. "How did you bring her back to life?"

Tegan's mouth fell open, but no comprehensible words managed to escape, so Tempest answered for her. "Vitani," she said. "I was never killed. I escaped."

The guild leader slumped against the wall. "Then you're of no use to me." She lifted her hand and waved towards the door. "Go. I want no part in your war."

"I think you do," said Clio.

Vitani looked up with a sharp gaze. "And who are you to make such assumptions?" she asked.

Clio swallowed the emotions that surfaced upon her face. "A mother without a child," she answered. "I recognize the look. How did you lose yours?"

A tear rolled down the side of Vitani's face, but the tension faded from her muscles. "Kaburem killed her for conspiring with rebels," she said. "I told her to stay away from it. I told her it wouldn't end well, but she had a pure heart. She couldn't stand by while others suffered, so they killed her, and now, they'll likely kill me."

"No one needs to know I've been here," said Tempest. "You can help us without putting yourself in danger."

"How?" asked Vitani.

"Connect us to the rebels your daughter consorted with," Tempest said. "We need Mage support."

Silence fell over the room as they awaited Vitani's response, and all Tempest could hear was the beating of her heart. "I'll send word to them," she said. "Where should I tell them to meet you?"

Tempest touched the emerald stone on her finger. "Firethorne," she said. "It's time to rally the dragons."

Vitani extended her hand. "Good luck, Dasha," she said. "I wish you good fortune."

"I wish the same for you," said Tempest, shaking the guild leader's hand.

32

*J*yles waited a short distance from the gates of Galdramir, his herbs strewn out over a table to trade. A woman stood on the consumer's end, fishing for coin in her pouch. The transaction was made as Tempest and the others approached. "Oh good," said Jyles. "You've returned." He hurried to collect his wares and stuffed them in a crate to be stored in the back of the wagon. "How fared the mission?"

"Things look favorable," said Tempest, climbing into the wagon with the others. In the corner sat the Kaburem soldier who'd attacked them earlier. "Has he given you any trouble?"

"He stirred a bit a short while ago, but another dose kept him quiet," said Jyles.

Tempest nodded. "Let's get him back to camp where he can be questioned."

"Right away, m'lady," said Jyles. He tied shut the wagon and jumped behind the reins. Before long, they were back in the confines of their camp.

Tempest assisted in carrying the unconscious soldier to a tanner's tent on the outskirts of the militia quarters. "See what you can get out of him once he wakes up," she said as they lay him on the ground. "I need to check on Neymar, but I'll return. No harm should come to the prisoner while I'm gone, understood?"

"Understood," said Clio, tying the prisoner to a post.

"Jyles, may I have a word?"

The Merchant stepped forward. "You may."

She motioned for him to follow, then stepped into the night air. When they were alone, Tempest voiced her concerns. "I fear the prisoner won't speak freely," she said. "Do you have anything in your stock that'll enhance coercion?"

"There are a few potions repugnant enough to make any man talk, but I've learned the easiest way to give a loose tongue is a little bit of this," he said, lifting a flask of whisky. "Give him enough and he'll tell you anything you want to hear."

"Good," said Tempest. "Get him drunk. I'll be back shortly."

Jyles lifted the flask as if to give a toast. "Now that, I can certainly do," he said, then he slipped back into the tent.

A short distance away, Tempest found her own quarters. Inside, Ava and Felix lay asleep on the ground. Neymar scurried around them. "It seems you wore them out," she said to the dragon, and she scooped Ava off the floor and carried her to the bed. Beside Ava, she placed Felix, then tucked them each beneath the furs. "You two would make fine Dragon Keepers," said Tempest, taking a seat on the edge of the bed.

She brushed a stray hair off Ava's face and took a deep breath. Looking down at the youthful pair, worries of the war surfaced within her heart. There were dark times that lay ahead. She'd been so focused on the task of building her forces that she hadn't truly thought about the cost until this moment.

In the long run, she hoped Ava and Felix's lives would be far easier if Tempest won this war, but until then, they would need to face things no child should have to. This fight would be a bloody one. From what she knew, Kaburem's force severely outnumbered her own, but loyalty was a fickle thing. Kaburem reigned with fear, while Tempest intended to rule with kindness. To which one people would gravitate, she figured only time would tell.

Tempest stood and plucked Neymar off the floor. "Best return before Jyles renders our guest invalid," said Tempest to the beast. He gave a chirp in response and coiled around her arm.

Upon arriving at the tanner's tent, Tempest found Jyles sitting at a newly set table with the man they'd captured. He'd woken now and held a conversation with Jyles that Tempest could not hear. When his eyes met Tempest's, he stood and bowed his head. "I must apologize for our previous interaction," he said. "My intentions were less than honorable, and for that, I am ashamed."

Jyles stood and gestured for Tempest to take his seat. "Will you be wanting a drink as well?" he asked.

"I will," said Tempest as she sat in the chair, and the prisoner followed her lead. "Now, I'm interested in hearing what exactly those intentions were. How did you know who I was?"

The prisoner took a sip of his drink, shackles clanging together with every movement. "Lazareth told us what you looked like," he admitted. "Though, he was wrong about the hair. Said it was red, not black. Anyway, there'd been a rumor passing through our camps about the soldiers from Mortem. Knights risen from their graves. When I saw you standing with them, I knew it must be true."

"You were correct in that judgement," said Tempest. "My name is Tempest. What is yours?"

"Morris," said the prisoner. "Pleasure to meet your acquaintance, but as much as I enjoy your company, I'd rather this not be prolonged. So, what is it you desire from me?"

"I think it obvious," said Tempest. "Don't you?" She poured another glass for Morris, then proceeded to answer his question. "I need information on Kaburem's forces."

Morris downed the liquid in his cup, then set the glass gently on the edge of the table. "I cannot, in the right, betray my brothers and sisters by telling you their secrets, but I can tell you about my homeland."

It wasn't entirely what Tempest wanted to hear, but she figured it'd suffice. Perhaps somewhere in that history there'd be something of use. "I'd like that," she said.

Morris reclined in his seat, gaze focused on some far off thought. "Kaburem was founded on an island years ago. According to legend, it's where society first developed. However, centuries ago, a volcano erupted, burying the land in ash. Only a few survived."

Tempest's breath caught. She knew this story. The guard at Firethorne had told her about it when she'd first arrived at the city. "The Midnight Dragon," she muttered.

"Ah," said Morris. "So you've heard of it." He poured himself another drink. "The lost city was not so lost after all. Those few survivors collected what they could and rebuilt the nation. They formed an empire. The architecture was made luxurious, large manors that look nothing like the crude, stone castles your people fancy. They built schools and taught us the ways of the world. They deemed magic to be heathenry and subdued those who used it."

This was useful, thought Tempest. Without magic, Kaburem gave the rebels the upper hand, if the Mages joined their cause, at least.

"As generations came and went, the savage lifestyle of the old societies faded to nothingness, leaving room for civility to bloom. Then one day, when I was a boy, a man washed up on our shores and spread mystical stories of a land called Alyria from which he'd been exiled. Our king found interest in these tales and brought the tide-born man into his circle as a political consultant. When the king died, he left the nation to this consultant, and thus the reign of Lazareth began."

Thoughts spun in Tempest's head as pieces to a puzzle she hadn't wished to solve fell into place. Her father had claimed to know Lazareth as a boy, and there was only one man she knew to have ever been exiled in his service.

"Forgive me, but you look unwell," said Morris. "Have I said something to disturb you?"

Tempest swallowed the remaining whiskey in her cup and dismissed his concerns with a wave of her hand. "No," she said. "How long ago did Lazareth arrive on your shores?"

Morris thought for a moment, then he gave his answer. "I'd say about seventeen years ago. I was only a child at the time." He filled Tempest's cup for her and continued his tale. "Lazareth taught us to hate your land. He said you were… uncivilized barbarians. While your lifestyle differs greatly from ours, I must say, you lot don't seem so bad."

From the corner of the tent came a laugh. "I wish I could say the same about your folk," said Jyles. "All you seem to do is murder."

"That was never our intent," said Morris. "We came here to teach you the ways of our society. We came peacefully, but we came at the wrong time."

"If what you say is true, peace was never in the agreement," said Tempest. "I've heard enough for the day. Thank you for your cooperation." She stood and departed without further conversation.

Wind howled through the air, pricking her skin with tiny ice crystals. Up above, a full moon loomed, staring at Tempest with a pale eye. She felt small under its glare.

Footsteps approached from behind her, and a gloved hand touched her shoulder. "Tempest," Clio said, "do you know something?"

Tempest stopped and shook her head. "No," she said. "It isn't possible." A tear rolled down her cheek, but she caught it with her thumb before the cold could freeze it.

"You can trust me," said Clio. "What happened?"

A tremor shot through Tempest's body, so she crossed her arms, trying to protect herself from the frigid air, but it was not the cold that distressed her. "Seventeen years ago, my father exiled his brother for attempting to assassinate me," said Tempest. "His body was never found. The time frame lines up. It could be him."

Clio froze, face twisting with shock, but with some thought, she composed herself. "It might not be. Go get some rest. We'll learn more tomorrow."

Tempest nodded and returned to her quarters. She constructed a bed at the edge of the tent, set Neymar beside it, and curled up beneath the thin blanket to sleep.

~~~

Through harsh terrains and bitter cold winds that carried the year's first snow, Tempest and her army drew nearer to the valley that stretched beneath the mountains of Firethorne. It'd been a quiet ride with only Morris and a gathering of the dead to keep her company. She wasn't ready to face the prisoner, and he honored the distance she wanted to keep.

Eventually, however, she knew she'd need to gather more information. Tempest swallowed her fears and cantered up to the prisoner's side. She dismounted her horse and walked it by the reins.

"I had no intention of upsetting you last night," said Morris.

Tempest turned to him and smiled. "You've done nothing wrong," she assured. "A piece of my history went missing a long time ago, and from your story, I think Lazareth may have had a part in it."

"Ah," said Morris. "Do you want to hear the rest?"

"I do," Tempest replied.

Morris took a deep breath and looked to the clouds. "In Kaburem, when a child comes of age, they are required to serve a year in the military. It is not like your nation where it's a choice. When it came my time to serve, I excelled and moved through the ranks with ease. About three years ago, they promoted me to the cavalry. They called us Dragoons. It was then that I met Lazareth for the first time."

"What was he like?" asked Tempest.

"He was like every other new king," said Morris. "He had bold ideas and boasted about them in a way that made everyone want to follow his lead. His first grand plan was to connect with the land he'd come from. He promised fortune and grandeur to anyone who joined him, so I followed. None of it was supposed to happen the way it did. No one was supposed to die."

"Perhaps not in the version they told you."

"If there is a different version, I'd gladly hear it," Morris said, so Tempest obliged.

"The first wave of your people came boarded on one of our ships that'd been sent out to find new land," said Tempest, recalling the details from her conversation with Prince. "They snuck into the castle to kill my father, but what they failed to foresee was that he was already dying. When my father met his death, they needed to make sure neither my mother nor I had claim to the throne, so they poisoned us."

"Oh," said Morris, fully engrossed in the tale.

"I got a warning, but my mother didn't." A lump formed in her throat with the memory. "I never got to say goodbye to them… not until Xudor took the immortal throne."

"That's your god of the dead, isn't it?" Morris asked. "Is that when you collected your knights?"

"It is," said Tempest.

"And what of the rest of your soldiers?" he asked. "You've got quite a strange array of them."

"Perhaps one day I'll tell you, but for now, I've said enough." She looked up the face of the mountain and found a moment of peace in her heart. "We're here." With a whistle, she summoned Neymar, and the beast spiraled down to join her.

From there on up, the road would be too perilous for the entirety of them to continue, so Tempest selected a small company of her most trusted to accompany her. The rest were left to set camp in the valley.

"How are we getting in this time?" asked Tegan as they wandered towards the path.

"I'm not putting all of you in my wagon," said Jyles.

A crumbled stone structure that peaked over the slope of a hill caught Tempest's attention "You won't need to," she said. "There's a mine in the area that empties out near The Claw. It was used as a holding cell for a game we played during training. I think there's an entrance down that way." She pointed towards the structure that'd captured her attention.

"Do you know how to navigate it?" Clio asked.

"No," Tempest admitted.

"Good thing I do," came a familiar voice from the brush.

A smile spread on Tempest's lips as Sagua stepped into view. "How did you know where to find us?" she asked.

"I saw your dragon flying through the clouds," Sagua said. "Once I got past the city walls, finding you was easy. Your army isn't exactly hidden."

"No, it's not," said Tempest. "So we can't remain long. Will you help us get inside?"

Sagua nodded. "I'll help you with far more than that," she said. "Come with me."

33

*A*ged, wooden posts upheld the integrity of the tunnel. They were a small enough company to pass through without disturbing it, but Tempest still worried. Dust drifted through the stone corridor, and the wooden beams groaned beneath the weight above them. But Sagua had assured their safety, and Tempest had no reason to doubt.

A breath of relief escaped her lungs when the exit came into view, however. The boards were stiff and reluctant to give in, but with enough pressure, the gateway opened. They emerged on the outskirts of The Claw, safely cloaked by the trees that covered the area.

"Welcome," said Sagua once the whole party had surfaced. "It's good to see you again."

Tempest brushed the dust from her clothes and smiled. "It's good to be back," she said.

With a nod of her head, Sagua addressed the others that'd accompanied the journey. "I see you've made some allies."

"I have," said Tempest, pointing first to the Necromancer. "This here is Tegan. She's been with me the longest."

Tegan outstretched her hand. "I'm the commanding officer of the Necromancer regiment and the dead." She bowed her head. "Pleasure to meet you."

Tempest gestured to the next two members of her party. "Cedric and Emil both work with rescued elephants," she said. "They were run from their sanctuary by Kaburem poachers, so we've offered them protection."

"At a cost, no doubt," said Sagua. "Tell me, are you prepared to pay it?"

Cedric nodded. "Not just a cost, but also a cause," he said. "We're prepared to face it."

"Good," said Sagua.

Stepping forward, Tempest introduced the next member. "This is Jyles," she said. "He's a Merchant who helped us in the Mage city."

Jyles bent at the hips and gave a grandiose bow. "Merchant by name, smuggler and apothecary by trade," he said.

"And this is Clio," said Tempest, introducing the final party member.

"Former military officer," Clio said. "I joined the rebels shortly after Kaburem usurped the crown.

Sagua greeted them each with courtesy. "I assume the rest are the knights of Mortem I've heard rumors about."

Tegan nodded. "We have ten per Necromancer in the force," she said. "Having already died, they're extremely resilient towards doing it again."

"As I see you've tested," said Sagua, touching the round bullet hole in the chest plate of one of the dead.

"We had a bit of a skirmish in Hekatia," said Jyles. "But the weapon was quickly subdued."

"Did the assailant give you any information?" Sagua asked.

Tempest shook her head. "Nothing of great importance."

"Ah," said Sagua, but Tempest could tell she'd sensed the lie. Eventually, she'd want to know the truth. "I'm sure you all are exhausted. You're welcome to stay the night in the officer barracks. We'll discuss further action in the morning."

The others followed Sagua to the barracks, but Tempest strayed from the group. She wanted, for a moment, to relive the memories of the past. It'd been nearly half a year since she'd finished training, but the time had seemed much shorter. Her feet navigated the woods with ease, and she soon found herself at her goal. The meadow was at peace this evening, and the trees swayed, barren branches tangling in wind dances.

She crouched beside the small pond and dipped her fingers in the ice cold water. Looking at the rivulets that scattered from her touch, she found her thoughts wandering to the boy who'd shared this place with her. It'd been some time since he'd reached her mind, but a sense of deep longing bubbled in her chest at the memory of him. She couldn't help but wonder if he was still here.

Her thoughts were soon interrupted by the crunching of approaching footsteps. "I thought I'd find you here," a friendly voice greeted from the brush. Despite the comfort of familiarity, there was still a twang of disappointment when Tempest realized the voice didn't belong to the one in her heart.

"Lyra," said Tempest as the girl stepped into view.

Lyra's dragon bounded into the field, chasing Neymar around. They played for a moment, snapping at each other and spitting small, harmless sparks.

"I came out here when I heard you'd returned. When you weren't in the barracks, I thought I'd check here. Cyrus used to come out here when times got tough... always sat by that little pond and watched the clouds."

A slight smile touched Tempest's lips as she looked up to the sky and saw a flock of birds drifting in the wind. There was a moment of silence before Tempest finally asked, "Is he still here?" Her voice cracked a bit, revealing more desperation than she intended.

"Sadly not," Lyra said with pity in her eyes. "A short while ago he was sent to Aquius to recruit from the northern sea islands."

Tempest gave no response, just sat by the pond, trailing her fingers through the sparkling waters. She'd write to him tonight, she decided. It'd been so long since she'd spoken to him.

"There's a room waiting for you in the barracks," said Lyra. "I can show you to it if you'd like."

"Lead the way," Tempest said, rising to her feet.

Together they walked with the moon to their backs, emerging from the trees that surrounded the barracks. The halls were familiar, but the energy differed. She had both fond and dreadful memories in this place, but the people she knew were mostly gone, and her sense of belonging was distant.

The room she'd been given was only a short walk from the main entrance. It contained only one bed and a desk in the far corner. She took a seat at the desk upon Lyra's departure and lit a small candle that sat on the edge. It'd been lit many times, and Tempest couldn't help but wonder who else had resided here. She was certain this candle could tell a wide assortment of stories.

In the drawer, Tempest found a blank sheet of parchment and a quill with a container of ink. She set the paper out and began.

Cyrus, she wrote.

I am reluctant to give out details of my location in the chance this lands in enemy possession, but I think you'll know it from the memories we share.

From what I hear, you're in Aquius now. I knew a man once who left for Aquius months ago. Perhaps you know of him. His name was Adrian. You'd do well to acquaint yourself with him. He has connections to some of the Naval sailors in the city. Perhaps one day, he'll sail you back to me.

Until we meet again,

She signed her name at the bottom of the page and folded it, stamping it with a wax seal. When morning came, she'd take it to the aviary to be delivered. For now, though, it was time to rest. Neymar curled into a small bed of straw in the rafters while Tempest settled into her own bed. Before long, they both fell asleep.

~~~

A soft rasp at the door drew her from her rest. The sun had yet to pass the horizon. Tempest threw on a cover and cracked open the door to see who was there.

Marius stood with an oil lamp in the threshold, shoulders hunched over with exhaustion. When the door opened, he straightened up and bowed his head. "Good morning," he greeted.

"Marius!" said Tempest. "You've returned!"

"Yes, m'lady," he said. "We came across a force of Mages upon our journey. They were led by a man named Avery. He's speaking with Sagua at the moment, though he's requested to meet with you next."

"That's good to hear. Were you successful with your mission?" she asked.

Marius hesitated before responding. "In some ways, yes," he said. "In others, not so much. I'll tell you about it soon. Sagua has called a meeting. She wants us all to gather in the guildhall."

"I'll join you there in a moment," said Tempest.

Marius parted, leaving Tempest to herself. She struck a fire in the hearth to warm the room, and threw on a newly crafted gown. With a pick, she combed out the tangles in her hair, then splashed some cool water from melted snow onto her face, shocking her senses into being more attuned. Neymar still lay in the rafters, sound asleep, so she left him there, not wanting to disturb him.

In the corridor, an array of sconces lit the way. She followed them to the guildhall where most of her party waited. They stood when she entered and only sat when she'd done so herself. Only a few moments passed before the rest joined them and took their seats. There was a new man amongst them who Tempest presumed to be Avery, and there was one missing as well. She'd have to remember to ask about it later.

"My apologies for the early summons, but it's important we begin," said Sagua.

Tempest sat upright and nodded. "How many rebels did we gather from the two missions?" she asked.

Avery was the first to answer. "Vitani's daughter paid a great service to us," he said. "When we got her call for help, the decision was made quickly. We've come with a force of two thousand."

"Are all of you Mages?" Tempest asked.

"Most of us are," said Avery. "Though, we have variety as well. They've all settled with your militia in the valley."

"And what of the west?" asked Tempest, turning her attention to Marius.

A glint of sorrow crossed his eyes, but he feigned a smile. "It took some effort, m'lady, but with the help of your letter, we managed to convince the rebels to join our cause. Seven thousand people followed us here, but only six thousand survived the journey."

Mutterings of shock and horror escaped the lips of all who were present, and Tempest swallowed the pain in her heart. "What happened?" she asked.

"It started with disease," said Marius. "When we arrived, we found many of the people ridden with illness. None of the Medics could pinpoint what it was. Theory is that it came from Kaburem. Hundreds had contracted it, and it spread with vicious speed." Marius paused, touching his thumb to the gemstone of a ring he wore on his little finger. It belonged to the girl who'd gone with him, Tempest realized. "Sarah caught the disease shortly after our arrival. She, along with many others, couldn't fight it off. She passed a few days later."

"Marius," said Tempest. "I'm so sorry."

"Don't be," Marius said. "It isn't your fault." He sat back in his chair and sighed. "With assistance, the illness was isolated and contained. Those unaffected followed us. They were eager to leave. All of us were. So eager that we overlooked something important. We were ambushed on the road by a host of Kaburem and Alyrian soldiers. They matched us in numbers but far exceeded us in strength. We shouldn't have made it out alive."

"Then why did you?" asked Clio. "They had a chance to cripple our forces. Why didn't they take it?"

"Pride is a sinister beast," said Sagua. "When a dragon hunts a herd of deer, it doesn't go for the weak and injured. Instead it goes for the strongest buck. I imagine Lazareth is doing the same. There's no glory killing an enemy in retreat, but if you kill the leader, the enemy crumbles, and the army is yours for the taking."

"Do you suppose they followed us, then?" asked Marius.

"Likely so," said Clio. "Odds are, they're in the valley with your new militia. You'll want to keep plans quiet from here on out."

Jyles lifted his hand, asking permission to speak. The room silenced to listen. "Pardon my interruption," he said. "But, we can't keep plans quiet if a plan doesn't exist. What is our next move?"

All eyes turned to Tempest, and she let out her breath, feeling the pressure heavy on her shoulders. "We've gained a lot, but we're still outnumbered," she said.

"Battles have been won with worse odds than this," said Sagua.

"Do we even know the odds?" asked Clio. "We've spent so much time preparing, but have any of us been watching the enemy? I haven't a clue where they stand."

"I've been tracking them," Sagua said, rising to her feet. She moved to the corner of the room and lifted a cloth cover off a table. A map of the continent was drawn on it, and bits of dragon bone scattered over its surface. "Most of the army is camped in the northern city, Aquius."

This detail caught Tempest's attention. According to Lyra, Cyrus was there too. The thought must have shown on her face because Sagua gave a nod.

"Cyrus has been keeping me informed of their position," she said. "They spend much of their time unloading weapons and stock from ships they send to their homeland. He estimates around twelve thousand to be in the city."

Tempest was proud of him but fearful all the same. If he got caught, they'd kill him. "What do we know of the west?" she asked. "Is there a larger force than the one Marius came across?"

Sagua shook her head, placing a handful of bones near the city of Sylvos. "This is the first I've heard of movement in the west," she said. "We didn't know they were there."

"Do you think they're still there?" Marius asked.

"They could be," said Sagua.

"But if you're right about their tactics, there won't be many left," Clio said. "Lazareth would have sent the majority of them here. We need to veer them off course."

A slight noise came from Marius' throat, and he scooted forward in his chair, deep in some thought. "On our way to Firethorne, we overheard talk of a celebration occurring in Alyria three weeks from now," he said. "It'll be the first anniversary of the new king's reign."

Those words struck like a bullet in Tempest's heart. She couldn't believe a year had already passed. The time had gone so quickly. "Lazareth doesn't know me," she said. "We could distract him with a battle in Alyria while our other forces take on the north and west. He'll assume it to be rash battle plans from a young commander."

"He wouldn't be wrong," said Clio. "It's too dangerous."

"But what if it isn't?" asked Sagua. "What if they hide as civilians within the crowd. They can strike from afar with a few warning shots to trigger chaos and pandemonium. As soon as it begins, they can retreat to a predetermined location. Therefore, no true battle ensues. Just terror."

"Could it work?" Tempest asked. "How many people would we need? It shouldn't be much. They'll be weak after Wynris. The illness is brutal in the city."

"It's struck our ranks as well. We'll send a couple hundred at most," said Clio. "Provided we have enough guns to arm them."

"I think I've got that covered," said Sagua. "We sent Tempest's gun to Vulcan while she was in training. With it, the Blacksmiths learned to replicate it. The newer designs are still in the works, but there's enough manufactured for most of your militia to carry one."

Tempest touched the edge of her gun. She'd not been told of its journey. "So we attack and flee," she said. "Do we hope they follow?"

Clio nodded. "Set the trap and lead them to it," she said. "We'll send a small force west to take an abandoned fort between Sylvos and Laurus. There, they'll make their presence known and draw out any remaining Kaburem fighters. It should be a simple task if what we predicted of their movements proves true."

"And to the north?" Tempest asked.

"To the north, we'll send our main force," said Clio. "We'll blockade the city and help Cyrus overthrow it. After you flee Alyria, get a fair distance away from the city and make a lot of noise. We'll meet you there to enclose the Kaburem forces and drive them to surrender."

Tempest thought on it for a moment, rolling endless outcomes through her head. It could all fail, but no war was won without taking that chance. "Let's do it," she decided. "Sagua, lead Jyles to the storeroom. We'll disguise the guns with produce and take them down to the camp. The rest of you remain. We have battles to plan."

Sagua and Jyles bowed their heads, but before they departed, Sagua turned to Tempest. "Add my name with a hundred Dragon Keepers to your soldier tally," she said. "I'm coming with you."

A smile touched Tempest's lips as she watched the guild leader vanish into the halls. "Let's start with Alyria," she said, moving to overlook the map.

34

One hundred militia soldiers had been selected to follow Tempest to the capital city. They infiltrated it slowly, sending small groups through the gates one day at a time. Tempest stood amongst the final group. There were three in total. She covered her face with the hood of her cloak and set Neymar upon her shoulders.

The day of the ceremony had arrived, and bells chimed through the air. Tempest and her men slipped into the city with the crowd of people that pressed through the gates. She glanced around, hoping to catch a glimpse of some familiar faces.

Down the street, her eyes found Clio with a small group of militia soldiers. They entered quietly into a building that stood at the edge of the square. Tempest nodded to her men, and they dispersed, taking their places for the attack. The goal was to spread thin so Kaburem would be unable to pinpoint their location, take the high ground and attack anonymously.

A whistle came from the shadows of an inn, and Felix stepped into view. "I'm ready, mum," he said with his chin held high.

Tempest handed Neymar to the boy and smiled. "Keep him safe, and stay far away from the fight," she said.

Felix took the dragon with care and slipped back into the inn. He'd been charged with the mission of seeking help if this ploy went awry.

Sheets of rain drenched Tempest's garb as she shuffled into the square for the ceremony. She stepped under an overhang that shaded the door to a shop from its pelting. A flood of people climbed an old staircase beside the shop, so she followed, winding up in the corner of a cramped room.

The windows had already been propped open in a futile attempt to hear the king's speech over the rain. With the amethyst ring visibly hanging around her neck, she easily parted a path to them. "I suggest you all return to your homes tonight," she announced, and Benjamin and Jensen entered the room, guns openly displayed. "We aren't here to hurt you, but I make no promises to what Kaburem will do."

This warning went to every room a rebel soldier occupied. A few of the people in Tempest's room heeded the advice, but others decided to stay, keeping their distance from the rebels. Whether they stayed for the king or to watch the king fall, Tempest didn't know, but she had other things to worry about right then.

Down below stood hundreds of Alyrian citizens who'd been crammed and stuffed into one area, all of them looked to an empty podium with a wall of armed Kaburem soldiers surrounding it. The murmur of the crowd went silent when the king emerged from the shadows of the temple, taking his place on the stand.

There was a moment of nothing, but to Tempest it felt an eternity. The only sounds were the pattering of rain on the roof and the shaky breaths that brushed through her lips, breaths carried on a cloud of steam from the cool winter air that bit at her skin. For some of her followers, these would be the last breaths they took, and Tempest suddenly wished it had never come to this.

"People of Alyria," said the king, voice echoing off the surrounding stone. "I come to you today with humble respect, for it is because of you that we may stand here today as a united front. However, it is my deepest sorrow to inform you that there are many amongst us tonight who wish to see us fall."

Tempest could feel her heart speed as gazes shifted to her and the rebels, but the true confusion unfolded far below. Individuals within the crowd dropped their cloaks and lifted guns into the air, barrels pointed towards the king. "Who are they?" Tempest asked.

"I don't know," said Jensen. "Is there another rebel group?"

Benjamin shook his head. "Look at the colorization of their guns," he said. "They're Kaburem."

A smile touched the lips of the king, and his guards circled around him. "I implore you, citizens of Alyria. Protect this great nation."

"Take aim," Tempest ordered, lifting her gun towards Lazareth.

Stones flew through the air from civilians who threw them at the fake rebels, struggling to disarm them. To Tempest's horror, the guns turned to the people, and the sound of gunfire erupted through the square.

With a deep rage burning in her heart, she pulled the trigger of her gun. It exploded with a thunderous crack and launched a bullet towards the king. It lodged itself in the back of one of his guards.

The guard fell to his knees, leaving an open path to the king. As Tempest reloaded, Benjamin took the shot. His bullet barely grazed the king's neck, but a message had been sent. Lazareth turned back for just a moment, and despite the distance, his eyes met with Tempest's. She readied her gun and pulled the trigger.

Before the bullet could land, the king was gone, pulled to safety by one of his guards. Tempest reloaded her gun and stuffed it back in its holster. "Get to ground level," she said. "Take out as many Kaburem soldiers as you can, but keep your focus on the civilians. Their safety comes first. When all are secure, call for retreat."

Benjamin and Jensen bowed their heads and departed, leaving Tempest alone with the group of citizens that remained. "What can we do to help?" asked a woman in the group.

Tempest sighed with relief. She was glad they'd understood the situation well enough to know she wasn't the enemy. "Come with me," she said. "We need to get the injured to a hospital."

They followed her without hesitation as she sprinted down the stairs and into the fray.

Body after body fell like moths to a flame, trampled and beaten by the stampede of people who were desperate to flee. The cries from those around her morphed into a blood-curdling howl as confusion turned to terror.

Tempest rushed to the aid of a man who limped from a wound to the knee. "No, my son... help my son," he pleaded, pointing to the young lad behind him.

The boy staggered by, dragging a dead woman by the arms. Tempest assumed her to be his mother. From a tear at the boy's neck, a stream of crimson bubbled.

She let the father go and ran to the boy, begging him to leave his mother and get out of range. "I'll get her to you, I promise, but you need to leave," she said, wrapping her arms around the boy to drag him out of harm's way. "I'm sorry." He kicked and flailed, cursing Tempest between every heart-broken sob. "Take this boy and his father to the rendezvous," she said, flagging down a fleeing militia soldier.

The soldier stopped and assessed the situation. "Yes, m'lady," he said, then pointed towards something behind Tempest. "You'll want to take a look at that."

Tempest turned back to the storm and found the temple in flames. Rain battled the sun-colored arcs in a dance fit for gods. She ran towards the temple, bracing herself for the intense heat within, but a strong arm stopped her path.

"There's no one inside," said Benjamin. "It's merely distraction. Keep your eyes on the battlefield."

Tempest looked to the windows with doubt, but she soon agreed. She glanced around, calculating her next move. Three Kaburem soldiers remained, and their rounds were likely dwindling. "Take position by the bakery in the far corner of the square," she said. "From there, you'll have a clean view of two Kaburem soldiers. I'll take down the last."

"Not alone, you won't," said Clio as she approached. She cocked her gun and nodded. "Let's go."

The Kaburem soldier stood in the center of the square, protected from retaliation by the clumps of people that stampeded past him, but the crowd was thinning, leaving gaps of time where the soldier was exposed. Tempest climbed a few of the temple stairs and took aim while Clio covered her back side.

From this position, Tempest could see a young girl charging the soldier with a fragment of stone. The soldier turned his gun to the child, and Tempest pulled her trigger, but she was too slow. The child collapsed alongside the soldier, clutching her ribs in pain.

"No," Tempest muttered. She grabbed Clio by the arm and sprinted to the child, dropping to her knees upon reaching her destination. After a quick inspection of the child's wounds, she looked to Clio for assistance. "Help me get her out of here."

"It's too late, Tempest," Clio said, and she drew her gun. "Stay with the girl. I'll cover you."

Tempest nodded and tore a shred of fabric from her gown to staunch the bleeding in the child's ribs. Rivers of blood soaked rainwater trickled through the divots of cobble beneath her.

The girl's ragged breaths convulsed with her body as it fought to keep her alive. "It's going to be okay," Tempest whispered to the child. The statement was a lie, and the child likely knew it, but she smiled anyway.

The bullet had struck the girl right between the ribs, and life slowly drained from her eyes. With one last halfhearted breath, she went still, that peaceful smile still written on her lips. It was the kind of smile only a child can give.

Blinded by tears and consumed by emotion, Tempest sat there in the rain, holding this poor girl who would never see the morning sun. Water soaked her hair and dripped through every crevice of her body, but Tempest could not feel the chill of it. She'd gone numb with sorrow.

Around her lay more corpses than she could count. A few of the rebel soldiers picked through them, searching for signs of life. There was none to be found in the bodies beside her. Tempest reached down, closed the child's eyes, and draped her black cloak over the girl's body. After giving a short prayer, she stood and turned to Clio, but the face she met was a different one.

"Patch... It wasn't us," she said, tears brimming in her eyes. "I promise it wasn't us. How could we do such a monstrous thing?"

"Shh, Tempest, I know," he assured, taking her hand in his. On his ringed finger rested the amber stone of the Medics. "We're doing everything we can." He glanced around at the wreckage of the square. "Do what you need, but we'll want you at the hospital when things settle down."

Tempest nodded and looked out over the square. There was much they'd need to take care of. The temple had burned, and the dead littered the streets.

Clio touched Tempest's shoulder. "Go with him," she said. "I'll take care of the dead. The living need you more."

"Thank you," said Tempest. "Meet me at the hospital when you're finished."

"I will," Clio promised.

Tempest followed Patch to the hospital. It wasn't a far walk, but in her condition, she drew many eyes. She wondered if any of the spectators recognized her. It'd been so long since she'd walked these streets.

"You changed your hair again," said Patch.

A chuckle arose from Tempest's chest. She found it odd that he'd noticed such a small thing in the chaos of their reunion, but even stranger was his ability to make her feel joy in the depths of so much despair. "Kaburem almost discovered me in Firethorne," she said, combing her fingers through the rain-soaked strands. "I dyed it black to confuse them, but I've run out of dye, and it's all nearly faded."

"I told you someone would recognize you," he said, nudging her playfully with his elbow. "You should have stayed with me. I've been invisible to society my whole life. Kaburem would have never found you."

"Perhaps that's true," said Tempest, thinking back to her time in Firethorne, thinking of Cyrus. Heat rose to her cheeks at the memory of their last parting. "But, despite the hardship, there was a lot of good too."

Patch stopped suddenly and turned to face her. "You fell for someone, didn't you?"

Tempest bit her lower lip, trying to contain the smile that threatened to give her away. "We have more important things to discuss right now," she said, hurrying her pace when the hospital door came into view.

"Indeed we do," said Patch.

When Tempest entered, she froze, overwhelmed for a moment by the insanity of the room. Medics bustled through the halls, tending to the many patients they had scattered through the building. Some were being treated on tables and shelves, others on the ground where space allowed. Beds were scarce, and the victim count was high.

Necromancers lurked in the corners, watching as the Medics worked and the Priests prayed, waiting for Odemus to claim one.

"Good gods, m'lady," said Jada from the corner of the room. "What happened to you? You've torn your gown to shreds."

"Come now, seamstress," said Patch, stepping into the hospital. "There are more important things to discuss." He gave a wink to Tempest then turned to face his work.

It amazed Tempest to watch him jump into action. He moved with unfaltering confidence. "Tempest!" he called from the bedside of a wounded man. "Come put pressure on this while I find a bandage."

The man groaned as her hand pressed down on the soaked cloth he had wrapped around the wound. She didn't want to hurt him, but she knew the pressure was needed.

"Thanks," Patch said, returning with a cleansed bandage. "Head up front. Liz has something for you."

Liz smiled when Tempest approached, and Felix stood up beside her with a bright smile plastered to his face. "I found help!" he said. "And I kept Neymar safe!" He held up the squirming creature for Tempest to see.

"Well done, Sir Felix," said Tempest. "Now, set him down, all right?"

"Yes, mum," Felix said, placing the dragon on the floor.

Neymar quickly took to the air and landed on Tempest's shoulders, nearly knocking her off her feet. He was much too big to do that anymore.

The young girl Liz tended giggled at the sight of the ecstatic beast. "This is Tempest," Liz told the girl. "She's going to help me with this, okay?"

The girl nodded, and Liz gave Tempest the rundown. "Her leg was broken in the stampede, and the bones need to be set back into place so they can heal properly," she said. "I need you to hold her hands so she has something to squeeze to relieve the pain." She then directed her attention back to the girl. "This is going to hurt, but I need you to be brave for me. Can you do that?"

Again, the girl nodded, gripping Tempest's arm tight in preparation. Her curious eyes gazed at the amethyst stone that hung at Tempest's neck. "You're going to talk to Tempest," said Liz. "On the count of three, I'm going to set the bones, got it?"

Once more the girl nodded, half distracted already by the question that boiled in her little head. "Are you a princess?" she asked, pointing to the ring with her free hand.

"I am, and one day, I'll be your queen," Tempest said as Liz counted one. "Are you a princess?"

The girl giggled and shook her head. "Only in play. Mother says I'm to be a Merchant, but I want to join the Army. Maybe then I can help save people from things like this."

On two, Liz set the bones and the girl cried in pain, digging her nails into Tempest's skin. When the girl relaxed and the pain subsided, Liz praised her for her courage.

"When we're finished here, perhaps you won't have to save any one. There will be no more darkness, no enemy," Tempest said, hoping in her heart that this child would not have to grow up in Kaburem's world of terror.

They continued into the late hours of the morning, helping the injured and assuring the victims that the rebels were not at fault. Some were convinced, but many still had reason to doubt. By the end, the tally of the dead had risen to sixty-three with hundreds more still clinging to life.

Outside, the sky still wept, washing away all evidence of the massacre. When the rains finally stopped, messengers were sent through the city to deliver sympathies from the king.

Tempest hid around the corner when one of the messengers entered the hospital. She stayed her breathing and closed her eyes, hoping the man hadn't seen her.

The room fell silent, filled only by the voice of the man who bore the letter.

"A message from the king," he said, then looked to the page in his hand. "There is an emptiness that comes with grief. A time when the tears stop falling and you have nothing left to give. Today we grieve as a nation for those lost in yesterday's attacks. Families lost a father, a mother, a brother, a sister, a son, or a daughter. Some even lost all.

"We keep them in our hearts and refuse to submit to these barbaric rebels. To fear them means they've won. We must stand together as one and fight for our right to live. I vow to end this rebellion once and for all. Help me bring them to justice."

35

*T*he sound of a child's laughter echoed through the hallway of the hospital. The night was young, and the sun had begun its descent, large clouds turning gold under its rays, but only a small amount of its light crept into the room Tempest stood in.

"Do you really think this will work?" asked Clio from the corner of the room.

Jada nodded, snagging a thin white cloth from her pile of material. "Hold this," she said, handing a corner of it to Tempest. With quick precision, she wrapped the cloth around Tempest's chest. "She's not the first woman I've disguised into a man."

The binding was tight, and it made breathing quite difficult. "Why would anyone voluntarily do this?" Tempest asked.

"Being a man in certain professions offers greater reward and less harassment," said Jada. "But truthfully, the majority of those who come to me simply feel more like themselves when they do it. I've helped men disguise themselves as women too." She stepped back and inspected her work, then, with another nod, she grabbed a wad of clothes and handed it to Tempest. "Tie up your hair and put these on. We'll meet you in the hall."

Tempest put on the shirt and trousers. A small mirror hung on the wall, and through it, her reflection watched. She hardly recognized the one staring back at her. Black streaked hair and mud caked skin. Perhaps that was a good thing. If she couldn't recognize herself, maybe Kaburem wouldn't either.

She twisted her hair atop her head and secured it with a pin. Over it, she put an old and tattered hat. When she was satisfied with the disguise, she stepped into the hall to meet the others.

"Ready?" asked Patch.

"Ready," said Tempest, taking Neymar from Clio's arms.

Clio pressed open the door and gestured to the path that lay ahead. "I've gotten word from a few of our men," she said. "They've begun to set up camp at the rendezvous. Meet them there. When everyone is accounted for, I'll join you."

Tempest paused and looked to Clio. "I'll see you soon," she said.

The door closed quickly behind them, and Patch took the lead, weaving through alleyways and shaded alcoves that kept the pair hidden from view.

He knew these streets better than anyone, thought Tempest, perhaps even better than her father had.

"There's a crowd gathered on the road just down that way," he said, pointing to a path that ran parallel to the city walls. "We'll have to cross it to get out. Keep your head low."

A soft chuckle arose from Tempest's chest. "Why is it," she said, looking at the scene before her, "that every time I'm with you, we end up fleeing the city?"

Patch stopped, a smile plastered to his lips. "I'll take none of the blame for that," he said. "You'd be fleeing the city whether I was with you or not."

"Right," said Tempest. "Suppose we ought to switch that." She peaked around the wall of the shop they hid behind, but her view was obstructed by a man who'd stepped upon a wooden box. "How many people do you see?"

"Looks to be about twelve," said Patch. "We should be able to blend well enough."

"Good," Tempest said, stepping out onto the path.

By the time they reached the man and his followers, a much larger group of people blocked the way through. They all stood with little space between them. Tempest wondered what had drawn them. This man must have been someone well esteemed.

"Fellow citizens of Alyria," he said, voice deep and calming. The way he spoke demanded a listening ear. "These are dangerous and confusing times, but I beg of you, for just one moment, lend me your attention. These rebels have proven to be the savages we feared they would become."

Tempest touched Patch's shoulder, halting his progression through the crowd. "I want to listen," she said.

Patch glanced around the street, then nodded. "Keep it short," he said.

Across the way, Tempest spotted a group of Kaburem soldiers patrolling the roads. She pulled her hat down to further conceal her face and wedged herself into the heart of the crowd where no one would pay her mind.

The man on the wooden box continued. "They attacked our city on a day of celebration and inflicted great devastation. There was no honor and no humanity in their tactics."

Murmurs of agreement rolled from the tongues of those throughout the crowd, their heads bobbing up and down as he spoke. It infuriated Tempest to see them accept his speech without any thought. She couldn't understand how all of them could so easily turn a blind eye to the changing world around them.

"How, though," said the man, "can we expect them to act humane when the majority of their army is made of the dead?"

His point stood strong in evidence, thought Tempest. There were many who would fear the dead, and Tempest counted on it. To face an army of corpses, no matter the odds, would require a bravery she wasn't certain Kaburem had.

"They are a ruthless people," said the man, "and we must stand up to them. It's time we stop mourning the loss of the good king and thank the gods for sending us a fighter to keep our nation safe from the horrors of rebellion."

A strong yet gentle hand grabbed Tempest by the arm. "I think it's best we leave now," he said, eyes flitting about.

The crowd was getting larger, and a wrathful energy buzzed through it. Tempest ducked her head and followed Patch to the gates. Where usually only two guards stood, there were four, each armed and ready. Patch approached them without fear. A change, Tempest noticed, from the last time they'd done this.

"Names and occupations?" asked one of the guards. He was a Kaburem man with the accent of their native land.

"My name's Patch, and this here is Janus. He's mute, so he won't be saying much. I'm a Medic. He's a Dragon Keeper." Neymar chirped in Tempest's arms, confirming the statement.

The Kaburem man inspected the pair, seemingly doubtful, but with a nod of his head, he accepted the tale. "What brought you to the city, and what is your cause for leaving?"

"We'd heard news of the upcoming celebration during our travels north, so we came. It's not often that us common folk get to see a king. As to our reason for leaving, well, you already know what happened. It's not safe here while the rebels are near. We're going home."

The man turned to his companions. "Let them through," he said.

They walked through the gates and proceeded without conversation until they broke the tree line. "So," Patch said once they'd made it a safe distance away. "Where is this rendezvous I keep hearing about?"

Tempest smiled, recalling their first journey out of Alyria. "The Wooden Serpent," she said.

~~~

Tents had already begun to be set up once they arrived. Only a quarter of her company was present. The rest were likely still within the city. Tempest pulled the hat from her head and ruffled her hair until it fell upon her shoulders.

"Tempest!" shouted the small voice of Felix from a wagon a short distance away. He alongside Benjamin, who sat flipping through the tattered pages of an old book, Jensen, who spoke of trade with Jyles, and a shackled Morris waited around a fire.

"Welcome back," said Benjamin, lifting a flask in greeting.

"I'm glad to see you all made it out all right," Tempest said.

"Same to you," said Benjamin. "There's a knight of Mortem waiting for you at a tent by the river."

"Oh? How long have they been here?"

"It arrived shortly after we did," Jensen said.

Patch stepped forward, jaw jutted forth in contemplation. "I'm sorry," he said, "I kept hearing that phrase from people in the city. What is a knight of Mortem?"

A slight smile touched Tempest's lips. Patch had, after all, given her the idea when they'd first met. "There was a boy, once," she said, "who taught me to fear the dead. He cowered away from Necromancers and was afraid they'd be capable of raising an army of corpses."

Amusement glittered in his eyes, but his features paled. "It was a childish fear," he said. "We can fear the dead all we want, but sooner or later, we'll all join them."

"But until then, dear boy, we'll be walking amongst them," said Jyles, taking a sip from his flask.

"Come with me," Tempest said. "I have much to tell you."

Together, they walked to the river, following its bends until they came to a tent. As expected, one of the knights waited on the back of a skeletal horse. In its hand was a parchment roll. "They're reanimated corpses," Tempest said. "The Necromancers control them through incantations. Though, with tasks as large as this, a stronger bond was likely necessary."

Patch circled the knight, studying the bits of flesh on the horse that remained unhindered by time. "Can they be killed?" he asked, backing away from the knight.

"All things with a life force can be killed," said Tempest. "If a knight's pilot dies, or if the connection is severed, the knight will return to its natural progression of decay." She bowed her head to the knight, and it returned the gesture.

Tempest unrolled the parchment and read the words on the page.

Tempest, the letters in the top left corner addressed.

I received your letter moments before a group of familiar faces arrived in this city. I hear from Sagua that you're moving now, no longer safe in the place that holds our memories. Maybe one day, we'll return there together, but until then, I have news. The city is ours. Sagua closed in on the perimeter, and I helped a few of them get inside the walls. We armed the people of the city and took Kaburem unaware, driving them from the docks. I imagine they'll be heading in your direction now, and thus, we shall likely follow. I'll see you soon.

At the bottom, it was signed, *Cyrus.*

Patch leaned forward, glancing at the page. "That's from them, isn't it?" he asked. "The one you love."

Tempest nodded. "He sent word from the north. They've overthrown Aquius."

The corner of Patch's lip twitched upward. "I could see it in your eyes. Will I get to meet him?"

"I hope so."

"Good," Patch said. "But, first and foremost, what happens next?"

Tempest looked towards the setting sun. "We sent troops west to take an abandoned fort that stands between Laurus and Sylvos. From what we know, Laurus is in shambles, and Sylvos has allied with Kaburem. One of my militia soldiers brought word of a Kaburem force in that area, but we believe it to have followed him to Firethorne. Our attack on Alyria was only meant to be a distraction. We were trying to redirect Kaburem's attention."

"So now they're coming here, leaving the west for the taking," said Patch, putting the story together.

"Exactly," said Tempest. "Word from them should arrive within the next few days. It'll give us time to collect ourselves before we continue on. What do you know of the villages north of Alyria?"

"Very little," he admitted. "There's only one that I know by name. It's called Tokun. I'm told it's where I was born."

There was a history in his words that Tempest hoped he'd tell one day. "Have you got any paper?" she asked.

Patch dug through his pockets and pulled out a crumpled page with old notes scrawled upon it. "I've only got this," he said, handing her the parchment and a small pencil.

On the back, Tempest wrote her reply.

There is a village named Tokun that stands like a bridge between us. It is there that we will meet again. I pray you recall our final game of Lumin. Perhaps it's time for a reenactment. You'll remember who I require to make it happen. Send them with utmost haste.

Tempest folded the paper and handed it to the knight. Before she could even mutter a word, the knight and the letter were riding north.

~~~

On the fourth evening, Clio arrived with the last group of rebels. "That's everyone," she said as Tempest walked to meet her.

"What's the status of the city?" Tempest asked.

"Recovering," said Clio. "Liz is still tending to many, but the numbers are lowering. More and more Kaburem soldiers filter into the city each day. The streets have gone quiet. They're preparing for battle."

"We'll build a memorial for the dead," said Tempest. "But we'll want to leave before long. I've been in touch with the north, and the next stage of the battle has already been set into motion."

"What of the west?" Clio asked.

Tempest lowered her head. "Nothing yet," she said. "We should prepare for the worst."

"There's still hope," said Clio. "The journey is long."

Tempest tried to believe her words, but with each passing hour, the dread relentlessly grew. She kept her mind occupied, helping with anything she could in the process of camp deconstruction. When time allowed, she collected large stones from the river bank, washed them in the stream, and piled them neatly into a mound at the center of the camp.

As the mound grew, other rebels began to join her. By the end, it stood almost as tall as she was. A crowd had gathered, intrigued by the stone structure she'd created. Tempest crouched down and scooped a handful of loose dirt into her palm. She spread the dirt over the top of the stones and muttered the words Sepora had told her when she'd visited the House of Xudor. "From dust we are born, and to dust we all return," she said. "Let this be memorial for all the souls lost in Alyria. Let this be a beacon of hope for better days to come."

A few of the others scattered dirt over the stones, whispering prayers to the pale moon that hung overhead. When all had paid their respects, they dispersed, each to their own paths, and Tempest to her tent. Neymar slept comfortably at the foot of her bed. She curled up beside him, careful not to disturb his rest, then closed her eyes to join him.

It was a short lived sleep. Tempest woke to the cries of the small beast beside her. When she opened her eyes, she saw him pacing by the tent entry. Something outside had disturbed him. "What is it?" she asked the beast, scooping him up and stepping into the night air. She had no knowledge of the time, but the sun showed no signs of rising just yet.

Once outside, Neymar squirmed, flailing and thrashing until she let him go. He flew to a tree branch and looked to the sky. Tempest followed his gaze and saw a great winged shadow cross before the stars. Whistles from the scouts spread sounds of warning throughout the camp.

"Is that a dragon?" Patch asked, emerging from the tent he'd been given to rest in.

"Coming from the west," said Tempest, hope budding in her heart, but in a single moment, that hope twisted to horror. The dragon's bone chilling cries tore through the air as the beast's wings failed to carry it. It plummeted to the ground, landing in the trees downstream of the river. "Gather a search party," she said. "Meet me at the bridge."

Patch nodded and got straight to his task while Tempest grabbed Neymar out of the tree. She placed him on her shoulders, then reached into her tent and grabbed a long coat for the journey.

At the bridge, she met with the gathering Patch had collected. There were six of them in total. Jensen and Benjamin stood together, each armed with a gun. Jyles leaned against the side of the bridge, flipping a dagger in his hand. Clio waited at the center with a rifle at the ready.

"Is this everyone?" Tempest asked.

"Yes," Patch said.

"Let's go." She pulled out her own gun and handed Patch her dagger. They followed the river downstream, searching for signs of the fallen beast. It wasn't long before they found it.

Its body was riddled with gashes and gunshot wounds that festered with infection. A saddle remained strapped to its back, but no rider accompanied it. "My gods," said Tempest as she approached the dying beast.

Neymar leapt from her shoulder and landed beside the larger beast, sniffing at the older dragon's wounds. The creature's breaths were few and labored. Only a short amount of time passed before it drew its last.

"What happened to it?" Patch asked.

Clio reached towards the saddle and unclipped a container that held a scroll. "This might tell us," she said, handing it to Tempest.

"Kaburem will have seen the dragon too," said Tempest. "We need to leave."

Tempest led the group back to the camp. When they arrived, Clio and the others parted to wake the remainder of the camp, leaving Tempest alone with the letter. She took a deep breath and sat beneath the moonlight to read. Her heart pounded as she fumbled clumsily with the seal that held the scroll of paper enclosed. When it fell loose, she held the writing in her hand for a moment, terrified to see what was inside.

A loose bit of parchment fell from the scroll, confirming her fears of a failed battle. The attachment had been stamped closed with the wax seal of the Army. Tempest set aside the main scroll and broke open the attachment.

Dasha,

It was addressed.

As the Army of the throne, it is our duty to fight for the person who sits it. We are not sworn to a single family and therefore cannot stand for you or your movement. Despite these conditions, I wished not to bring any more bloodshed than this war of yours has already caused, so when we came upon your rebels, I called a cease fire unless first fired upon. To my displeasure, the ceasefire did not hold. Those that so bravely manned the fort walls have been laid to rest, and their belongings have been sorted. Amongst the dead, I found this document with record of the events written by one of your troops. I've sent it to you as a sort of attempted condolence. It was certainly not a loss without a great fight.

It had been a small force sent to Sylvos, and they had been met with the Alyrian Army. Sagua's predictions of enemy movement had gone astray. By the sound of things, none of the soldiers would be returning. Tempest's face paled at the thought. Men, women, and beasts, all sent to an early demise for a war that was dying after only one week of fighting. Her revolution was failing.

With shaking hands, Tempest drew open the main scroll. It was a collection of journals documenting the nights leading up to the battle. Signed at the bottom corner of the page was the name, *Quinn*

This marks seventeen days on the road to Sylvos, it read. *They've sent us with a small collection of Mages and common folk, me being one of only four Dragon Keepers selected. The elephants and undead all went north to face the main force of Kaburem. By this point, I know the faces, if not the names as well, of most of the people in this company.*

Beside me now is a well-aged couple, wed for over thirty years. Artel is a sailor, Virginia a performer. Together they travel the world. They were once the most well-known performers in the river lands down south near Mirenor They call those years the golden days. At that time, I'm told they were living lavishly in the second most beautiful city in the realm. Virginia tells me it looks like an ancient sea temple with massive gardens that decorate each tier, spilling over the walls in utmost beauty. I love watching her talk of the city and their time touring the south. Her eyes light up, and a smile graces her lips that evokes one's greatest memories.

Many nights, I fly over the company with the other three Dragon Keepers, keeping watch over the people below, but my favorite hours are spent down with them. I love to hear their stories and adventures. Artel will often pull me aside to make some remark on the beauty of his wife, wanting to make sure I saw it too.

"Do you see, Quinn, how her black curls shimmer in the sunlight?" he'll say. Black curls that were now streaked with grey, but it made no difference to him. One time, he said, "Look! Look how stunning her silhouette is in the sunset," as she looked out over the mountains. Another time, he said, "Look at her smile... it gleams brighter than the moon itself. She is a portrait painted by the gods." Not a day goes by without these comments, but I don't tire of them. It gives me hope that a love so strong exists in this world. Perhaps, after this war, I will find it for myself.

Aside from Artel and Virginia, I have become quite well acquainted with a young boy named Alex. He's the age of my little brother and gives me a small taste of home, even when I'm so far away. It's getting late now, and I can hardly keep my eyes open. Until next time, dear pages.

The writing broke there, separated by a crooked line drawn between entries. Tempest lit an oil lamp and continued reading.

We arrived on the outskirts of our destination this morning. There's a smaller fortress a short distance away. A few Kaburem soldiers have made camp within it, but we plan to drive them out. Our company is in dire need of provisions. Food is scarce and hunters return empty handed. To take this base would give us enough food to finish the journey—The horn just sounded.

Then, on the next line:

The raid proved successful. The halls smell of cooking food, and spirits are high. There is music everywhere, and smiles touch the faces of those who haven't let one show since the start. I'm watching a young woman dance to the tune of a fiddle right now. There is so much love and hope in her heart. I can't help but share her joy. In it is the promise of tomorrow.

Tempest flipped the page; the pen strokes on this side were weakly pressed and shaky with effort.

We woke this morning with a company from the Alyrian Army at our door. They gave us a choice. Surrender the fort or die defending it. We never stood a chance. We were told not to fire first and for the longest time, no bullets flew. It was like two lions standing their ground, waiting for the other to attack. I don't know which side the first bullet came from, but after it launched, everything plummeted. My dragon was shot down in the fight. I fear I may have broken a few ribs in the fall. It hurts to breathe. I almost wish my body would just give up.

The pain in my heart is as bad as any physical injury I've endured. I sit now amongst friends who have already gone. Artel and Virginia in the far corner... young Alex stares with empty eyes at the stars. Beautiful stars that I look upon now, dancing up in the heavens for all eternity like the souls of my dear friends. Soon I will join them.

Tempest trembled as she folded the page back to its original state, tears welling in her eyes.

36

empest moved slowly, every step heavy with the weight upon her shoulders. She pressed her palm to the stones of the memorial and gave a prayer. She prayed to the gods of war, giving words to the patrons of victory and protection.

Patch stood a few paces behind her. He waited patiently as she finished her words. When she was done, she turned to meet him. She felt hollow, heart searching for an answer in a void that held none. She opened her mouth to speak, not sure what to say but hoping Patch would have an answer.

"Patch..." she began, voice as frail as she felt. "How am I supposed to win this?"

He took her hands in his and looked into her eyes as he responded. It was a gesture that seemed to be the only thing keeping her on her feet. "Not alone, for starters," he said. "Your army is different than theirs, so use it. Attack them like the wolf pack does the bear. Spread them thin so they can do nothing but defend. We know they're heading this way, likely towards Tokun. There's still hope in this, Tempest. Don't give up on us yet."

He held out her dagger, and she took it carefully in her hands, sheathing it in the leather pouch she'd tied to her leg. "Come with us," she said when the weapon was secure. "We need your skills on the field, and I need a friend."

"I can't," he said. "Liz... and the hospital."

"Will all be here when you return," said Tempest

He thought on it for a moment, and Tempest feared denial, but she could see the familiar spark of adventure in his eyes. "I'll come."

~~~

At a day's distance from Tokun, Tempest rode ahead with Patch and Jensen to inquire with the locals about Kaburem's position. A short detour from the trail led them to a small town with an elegant wooden sign at its gates that bore the name, Nuvia.

Once through the gates, they approached a local tavern. Its door swung open and closed in the wind. Tempest's stomach grumbled at the smell within, and the thought of fire warmed her inside. The days had been cold, and the nights bitter.

The trio tied their horses to a bannister outside and entered. There were travelers and locals alike scattered throughout the hall. Tempest sat at a long table that marked the center of the room. Across from her sat a woman who talked to a gathering of travelers about the war brewing throughout the realm.

"It's terrible what's happening," the woman muttered to another. "All this violence... My brother went and joined the rebellion. He wanted to make a difference. Stupid decision if you ask me. Better to remain unnoticed in times like these. That's how you survive."

Tempest leaned forward. "I don't mean to intrude," she said. "But you've sparked my curiosity. Have you heard anything about where the two sides are? My family is trying to stay as far from the bloodshed as possible."

The woman shook her head. "I've heard rumor that a group of rebels has taken a village not too far from here. I figure if I've heard that information, then Kaburem's got wind of it too. It'd be best for you to leave if avoiding blood is your goal."

Tempest thanked the woman and stood, looking around the room for her companions. Jensen caught her gaze from the far corner of the room and shook his head. Nothing useful from his end. At least the woman had given insight to one thing.

Patch and Jensen joined her at the door of the tavern. "What have you got?" asked Patch.

"We need to get to Tokun," said Tempest.

"Have the people you sent for arrived?"

"I believe they have."

Jensen opened the tavern door and gestured forward. "Then we best not waste time," he said.

They retrieved their horses and returned to the road, riding full speed towards Tokun. Just as Tempest had hoped, the Mages were camped outside the village. Avery approached the three of them on horseback, greeting Tempest with a bow of his head. "What would you have us do?" he asked.

Tempest dismounted and surveyed the lay of the land. "We need tunnels," she said. "As many as we can get."

~~~

Once the tunnels were drawn out for reference, Avery and his gathering of Mages set to work. The feat of it fascinated Tempest. The way the dirt caved in looked like a giant snake had carved the land. It reminded her of ancient legends from a time before the gods. They were legends that told of the creation of the world. She'd read them in the old and beaten scrolls hidden in the depths of the Alyrian library.

In their mythologies, giant creatures descended from the stars and trampled the ground into its shape. The snake had carved the rivers and canyons, the twin bears raised the forests with their claws, and the ox pushed the ground into mountains. Here, however, there was no snake involved, only magic.

The Mages had nearly finished by the time the rest of her company arrived in the village with Clio at the lead. Tethered to Clio's horse was a man Tempest didn't know. He walked with a limp and spat at Tempest's feet when she approached.

"Who's this?" Tempest asked.

"William," said Clio. "He's Kaburem native. We found him trying to free Morris late last night."

Tempest's brow raised with curiosity. "You managed to sneak into a camp one hundred strong without a soul seeing you, surely you knew what you were doing. How did you get caught?"

William bared his teeth like a beast and glared at the Kaburem prisoner behind him. "He's a bloody turncoat," he said.

"Morris turned him in," said Clio. "What will you have us do with him?"

Tempest thought a moment. She could use William to her advantage if she played this right. "Set up a tent for questioning," she said. "I'll meet with both prisoners momentarily." She turned then to a wagon just a short distance away and called to its owner. "Jyles," she said. "A word?"

Jyles leapt from the wagon front and jogged up to meet her. "What do you need?" he asked.

Tempest didn't answer until they were well away from listening ears. "I need you to do something for me," she said. "Something that may not make sense but is imperative to the success of this mission. Can you do it?"

"What is it?" He was cautious of her request, and rightfully so.

"I need you to smuggle William out of our camp."

His eyes widened at the request, and his lips parted to form a befuddled noise. "What for?"

"I need you to take him back to his own camp," she said. "Bring him only as close to it as you think safe." She paused then, and Jyles noticed.

"There's something you're hesitant to tell me," he said. "What is it you'll have me do upon delivery?"

A chill ran down Tempest's spine as she uttered the next directive. "Kill him quietly, and leave a letter in his hand. Kaburem will need to think the letter was worth dying for."

Jyles' lips pressed together in thought. "When will this occur?" he asked.

"Tonight," said Tempest.

He nodded. "I'll be waiting."

Tempest thanked him, then she left to write the letter Jyles would deliver. The daylight was fading, so she set up a table outside her tent and began to write beneath the setting sun.

Issakar, she addressed it, not daring to write the name of anyone living.

I write to you today in hopes that I may convince you to join my cause. While we took heavy rebel loss in the west, and severe civilian loss in the capital, our numbers remain strong. My army managed to overthrow Kaburem in Aquius, but I remain in a village called Tokun with those that followed me to Alyria. We stand merely a hundred strong in this village, but in total, my army commands fifteen thousand. If you join me, we can double that. I hope you will consider. We are on our way to Laurus to connect with further support, including yours if you're willing. It is there that we will unite all our forces. It is there that the true rebellion will begin.

She signed the bottom with the name she'd been born with and sealed it shut with the wax crown of the Royal House. The letter had been riddled with lies, but she hoped Kaburem would believe them. Her army would not be returning to the west as the paper said but would rather be uniting right here in the village of Tokun. If Kaburem thought the rebellion was vulnerable, they'd attack carelessly, allowing the rebels to gain the offensive hand.

Across the way, Tempest saw Jyles take a seat beneath a tree. She picked up the letter and walked to join him. "Are you ready?" she asked.

"Always am," he replied.

"I plan to talk to Morris first," she said, handing the letter over. "Once he's gone, I'll distract the guard. The rest is up to you."

He took the letter and stowed it in the inner pocket of his coat, so Tempest stood, brushed the dirt from her clothes, and approached the guard of the tent. He was a young militia soldier that'd come with Clio and Marius. "Right on in, m'lady," he said, lifting the tent flap for her entry.

Morris greeted her kindly, rising to his feet and bowing his head, but William remained in his seat, fury in his eyes.

"Clio says you're the one to thank for the capture of this new prisoner," said Tempest.

Morris nodded, taking a seat once Tempest had done so first. "I am," he admitted.

"What spawned the change of loyalty?"

There was no hesitation in his response. "Alyria," he said. "When we first spoke, you told me of Lazareth's horrible intentions. I didn't want to believe you at first, and I still find myself doubting, but in Alyria, your words proved true. Whether their mindset is old and long planned, or if it has recently developed, my people have become violent beyond compare. That is not the nation I sailed here to support."

Tempest shifted in her seat. "How do you know what happened in Alyria?" she asked. He'd stayed with those who couldn't fight at a camp outside the city during the battle.

"Even from beyond the walls, we could hear the screams," he said. "That boy, Felix, he told me what'd happened when he and the others met with us at the bridge. There's a raw truth that children tell, and his truth terrified me."

"It was something he ought never have witnessed," said Tempest. "I'm afraid I can't offer much in reward outside of small liberations. You'll be given permission to roam the camp, but the shackles will remain until you're further trusted."

"Understood," he said, bowing his head.

"You're dismissed," said Tempest, gesturing to the exit.

Morris stood and left, leaving her alone with William.

"You'll have no such loyalty changes from me," he said. "I knew what Lazareth was before I made this journey, and, dear child, he is powerful."

Tempest drew her knife and touched the blade of it to her skin. "You'll find," she said, "that albeit in different ways, so am I." She dragged the blade across her arm, then stowed away the weapon.

A look of confusion plastered itself upon William's face as Tempest slipped out of the tent and into the night air.

"Forgive me," she said to the guard whose face twisted with horror. "I can be a clumsy fool sometimes. Will you send for Patch to help me tend this?"

"Right away, m'lady," said the guard, and off he went.

Tempest staunched the bleeding with the cloth of her dress and looked up to meet eyes with Jyles. The smuggler took the hint and slipped quietly into the tent.

"What happened?" Patch asked when the guard brought him to her.

"Nothing serious," Tempest assured.

"Did he attack you?" asked the guard.

Tempest nodded. "He tried. But, I'm afraid I got to myself before he had the chance to."

The guard stepped into the tent and uttered a curse. "M'lady, he's escaped."

"What?" she asked, following the guard in.

A blade had sliced an opening into the fabric of the back wall. Tempest figured it'd been where Jyles and the prisoner made their exit.

"Should I gather a patrol?" asked the guard.

Tempest shook her head. "He's not worth our efforts. There's a battle coming, and we must prepare."

Patch wrapped Tempest's wound with a bandage and sat beside her. "That was a clever ruse," he said once the guard departed. "What's your goal?"

"To send Kaburem a message. Come with me. There's work to be done."

Patch followed her through the scattered tents as she collected a small group for the task at hand. She nodded her head, satisfied with the turn out. Ten soldiers stood together at the edge of the camp, each awaiting her directive.

"As you are all aware, there is a village nearby called Tokun," she said. "It will be host to one of the bloodiest battles in this war. Our goal tonight is to ensure none of that blood spills from innocents. All villagers are to be relocated to our camp. Leave no one behind."

They each took a horse from the stables and made their way to the village. Tokun was a small village with no walls to protect it. A group of patrolling citizens rode up to meet the new arrivals. "We'd heard rumors that you were coming," said a woman at the forefront of the group. "I'd hoped they weren't true."

"I wish I'd come to tell you they weren't," said Tempest. "But you all need to leave. We'll set up a camp for you near our current one. Stay there until you can no longer hear the sounds of battle."

"What of our homes?" the woman asked. "Are they to be ransacked?"

"Not by us."

The woman's lips pressed together, but she bowed her head. "Do what you need."

Tempest motioned her people forward, and each dispersed to various homes. Residents peered from their windows, watching their group as they rode through the streets. Tempest dismounted her horse and walked up to the nearest house. She lifted her fist to knock, but a young boy near fourteen years of age opened the door before she could. He stood proud, ready to protect his family.

"We aren't here to harm anyone," Tempest assured. "We've come as a warning. The war is coming and it'd be best if you all weren't here when it arrived. Gather whatever you can, and we'll take you to our camp to ride out the battle."

The boy looked wary but motioned to two others who stood hiding around the corner. Tempest watched as they moved. There was a girl the same age as the boy, and another who was younger. The house was scarce of material things, and the clothes they wore were ragged and old. The roof over their heads was all they seemed to have. No parental figure was present. Tempest helped them pack what little things they had, and the children followed her out.

By midnight, the village had been evacuated. Tempest's group of ten took care of the villagers, helping them set up tents and settle down before the battle to come. When finished, Tempest summoned the leaders of her gathering.

They each sat around a small wooden table, illuminated by nothing but the dim, flickering glow of candles. Tempest pulled out a paper and pen, then drew a crude representation of the land, using dotted lines to signify the locations of the tunnels. "The success of the upcoming battle relies entirely on deception," she said, pointing to the tunnels on the map. "I know from experience that Mages are well versed in the art of it."

A smirk touched Avery's lips. "You'd be correct."

"I'm counting on it," said Tempest. "I'd like to create a mirage within the village. It must resemble a full functioning, occupied village. Images of rebel soldiers and civilians should exist within the mist. Is that possible?"

"It is, but we'd need to be inside the village to do it."

"That's what the tunnels are for," said Tempest. "The rest of us will be waiting inside them. We'll conceal the entries and wait for Kaburem to let down their guard. When they've decided their victory is certain, we will attack from the shadows. As soon as the bullets start flying, break the mirage and join us in the tunnels." Tempest traced the path of the tunnels to the points at which each surfaced. "We'll hit them from every direction, forcing them into unsettled lands, then we'll disappear into the ground."

"And when we've exhausted the length of each tunnel?" Clio asked.

"We'll collapse them," said Tempest. "That way, no Kaburem soldier can follow us through. When every tunnel has fallen, hide in the brush and attack at random intervals. Pick at the edges and keep their forces confused. We'll want to push them towards the east. Sagua and the rest of the army will come through Tokun to help us. We'll reconvene when she does."

"The Alyrian Army that caught us unaware will be heading this way, don't you think?" asked Clio.

Tempest shook her head. "I wouldn't anticipate them coming any time soon," she said. "I provided them with false intelligence that points to an impending battle in Laurus. They'll keep the Army there for protection until they realize the falsity of the claims." She paused a moment, looking to the faces that surrounded her. "However, I can't assume the intelligence will ever reach its targeted audience. We'll keep eyes to the west and prepare for battle on two fronts."

The tent flap opened, and Jyles stepped through the entry. He took off his hat and smiled. "Message delivered and received," he said. "It caused quite a stir. We should expect them by morning, I think. Thus were the final words of our messenger. He claimed they'd have us trapped and surrounded like a flock of sheep, and I have no cause to deny it."

"Well done, Jyles," she said. "All of you, get some rest. We'll meet again before the sun rises. I'll divide our force into designated tunnels. Each of you will lead your own divisions."

No other words were said. The weight of coming battle hung heavy in the air. The others stood and left, each going their own way, but when Tempest turned back to the table, she found Patch still sitting.

"You'll be up a while longer, I imagine," he said

"Likely so." She took a seat beside him.

"Do you mind if I keep you company?"

"I'd prefer it," she said, rubbing her temples with the tips of her fingers.

Patch chuckled. "Crown getting heavy?" he asked.

"It always will be."

"You know," said Patch. "When I was a boy, I was appointed King of a mischief of rats."

"Is that so?"

"I'd never lie to you," he said. "I gave these rats discarded treasures and fed them when I could. As long as you do that much, you'll at least be a decent queen."

"I haven't got any treasures," said Tempest, "nor have I got much food, and I certainly don't have a kingdom to make any of this needed."

"Well," said Patch. "I, Lord Patch, King of the Rats, do declare we change that." He grabbed the map from the center of the table and flipped it over, snatching the quill from its jar of ink. "How many soldiers have you got here?"

"About sixteen hundred," said Tempest. "Most of them are Mages, with the exception of those I took to Alyria. We'll only want about fifty of them inside the village for the mirage, some to create the image, some to make noise. Kaburem needs to believe we're all inside. As far as they know, there's only a hundred of us here."

"That leaves over fifteen hundred to your disposal in the tunnels, and only six commanders to lead them."

"We'll need to raise that number," said Tempest. "There are thirty tunnels that need commanded. I'll have Avery and Clio appoint ten each. The rest I'll gather myself. There are many who proved their worth in Alyria."

"Thirty commanders, then," said Patch, jotting the numbers down on the paper. "That's about fifty soldiers per tunnel. You'll be ready."

Tempest looked to the paper and smiled. "Patch," she said. "I need to tell you something."

"What's that?" he asked.

The thought had first come to her in Mortem, and it'd crossed her mind a multitude of times since then. She looked up to meet his eyes. "If I should fall in this war, I need you to take my place. I need you to lead these people to freedom."

He shook his head. "Fear not, princess," he said, placing his hand on hers. "You'll not be dying if I have any say in the matter. Our promises still stand. You're not allowed to die."

37

old wind howled through the trees, carrying with it the sounds of the decoy village. Tempest crawled through the brush, giving one last glance to the lodges. The mirage had been set an hour prior. False characters patrolled the village in rebel garb while false residents went about their day. Looking at it, Tempest could almost believe it was real.

In the distance, she heard a war drum beat like the heart of an approaching beast. "They're coming," she whispered to a young lad beside her. "Return to the tunnel and sound the alarm. I'll join you in a moment."

"Yes, m'lady," said the soldier, then he turned and slipped behind the pile of greenery that hid the entrance to the tunnel.

A short time after, a horn bellowed through the air. Tempest watched as the false soldiers took post in defensive positions, and the false villagers retired to their homes. She knew she ought to get under cover soon, but she wanted to see their numbers first. Twelve thousand had been driven from Aquius, and more had likely followed from Alyria. There could be ten Kaburem soldiers for every one of hers. She hoped Sagua would arrive sooner than later to bring balance to those odds.

Through the ground beneath her, she heard the rumble of thousands of marching footsteps. She inched forward, pulling herself to the crest of a small mound. From there she could see most of the village and the trees that surrounded it.

The branches swayed and danced in the wind, black and crimson shapes shifting through them. The enemy emerged from the tree line in a silent mass, surrounding the entirety of the village. A horseman with a feathered tricorne on his head rode forth, stepping just barely into Tempest's view. He had his back turned to her, but she could still hear his voice. It was loud and commanding.

"Ready arms!" he said, and his men fell into formation, aiming their guns towards the village. "Your army is a day behind us, Dasha. You cannot hope to win this."

Twigs snapped beneath the heavy footsteps of approaching Kaburem soldiers who were taking their positions. Tempest crawled back to the tunnel entry and slipped inside to confront the men and women in her division. There were many faces before her. Some were worn with age, others young and bold. She wished she'd known them better.

At the forefront of the group, a Mage opened their palm, conjuring a small orb of blue light. Tempest hadn't seen one since her days playing Lumin. It warmed her heart to remember the thrill of the games, but this was not a game anymore.

"Take positions," she said. "They're here."

One by one, her soldiers took leave of the tunnel and took their places within the brush. When all had left, Tempest followed, submerging herself in a patch of tallgrass behind the Kaburem force. She cocked her weapon and aimed it to the back of a Kaburem soldier. "On my call," she whispered, and the others nodded.

"I ask you once more," came the voice of the Kaburem commander. "Surrender yourself before there's more blood on your hands. We have you surrounded."

Atop the village watch tower, a great bell began to toll, and a black flag lifted for all to see.

"So be it," said the commander, and he returned to his ranks.

"Fire," said Tempest, pulling her trigger.

Bullets tore through the backs of the Kaburem ranks, felling many with a single hit. It was a horrible spectacle, but there was no time to see their reactions. Tempest jumped to her feet and sprinted with her division back to the tunnel. Their footsteps beat at the ground like thunder, and the dirt walls around them shook to its fury.

At the rear of her division, the Mages collapsed the land, closing the tunnel as they ran. There was no turning back now. Tempest sped her pace, leading the charge towards the next surface point.

Dust rained from above as Kaburem scattered their ranks, and gunshots sounded through the air. When they stopped to reload, Tempest led her division out of the tunnel once more. They surfaced on the south side of the village this time, hidden by thick, unkempt brush.

"Ready arms!" called the Kaburem commander.

Their guns aimed in all directions, leaving their ranks vulnerable. Tempest lifted her hand to hold her division's next wave. They remained low, shielded by tree trunks and foliage.

From the north, two of the rebel groups made their attack, drawing Kaburem's focus back to one side. Tempest waited until the gunfire faded before she gave the command.

"Fire," she said when Kaburem stopped to reload.

They struck again, catching Kaburem unprepared. Wails of the injured joined the chorus of gunfire, and Tempest and her division returned to the tunnel. They stormed towards the final surface point where they joined the rest of the divisions on the western flank.

Tempest was the first to surface, but the others followed close behind. On either side, she watched the other divisions flood from their tunnels. They moved like shadows through the woods, spreading wide to press the Kaburem force to the east.

"When the shooting begins, collapse the rest of the tunnels," Tempest said to the Mages beside her. "Take to the brush and pick at their sides. Whatever methods necessary, force their retreat."

They each nodded and moved to spread the word. When all were positioned, Tempest prepared her weapon, signaling the others to do the same.

"Fire at will," she said.

Gunshots rang through the air, and her company charged through the woods. Tempest whipped through the trees, attempting to lodge a bullet in any Kaburem soldier she encountered. She felt like the hawk who hunted a flock of small birds, removing the isolated strays on the edge.

The Kaburem force pressed inward to the heart of Tokun, but there was no protection to be found. Tempest watched as a group of Mages cracked the ground beneath the enemy soldiers. The Kaburem men scattered, a look of horror on their faces. She wondered if they'd ever seen magic used in such a way.

With a quick reload, Tempest fired again, this time aiming at the commander. The bullet whizzed through the feather on his hat, and he looked about with frantic eyes, trying to pinpoint the location of the rebels. After a moment, he shouted the word Tempest hoped to hear.

"Retreat!" he called, and the war drum sounded it off.

"Stay on them!" Tempest said to the rebels around her, and they obeyed, chasing Kaburem out of the village and into the woods. She ran beside them, poking and prodding the outskirts of the Kaburem force whenever opportunity allowed. After nearly an hour of doing so, she reached into her pouch of rounds and found it nearly empty. The sun had begun to set, but Kaburem still ran.

"Hold your fire!" she shouted to the rebels when they'd reached the top of a hill.

The sound of gunfire faded to silence in a matter of minutes, and the rebels halted their pursuit while the Kaburem soldiers sprinted down the hill and leapt into a stream that crossed its valley.

Sweat poured from Tempest's skin, and her palms were caked in mud. Behind her, soft footsteps approached, and a hand reached out to touch her shoulder.

"We should rest here," said Clio. "We can keep an eye on Kabrem while we gather our strength. They'll likely set their own camp on the other side of that stream."

"Agreed," said Tempest. "Will you send for the camp followers. We'll need tents up by nightfall."

"I will," said Clio. "What of Tokun's residents?"

Tempest wiped her brow with the sleeve of her coat. "Tell them the battle is finished," she said. "They may return to their homes."

Clio nodded and set off on the journey back to Tokun. As she vanished behind thick tree growth, Tempest's other commanders drew near. None seemed to have taken much damage, but they all looked as exhausted as she felt.

"We'll rest soon," she said to each of them. "But first, we'll need to search the woods. Gather the injured, the dead, and the valuables. Bring it all here. Any Kaburem injured are to be treated with civility."

Her commanders divvied up the land that needed covered, then relayed the order to their men. "Patch," Tempest called before he strayed too far.

He turned to meet her. "Yes?" he asked.

"Have you got any material for healing?"

"Only a small surgeon's pack," he said. "There's more with our things back at camp."

"It'll be arriving soon," said Tempest. "Gather whoever you need and set up a blood tent."

Patch left to begin his task, and Tempest turned to the remaining rebels. "Follow me," she said. Together, they walked through the woods. The trees had changed in the light of the sunset, standing now with outstretched shadows in a dim, golden glow. Tempest kept her eyes to the ground, searching for signs of the battle.

The first sign came from behind a tree where a soft voice muttered unrecognizable phrases. Tempest moved to inspect and found a young Kaburem man propped against the tree's trunk. He held his hand to his stomach where a bullet had pierced through him, but he couldn't seem to slow the bleeding.

"Take him to Patch," Tempest said to two of her men, who then lifted him up and carried him towards the hill.

At the base of the tree, Tempest found the Kaburem man's weapon and an abandoned sack of things. The gun was one of the longer versions, and it had a sharp blade attached to its barrel. She passed the weapon to one of the Mages then pulled open the strings that held the sack closed.

Inside was a pouch of bullets and powder packets, some uneaten rations, a few stray coins from his homeland, and a letter from a woman named Annabelle who appeared to be his wife.

Tempest draped the strap over her shoulder and continued her search through the woods. She found an assortment of things on the way. Jewelry, blades, and corpses amongst them.

When she'd cleared a portion of the land, she returned to the hill. A pile of spoils gathered from the dead had begun to form at its center. To its left, another pile formed, this one made of fallen rebels. Five of her men had been killed in this battle. It was nothing compared to the Kaburem casualties found throughout the woods, but it was five more than Tempest hoped.

She walked over to the corpses and studied each of their faces. Three of them had been members of her militia who'd come from the southern villages. The other two were Mages who'd followed Avery to her services.

Tempest said a short prayer over each, then turned to seek the blood tent. She found it a short distance away, though as of yet, it lacked any semblance of a tent. Patch had assembled a small gang of Medics and steady handed regulars to heal as many as they could. The injured lay on stone pallets pulled from the ground by the Mages. Some of the healers stayed only with the rebels, reluctant to help Kaburem, but Patch jumped between the injured with no thoughts of enemy or friend. He set a good example, thought Tempest.

"Has Clio returned with the others yet?" Patch asked between patients. "I need medicines from Jyles' wagon."

"I haven't seen her yet," said Tempest. "I'll check when I'm finished here. Have you any idea where I can find a man with a bullet in his stomach?"

Patch pointed to a pallet in the corner of their setup. "That'd be him," he said. "But the bullet's been removed."

Tempest moved to stand beside the man she'd found earlier, leaving Patch to his work. The man was awake, but he looked weak. She wasn't certain he'd survive the night. He peered at her through faded eyes, and his hands trembled when he reached towards the sack she held.

She pulled the rounds from his collection and returned the rest to his keeping. She wanted to ask him about the woman in the letter but figured he'd want to rest, and she had other things to take care of before the night fell.

Campfires were set along the hill, and when the camp followers arrived, tents were erected around them. Tempest found Felix and Ava in one of the wagons, feeding Neymar a strip of raw meat. The dragon chirped when she approached, but his focus remained on the food.

"Good evening, mum," said Felix. "Did you win the battle?"

Tempest nodded. "We won this one, but there are many more to come," she said.

"Will I be able to fight in the next one?" he asked.

"No, Sir Felix," said Tempest. "I need you to guard Neymar until the other dragons arrive."

"After that, then?"

"I'll think on it," Tempest promised, though she hoped Felix would forget about it by then.

A smile painted his lips with joy. "They'll be here soon," he said. "We saw them flying through the clouds on our way here."

"Is that so?" Tempest asked, and the boy nodded. "Help your mother set up your tent. I'll take Neymar to greet them when they get here."

Felix scooted out of the wagon and helped Ava behind him. The two scurried off to find their parents, leaving Tempest with Neymar. She scooped the dragon into her arms and walked to the edge of their camp. Up above was a canopy of stars, glittering beneath the moon in elegant glory. Down below, like stars of their own, fires from both the rebels and Kaburem burned.

She lost herself in the spectacle of it all. Sparkling lights in a sea of darkness, some shining in the abyss, some illuminating the tasks of nightly lives. A man's voice interrupted its tranquility. Avery, she realized upon turning to meet him.

"They're here," he said.

38

A t the forefront of the army, Tegan and Marius rode side by side. Up above, in the swarm of dragons, Tempest spotted Sagua on the back of Zauryn. The guild leader flew down to meet her, landing only a short distance away. Tree branches bent beneath the breeze the beast created as it neared.

"Welcome back," said Tempest. She was happy to see each of them, but she couldn't refrain from scanning the faces behind them for Cyrus. He seemed not to be there. "I'm sure you're all exhausted after your journey. Get some food, and rest a moment. We'll meet in two hours to assess our next move."

Marius sped his pace, rejoining his friends at Clio's side. The others dispersed, seeking open land to set up their tents, but Sagua remained. She tapped Zauryn's leg, and the beast took flight, returning to its com-panions in the sky.

From Tempest's shoulders, Neymar watched the sky with wide eyes. He pressed his talons into her skin and wriggled with excitement. "Go on," Tempest said to the beast, and Neymar leapt into the air, joining the dragons in the clouds.

Sagua smiled as she watched the young dragon ascend. "I've brought something for you," she said when Neymar vanished into the twisting flock of scales. "It's a letter from Cyrus."

"A letter?" Tempest asked, saddened by this news. She'd hoped to be reunited with him once Sagua returned from the north.

"Yes," she said, pulling out the folded parchment. "On the day we planned to leave, he came upon a man named Adrian. He told me it was very important that he stayed to talk to this man, and he said you'd understand."

Tempest plucked the letter from Sagua's fingers and inspected the writing on its front. The lines were fluid and beautiful like his voice, and they curved elegantly into the shape of her name. "Thank you," she said.

Sagua bowed her head and continued forward, leaving Tempest alone with the words in her palm. She held them with care and carried them to a cook fire burning in the center of the camp.

There were others around the fire too. Patch sat on a stone, warming his hands by the flames, and Benjamin sat upon a log stool, reciting an old legend to a gathering of children from various rebel families.

The tale was one of a Dragon Hunter who strayed into a cave, searching for a renowned beast, and discovered Zalder, the god of fire, instead. Zalder had heard of the hunter's lifelong achievements and lamented over the creatures this man had slain, so he turned the hunter into the creature the man had spent his whole life killing. Great leathery wings stretched from his back, and his skin turned to scales. He grew in size until even the god looked small.

One day, years after the hunter had gone missing, his sister came searching for the legendary beast. She believed it had killed her brother. "Perhaps it had," said Benjamin to the children. "For there was no more humanity left within this beast."

Tempest took a seat beside Patch, and she pulled Cyrus' letter from the envelope that contained it, tuning out the tale of the dragon and the huntress.

Tempest, it addressed.

I regret that I'm unable to give these words to you in person, but there are things in the works now that I must finish. I know this letter is being delivered by safe hands, so I'll speak freely. You'll recall the man you suggested I meet; the one named Adrian. I ran into him at a tavern this morning, and we got to talking about the war. He's spent his time in the city acquainting himself with a group of Naval captains who have secured ships for our cause. We intend to dispatch them in two days' time. I will remain with them until it's done. When we near the coast, I'll send my dragon to signal our arrival. Wait for me, Tempest. We'll be together soon.

"Good news?" Patch asked, glancing to the words on the page.

"Very much so," said Tempest. "I'll tell you what it is at the meeting."

"Good," said Patch. "That gives us time to hear the end of Benjamin's tale." He lifted his cup in toast to the storyteller, then took a drink in his honor.

Tempest reached into her bag and pulled out the old, well-traveled notebook. She thumbed through it and placed Cyrus' letter between the pages that contained their memory of the Nyoka. When the letter was secure within the binding, she turned to an empty page and began to draw the scene before her. Benjamin sat tall, reciting a great battle between dragon and huntress to the children all around him. In the end, the dragon was slain, and in its dying moments, it transformed back into the man it once was, and the huntress realized her terrible mistake.

When the story was through, the children stood, eager to play. They started up a game that resembled the story they'd heard, but it was a game much older than Benjamin's tale. One child transformed into a dragon and chased the others around the fire. Each time he captured a player, the victim turned into a dragon too. It would continue until only one human remained.

Tempest returned her gaze to her pages, flipping through all the memories. There'd been so many throughout the year. Before she could linger on any one in particular, smooth hands pulled the book from her grasp. She looked up, eyes meeting with the pale green gaze of her friend.

"That's enough of this old thing," Patch said, scanning the pages inside. His lips curved into a slight smile, then he closed the notebook and set it aside. "Come on, get your head out of the book and live a little." He grabbed Tempest by the arm and pulled her to her feet. She groaned but put up no resistance.

They didn't go far, just around the fire to where the group of children played. Tempest glanced back at her notebook, then turned her focus to the children. One of the older ones ran about, flapping his arms as if they were great wings while the others ran from him.

Patch stopped the first dragon and whispered something into his ear. A broad smile painted the child's lips, and his direction changed, aiming now at Tempest. Her eyes widened as she spun on her heels and began to run.

The child was quick and caught up to her with ease. With the tap of a hand, Tempest was decreed a dragon. She wadded the cloth from her coat into her hands and spread it out like the thin membrane of a dragon's wings. The remaining children screeched and ran, but Patch stood still, laughing. He likely thought himself immune to the sudden dragon infestation, but Tempest was determined to prove him wrong.

He fled from her approach, but it was too late. Tempest reached out her hand and grazed Patch's back with her fingers, converting him into a dragon. The children giggled and screamed as they scurried about, barely avoiding capture. In the end, only one remained. She was small and quick, with a burning determination in her eyes. Tempest scooped her up in her arms and lifted her above the rest, proclaiming her the champion. The child flashed her teeth with a wild grin that grew contagious on the faces of the others.

Out of the corner of her eye, Tempest caught Marius approaching with two drinks in hand. She set the child down and stepped forward to greet him. He handed one of the drinks to Tempest and bowed his head to Patch.

"The rest of us have gathered at a fire just down that way," said Marius, pointing to a dim glow in the trees. "Would you prefer we meet you here, or will you join us?"

"I'll come with you," Tempest said, then she collected her things. "Patch, Benjamin, come on. There are plans to be made."

The two nodded and fell in behind her. The next fire was only a short distance away, and around it sat those she trusted most. They all stood when she arrived, silencing any conversation that may have been occurring.

"We shouldn't have this discussion here," said Tempest. "My tent has been prepared for the meeting. Is everyone ready?"

"Always," Clio said. "Lead the way."

"Follow me." Tempest turned on her heels and guided the others to her tent. Ivy and Callum were set to guard the entrance, and the rest stood around the table that'd been placed at the center of the room.

When all had taken their seats, Tempest began. "I come to you all tonight with news I had not anticipated receiving," she said. "My contacts in Aquius have secured a fleet of ships for our cause."

A murmur arose from the lips of all who were present as the implication of the statement set in. "This changes everything," said Marius.

"Not yet, it doesn't," Clio said. "We'd have to push Kaburem closer to the coast for it to make a difference."

"We're not far from the coast as is," said Tempest. "A few more attacks could push them the rest of the way."

Clio nodded. "We should expect retaliation. We've lost our surprise element."

"Not if we attack tonight," said Jensen. "They'll be unsuspecting of another hit so soon after the last."

Tempest leaned forward, intrigued by his idea. "What would you suggest we do to them?" she asked. "We don't have time to gather many men."

"Well," said Jensen. "We have the Dragon Keepers now. Let's smoke them out like rabbits."

"The wind is harsh, and the forest is dry," said Sagua. "The fire would spread rapidly. You won't be wanting to use more than ten dragons. Anything more will result in a flame we cannot control, even with help from the Mages."

"Ten dragons, then," said Tempest, "and as many Mages as we can get. What next?"

"We gather our strength for a third wave," said Clio. "No matter how strong an enemy is, it will always submit once courage has been beaten out of it."

"Your soldiers of Mortem ought to do that well enough," said Emil. "They certainly gave me a fright."

"I'm sure Kaburem was terrified the first time they saw the dead," said Tempest. "But, now the shock has likely subsided. We need something stronger."

Patch lifted his hand. "May I make a suggestion?" he asked.

"Please do," said Tempest.

"Kaburem has already faced your armored dead, correct?" he asked.

"Yes," Sagua answered. "In Aquius."

"But they have not faced their own dead," said Patch.

"You want to raise their dead against them?" Tegan asked.

Patch nodded. "Imagine the terror when their fallen comrades storm their ranks."

"It's a cruel thing," said Tempest.

"No crueler than setting their camp aflame with them inside it," Clio said. "This is war, is it not?"

"Can it even be done?" asked Tempest.

"We'd need to leave some of the knights behind," said Tegan. "But yes, it can be done."

Tempest stood and paced around the room. These were unforgivable things they were planning. She wondered at what cost victory would come. "Will it get us close enough to the shore?" she asked.

"As close as we should dare until your contacts arrive with the ships," said Clio. "Kaburem will likely have ships of their own that we'd best avoid."

"Have scouts seen anything coming from the west?" Tempest asked. "We don't want to be caught unaware. If the Alyrian army is coming, they should be arriving soon."

Jyles shook his head. "Nothing yet from the west," he said. "I spoke to Morris this morning. He's reached out to a Kaburem soldier who believes he's still loyal to Lazareth. According to this soldier, word of the ploy has yet to reach the Alyrian army. They remain in Laurus. We shouldn't expect them any time soon."

"And do you trust his word, Tempest?" Clio asked.

"I trust it enough," said Tempest. "Avery, Sagua, go prepare your men for tonight's battle. The rest of you, keep your wits about you. If there's anything I know about war, it's that the direction of it changes like the wind."

~~~

Tree branches bent to the will of the breeze, swaying and dancing around the rebels as they silently crept towards the stream that separated them from the enemy camp. There was a storm coming in, and it was bound to be a violent one.

Tempest rolled the cuffs of her pants to her knees before stepping into the frigid stream. She was glad for its shallowness. Anything deeper would have rendered her entire lower half frozen.

With a breath, she stepped forward and waded through the black waters that traced the hill's valley. A hand reached out from the ledge of the other side and pulled her to solid ground. "Thank you," she said to the Mage.

Down the stream, she found Avery climbing from the water. "This should be everyone," he said, wringing the water from his clothes.

"Send your men to surround the Kaburem camp," said Tempest as she looked to their target in the trees. Camp fires still burned, but they were dwindling, and there were no voices to interfere with the night's silence. The Kaburem regiment seemed, for the most part, to be comfortable in their beds. "Use any means necessary to keep them trapped in the inferno. We won't be able to hold them, but we'll be able to guide their escape."

Avery relayed the orders to the other Mages who'd come along on the mission, then he returned to Tempest's side. "Which flank will you be joining?" he asked.

"Yours," said Tempest. "The eastern flank will be the one we break to allow their escape. I want to be there when it's done."

"I'll wait for your signal," he said. "Let's get this over with, shall we?"

"Let's," said Tempest. She took hold of her gun and walked with the others into the shelter of the trees. There were just over a thousand rebels with her, and they moved like whispers in the wind, winding through the foliage towards the sleeping Kaburem camp. Tempest stepped with care over the roots and fallen leaves, trying to keep as quiet as she could.

Kaburem guards paced along a wood spiked perimeter, watching their surroundings with a warry eye, but they didn't seem to see Tempest or her company. "Signal the Dragon Keepers," Tempest directed.

Avery pulled a small paper dragon from his pocket and held it in his palm. With a conjured gust of wind, he sent it soaring towards the Dragon Keepers that lay in waiting on the other side of the stream. Within a mere few seconds, their silhouettes blotted out the stars in the sky.

"Dragons!" cried one of the Kaburem guards at the edge of the camp. He grabbed his gun and sprinted through the tents, calling his comrades to arms. "We're under attack!"

His warnings didn't last long. One of the dragons landed before him and set his body aflame. The other Dragon Keepers landed beside the first and joined the stream of fire. Kaburem's tents lit up as though the sun had consumed them, and the camp glowed like a candle constructed by the gods.

Tempest watched as the Dragon Keepers slipped from the licking flames, and the camp came alive with the sound of screams. Waves of heat rolled through the trees. She could almost imagine the fire god himself dancing in the glow. Wails of the enflamed echoed through the woods, and humanoid figures fled from their tents, burning bright against the dark blue of night.

"Cage them," said Tempest, and Avery launched a red light into the sky for all the Mages to see.

The ground shook as walls and chasms formed around the camp, trapping the Kaburem soldiers inside. Any flames that surpassed the barrier were extinguished, and any soldier that dared to cross met a similar fate.

Tempest watched in horror as a Kaburem man clambered over twisting roots that ensnared his every step. No matter how hard he struggled, he could not escape the fire's hunger.

Another man stood trapped between the flames and a rock wall that towered over him. His fingers dug into the rock, painting red streaks in the stone, but the fire caught him before he could make his escape.

All of this made Tempest's soul ache, but nothing compared to the third man she spotted. He looked to his comrades who burned despite all attempts of escape, then he lay down his weapon and walked directly into the flames. There was no hope, no spirit left in that man.

"That's enough," said Tempest. "Release the eastern flank."

The Mages halted their assaults and left the east open for escape. Just as they'd intended, the Kaburem soldiers fled towards the coast like a frightened herd of sheep.

39

$\mathcal{M}$ ilitia soldiers stood armed and ready around the rebel camp. They looked tired but alert. Their guns aimed towards Tempest and the Mages as they emerged from the shadows of the trees. "Lower your weapons!" Benjamin shouted to his defensive line.

The soldiers dropped their aim and stowed away their guns. Clio and Patch rode forth through their lines and dismounted beside Tempest. "So it's done, then?" Clio asked.

"It is," said Tempest. "Benjamin, your men may retire for the night."

"You heard her," he said to his ranks. "Get some rest."

The militia line broke and scattered throughout the camp. Tempest looked back at the smoke filled sky, then turned to her companions. Her heart ached at the remembrance of the battle, but she could not deny the effectiveness of the strategy. "Most of them fled with nothing but their guns and the clothes on their backs," she said. "Sagua is tracking them from the sky as we speak. They're weakened without supplies. We could end this all tomorrow."

Patch's eyes widened at the statement. "Do you really think so?" he asked.

"I do," said Tempest. "If you had seen their terror, you'd think so too."

"Let's not get ahead of ourselves," said Clio. "We have yet to learn where they're headed. It's best we take this conversation inside the camp."

"Avery, dismiss your men," said Tempest "We'll reconvene for an updated plan in the morning."

"Yes, m'lady," he said with a bow of his head.

Once they'd returned to the heart of the camp, Tempest sent Felix to retrieve Neymar for her, and the boy departed with haste. She then lifted the flap to her tent and turned to Clio. "When Sagua returns, will you send her to me?" she asked.

Clio nodded. "Of course," she said, then split off to join her men.

Tempest turned to Patch, the last remaining of the group. "Will you wait with me?" she asked. "I'd enjoy the company."

"That depends how long you anticipate waiting," said Patch.

"Do you have somewhere better to be?"

"I might." He smiled. "After our last conversation, I've been thinking about resurrecting my rat kingdom. Maybe we can be allies when all this is through."

"A valuable alliance," said Tempest. "But the rats will have to wait for their king tonight."

"I'll beg them to forgive you," he said, stepping into the tent. "What's on your mind?"

There were a million things on her mind, but she hadn't the heart to give them life with words. At the forefront were the screams of the Kaburem soldiers as they fled their flaming tents. They mirrored the sound of the screams from Alyria, she thought. Wails of terror and confusion. She shook the thoughts from her head and said, "Nothing."

Patch looked over to her and nodded. She could tell he saw through her lie, but she was thankful he didn't question any further.

"Will you tell me more about your old rat kingdom?" she asked, sitting across from Patch.

A chuckle arose from his chest, and he leaned back in his seat. "Where do I begin?"

"At the start, of course," said Tempest. "How did you find them?"

"Well," he said. "They lived in an alleyway between a butcher's shop and a tanner. The Merchant that owned the butcher's shop was kind to me, so I stayed in the alley with the rats. He'd give me unsold, aging meat, and I'd give the remains to the rats. I felt for them. In them, I saw myself. They were alive, they were set aside, and they were afraid, just like me. So I fed them and kept them safe."

"And yet," said Tempest, "even after all that, you didn't know you were a healer."

Patch shook his head. "As I've told you before, I didn't think I'd make it long enough to find out. Children don't last long when they're alone on the streets."

"We can change that, you and I," Tempest said, placing her hand on Patch's shoulder. "Once this war is through."

"I know we can," he replied. "And we will."

The tent flap opened, putting a halt to their conversation as Sagua and Felix stepped inside. The boy seemed to be bombarding the guild leader with questions about dragons. "Pardon our interruption," Sagua said upon their entry, silencing Felix's torrent of inquiries for just a moment.

Tempest stood to meet them and took Neymar from Felix's arms. "What did you find?" she asked.

"Kaburem has taken refuge in a town less than a league from the coast," said Sagua. "I spotted a farmhouse not far from it, which may be of use."

"Could you draw up a map from memory?" Tempest asked.

"If you gave me some time, I could have one by morning," said Sagua.

"Perfect. Bring it to the briefing."

Sagua bowed her head, then with Felix at her side, she left once more, giving the room to silence. It was in this silence that Tempest's thoughts and fears reigned. She couldn't keep them at bay, no matter how she tried.

"Will you be all right tonight?" Patch asked. "I can stay a while longer if you need."

She wanted his continued company more than anything in that moment, but they had a long day ahead of them, and they both needed their rest. "I'll be fine," she promised. "Thank you."

"Of course," said Patch, then he collected his things and parted ways for the night.

The camp quieted in these late hours, and so too did Tempest's mind. She stripped off her gown and huddled under the furs of her bed. They were warm and comforting in the chill of the night, but they could not keep the memories from her head.

Images of the fire burned into her dreams. It was bright, and it roared with a horrid song. Her aching soul begged to turn away from the screams, but her eyes stayed forward. She knew this was the cost of her war, haunting images that would linger in her mind for all time, but she was determined to face them.

At this revelation, the dream began to shift. The fire condensed and expanded, twisting into a familiar shape, until finally, where once was a burning camp, there stood a lion the color of the sun.

~~~

Tempest rose early from her rest, perplexed even still by the dream that'd come to her in the night. She sat up and sighed, giving up on any thoughts of further sleep. By the entry to the tent, she saw Neymar, pacing back and forth. He chirped and whipped his tail as the sound of footsteps neared.

She couldn't tell who they belonged to, so she donned a cloak and strapped her dagger to her thigh.

"I have important information m'lady will want to here," said a woman's voice from outside.

"I'll determine its importance," her guard replied.

"I'm a Merchant from Isigodi," The woman said after a moment's pause. "While on sentry duty, two boys from a local town came to our borders. They claim to have information on the enemy and wish to meet with m'lady. Will you tell her when she wakes?"

Tempest ducked through the tent threshold and turned to the woman. "Show me to them," she said.

"Yes, m'lady," said the woman with a bow of her head. "I apologize if I was the cause of your waking."

"I was already up when I heard you coming," Tempest assured. "You said you're from Isigodi?"

"Yes, m'lady," said the woman once again, turning on her heels to return to the boys she spoke of.

"I remember your village quite fondly," Tempest said. "Nikita was the first to show us any kindness on the road. May I ask your name?"

"Amara, m'lady," said the woman.

"Please," said Tempest. "Call me Tempest."

Just as Amara had said, two boys waited on the outskirts of the camp. They rose to their feet and lowered their hats as she approached. One looked to be about Felix's age. The other seemed only a few years younger than Tempest was.

"I'm told you have information on the enemy."

The younger boy nodded with vigor. "We do!" he said, a bright smile on his face.

"Be still, Amir," said the elder. "This is not one of your silly games."

Amir returned his hat to his head and stood silent, watching the other boy intently.

"My name is Elias," said the elder boy. "This is my brother, Amir. Our parents are farmers in the town Kaburem took. We were out in the fields when they arrived, but we managed to slip away without their noticing. When we left, they were forcing our people to build a barricade around the walls."

Tempest lifted her hand to silence the boy. "The trees have ears," she warned. "Let's take this to my tent where we can speak freely." She turned to Amara. "Summon Clio and tell her to gather the others."

Through the camp, she led the boys with a collection of guards behind them. When they were secure within the tent, she turned to Elias and said, "Tell me more."

Elias stood tense, eyes flitting between the armed guards and the small dragon that stood with them in the tent, but Amir showed no such fear. The young boy took a seat at the table across from Tempest and waved for his brother to join him. Not only was he of age with Felix, but he had a similar heart as well, thought Tempest.

"You said they were constructing a barricade. Did you see how they did it?"

Elias nodded. "Our walls are made of wood, not stone," he said. "We've never been a wealthy people, but Kaburem paid no mind. They built a mound around the walls and stuck sharpened logs in the dirt for protection. Odds are, our people won't like the sudden occupation. We have little enough as is, and Kaburem is known to take without remorse."

"They are, indeed," said Tempest. "Would you like to help us do something about it?"

"Absolutely!" said Amir, and Elias agreed.

~~~

Within the hour, the rest of the rebel leaders had gathered inside her tent, and when all were present, Tempest began the briefing. "Elias here," she said, gesturing to the boy, "has brought information on the Kaburem camp. Sagua, do you have the map?"

"Right here," said Sagua, lifting a parchment into the air before placing it at the center of the table.

Tempest pushed the map towards Elias. "Does anything need correction?" she asked, and the boy leaned forward to inspect it.

"Up north, here, by the lake," he said, pointing to a small strip of land that separated the town from the water. "It's too marshy to be fortified. We call it the smugglers road. It's the only path safe enough for traders to transport crops for the black market."

Jyles perked up at these words. "How many people do you think could slip through there unnoticed?" he asked.

"Two or three at most," Elias said, defeated, but Amir giggled.

"Bet we could get a whole lot more with a proper distraction," he said.

"Aye, and what do you suppose that distraction would be?" Elias asked, ruffling Amir's hair. "Do you intend to run through the streets screaming fire?"

"I might!" said Amir, excitement flaring in his eyes.

"It'd never work, but—" Elias paused. "Oh," he said. "It just might. The old whittler's house isn't far from the route. He died from Wynris' touch this winter. No one would miss it if it burned to the ground."

"I imagine Kaburem isn't too fond of fire these days," said Tempest. She could hardly stand the sight of it herself, and she'd only watched the inferno from afar. These soldiers had been inside it. "We'll set to lay siege in the morning. Blockade the roads; let no one in and no one out. Elias, Amir, return to your home. Tell anyone in support of our cause to mark themselves with an ash paste before they go to sleep. Draw a line with it down the center of your face. Anyone marked will go unharmed during the battle."

"And the fire?" asked Amir. "When should we light it?"

"In the darkest hours of the night," said Tempest. "When no one is awake to catch you."

Elias stood and bowed his head. "It will be done," he said. "We should head back. People will wonder where we've been.

"You take care of your part, and we'll take care of ours. You mustn't forget a thing."

"We'll be ready," Elias assured. "Come on, Amir. Let's go home."

The two boys made their way back towards their town, escorted as far as possible by Emil, and Tempest sat down to continue planning. "We'll leave for the siege tonight," she said. "There's much that needs prepared."

Tempest pulled the map closer and searched it for opportunity. "This farmhouse you told me about," she said, looking across the table to Sagua. "We'll station Tegan and her Necromancers inside it. Clio, you'll lead a militia regiment to protect them. Their safety is imperative."

"Will we be raising the Kaburem dead as was the initial plan?" Tegan asked.

"Yes," said Tempest. "They'll be the ones to slip into the town during the fire. Jyles, you will be their guide. I need a living soul there to make sure nothing fails. Any ash marked citizens are not to be touched, but Kaburem and their supporters are to face Xudor's wrath. Ensure every Necromancer knows it well.

"The Mortem knights replaced by Kaburem will stand post around the camp to ward off attackers. The rest, alongside the Dragon Keepers, will be scattered through three companies to blockade each road that enters the town. Benjamin, your men will remain here to watch over the camp followers. We'll send for you when the battle is through."

"Where will you have us take the elephants?" Cedric asked.

"You and Emil will remain here as well," said Tempest. "Tend to the elephants as needed. We'll want them at full strength when we face Kaburem on the field once more.

"All other soldiers who are not placed in either the blockade or protective companies should take position in the fields. They are to hide amongst the crops where they will capture, kill, and drive out any enemy soldier that attempts to flee. If they are reluctant to run, we'll pursued them."

~~~

On the breeze rode a pungent scent that drifted towards Tempest and her company. It was almost worse than the smell of the Mortem knights when they were fresh from their graves. The bodies that lay scattered here in the ash covered grass were charred and melted. Some could hardly be recognized as human, and flies had already taken to their flesh.

Tempest pressed a cloth to her nose, stifling out the reek of the bodies. "Gather anything that can be of use," she said, looking out at the blackened Kaburem camp. "Avery, send signal to the Necromancers. With any luck, some of these bodies may still be whole enough to raise."

Patch walked up beside her, holding a small pile of ash in his hand, but a gust of wind sent each fragment dancing through the air. "I knew a girl named Dasha once," he said, turning to face Tempest. "She would have fainted at the sight of this. You're much stronger than she was."

His words were kind, but they stung all the same. "Do not mistake this for strength," she said. "I'll never forgive myself for what I've done."

"And there lies the difference between you and them," said Patch, nodding to the deceased. "They'd have shown no remorse."

"They've got one!" shouted a Mage from a few paces away.

Tempest stepped carefully over a body and shifted closer to the one being risen. Its muscles twitched and writhed as if movement was a foreign concept, but soon, it found its feet. Broken parts snapped into place, and melted flesh slipped from the bone. It made Tempest's skin crawl. The knights of Mortem had always been covered by their armor. To face the dead and look them in their eyes was an experience like no other.

40

$\mathcal{B}$irds sang through the silence of the standoff, their voices shrill, yet peaceful. It was an odd tension of feeling, the tranquility of nature against the suspense between enemies who stood no more than a thousand yards apart.

Tempest watched the Kaburem soldiers through a spyglass as they hid behind dirt mounds with long wooden spokes, resting their guns on the crest. Where fortification was slim, civilians of the town were made to dig barriers. Behind them were the wooden walls that protected the town from unwanted creatures.

A cool breeze moved the air, but spring was nearing, and with it came Zalder's warmth. It was a welcome change to the chill of winter, but moisture lingered in the air, making it harder to breathe.

"M'lady," said a Dragon Keeper perched on the shoulders of a silver beast behind her. "There appears to be a tradesman coming up the road."

Tempest turned her sights to the path, and on it, she saw a man who rode a wagon down the dirt road, led only by a single horse. "Come on, Neymar," she said, whistling for her small creature. "Let's go meet the traveler."

Neymar padded along beside her, content. He'd gotten larger in the recent weeks. There was more game in these woods than there'd been down south, and with the help of the hunters and other dragons, he'd been eating well. Soon, however, there wouldn't be much left. They'd picked the woods clean, and hunting parties were required to travel further to find anything sufficient. She hoped, if not for anything else but the sake of food, this war would end soon. Dragons, elephants, and men were all very hungry creatures.

"This is outrageous!" said the Blacksmith on the wagon. He stood on the ground now, face red with rage. "I make this trip every week to sell my tools to the farmers. Let me through!"

"Every week but this one," said Tempest. "Trust me, you won't want to be in there tonight."

He threw his hands in the air and huffed. "I won't be long," he said. "In and out, I assure you."

"You can make your trade with my men," said Tempest. "You'll not be entering the town."

This man wasn't the last to attempt entry. There were many who flowed through this little farm town. The numbers slimmed, however, as the night progressed and the moon began its journey through the sky.

A yawn escaped from her lips, and Tempest held her palms up to a small fire at the edge of their encampment. The hour was late, but the night was still young. It'd be a while longer before anything happened in the town, and Tempest found that time only served to heighten her nerves.

"You look tense," said Morris. He'd requested to fight for her in the upcoming battle in exchange for the removal of his shackles, and she'd allowed it. "Take a sip of this."

Tempest wrapped her fingers around the flask he offered and brought it to her lips. It had an odd smell to it, and an even stranger taste. "Gods," she said, passing the flask back to Morris. "That's awful."

A chuckle arose from Morris' lips, and he took a deep swig. "We call it grog," he said. "It's served to soldiers back home. I found a cask of it in the spoils of your previous battles. None of your men seemed to have any interest in it."

"I don't blame them," said Tempest.

"Neither do I." He stowed away the flask and sat on a stump beside the fire.

"Can I ask you a question and have you answer it with full honesty?" Tempest asked.

"As long as speaking truth won't get me killed," said Morris.

"You have my word," she promised. "Tell me, from your perspective, are we in the wrong here? Have my methods stooped to the same cruelty of my enemy?"

Morris sucked in his cheeks and whistled. "I'll not lie and tell you your methods aren't harsh, but there's one thing that keeps you divided from Lazareth. You attack only on the battlefield, and you spare as many as you can. He holds no such regard for any life outside his own."

"Nor a regard to kinship," said Tempest, but Morris didn't seem to catch her words. "Thank you for your council," she said, louder this time.

Morris stood and bowed his head. "You're welcome to request it at any time, but for now, I'll leave you be."

~~~

An infinite array of stars scattered through the sky, and drifting towards them was a plume of smoke. "They've done it," Tempest muttered, leaping to her feet. "Spread the word, and ready your men. The battle has begun!"

Her soldiers scattered through the alfalfa fields, and Tempest mounted her horse. Shouts from her readying army lifted in a thunderous chorus that made the Kaburem soldiers on the barricade squirm. She dug her heels into the horse's sides and cantered down the line of her ranks, watching the town for signs of panic.

The wait was a short one. Bells sang, and people wailed. Tempest knew the dead had succeeded in breaching the walls. She prayed Amir and Elias hadn't forgotten to warn the innocent.

With the spyglass, she watched the barricade. Those that manned it looked warily around as the sound of gunfire echoed within the town, but one man stood at the zenith of the mound, shouting commands to keep them still. Tempest wished she could hear what he said to hold the Kaburem men at their posts, and she wondered if his words would keep them strong when the men were faced with their own dead.

The first boney hand wrapped around the wood posts of the wall and pulled a walking corpse over its edge. The men closest to it in the barricade aimed their weapons towards it. They riddled the corpse with bullets, but none felled the creature. Tempest watched as the dead soldier drove its sword through the hearts of its living brethren. It did not stop until the blade of an ax split its skull, severing the connection between the flesh and the Necromancer.

The Kaburem men cheered at the killing of the dead soldier, but their joy was short lived. Others dropped from over the city walls and wreaked havoc through the barricade.

This seemed to be the point at which their ranks shattered. Every man and woman that manned the barricade fled into the safety of the fields, unaware of the threat that lay waiting beneath the growing thatch. Tempest put away the spyglass and rode towards Sagua.

"What will you have us do?" the guild leader asked from atop her dragon's shoulders.

"Fly over the town," said Tempest. "Drive out any Kaburem soldiers that remain. I'd like you to refrain from setting more fires. We need the town, and we need their crops."

Sagua bowed her head, and a torrent of wind beat downward as the dragons took wing and made way to the town. They swooped and snarled, snapping at any Kaburem soldier that dared to come near. By Tempest's side, Neymar hissed, eager to join the fight, but he listened when she forbade it.

The drums and cries of retreat lifted into the air, and Tempest watched her enemy flood through the gates and veer course for the sanctuary of the trees. Some were met with a bullet, but others managed their escape.

"Should we pursue them, m'lady?" asked a militia man beside her.

"No," said Tempest. "The town is ours."

~~~

At the forefront of her army, Tempest rode through the main gates. The rebels were met with both cheers of triumph and terrified stares as they marched through the streets. She couldn't blame the citizens for being afraid. Kaburem bodies lay mutilated on the ground anywhere one looked. There'd been no dignity to their deaths.

One of the risen Kaburem corpses met Tempest in the middle of the road. It lifted its hand and gave a grandiose bow, to which Tempest returned, then it collapsed and gave way to death.

"Welcome," said a man who approached with the ash markings on his face. "We have much to discuss."

"That we do," Tempest replied, dismounting her horse. "You're in charge of this town, I presume."

"As of tonight," said the man. "The former leader did not support your cause, so we abstained from telling him of the markings."

"Ah," Tempest said. "Then our victory brought favor to us both."

"It did," said the man. "One can hope it does so for a prolonged period of time." He extended his hand in greeting. "My name is Arthur. I believe you've already met my boys." With a gesture, Amir and Elias stepped into view.

"I have," said Tempest. "We owe much of our victory to their help. If you'll allow it, I'd like to reward them."

Arthur bowed his head. "I'll not require it, but you may do as you please. Your men will be wanting rest, I imagine. You're welcome to set up camp within the walls. All I ask is that any houses you occupy belong to the dead."

"Of course," Tempest said, then she turned to her men. "Jyles, you'll go with Morris to retrieve Benjamin and the camp followers. Clio and Tegan should be joining us soon. Patch, set up a blood room for the sick and injured. Avery, take your men with the advice of the militia Fire Keepers and put out any flames that remain. The rest of you, loot and bury the dead."

Her soldiers scattered in every which way, and Tempest followed Arthur to the center of the town. The two brothers followed close behind, dropping bits of food for Neymar as the dragon trailed at their rear.

Arthur pointed to a manor on the corner of two roads. "That's the former residence of our deceased lord. It's yours while you're here. My boys will water your horse."

"Thank you," Tempest said, bowing her head to her host. "Your aid will not be forgotten." She whistled for Neymar to follow and walked into the manor. It was old but well kept, and a great candled chandelier hung from the rafters.

Tempest crouched down and lit a fire in the hearth. Temperatures had dropped with nightfall, and a damp chill settled in her bones. The flames lifted into the air and brought warmth back to her body. She flexed her fingers and took a breath, setting her mind to the next task. Her stomach was empty after the long night, and stress had kept her appetite at bay.

Behind the dais, she found a wooden door that led to the kitchens. Half prepared food lay strewn across table tops. She figured it was meant to be the former occupant's breakfast had he not perished in the night.

Tempest grabbed a loaf of bread and a portion of cheese to accompany it, then she descended into the cellar to find meat for Neymar. There was no warmth inside it, and hardly any light, but she managed to find what she needed.

A skinned rabbit dangled from wood beams. It appeared to be a decently fresh kill. Tempest cut it down from its strings and carried it to the kitchens for the beast. He chirped as she approached with it, and hummed when she tossed it to him

"Let's go find the bed chamber," she said to the dragon, and he happily followed her up the stairs.

Great tapestries hung over the walls, and deer pelts wrapped around the rafters. A bed sat in the middle of the room, piled high with wools and fur. On the floor, staining the wood a deep crimson, was a drying pool of blood. She figured it must have been where the man who'd lived here died, though his body had been removed. She hoped he'd been buried with respect.

Neymar curled up beneath the bed and lay his head on the floor, closing his eyes for sleep, and Tempest followed his lead. She undressed for the night, washed her skin with a cloth and a small bucket of ice cold water, then lay beneath the furs to rest.

Come morning, she woke early to the sounds of birds at her window. There was a tree that stood just beside it, and a lark sat in its branches, building a nest for the spring. A smile touched Tempest's lips at the sight of the bird. She felt it a sign from the gods. Perhaps they were behind her in this after all.

"Wake up, Neymar," she said to the sleeping beast, nudging him gently on the head. With some motivation, he rose.

Tempest slipped into her gown and walked with Neymar into the streets. There were many out and about, recovering after the night's affairs, but down the road a bit, she found familiar faces.

"Benjamin!" she called, and he turned to greet her with a warm smile. "I'm glad to see you've made it. Is the rest of the camp settled in?"

"They are," he said. "The town has welcomed us kindly."

"Good," said Tempest. "We'll be meeting soon. Gather the others and find me at the manor." He bowed his head and left to do her bidding.

Where he'd stood, Jada shifted to take his place. "M'lady, will you require repairs to your gown?" she asked, looking to the scuffs and tears.

"Not just yet," said Tempest. "I have another task for you to do first. The two brothers that helped us win this battle, I'd like you to craft them each a sword. Come to the meeting with us today to discuss it with their father."

"Yes, m'lady," she said.

An elephant trumpet disrupted the conversation as Cedric rode down the street upon the back of one of the larger creatures. "Good morning," he said. "I hear we have a meeting to attend to."

"We do, indeed," said Tempest. "I'm off to retrieve Arthur. I'll be back. Please ensure the elephant doesn't follow you into the manor."

"Oh, but Tempest," said Patch from the midst of a group of training soldiers. "Would it not be fun to watch the beast try?"

"Did I permit you to speak?" Morris asked.

"No, sir, you did not."

The rest of the training group found amusement in this, but Morris only rolled his eyes. "Load firelocks!" he shouted, and the trainees obeyed.

Tempest watched them work for a moment, soaking in as much of the lesson as she could. She was happy to see Morris helping the others. She'd stolen moments of training herself when time presented itself. He was the only one professionally trained to wield these weapons, and that knowledge needed to spread.

Down the street a bit, she spotted Arthur, so she separated herself from the group and moved to join him. "Good morning," she greeted. "I must thank you again for your hospitality."

"The pleasure is mine," he said, taking a bite from the apple in his hand. "What comes next for your lot?"

"We'll be deciding that this morning," said Tempest. "Since this is your town, I'd like you to be present for the discussion."

"I'd like that too." He gestured forward. "At your lead, m'lady."

By the time they made it back to the manor, the others had found their way inside. They sat around the long table in the center of the hall, and they stood when Tempest entered. "Let's begin," said Tempest, taking a seat beside Arthur on the dais. "Tegan, have the dead been laid to rest?"

"They have," she assured. "All of them, even those we raised from the fire, have been returned to the gods."

"Thank you," Tempest said. "With luck, the knights of Mortem will soon do the same, but until then, there's work to be done." She lifted her hand and gestured to her seamstress. "Arthur, I'd like you to meet Jada. She's a Blacksmith, and a brilliant one at that. I've asked her to make your boys swords for the help they gave."

"They'd be honored to receive such a gift," said Arthur. "I'll arrange a meeting with my sons so details can be determined."

Jada smiled, and Tempest continued. "The next thing I'd like to discuss is the length of our stay. I don't wish to remain longer than we're welcome, so I've brought a proposition."

Arthur leaned forward, ready to hear it.

"We're waiting for a signal," she began. "A dragon in particular. One close in size to my own. It will bear word of reinforcements. I'd like to stay until that dragon arrives. It should be no more than a week's time, and we will not be staying without contribution. We'll help where needed, and perhaps a trade relation can be made between my army and your farmers."

"A simple negotiation," said Arthur, holding his hand out to bind the agreement. "I accept your terms."

Tempest took his hand in hers and smiled. She was glad for his support. It would allow them to regroup behind the safety of walls. "Have we any knowledge of where Kaburem has fled?" she asked, turning back to the others.

"None," said Clio, disheartened by the claim. "We don't even know where to begin looking. They scattered in all directions."

"They did," said Arthur. "Which brings question to something important. Why did they retreat?"

"He's right," Patch said. "They should have surrendered. Something is keeping them hopeful."

Tempest leaned back and closed her eyes. "The same thing that's keeping us hopeful," she said. "Reinforcements. They must have ships near the coast. Search for their camp in that direction."

~~~

Four days had passed since their arrival, and still no word from Cyrus came. Tempest worried something terrible had happened. It was a long journey, and Rhumir had not been kind of late. Storms reigned the sky, day and night.

Tempest huddled beneath a tarp and watched the people of the land from the parapet. Despite the rain, they still worked their fields, trying to maintain the crops. Sunlight faded as the hours progressed, and the work began to slow. Off in the horizon, silhouetted by golden light beams, she saw a man riding hard for the town.

"Horseman approaching!" she shouted to the guards that manned the barricade.

The horseman paid no mind to the guns aimed towards him. He kept a steady pace and dismounted only a few feet away. "M'lady," he said, bowing his head. Mud caked his face, and rain matted his hair, but Tempest recognized him as one of the scouts she'd sent to track the Kaburem camp. It'd been found the day before.

"Has something happened?" she asked, motioning for the guards to lower their weapons.

"Kaburem," he said, breathless from the ride. "They're gone. I got to the camp this afternoon. It'd been abandoned with haste. Their night fires still burned when I arrived."

"Go, find Clio," said Tempest. "Bring her to me, and tell no one else what you saw."

"Yes, m'lady," he said, then he sprinted through the gates, leaving the horse to Tempest's care. She grabbed the reins and walked it to the stables, passing the beast to the one armed man who watched over the creatures.

Clio rounded the corner and sped her pace when she caught sight of Tempest. "You sent for me?" she asked.

"I did," said Tempest. "I need you to ready the army. We'll be marching at first light. Kaburem has vanished from their camp."

"It could be a trap," said Clio. "We'll need to proceed with caution."

"Agreed." Tempest touched her forefinger to her lips, thinking, then she crouched to the ground and scooped some dirt into a pile. At the top of her makeshift hill, she placed a rock, signifying the Kaburem camp. "We'll send half of our force to inspect the abandoned camp. The other half will hang back in the shelter of the valley to watch for any signs of ambush. Kaburem is weak. If they're smart, they won't attack until they have their ships to back them."

"Why would they leave if not for the sake of an ambush?" Clio asked.

"Perhaps their ships arrived," Tempest offered. "It'd be a beacon of safety they'd certainly want to flock to in their current state. Would we not do the same in their position?"

"Where should we meet if something goes wrong?"

Tempest bit her lip, deep in a thought. "Samak," she said. "It's a fishing town I learned about in my studies as a girl. It's a formidable place on the coast that'd be large enough to host us until Cyrus arrived."

"I'll spread the word," said Clio, and by morning, the rebel army was on the move.

~~~

Tempest led the first half of the army through what remained of the Kaburem camp. The cook fires had died, but everything else seemed hardly disturbed. Tents lay abandoned, and wagons brimmed with food. Whatever was to happen, Kaburem seemed to have no intention of the war lasting beyond the day. Tempest hoped they were right.

"They're gone," said Clio. "No sign of them anywhere."

Sagua flew down from the sky and confirmed Clio's statement. "There's nothing but stillness."

"Keep to the skies and alert me if that changes," said Tempest. "Clio, bring the rest of the army up. Gather any ammunitions, powder, provisions, or weapons that you find."

"Tempest," Clio said when Sagua had departed. "Something isn't right. We shouldn't take their disappearance lightly."

"I agree with Clio," said Benjamin as he dug through a pile of coins. "This is unnerving. They wouldn't leave this much behind if it wasn't a trick."

Red scales barreled down from the clouds, crimson wings stretching from either side. When the dragon landed, Sagua jumped down to join them once again, panic in her eyes. "We've spotted them," she said. "They're marching towards the town."

Tempest's heart dropped. They'd left it, for the most part, undefended. She'd never imagined Kaburem would return to it. "They wouldn't dare try to take it again, would they? They'd never manage to hold it."

"They don't need to hold it to send a message," said Clio.

"Dear gods," Benjamin muttered.

"Sagua, fly back with the Dragon Keepers," said Tempest. "Benjamin, take a small group and ride for the town. Help Sagua evacuate the area. We'll be behind you with the army. Go now. There's no time to waste."

Her friends scattered to do her bidding, and Tempest was left alone. Voices shouted as the army collected itself and prepared to march. She prayed Benjamin and Sagua would make it in time. There were so many they'd left behind. Felix and Ava with Neymar; Jada, Amir, and Elias with their father; the families of every one of her soldiers, and the families native to the town. If Kaburem got there first, the devastation would be unfathomable.

Tempest mounted her horse and rode through the ranks, waiting at the lead for everyone to take their formations. Down the slope of the hill, she watched as Benjamin and fifteen others galloped towards the town. When the army was ready, she followed in their lead.

They moved slowly through the forest, and each hour brought further anxiety to Tempest's heart. She couldn't bear the thought of what would result from failure.

"Soldiers in the distance!" Clio shouted from atop her horse. She rode forward, inspecting the approaching group. "Ready arms!"

Tempest moved to join Clio, locking her gaze on the distant figures. Flying above them, she spotted Neymar. "They're friendly! Lower your weapons!"

She dug her heels into her horse's sides and sprinted towards the group. At their lead was Benjamin.

"We got as many as we could," Benjamin said, head hanging low. "Tempest, we were too late."

She glanced at the faces around her. Felix, Ava, and their parents stood huddled together behind Benjamin. It was them that Neymar protected. The beast's mouth was red with blood, and he had a wound across his chest.

"He saved us, mum," said Felix. "There was a man who tried to kill us. He didn't know we had a dragon." A smile touched the child's lips. He was the only one who seemed to find any joy in the situation.

Not far from them, Tempest spotted Amir and Elias. The younger boy stood sobbing in his brother's arms. Tempest figured it meant Arthur would not be joining them.

The cries of dragons echoed through the air as the Dragon Keepers flew overhead with more of the refugees. From what Tempest could see, between those on the ground and those in the sky, they'd manage to save at least a couple hundred of the citizens and camp followers. She expected Sagua to come down and meet them, but the guild leader continued flying until none of the dragons remained overhead.

"Kaburem's close behind us," said Benjamin. "We need to leave."

Tempest turned to Clio. "Scatter the men," she said. "Divide the ranks and send them in all directions. We'll rendezvous at Samak." She called Neymar to her side. "Benjamin, take the lead. I'll follow up at the rear. When you reach the army, send the Necromancers to me. The dead should dissuade any thoughts Kaburem has of pursuit." She didn't wait for an answer. There wasn't time for counterarguments. With Neymar flying at her side, she raced to the back of the refugee host.

No more than an arrow's flight away, the Kaburem soldiers marched. Tempest's heart pounded in her chest as they drew near, and she pulled out her gun, prepared to fight. Beside her, Jada stood, sword drawn for battle.

At the forefront of the Kaburem army, Tempest found a familiar face. She'd met him long ago. It was the guild leader of the Alyrian Army, and in his hand, he held the severed head of Arthur. He lifted it into the air, halting the progression of the enemy. A moment of silence fueled a fire of tension between Tempest and the guild leader, broken suddenly as the Necromancers and the dead fell into formation beside her.

She didn't know how the Army had gotten here, nor why they'd heard no word of its travel, but none of that seemed to matter in the moment. Tempest rode forward alone, stopping twenty feet from the enemy. Their guns aimed towards her, but the guild leader's hand held off their attack.

"How could you do this?" she asked him. "You've gone against every word you ever spoke to me. Look around," she said, gesturing to the refugees that huddled behind the dead. "These are the people you swore to protect. You've disgraced Alyria, and you've disgraced my father." She spat on the ground, fury in her heart. "I pray, upon death, the twin lions devour your soul." She reared her horse and returned to the safe keeping of the Necromancers.

As she'd hoped, the Alyrian soldiers did not follow when the rebels retreated. Instead, they stood at the guild leader's command, and they waited.

41

*R*ed sparks danced towards the heavens from a small fire Tempest sat beside. There was a light breeze that chilled parts of her body, but she knew the sun would warm the air when daybreak came.

She'd spent a lot of time on this wall since their arrival in the city of Samak. It gave her mind rest to know she'd be the first to spot Kaburem if they'd decided to follow. She doubted they'd show at this point. Days had passed with no sign of the enemy, yet still she stood, watching.

There was a peace at the top of this wall as well. Tempest enjoyed its feeling. From the top of it, she could watch as travelers entered and left the town, tiny glimpses of other lives that crossed hers in a fragment of a moment. She imagined this to be what the gods felt whenever they looked down upon their creation. To watch the world from above made things seem small. It was a feeling she only ever experienced on the backs of dragons.

Tempest took a deep breath, sucking in the fresh morning air, then she turned her gaze back to the flames. Within them, she sought her patron god and said a prayer for Cyrus. He'd been as silent as Kaburem, and word of his arrival had yet to come. At the end of her prayer, she poured libation into the flame, watching the smoke carry it upwards to the realm of the gods. It disappeared on the wind, riding with the call of a horn from the watch tower.

"What is it?" she asked, standing to meet one of the rampart guards.

"Looks to be a dragon," he said, pointing to a small silhouette in the distance, then he turned to look at Neymar. "If I had to guess, it's about the same size as yours. I think this is the one you've been waiting for."

Her fingers clasped the amethyst stone at her neck, and she smiled. She whistled for Neymar and sent him into the sky to guide Cyrus' dragon to her. The two beasts played and tumbled in the air, spitting small fire balls at each other as they neared. They landed side by side on the parapet, and Tempest reached out to stroke each.

Cyrus' dragon was a brilliant gold color that matched Neymar's wings. Tethered to its hind leg, she saw a small white cloth. She untied the cloth and unraveled it, revealing a painting of a dragon with Neymar's likeness standing on a shattered bone crown. Above the dragon's head were three suns. "Three days," she said in a breath. "Sound the bells."

All along the walls, bells sang for the news, summoning her commanders and friends to a hall at the center of the town. She gave Cyrus' dragon a chunk of meat for the journey and sent it on its way. Neymar chirped as the golden creature flew back to where it came from. His head tilted, and his eyes brimmed with curiosity.

"Come now, Neymar," said Tempest as she made her way down the steps. He spun in a circle, then launched into the air, following her to the hall.

Merchants shouted and bartered in the streets as people wandered about. Up until Tempest's arrival, it seemed as though this town had managed to go untouched by this war. She hoped her presence wouldn't result in catastrophe like it had for the last town they'd taken.

When she arrived at the hall, she found the others waiting around the table. On one end sat Jyles and Marius. She was happy to see them returned. They'd been on a scouting mission to track the Kaburem army. Fresh from the journey, their skin remained painted with dirt and mud.

"I've received word from Cyrus," she said, and the energy in the room brightened. They'd gone too long without hopeful information. This was sure to lift their spirits. "He and the ships will be here in three days. What do we know of the enemy?"

All eyes turned to Jyles and Marius. They were the only ones who'd know much of anything. Jyles scooted back in his chair and stood to address the room. "They've all gathered on the beach two miles north of here," said Jyles. "The Alyrian Army is with them. We believe Morris' contacts knew of his desertion, and thus provided us with false information about the Army's location. While I trust him, there are many who don't. I suggest he be shackled again until a proper trial can be held."

"I thank you for the advice," Tempest said. Morris' alleged betrayal was a matter she'd need to confront, but it was not the thing at the front of her mind. "Tell me more about their position on the beach."

Jyles leaned against the table and exhaled through pursed lips. "There are many of them, I'll not lie," he said. "Despite our victories, they still outnumber us. But, what we lack in numbers, we have in diverse strength. With that, we'll also have the ground. The land slopes down towards the water, making the beach the lowest point." As he spoke, he drew a rough representation of the land on a piece of parchment. "They have thirty-two ships anchored on the beach. They've lined the ships and shore with explosive, miniature trebuchets called cannons. At the edge of the beach, they've hung the former guild leader of the Army. He was publically executed on the day we arrived for letting you go after the standoff."

Patch rubbed his neck and his face twisted. "It's a horrible way to die," he said. "The gallows should be reserved for the worst of people."

"His death is not our current concern," said Tempest, though she was as shocked as the others to hear of it. She pulled the map sketch closer and grabbed the pen Jyles had used to draw it. "We mustn't mistake the sloped land for an advantage. They're pressed against the sea with hardly any means of escape. Their will to survive will be strong."

Sagua's head tilted, and she smiled. "Death ground, I believe is what your father called it the day you and I first met."

Tempest nodded. "If the guild leader heeded his advice, the Alyrian Army will have been trained to fight on that ground. They hold the advantage, not us."

"So, what do you propose we do about it?" Clio asked.

"We don't have enough guns to meet them head on in the field with their fighting style, so we'll give them a taste of our own. Once we break the tree line, the dead will form a shield wall at the forefront of our army. Tegan, you and the Necromancers will remain here for protection."

"We'll use the town's temple," said Tegan. "The connection will be strongest there."

"Good. Behind the dead, we'll form a line of gunmen. Upon my command, the wall will split for the guns to fire. The archers will listen for this command as well. They'll stand the line behind us. After the first volley, Sagua, you'll lead the dragons to set fire to the enemy."

"A perfect moment for an approach if you can keep the stream of fire controlled," said Clio.

Tempest circled the table, thinking. "We'll bring forward the two ends, curving into a horseshoe formation. Swordsmen, regulars, elephants, and Mages will take the ends. When the dragons are through, we'll thrust forward from all sides. Cyrus will take care of the ships. If he manages it quick, he and his men will hopefully join us to box the Kaburem and Alyrian armies in. We will force two options upon them. Surrender, or death."

"Where would you like the blood tent?" Patch asked. "I fear we'll need a large one for this."

Jyles stood from his seat. "If I may suggest something," he said, looking to Tempest for permission. When she nodded, he continued. "There's a water fall at the top of the hill. It's formed a small basin that could provide protection for the Medics."

"Fresh water too," said Patch. "We'll need plenty of that."

"It's settled, then," Tempest said. "We'll march at dawn three days from now. Do what you need to prepare, and may the gods be with us all."

~~~

From the top of the hill, Tempest could see the endless ranks of Kaburem soldiers that stood ready before the Alyrian ships. They'd corrupted the ships with black sails, boasting the bone crown of King Lazareth. Great wood hulls creaked with each motion of the waves, but there was no sign of Cyrus amongst them. Not even on the distant horizon.

"Will you have us wait until he arrives?" Clio asked.

"No," said Tempest. "We'll use this to our advantage. Cyrus will join us when the sea allows it. Ready the men. It's time we end this."

She tucked the amethyst ring away, protecting it from whatever was to come. Shouts and commands rallied her soldiers into formation, and Tempest's heart beat heavily in her chest. The outcome of this battle was likely to determine the victor of the war. With a whistle, she summoned Neymar from the sky and took him to Sagua's care.

"Keep him alive for me, will you?" Tempest asked.

"He'll be safe within the flock," Sagua promised. "You need only worry about keeping yourself alive. Remember what I've taught you. We can win this, Tempest, but only without fear."

Tempest bowed to her mentor and smiled. "I'll see you at the other end," she said. "If Cyrus hasn't arrived by the time we send signal, burn every last ship."

Zauryn lowered his head and gave a rumbling growl. It was as though she'd given the command to him, and he'd accepted it willingly. The beasts around him picked up the sound, and soon, much like the men, they began to roar, wings flapping in a fearsome display.

Tempest hoped Kaburem could see it from their place at the bottom of the hill, men the size of ants crawling along the crest of the hill with Zalder's beasts behind them. She'd be frightened if it were her looking up at the spectacle. She touched Zauryn's snout, then left to find Patch at the blood tent.

Jyles had been right about the waterfall. It cascaded from a cliff top and landed in a pond at the edge of the small basin. Around this plot of land stood large rock walls that protected the tent from ambush.

"I'd consider this place to be beautiful had it not been destined to hold the dying in just a few hours," said Patch as he set down a bucket of water. "This stream, that beach. It'll all be red with blood when the day is through."

"Is it worth it?" Tempest asked. "To pay such a price."

The question seemed to catch him off guard, but there was no hesitation in his answer. "Yes," he said. "And if you find yourself doubting, think of Felix and Ava. Think of every child in our camp, and think of every child who has yet to be born. We win this fight for them, no matter the cost."

Tempest took his hand gingerly in hers and pulled him into a hug. His muscles went rigid with the surprise of her action, but then he relaxed and enclosed her in his arms.

When they separated, Clio stepped forward. "We're ready."

"Wait!" Jada said, jogging up to them with a cloth wrapped item in her hands. She'd come along this time to help Patch in the blood tent. "You'll want to be taking this with you." She unwrapped the cloth and held out a beautifully crafted sword. An emerald stone had been pressed into its hilt. "When the two sides clash, a blade will serve you better than a gun."

Tempest thanked the Blacksmith and took the sword. She carefully unsheathed it, testing its balance. It was easy to hold and graceful in its movement. Fresh from the forge, she had no doubt in its sharpness.

She bowed her head to the Blacksmith, slipping the blade back into its scabbard, then she followed Clio to the forefront of her army. She found a sloped boulder and climbed to the top. At its peak, she could see most of her ranks, and they could see her. Their gazes fell to her when she lifted her hand, so she began to speak.

"When I was a girl, I read stories about warriors like each of you," she said, and the rocks around them echoed her words. "I never dreamed I'd have the honor to stand and fight beside you, but over the past months, I have done just that." She looked to their faces then, remembering each. "In Alyria, when Kaburem slaughtered the innocents, I watched you defend them. In Tokun, when we faced the entire Kaburem army with only a thousand men, I watched as you held your ground. In each of your cities, your villages, your towns, I watched you rise from the ashes. I watched as the lamb became the lion.

"Now we stand here once more, and perhaps for the final time. I will not sit here and give you false pretenses of glory. I will not promise that each of us will make it to see the morning. I know none of this is true. But, I'll tell you this. We will not go gently, and we will show no mercy."

A cheer rose from the hearts of her soldiers, joined by the clamor of swords against shields. She jumped from the boulder top and stood by Clio's side, joining the ranks of gunmen just behind the dead. "Forward march!" Clio shouted, and they began their descent.

Their steps beat out a cadence against the earth, met by the distant drumming of the Kaburem army. A silence loomed over the soldiers that was only ever heard in the moments just before battle. She'd grown to hate this silence. It carried the unknown.

The trees grew thin as they neared the base of the hill, and soon, instead of grass, beneath their feet was sand. They stood now less than a hundred paces from the enemy. "Shield wall!"

As one unit, the dead lifted their shields, interlocking them in an impenetrable pattern. Tempest closed her eyes and drew in a breath. "Ready arms!" came Clio's command.

Heavy breaths rolled from the lips of every soldier that stood beside Tempest, each exhalation sang the song of fading time. How many more breaths, she wondered, would any of them take? She bent her knees and planted her feet, grounding herself in the sand that shifted beneath her. With the pad of her thumb, she pulled back the hammer and cocked her weapon. Behind her, she could hear the creak of bowstrings as the archers drew back their arrows.

They waited there for a moment that seemed infinite, each breath counting down, but then the next command came, and Tempest realized the dreadful silence had been a far kinder sound than what was now to follow. "Fire!" Clio shouted.

The shield wall split in just enough time for Tempest and the other gunmen to fire. Their bullets whizzed through the gaps of the barricade, landing somewhere within the Kaburem lines. Only a mere few seconds after, the return volley came. Through the same gaps they'd fired through, Kaburem's bullets flew, one piercing the flesh of the man beside her. He lifted his hand to his throat where the bullet had shot clean through. Blood spilled from his lips, and he fell to his knees. Tempest kept her eyes forward but said a silent prayer for the fallen.

To her relief, the bullets that struck the dragon scale shields did not break through. "Forward!" Clio called, and with three great chants, the army inched forth, swallowing the deceased in a sea of soldiers. As they moved forward, the dead closed the shield wall, giving the rebels a moment to reload, but Kaburem was given no such time.

Tempest whistled, and the sound was carried by the soldiers until it reached the ears of Avery. A flash of light launched into the air, signaling the wave of Dragon Keepers. They took to the skies, scales glimmering beneath the rising sun. Tempest found Neymar soaring amidst the flock. He was smaller than the rest, and more agile too. His wings beat fast as he fluttered around the flock, never staying in a single spot for long.

Kaburem turned their guns to the skies, but they were too late. Tempest couldn't see much of the fire, but she could feel it. It drew sweat from her pores at even this distance away. Despite the heat, a chill ran through her spine, and her palms went cold. The wails of burning men carried her mind back to the night she'd lit their camp aflame, and the memory tore through her heart like a knife crafted of ice.

"The floor is yours," said Clio, drawing Tempest back to the present.

She peaked through the cracks of the shield wall, watching as the ships and soldiers caught flame. "Begin approach!" The two ends of their line arced forward while Tempest held their center. When the dragons cleared the field, she gave the next command. "Fire!"

They let loose another round, met only by unorganized retaliation as Kaburem gathered their wits. "Close them in!" Tempest shouted, and the arced line pressed forward.

She watched the horizon but found no friendly sails. There was only smoke billowing from the burning masts of the Kaburem ships. From this smoke came deafening sounds. Large metal balls flew through the air, sabotaging the front lines of the shield wall. When the balls struck the ground, the earth shook. Dirt sprayed in a fountain of fire, and the soldiers who'd been close to them collapsed to the earth.

Bodies dropped everywhere Tempest looked. "No mercy, no fear," she said, voice lifting above the chaos. Her words echoed from the lips of all who surrounded her.

The knights of Mortem drew their swords, and Tempest did the same, switching her gun to her left hand. She opened her mouth and let out her fury in a guttural scream, charging forward with the masses. Gun fire and cannon fire met the trod of a stampede as the two armies clashed. Salt soaked sand quickly turned red in the storm of battle, bullets like thunder and blood like rain. She couldn't tell which side was spilling the most. All she could see were those that fell around her.

She knew then why they called it death ground. It was one thing to hear of it; it was another to witness it. The way Kaburem fought was driven purely by the innate need to survive. She'd seen the look once before, in the eyes of Klaus just before he died.

A gunman charged towards her, thrusting the blade at the tip of his barrel into a Mortem knight who stepped in his way. It was a brilliant weapon, thought Tempest, dodging a charging elephant. Fatal in more ways than one. Just before the attacker reached her, one of the knights drove a sword through his back.

Tempest ducked and swung her blade, opening the stomach of a man behind her. He fell with a gargled grunt, clutching his innards as though it would stop his dying. With a bullet, Tempest removed his misery.

From the sky came a dragon. Its rider stayed low and close to the creature's neck, swinging a sword left and right as the beast sent a stream of fire through the Kaburem lines. Any soldier that dared approach was met with the bite of sharp teeth.

Tempest stepped back from the dragon, and her foot sank into the shattered skull of a dead rebel soldier. There were many that littered the ground. Some she knew but some she didn't. She swallowed the pain that threatened her heart and pressed onward.

"Watch out!" cried a Kaburem woman, eyes locked to the clouds. When Tempest looked to see what caused the woman's fear, she saw a dragon plummeting towards them. She sprinted away, leaping over cadavers as the falling beast barreled into the ground. Her balance faltered, and she reached to touch the ground, trying to keep her feet beneath her.

The hand of a Mortem knight grabbed her by the arm and steadied her, then the corpse collapsed with nine others. For a moment, Tempest feared the Necromancers had been breached within the city, but behind her, the dead dragon roared.

"Dear gods," she muttered, turning to face the beast. Its eyes were white, and it moved unnaturally. By the looks of it, this was the first dragon the Necromancer had ever risen. This fact, however, did not stop them from wreaking destruction. The fire in the beast had extinguished, but the creature had many other methods of killing, and the Necromancer used them all.

Tempest ducked and covered her head when the thunderous crack of a firelock tore through the air. Before the bullet could strike, a small rock wall shot from the ground, intercepting its trajectory. Tempest lifted her gun and shot the man who'd fired at her, but the squelch of severed flesh turned her attention to the Mage who'd saved her.

Avery stood no more than a few paces away with a serrated blade through his heart. He'd left himself vulnerable to save her with magic, and he'd paid the ultimate price. His slayer pulled the blade out and swung it towards another, but it never reached its goal. Tempest reloaded her gun and readied to fire. As the man's blade sliced towards the other rebel, she put a bullet in his head.

Clio fought beside her now, thrashing at the enemy with two curved blades. "We're losing too many," she said, breathless.

Tempest could see the truth in her words, but she refused to accept defeat. She would not let Kaburem have this victory. They could still win this, she knew they could. The cost would be great, but victory was worth the sacrifice. She picked a hatchet from the earth and threw it into the leg of an enemy soldier. "We'll hold strong," she said, and Clio rose no further question.

Rebel soldiers fell back towards the safety of the trees where life was promised, abandoning the ones doomed to death on the beach. They ran past her, fleeing a seemingly certain end. Tempest did not follow them. Instead, she lifted her sword and charged straight through the enemy lines, whistling to summon Neymar from the skies.

"Protect your queen!" Clio shouted, following Tempest into the fray. The others followed too.

Neymar descended from the clouds, guarding Tempest with streams of fire. His talons dug into the dirt, and his roar sent her soul shivering. A burst of flame ignited a Kaburem warrior, but the soldier did not stop. He swung a great sword in a vicious arc through the air. Tempest dodged the blow and rolled, slicing the back of his heels as she passed. When she stood, her eyes caught the golden glint of Cyrus' dragon flying through the air.

Nineteen ships anchored behind the flaming Kaburem fleet, and the men and women that manned them drifted onto the beach in whale boats. At their lead, Tempest caught a glimpse of Cyrus and Adrian.

A triumphant cry burst from the lungs of the rebel soldiers as fresh fighters joined the battle. Victory turned from a distant prayer to reality, and a new energy surged through both her men and herself. She swung her blade with no remorse, sinking it into the flesh of any Kaburem soldier that neared.

One kill for the Necromancer who'd stood his last guard over her mother's soul before Kaburem murdered him. One kill for the Medic who'd joined the Necromancer's side to give Dasha a chance to flee. She would not flee today. One kill for her mother, innocently slain. One kill for Prince, who'd given his life to begin the revolution. Tempest did not stop until she saw a white flag hoisted up the mast of a collapsing Kaburem ship.

The battle was won.

42

*T*empest held a scarf to her nose, stifling the reek of the hanging man before her. He'd been there for days, and the elements had taken their toll. His hands were bound with rope, and he was dressed in fine clothes. On his ringed finger, he still wore the olivine stone that marked him guild leader of the Army. He seemed to have accepted his end with honor.

"Bring him down and bury him with the rest," said Tempest to the two militia men who'd brought her to the gallows.

A chill set deep within her bones, and she couldn't tell if it was the grotesque disfiguration of the hanging man or the cool, damp wind of the night that caused it. She shuddered, watching as the black waves lapped forward onto the beach, only to retreat with a collection of bloodstained sand particles.

Most of the carnage had been cleared at this point, but the evidence of this battle would remain rooted in the land for many weeks to come. Gulls flew with the dragons overhead, and crows flocked beneath the moon, summoned by the scents of rotting flesh.

A large hand touched Tempest's shoulder, startling her from her thoughts. When she turned, she found the smiling face of an old friend. "Adrian!"

He stepped back and gave a theatrical bow. "At your service," he said. "Did you miss me?"

Tempest chuckled at the prospect. "Of course I did."

He pressed his hand to his heart and feigned surprise. "I'm shocked to hear truth in those words," he said. "But I know there's someone you miss more. Come on, I'll take you to him." He held out his arm and escorted her to the shore where a small whaleboat bobbed with the waves. Up above, Neymar circled, still on edge from the morning's fight.

With Adrian's aid, Tempest climbed into the boat, steadying herself as it rocked. When she was seated, he waded into the water and pulled the boat away from the shore before joining her inside it. She watched him row, pushing them towards a distant ship with each stroke. The slow rhythmic pulse of it mirrored her heart. There was an inexplicable nervousness in her gut, one that had grown in the months she'd spent apart from Cyrus. She wondered if she'd changed in that time. If she had, then perhaps so had he.

Water cascaded from the sides of the great ship, and wood groaned with each wave that rolled beneath its hull. Ropes swung down from the deck, and Adrian tied them to metal ringlets on the whaleboat's edges, shouting to the one above when the knots were secure.

Their little boat swayed and pitched as the men above heaved them to the top, but Tempest found the motion soothing. She was glad, nonetheless, when the swaying stopped. It, combined with the rocking of the ship, made her head spin. She clambered over the rail and planted her feet sturdily on the deck, wiping her salt crusted palms on the folds of her clothes.

When Adrian joined her, he nodded towards a figure who stood in the shadows, overseeing a group of Kaburem prisoners being loaded into the brig.

"Cyrus!" Adrian shouted, and Tempest's heart sped. "I've got another prisoner for you!"

Tempest whacked him with the back of her hand. "I am not a prisoner!" she scolded.

Cyrus' back straightened at the sound of her voice, and he turned, stepping into the pale blue light of the moon, a smile broad on his face.

Adrian leaned close. "It is only the truth," he said to her. "The fates have you both shackled to each other, whether you know it or not."

"You speak too freely sometimes," said Tempest with a playful glare.

"I always will," he replied, then he left to take over Cyrus' task.

A flush crept to Tempest's cheeks as Cyrus strode towards her. There'd been truth to Adrian's words, and she knew it well. When Cyrus stopped before her, she lifted her hand and placed it gently on his chest as though it were the only way to prove this moment was real. The solidity of his presence was something she had not realized she needed so desperately.

He took her hand in his, and his features softened. He said no words, and neither did she. She simply stood, taking it all in. Her trance only broke when Cyrus' lips pressed to hers. With his kiss, her fears seemed to melt away. She knew, in that moment, no matter what was to come, things would be okay.

Tempest's fingers curled, clutching to the white fabric of his shirt. "Five months apart," she whispered, finally answering the question he'd asked so long ago.

"That's far too much time."

"So much has changed."

Cyrus touched her chin with the curve of his forefinger, and he smiled before pulling away. "Come with me," he said, and Tempest followed. He led her up the stairwell to the quarterdeck where a man stood watching over the whole of the ship. "This is Captain Edwards," he said, and the man turned to meet them. "He's one of the main reasons our mission came to fruition."

"I'm honored," said Tempest, bowing her head to the Naval officer.

He returned the gesture with gallantry. "The honor is mine," said the captain. "I should apologize for our delayed arrival. Rhumir put us through many challenges on our way, and there's no greater fury than a storm on the sea."

Tempest dismissed his worries. "Delayed or not, I'd say you succeeded the god's challenges."

"I must agree," said Cyrus. "Look at the sky, there's not a cloud in sight."

Tempest did look to the sky. It was the first time she'd done so all night. She'd been so caught up with the calamity on the beach, she hadn't thought to look above it. The beauty of the stars was a welcome change. Dark waves reflected their glittering extravagance, making the black abyss seem endless.

"I once read a journal written by a Priest from long ago," she said, returning her gaze to her two companions. "In it, he wrote that the gods created us, our world, and the stars with the same material."

Cyrus' brow lifted at the thought, and the captain shared in his curiosity. "Do you think he was right?" Cyrus asked.

"I do," said Tempest. She was confident in her answer. "When I visited Mortem, Sepora told me that, in death, our bodies return to the dust we were born from. Perhaps one day, that dust returns also to the stars."

"Maybe that's why the sailors are drawn to them for guidance," said Cyrus, eyes fixated on the speckled sky. "Thousands of lives contained in glowing dust fragments. If anyone were to know the secrets of the sea, it'd be them."

"What wonders we could learn from the stars," Tempest marveled.

"After years at sea, I can certainly attest to their boundlessness," the captain added. "But, the question we must ask ourselves now, m'lady, is which ones shall we be following next?"

A smile graced Tempest's lips as she spoke the next words. "We follow the ones that guide us to Alyria. It's time we take back our homes; don't you think?"

~~~

A cool breeze tugged at the loose cloth of Tempest's new gown. She liked the way the wind gave life to its layers. It was a sharp wind, one blown by the fading breaths of the winter goddess, and it sliced through her body like a million ice crystals. Izasel had come at last with spring, putting an end to death's reign, and illness, while spread far and wide, had not struck as harshly as it had the previous year.

With the palms of her hands, she pressed back the whipping strands of her hair that joined in the wind's dance. Streaks of it remained blackened from the dye she'd put in it, but by this point, its auburn color had mostly returned.

An icy mist pricked at her skin as the breeze carried a spray of water from the river that lapped before her. It was a humid morning on these docks that made the air seem colder, but she found comfort in it. Grey clouds drifted through the sky, and thunder rolled from within them. She thought that perhaps Prince had been right in giving her the name he had. A storm had come indeed.

Hollow footsteps knocked with musicality on the wood planks that stretched into the fog. An array of fishing boats and ships lined the docks, each of them bustling with activity, but these footsteps belonged to someone familiar. She walked forward, meeting Cyrus on the edge of the pier. Even though she'd gone months apart from him before, after reuniting, these past weeks separated by travel seemed eternal.

Captain Edwards stood by Cyrus' side, barking commands to the men who were charged with the task of unloading the Kaburem prisoners. They were to be marched to the temple ruins where the newer prisoners were being kept. The rebels had taken the city with ease upon their arrival. Most of the Kaburem soldiers retreated to protect the castle when the army drew near.

"M'lady," said Cyrus, extending his hand towards her.

She accepted it graciously, and he escorted her through the port. Their two dragons followed on either side. "I meant to ask this earlier," she said, looking to the golden beast she'd encountered a number of times, yet hardly knew. "What did you end up naming your dragon?"

It was one of the first conversations they'd had in the early days of their training, but Tempest had been so afraid of Cyrus in that moment, she'd never heard his response.

"I named her Zuri," he said, and a pang of sadness lingered in his voice at the mention of the name like always, but there was something new to accompany it. In his eyes, Tempest found joy. "What about you?"

Tempest gave a pleasant sigh. They'd both named their dragons after people they'd lost. "Neymar," she said.

They stopped before the entrance of one of the riverside taverns, and Tempest took a breath, preparing. When she looked up, Cyrus' eyes met hers, deep pools of honey in the light of the sun. His brow lifted. "Are you ready?" he asked, and she nodded, so he pressed open the door. Inside waited near every person who'd helped her on this journey.

Cyrus kissed the top of her hand, then moved to take his place amongst the others. A map of the city lay strewn across the table with dragon bone figurines placed where Kaburem reinforcements were known. Tempest stepped forward to look at it. She'd seen many maps in the recent months, but they'd all been foreign to her. With each line of this one, however, she could visualize the layout with clarity.

The curved path to the main gates she'd walked any time she ventured to the city. The woods to the west of the castle she'd look at through her bedroom window. At night, in the summer months, the trees would light up with tiny glowing insects. She'd always found them fascinating. Each pen stroke held a memory from her childhood that brought joy to her heart. With a breath, she took in the moment, relishing in the knowledge that she was finally home.

"I have asked the world from each of you," said Tempest, "and you have all delivered it. Tonight, I ask you to do so once more. It is my fullest intention to negotiate with Lazareth. I wish to end this war with peace, but I know he won't accept. He is plagued by wrath, and wrath is a flame not easily extinguished."

"Cut away the oxygen, and all flames will die," said Clio. "If we wish to preserve both rebel and civilian lives, it's in our best interest to lay siege. The king and his men are trapped within the castle walls. We can force their surrender through starvation."

"Forgive me," said Marius, "but starvation takes time I'm afraid we don't have."

Tempest was glad to hear his voice. He'd remained quite silent since Sarah's death, and his optimism had depleted in the weeks that followed. She wondered if this hesitation was a product of desperation or if his claim held conviction.

Once he'd captured the silence of the room, he explained himself. "Last night I shared some drinks with a few of the locals. They were under the assumption that I was no more than a common sea farer, so they told me secrets a bit too freely. There is unrest in this city, and we've only amplified it with our arrival. They still blame us for the massacre at the temple."

"Drunken murmurings, no doubt," Adrian assured. "I've seen men talk of glory they'll only ever find in liquid spirits. If these folks were fighters, they would have already picked their side of the war. Odds are, they'll be no threat to us."

"You'd be amazed what a bit of fire and opportunity will do to the average man," said Benjamin. "Do not discount them. They are much like us, so we must show them we stand with them. We must show them we are not their enemy."

"Then we'll do that," said Tempest. "We'll send out aid groups. Medics, food, supplies, whatever people require. It may not be enough. We've been convicted of an unforgivable thing, and bribery does not earn trust. We must prepare for everything, be it siege, assault, or peace."

~~~

Tempest placed her right foot on the dangling stirrup of the horse's saddle and swung her other leg over the creature's back. When she'd mounted, Patch reached up and handed her the white flag that signified their peaceful intentions.

"Are we ready?" asked Cyrus who'd mounted the horse beside her.

"Let's go," Tempest said, lifting the flag above her head.

Together, Tempest, Cyrus, and Clio rode forth towards the castle gates with ten Mortem knights at their flanks for protection. The portcullis opened as they neared, and a group of equal size emerged. At the forefront stood a young envoy. Tempest had seen him before. He'd held the king's banner at Prince's execution.

"Have you come to offer your surrender?" the envoy asked.

Tempest laughed. "For your king, perhaps," she replied. "I've come to offer him an honorable end to this war. No one else needs to die."

The envoy shrugged. "He'll not have your negotiations unless they're on his terms."

"And what terms are those?" asked Clio. "Your king is in no position to make demands."

"You come to him," the envoy said, as though it were an obvious answer.

"That'd be certain death," said Tempest. "We'll meet on neutral ground, or there will be no negotiation."

"It is the chance of your life or the lives of your people. Consider this with care." He spun his horse around and galloped to the castle, his companions following close behind.

"Set a guard by the gates," Tempest said to Clio. "If anyone leaves this castle, I want to be the first to know of it."

Clio nodded and dug her heels into the sides of her horse, which kicked clumps of dirt as it rode off. "What did he mean?" Cyrus asked. "Your life or the lives of your people. What can the king do, trapped within his walls?"

"I fear we may soon find out," said Tempest. "Let's go."

At the bottom of the hill, Patch still waited. "What's the verdict?" he asked.

"Prepare the hospital," said Tempest. "Kaburem has something planned."

"I'll tell Liz." He lifted his arm to help Tempest dismount, but his gaze stayed focused on Cyrus. "While I'm away, you'll ensure she does nothing rash, I trust."

Cyrus chuckled, amused. "I'll not let her turn herself in, if that's your meaning."

A smile twisted Patch's lips. "You and I will get along just fine."

"There are other things than me to worry about," snapped Tempest.

"There are always other things to worry about," said Patch. "Let me enjoy the little things for once." He climbed onto the horse Tempest had borrowed and left to join Liz at the hospital.

"Where did you meet him?" Cyrus asked, lowering his hand to pull her onto the saddle.

Tempest took his hand and clambered up the side of his horse. When she'd settled in front of him, she gave her answer. "Here, actually. I met him in the city the month before my parents died. He was one of my first true friends."

"It seems you've made plenty more in the year that followed," he said, wrapping his right arm around her waist as he spurred the horse forward. He was warm and solid against her back, and she never wanted to leave his hold. "Will you tell me their stories over supper? I want to know everything I've missed."

"I will," said Tempest, and so she did. They found a table at an inn near the edge of the city, and Tempest told him everything, from Mortem to the day they reunited. When she'd finished, Cyrus did the same.

Shortly after training, he'd been sent to Aquius for his first mission as an officer. His task was to recruit for the guild and introduce the northern youth to the dragons their guild was charged to protect. Tempest wondered if Jax had been doing the same when she'd seen him in the streets of Alyria.

According to Cyrus, he'd been sent to Aquius to watch Kaburem as well. Sagua wished to keep a close eye on the ports to monitor their power. He spent his mornings at a tavern on the docks and counted the ships, men, and supplies that filtered through. It was this that enabled the rebels to recapture the Naval city a while back.

When the city fell, and Kaburem retreated, He'd recalled the letter Tempest had written and set out to find Adrian, but it was a big city, and he'd had no luck. On the day they planned to leave to join forces with Tempest's few, he'd walked into the tavern once more to pay his bill. At the bar was a man with a group of Naval officers. He heard them call this man Adrian, so he joined them. When he was sure he'd found the right man, he showed Adrian the letter, and they began their plans to sail to the eastern coast.

"It was fate that he was there the day I planned to leave," said Cyrus. "I'd never have predicted it."

"Fate is as unpredictable as a flame," Tempest said, swallowing the last bit of drink in her cup.

When she set the empty canister down, the front door swung open with a frightening urgency, and one of her militia men entered. "M'lady," he said with a bow. "There's a rider coming from the castle. He appears to be a messenger."

Tempest stood and shrouded her face with the hood of her cloak. "Show me to him," she said.

They didn't need to travel far. As soon as they left the tavern, the rider rushed past them. It seemed to Tempest that he was headed for the square.

Whatever he planned to do, he expected an audience. Tempest followed his path, stopping only when she reached the edge of the square. Cyrus stood at her side, watching the many faces that strolled about.

The messenger shouted summonings, drawing in the audience he desired. When enough people had gathered, he unrolled a sheet of parchment and held it up to read. "Let it be known," he said in a voice that echoed off the surrounding stones, "that an agreement of peace was offered to the rebels, and they declined it. We ask you citizens to help us prevent the war they demand. Turn over the rebel queen, and all this will be over. Keep her hidden, and the city will pay."

A gunshot burst through the air, and the crowd ducked in terror, but Tempest stood and watched as the bullet landed between the messenger's eyes. She hadn't a clue who'd fired it, but she knew the blame would fall on her. Cyrus seemed to know it too. He took her hand and quickly pulled her away.

43

*W*aves of steam lifted from the ham and eggs that sat on the plate before Tempest. She took a deep breath, savoring the warm scent of the fresh morning meal that'd been delivered to her residence.

At her side, Neymar chirped, head tilted as his eyes focused on the meat. She cut a portion of the ham and fed it to the creature, who hummed graciously in return. He swallowed it down and nudged the leg of the table with his head, but Tempest refused to give him more. He'd get his share of food on the hunt later in the day.

As she scooped up her first bite, she was interrupted by a sudden guest. She sighed as a familiar gait drew near, and Clio plopped down in the chair opposite her with a sheet of paper clutched in her hand. "Good morning," said Tempest, setting down her fork.

Clio did not return the pleasantries, just spread the paper out for Tempest to see. "Lazareth wishes to play games with us," she said.

Tempest came to the same conclusion. On the paper was written a decree that deemed any aid to the rebel army a crime against the crown, condemning the entire city. For each account, a punishment was promised, and the first punishment had already been fulfilled.

"They've taken much of the livestock to Odemus in a most horrid fashion," said Clio when Tempest looked up from the page. "Horses and cattle have been mutilated. They even killed some street cats for a reason only the gods know."

Dread formed in the pit of Tempest's stomach, and the food on her plate was forgotten. "What of the elephants?" she asked. She'd sworn to protect them, and she'd never forgive herself if she'd failed to do so.

"I don't know," said Clio. "But they're surrounded by soldiers. No one brave enough to try would be smart enough to succeed."

Tempest stood and threw on her cloak, but Clio stopped her before she could reach the door. "Let me go," said Tempest.

"Have you forgotten the crown has called for your head?" Clio replied.

"I will not cower in this room while my people suffer. I'll take a guard if I must, but you can't make me stay."

Clio took a deep breath, then she dropped her arm and opened the door. Outside waited Callum, a knotted blade of grass between his fingers. When Tempest stepped through, he let the grass piece fall, and he stood to greet her. "Are we going somewhere?" he asked, touching his arm to summon the dead into action.

"Down to the camp," answered Tempest, pausing only long enough for him to collect his Mortem knights.

Clio had spoken truthfully. Stablemen carried murdered horses from their stalls, chickens lay in the streets with broken necks, and street cats lay bloodied beside them. As they neared the farms on the outer edge of the city, pigs joined in the slaughtered masses, and sheep had their coats turned red with death.

In the mud, she found the body of a man garbed in all black with a bullet in his back. Clio had been right about this too. This man appeared to have tried to reach the elephants and paid for it with his life.

Militia soldiers sat around the small heard of elephants with their guns loaded and ready. It appeared that every beast was accounted for, which brought relief to Tempest's heart.

One of the young bulls lifted its trunk and wrapped it gently around Tempest's arm. "He thinks you've got food," said Cedric as he approached with clumps of tall grass in his hands. He passed a portion of it to Tempest, and the elephant probed at it with the tip of his trunk. "Hold it up to his mouth."

Tempest did as he directed and hovered the grass beneath the elephant's trunk. It opened its mouth in return and patiently waited for Tempest to place the grass inside.

"I assume you didn't come just to feed the elephants," Cedric noted, and Tempest shook her head.

"I came to ensure the elephants survived last night's attacks," she said.

Cedric sat on a log stool and smirked, gesturing to the body still laying in the mud. "I don't think the poor man had ever seen an elephant before they'd sent him off to kill one. He was absolutely terrified." He paused, placing his palm to the forehead of the little bull. "We've dealt with far smarter assassins than his lot."

"Regardless of their intelligence, this action was premeditated," said Clio. "No one left the castle, so they must have people within the city. Odds are, they'll strike again."

Tempest let out her breath, contemplating the various extremes Kaburem could go to if they allowed this game to continue. "We'll expand the night watch," she decided. "We won't catch everything, but perhaps we'll at least see something. Until then, we need to help the city. Gather what men you can and set out in groups to cover sections of the city. Clean up any corpses and salvage any meat or pelts you can. We'll promise farmers compensation for the slaughter. Quell any retaliation or riots with solidarity. We must show them we are not their enemy."

~~~

All through the day, they gave aid to the city. Tempest walked over stone streets, feet heavy with exhaustion, but the work was not quite through. She lifted her hand to cover a yawn, then plastered a smile to her face. A group of young children had gathered in the street. They sat around a fire and listened to stories told by Benjamin. His words flowed like music from his lips as he narrated old tales of dragons.

Sparks of wonder glowed in the eyes of the children. His words struck the heartstrings of the soul, emphasized by the scaled beasts that roosted all around. He paused his story when Tempest approached with Emil and an elephant at her side. The children gasped and ran up to the grey creature, touching its rough skin with their palms.

She wondered what thoughts were blooming in their minds. The rebel army in their streets, dead men walking, elephants and dragons ambling about. It was all quite absurd. If she had seen this as a child, she'd have been struck with awe.

Tempest reached into the basket strapped to the elephant's left side, and she pulled out sacks of breads and cheeses, passing a handful to each child. They took the food with gratitude, then returned to their seats around the fire, eager to be immersed once more into Benjamin's words.

When all had settled, Tempest and Emil continued down the street, not stopping until the designated food had been fully dispersed. The moon hung high in the night sky when they were through, and her eyes weighed heavy in their sockets, but despite it all, she felt at peace. Order had been maintained in the city, and a kindly relationship began to bud. There were still many who mistrusted the rebels, but after the night's attack, their anger lay with Kaburem.

Seeing the people in the streets, content and celebratory for even just a moment, Tempest could almost convince herself that the death and suffering was through, but the reminders of war came once more while Tempest lay asleep in her bed.

She woke, startled by the sound of a woman's scream. Neymar lifted his head, silhouette barely visible in the black of the room. He rose to his feet, following Tempest, and brushed against her leg as she fumbled her way to the hook that held her cloak.

By some grace of the gods, she managed her way to the door without too much blundering, and she pressed it open, letting the pale light of the moon and stars guide her towards the source of the scream. The Necromancer set to guard her quarters in the night stood waiting with his Mortem knights. He seemed to have expected her curiosity, and a hint of intrigue gleamed in his own eyes.

"It came from that direction," he said, gesturing down the dimly lit path.

Tempest started down the street, Neymar and the dead behind her. Her eyes flitted to the dark alleyways along the way where fear lurked in the shadows. She knew she was safe with the Necromancer's protection, but there was no telling what dangers lay hidden from the moonlight.

A small group had gathered in the street by the time Tempest reached the source of the cry. They stood around a youthful boy who lay in a puddle by the well, pale with blue lips that glistened, wet from the poisonous water that'd killed him. She knew this look all too well. Whatever this boy drank had contained the same toxin that'd killed her mother.

Tempest crouched down and took the boy's hand. "Who is he?" she asked, looking to the faces that gawked at the boy.

"I seen him at the stables, m'lady," said a large man at the edge of the circle. He was broad shouldered and wore the thin clothes of a Farmer. "Must ha' come to fetch the horses water and taken a sip himself. He's got no kin that I know of, just the stable master who looks after him."

Tempest's guard stepped forward and lay his hand on the child's brow, whispering a prayer that'd carry the soul to Xudor's hall. "He should be buried," said the Necromancer. "Notify the stable master of his death."

The farmer left to do so, and in his place stood Clio, a paper in her hand. She stepped forward and held the paper forward for Tempest to read. "They've played their second hand," she said. "I've ordered the wells and rivers to be blocked off. Have you ever seen a poison like this?"

Tempest nodded, standing to meet the others. "It's Lazareth's favorite weapon."

"A coward's weapon," muttered Clio, and a few in the crowd agreed.

"He used it on my mother," said Tempest, clutching the amethyst ring at her neck. The crowd hushed and craned their necks forward. This part of the story had never been told. Tempest stood up and continued in a voice loud enough for all to hear, telling the true story of the night her parents died. She told of her father's illness and the aid that came when he perished. She told of the poison and of the boy, Prince, who helped her escape. She told of the Medic and the Necromancer who stood hand in hand in the face of death to give her time to flee. She told it all, and the people listened.

"Do with this knowledge as you will, but I hope you spread it," she said when she had finished. "You and I, we're on the same side, and I hope one day, you'll see that."

The crowd stayed silent, digesting the spoken words, but mutterings began once more when the Farmer returned to the scene. In the commotion, Tempest, Clio, and the Necromancer made their escape.

"What are we going to do about this?" asked Clio when they'd gotten a safe distance away. "Even trapped in his castle, Lazareth still manages to hurt people. We can't sit idle while he does."

"Would you have us attack?" Tempest asked. She felt helpless in the mess of it all.

"I suppose that depends on your goal," said Clio. "We could end this tonight and save the city from whatever other sufferings Kaburem has planned, but we'd lose hundreds of men in doing it, or we could continue to wait and watch as hunger makes even the boldest fall to desperation. But, the longer we wait, the longer the city is at risk."

"There's one more option... We could agree to his terms of negotiation," Tempest offered. "I come to him. He won't meet us on neutral ground for the same reason I won't meet him in the castle. There's no trust that peace will be upheld."

"There could be if we enforce it. We bring the army to the castle gates and threaten to attack if the momentary peace should falter."

"If it comes to that, battle will be our only option. We'll keep waiting."

~~~

The wait proved unbearable to Tempest's restless mind. As the night hours settled over the land, her mind began to turn over every possibility that lay ahead. There was a certain dread that came with knowing something was coming but not knowing when or where. She stroked Neymar's scales and let his hums of contentment sooth her worried heart.

Hours passed without sound, and she found herself hoping they'd gone one night without a new attack, but that hope crumbled when the alarm bells began to sing. She stood, already dressed, and stepped into the night.

Smoke billowed through the air, and chaos erupted as the city woke to their buildings burning. Citizens ran from their houses, heaving water from the wells to douse the flames. Tempest joined in, hoping the toxins had faded.

The Mages battled to contain the flames, and Fire Keepers ran into the burning structures, braving Zalder's heat to rescue anyone trapped inside. Tempest didn't know how they did it. Even outside, the smoke made her throat raw.

Wind carried the tendrils of flames to other buildings. It danced and breathed like a living creature. She imagined if the dragons were not contained by scales, they'd look a bit like this. Burning, uncontained rage.

Sweat poured from her skin as she ran to and fro between the well and the fires. She couldn't feel her legs by the end of it, and her lungs begged for clean air, but she continued alongside the rest until every last fire had faded to a dull, ashen ruin. The sun had risen, taking the cool winds of night away.

Tempest took a breath and leaned against the well, dabbing her brow with a cloth strip. It came away caked in ash and sweat. "Need a drink?" asked a voice that made the night's toil seem distant. Tempest looked up, eyes meeting with Cyrus'. He held a flask of water in an outstretched hand. "It's pure," he assured.

"I should hope so," she said with a slight laugh, then she took a deep gulp of it, feeling the liquid journey down her throat. When she lowered the flask, she saw two others approaching. It was Jyles and a tall, lanky boy whose hands were bound.

The boy dropped to his knees before her, aided by a shove from Jyles. "We caught him fleeing the powder stores after failing to set his fire," Jyles said.

Tempest crouched before the boy and looked him in the eyes. They brimmed with tears, and his hands trembled with fear. "What's your name?" she asked.

"Joshua," he murmured, then in a louder voice, "I didn't want to set the fire, m'lady. I only agreed to it because Kaburem promised me coin. I haven't got any parents, and I've got a little sister to care for. I had to try for her. I beg your forgiveness... please."

His voice shook with as much terror as his hands, and Tempest pitied him. She reached forward and untied his cloth-bound wrists. "On your feet, Joshua," she said, rising to her own. "I'd like you to meet a friend of mine."

She led Joshua to the hospital and introduced him to Patch who'd been working since sun rise, treating burns and other ailments from the fires. "Joshua, meet Patch," she said, and the boy's eyes flared with recognition.

"I've heard of you," said Joshua. "You're the healer that helps kids like me." He paused. "But you vanished after the massacre. There were stories that the rebels took you as captive." His cheeks reddened with a sheepish glow. "You joined them, didn't you?"

Patch nodded. "I joined them long before that day," he said with a smile. "I was a nameless kid living on the streets, but one day, I stumbled upon a strange girl hiding on the roof tops." His eyes flitted to Tempest. "One month later, this girl became an exiled queen, and the fates began to weave their tapestry." As he spoke, he weaved a thread of his own, suturing the wound of an unconscious man.

Tempest stepped away, letting the two converse about experiences she'd never know. She found a seat in the corner, and Cyrus sat beside her. "I spoke to Clio last night," she said, taking his hand in hers. "She convinced me to keep up the siege, but after tonight, Cyrus, I want to turn myself in."

His eyes flashed with worry, his grip tightened, and he inhaled sharply, but otherwise, his composure remained stoic and calm. "Why?" he asked, voice barely rising above a whisper.

"I keep telling myself it's a final effort to reach a bloodless peace, but I know that's not how this ends."

His lips pursed, and Tempest could see the pain he held back. "We have the strength to storm the castle," he said, seeking an explanation. "Why turn over and give negotiations a second chance if you know they will fail?"

"Because it's not negotiations that I'm hoping for, and neither is he." She leaned back in her chair and closed her eyes. "I've realized recently that I've known of Lazareth my whole life. Only then, he had a different name than this one. Growing up, I knew him as Atticus."

"The king's brother?" Cyrus asked, just as confused as Tempest had been. "Isn't he dead?"

"Exiled," Tempest replied. "My father felt that a far worse fate. He was chained to a boat and sent into the sea where he was never seen again... At least by any citizen of Alyria. According to one of our prisoners, it was around this time that a man named Lazareth washed up on the beach of Kaburem's island."

"You think it was Atticus?"

Tempest nodded. "In Mortem, my father told me he knew Lazareth. It all lines up. This started long ago, before anyone knew it was coming. It has always been and will always be between him and I... until one of us is dead."

"So you wish to offer your head on a platter?" He spoke with staccato, tensions of clashing emotions bubbling in each word.

"And kill him upon delivery. You remember my telling you about Markus, yes?"

"The one with the dreams."

"Yes. If his dream comes true, which they always seemed to do, Lazareth's death is certain."

"And your survival is unknown."

"Better odds than his, I reckon." A slight smile twisted her lip. "I have to try."

"Will there be no changing your mind, then?"

"No," said Tempest. "I'll tell the others tomorrow morning. These people can't afford for us to wait longer than that."

"And until then?" Cyrus asked.

"We have ruins and rubble to sift through."

44

andlelight flickered in the dark room Tempest lay in. There was little furnishing, and cobwebs stretched in the corners. The tiny flame of her candle threw the shadows of these objects against the walls. It fascinated Tempest, looking at the flame. Fire seemed to hold the world's deepest secrets, and she thought maybe if she stared at it long enough, it'd show them to her.

She hoped that it would. Answers were slim and few these days, and doubt plagued her every decision. This, to her, was a battle greater than any physical one, a constant mental debate between what was right and what was wrong. The verdict of her choice would determine the fate of everyone. It was a horrible power to bear.

Tempest sat up, shedding the furs that covered her. Carefully, she placed her feet on the cold, wooden floor and stood, stepping over Neymar who lay sleeping between the bed and the desk. She lifted the candle and carried it with her, taking a seat in the chair. When settled, she reached into the desk drawer and pulled out her notebook.

The pages only held a year's worth of memories, but the time had seemed far greater. She turned to the last pages of the book where Cyrus' flower remained pressed within, and she dipped a pen into black ink, not yet certain what she intended to write. Despite not knowing, she put the pen to the paper and let her thoughts take physical form.

To whomever may discover this, she began. *I pray it is known that everything I've done, I've done in the interest of protecting my people. Tomorrow, be it destiny or mistake, I will do so once more. I will return to the beginning and face the man who robbed me of everything I knew, yet gave me a life I'd only ever dreamed of. Fate is a fickle thing.*

I know the king will choose death before he surrenders. This castle is as much his home as it is mine. To return after seventeen years of exile, he'll not want to leave.

The Kaburem people, however, are motivated differently. Their homes are across the sea. They'll want to go back to them when all this is through. If the king is dead, their surrender is imminent.

So, you see, even this I do in the interest of protecting my people. It must be done, no matter the personal cost. If I die tomorrow, I pray it is a death with meaning. I pray I have done enough.

With the last period came a knock at the door. Tempest closed the journal and pushed it aside, rising to meet her guest. "Come in," she said, covering herself with a thin night robe.

The doorknob twisted, and in stepped Cyrus, shirt loosely tucked and coat hurriedly thrown on. It seemed as though he'd made the decision to come in a rushed flurry of thought. His eyes were sunken with exhaustion but remained alert and focused entirely on her. "Did I wake you?" he asked, gaze flitting for only a moment to the disturbed furs on the bed.

"No. I couldn't sleep," she said, crossing the room to stand before him. He lifted a hand and gently touched her cheek. With this action, the uncertainty that tumbled through her mind came to an abrupt stop. He was warm and steady, and it brought her comfort. "Have you come to change my mind?"

"No." His thumb brushed over her lips, gaze boldly meeting hers. "I came because I'm scared," he said, grasping her hands and pulling her close. He smelled of pine and old parchment, with a hint of smoke from the fires. Tempest found it quite intoxicating. "And if I'm scared, I figured you must be terrified."

"I am," she said, admitting it to herself as much as she was to him.

"Then I came to be with you, if you'll have me."

Tempest entwined her fingers with his and answered him with a kiss. "I'll have you," she said when their lips had drawn apart.

The soft reflection of the candle glimmered in his eyes; the flame seemed to mirror his soul. She'd seen it before in the meadow of Firethorne, that burning glow of passion and curiosity.

"What are you thinking about?" he asked, and she blinked, startled from her thoughts, then a shy smile touched her lips

"A boy made of fire, sitting in a meadow," she replied.

"Oh?" His brow raised in mock suspicion. "Who is this boy?"

"My love," said Tempest, and a deep hum vibrated within Cyrus' chest.

"Is that what we are, then? Lovers?" The word rolled from his tongue like a gentle breeze, and it made her heart flutter.

"If you'll have me," she said.

"I'll have you," he replied. "Until the end of time."

She broke away from him then and sat on the edge of the bed, conflicted. "Even if my time ends tomorrow?"

"It won't," he said, joining her. "It can't. I can't bear the thought of it." He took her hand in his and held it tight. "Everything in my soul tells me not to let you go…"

She hooked her forefinger beneath his chin and turned his gaze to her. "You don't have to." If this was to be her last night amongst the living, she wished not to spend it alone. "Not tonight. Will you stay with me?"

He leaned forward slowly and answered with a kiss.

~~~

Tempest woke in the predawn hours. A fog had set in overnight, leaving the room damp with humidity. She took a deep breath, calmed by the scent of it.

Cyrus lay beside her, breaths long and heavy, the light blue tint of morning soft on his skin. Tempest reached forward, touching the point where his shoulder blades met. She followed his spine down his back, feeling each bone, each muscle.

He stirred, waking to her touch, and he turned to face her with a smile. "Good morning," he said, voice low with the raspiness of freshly waking.

"Good morning," she replied, pulling her hand back. "I didn't mean to wake you." She felt suddenly quite shy, memories of the night before playing in the back of her mind.

Cyrus didn't answer with words. With his right hand, he enclosed the one she'd pulled away and brought it to his lips, then he propped himself on his elbow and leaned forward for one final kiss to end the blissful night, but he stopped midway as the doorknob turned, two voices arguing behind it. Tempest covered herself quickly, and the door swung open.

"I'm sorry, m'lady; he insisted on getting through," her guardsman said, keeping his eyes on the floorboards. His head tilted to the left, addressing Patch, who stood frozen in the doorway.

"My, my!" said Patch with a grin. "I regret that I must interrupt this, but there's something the two of you ought to see."

Tempest closed her eyes and sighed, mentally preparing for whatever was to come. "We'll meet you outside," she grumbled, and Patch and the guardsmen departed.

"Do you think it's Kaburem?" Cyrus asked once they were alone again.

"It must be," she answered, untangling herself from the furs. The air was cold on her bared skin, and tiny bumps rose from her flesh. She rubbed her palms against them, hoping to restore the warmth that'd once been there.

Sunlight crept through the window, but it was not yet enough to fill the entirety of the room. There was a dim surrealism that lingered within these walls. Fragments of the night gone by. But, with the growing light came the responsibilities of the day. Tempest dressed quickly, not wanting to prolong them.

"Ready?" Cyrus asked, garbed once again in the black frock he'd worn the night before.

"I'm ready," she said, taking the hand he held out for her. Neymar, having freshly woken, followed groggily behind them.

"I must warn you," said Patch once they'd reached him. "It is not a sight for those with weak constitution."

Tempest swallowed the lump in her throat and nodded, following Patch to the square. At the center of it stood a crowd, murmuring their discomforts of whatever lay before them. As Tempest neared, they parted, giving her a full view. The orphan boy, Joshua, hung from a crudely constructed gallows, body slit open so that his blood dripped wherever the wind carried it, painting the stone floor crimson.

"We think his cohorts did it. The ones who set the fires," Clio said, sitting beside the structure with a weeping girl in her arms. "They left this." She handed Tempest a crumpled piece of paper marked with the teardrops of the child.

Tempest unraveled the paper and read the words out loud. "By order of the Kingsmen," it said. "Joshua: Executed on the charge of treason for colluding with rebels. Let his blood be a reminder of the massacre, lest we forget who the enemy is."

Her voice faded as she read each word, despair and rage boiling in her heart. The only thing that kept her steady was Cyrus' touch. She turned to the onlookers who watched, curious and horrified all the same.

"Lest we forget who the enemy is," Tempest repeated, loud enough for all to hear. "That's what they want of you, so I say listen. Listen when I tell you, we had no part in the massacre. We came only for the king. It was his men who slaughtered the innocents. It was him who fled.

"We stayed. Despite the danger, we stayed and protected you. We stayed and healed you. We are not your enemy. We never were. The enemy sits like a coward on his throne, ordering his people to suffer in the name of a war he's already lost. Stand with me against him; I beg of you. Stand for yourselves."

They did not rally, hearts suddenly changed, but neither did they protest. A part of them, thought Tempest, knew her words were true. "Call a meeting," she said to Clio. "I want every commander, every leader, and every friend to be present."

"Will we be planning an attack?" asked Clio.

"We will," said Tempest.

~~~

The sun's daily journey was well underway by the time all had gathered. Her people shuffled into the room, some still dreary eyed from the night. Once each had taken a seat, the doors were closed, locked, and barricaded from further entry. Tempest stood to address her companions, bowing to the lot of them before she began.

"At the end of this road, there sits a false king in a stolen castle with hardly an army to defend it," she said. "Tonight we take it back." Murmurs of agreement washed through the hall, settling when Tempest lifted her hand. "The path we go about it might seem odd, but I ask you all to trust me. You will line your ranks as was planned the day we arrived, but I will not be with you. Instead, I will be within the castle, making negotiations under a truce that will not hold."

"Will we be the ones to break it?" Clio asked.

"No," she replied. "Lazareth will try to kill me. If I'm correct in assuming his history, he'll not throw away this chance."

"Forgive me," said Patch, running his fingers through his sleek black locks. "Why offer negotiations if you know Lazareth will break the truce?"

"Because when he does, I'll be close enough to kill him." She drew out her dragon hilted dagger and lay it on the table. "If Lazareth dies, Kaburem will surrender. This is not their fight. It never has been. They want no more casualties than we do."

"You can't possibly think we'd let you go through with this. It's suicide," said Patch. "Cyrus, you swore you wouldn't let her do this."

"I'm not asking for approval. I'm asking for your help," Tempest said before Cyrus could respond.

"Lazareth would certainly not expect it," said Clio. "Take out the foundation, and the house will crumble. It only takes a bit of force."

"What if he kills you first?" Patch asked.

"Then you'll swear to do what we discussed," she said with a somber smile. "You'll pick up the crown and finish what I started."

All eyes fell to Patch. Whether he'd wanted it or not, she'd publically named him her successor. For the sake of her memory and the sake of the nation, he'd have no choice but to accept.

"Are there any further oppositions?" Clio asked, and the answer came in the form of silence.

"It's settled, then," said Tempest. "Gather your men and meet atop the hill in six hours."

~~~

Horses whickered and shook their manes as they were corralled into the street. There was an excitement and a terror that came with impending battle. It was that innate thrill of the fight coupled with the dread of death. It flourished within the gathering crowd and settled deep in Tempest's chest.

"Tempest," said Cyrus, pointing down the road. "Look."

She followed the line of his finger to the approaching figure. It was Patch, dressed for battle with a gun in his hand and a pack of supplies strapped to his side. "Does this mean you've forgiven me?" Tempest asked once he'd neared.

"For the moment," said Patch, tugging her into an embrace. "That's why I'm coming. Liz will be watching the hospital, and I'll be watching you. After all, someone's got to make sure you don't break your promise. Odemus will not be meeting you tonight."

Tempest smiled and held him tight. When they drew apart, her fingers reached for the clasp at her neck, and with careful precision, she unhooked it, letting her mother's ring fall into her palm. "Return this to me when I've made it out alive," she said, placing it in Patch's hand.

"I will," he promised, tucking it away for safe keeping.

Tempest climbed onto her horse, and the others followed. Together they rode up the hill to where the army waited. Clio sat mounted at the forefront of the ranks, preparing to make the calls for battle. Behind her, the rebels stretched far into the tree line, thick foliage canopied above their heads. In some of the larger trees, Tempest could see dragons perched in the branches. The others flew through the sky, Neymar and Zuri amongst them, casting large shadows on the ground as they swarmed.

She whistled to summon Neymar from the sky, and two Mortem knights stepped forward from the ranks, drawing her attention back to the ground. Somewhere within the Alyrian graveyard was Tegan, puppeteering the knights from afar. Tempest cantered forward to meet them. They bowed to her in unison, signaling the evening to begin.

"Let's try this again," said Tempest, and Cyrus held out the white flag of truce. Their fingers touched for only a moment as she took the flag from him, but it was enough to make her heart soar with longing.

"Promise you'll come back to me," said Cyrus.

"Always," Tempest replied, then she spun her horse to face the castle. With a deep breath, she squeezed her heels into the horse's sides and began her journey forward, the two Mortem knights and Neymar at her side.

As they drew near, the castle's portcullis opened with a deep groan, and the king's envoy rode out from beneath its wooden teeth. Tempest's focus was not on him, however. Instead, her gaze locked above where Lazareth stood, looking over the parapet.

"Have you come to talk or to fight?" asked the envoy, glancing behind her to where the army stood.

Tempest looked forward to meet his eyes. "That depends on your king," she said. "I'd like to reopen negotiations."

The envoy's brow raised. "On his terms or yours?"

"His if he's willing." She leaned forward. "There will be a truce, of course. My safety must be ensured. Otherwise, well—" Her voice trailed and she looked back at the waiting army. "You get my meaning."

The envoy gestured towards the gate. "Right this way."

They proceeded forward through the gullet of the castle entrance. Once through the first gate, Tempest and the envoy dismounted, and the horses were led away. The Kaburem guardsmen closed the first gate and opened the next. Tempest walked through them, stepping inside for the first time in over a year.

It felt odd to her, walking through these halls. She seemed to know them, yet at the same time be entirely foreign to them. Something had changed and she couldn't decide if it was the castle or her.

Memories of childhood flooded through her mind as she continued through the castle. They were memories of a life gone by, of a girl who'd died the same day Kaburem came. She wondered if the girl she'd been would even recognize the girl she was now. Dasha had been a dreamer, desperate to flee the burdens of Royalty. Tempest had taken those burdens willingly and bore them with great effort.

The ornate, brass hinges of the throne room doors groaned as they opened. "Have you any weapons?" asked the envoy, inspecting Tempest and the knights warily.

They had nothing to show but empty scabbards, but concealed beneath Tempest's coat was the dragon hilted dagger. "We brought none," she said. "This is a peaceful meeting, is it not?"

The envoy appeared doubtful, but after a quick check, he resigned his suspicions and turned to leave. "Lazareth will meet you here momentarily. Best you don't wander far."

Tempest stepped through the threshold, listening to the hollow steps of the envoy as he vanished down the hall. The room was much the same as she'd last seen it, but from the rafters hung long Kaburem banners. She looked forward to demounting them.

On the dias sat the throne. It'd been carved intricately from a dark wood, accents of silver weaved within the grain. She could see her father sitting there, addressing political matters with a member of the Law Enforcement at his side. He'd spent hours in this seat. Tempest reached forward, touching the edge of the armrest where the wood had been carved into a lion's head.

"Envisioning yourself up there?" asked a voice she'd heard only once.

"Envisioning my father," she said, turning to face Lazareth, who stood momentarily in the doorway with two guards. "Truth be told, I never wanted this throne. I had half a mind to stay in Firethorne and make a new life for myself, but a dear friend convinced me otherwise."

"Pity," Lazareth muttered.

Tempest ignored the remark. "The moment I left training, I saw the reason why. The people deserve better than this."

"And you think you can give that to them?" His laugh echoed boldly from the walls. "Child, you have no idea what it means to rule a nation."

"Perhaps I don't, but I can't do much worse than you."

His eyes narrowed and his jaw set. He looked ready to rebut, but he held his tongue. Tempest walked down to meet him, daring to get as close as she could.

He stood tall, features boasting dark hair, sharp lines, and deep sunken eyes. He looked entirely different from her father at first glance, thought Tempest, yet at closer inspection, the resemblance emerged. They were subtle similarities that'd only go noticed by someone who knew the two were kin.

Any doubt she had of him being Atticus shriveled away when he sat upon the throne. He carried with him the same kingly presence her father always had. "You wanted negotiations? Well here's my offer." He leaned forward, green eyes staring into hers. "I'll let your army walk free if you surrender yourself to me."

She almost laughed at his preposterous suggestion. "No one can ever walk free while you sit that throne." She touched her finger to her lips and walked a few paces, feigning thought. "I propose you leave. Take your men back to Kaburem, or let them stay if they desire, but you will leave, and you'll never return. You'll be exiled once again, Atticus."

He stood with a smirk and bowed, accepting the name. "We both know what it is to be exiled, so you'll understand, I'm not inclined to do it again."

"You can't win this," said Tempest. "You must know that."

Atticus walked towards her, stopping only inches from her. He leaned forward, breath hot on her skin. "I'll die in this crown before I let you take it from me again." He lifted his hand, and the sound of gunfire rang through the hall. His guards had shot her Mortem knights clean through the head, severing their connection to Tegan.

Neymar chirped in distress, digging his claws into the floor as he hissed and spit sparks at the nearest gunman. "Kill them," said Atticus.

For a moment, the world seemed to slow. Tempest had read accounts of this occurring when the mind knew death was approaching. She grabbed the hilt of her dagger firmly in her hand, then plunged the blade through Atticus' ribs. With its landing, two more bullets flew. One of which struck Tempest in the side. She didn't know where the other had landed, but she prayed it'd missed its goal. Her hand lifted, clutching the point where the bullet had entered. It felt aflame beneath her touch, and it sucked away her energy.

Tempest fell to the ground, eyes locked lazily on the collapsed figure before her. Something in the back of her mind knew it to be Atticus, the dagger still lodged in his back. Elsewhere in a distant thought, she heard the sounds of screaming men. Her heartbeat slowed, and her breaths became laborious. She blinked, drawn relentlessly to the lure of sleep. When she opened her eyes once more, the room had consumed itself with fire and smoke.

She found it beautiful in a strange way. Billowing arcs of orange and red. She felt as though she were floating within its colors, body in such searing pain that she could hardly process it as her own.

Neymar landed in front of her, head tilted with worry, black and gold scales gleaming in the firelight. It was the last thing she saw before the world fell to darkness.

45

yrus fumbled with the reins of his horse, growing impatient with every passing moment. With a soft squeeze of his legs, he spurred his mount into motion, pacing in a small circle to steady his mind.

"Have patience, Cyrus," Clio urged, snagging the reins of his horse to stay the beast. He paid no mind to her words, restless eyes focused on the sky where grey clouds gathered.

"She'll make it out," Patch said, his eyes lingering too on the clouds above. There was menace in their looming. "She always does."

A sudden flash of red illuminated the clouds, and Cyrus' head turned to the direction of the graveyard from whence it came. Clio and Patch seemed to have seen it too. They fell silent, gazes locked on the distant signal. There was only one thing it could mean. The peace was broken.

Behind them, the dead snapped to attention, readying for the inevitable battle. Cyrus shifted his eyes to Clio, fear rising in his chest. He was not afraid of the dead, nor was he afraid of dying. What terrified him was the accuracy of Tempest's prediction, and thus the likelihood of her demise.

Clio stared forward, eyes narrow as she calculated what lay ahead. Cyrus did the same. A Kaburem man walked along the rampart, purpose in his gait. He stopped and leaned close to one of the commanders on the wall. An order echoed through the guardsmen that manned it. Their guns trained forward, preparing to defend.

"Send the signal," said Clio at last, and a flash of red light shot from the Mage who stood at her side.

With the deliverance of the responding signal, the Mortem knights charged forward. A chill set deep within Cyrus' bones as he watched them scale the castle walls like insects, impervious to the onslaught of bullets that struck them.

Some of the knights fell limp to perfectly landed wounds, but many made it to the top where the Kaburem lines scattered. Those caught by Xudor's soldiers found no grace in the way they died. The rampart cleared of gunmen quickly, and the dead wreaked havoc within.

Clio called next to Cedric who sat atop one of the elder elephants that'd been armored and armed with battering rams. His partner, Emil, had been left to tend to the younger beasts in the safekeeping of the city. Another command was given, and the great beasts charged forward in a rumbling stampede, their trumpets echoing through the air in a terrifying song as they slammed into the stone walls of the castle.

The portcullis gave way first, then bit by bit, the walls began to crumble, bowing to the god-like drum of the elephants' tread. They stamped and ran in all directions, trampling anything that stood in their path.

"Ready the militia," Clio said, eyes never leaving the battle ground ahead.

Cyrus cantered towards the rebel ranks and rode along the front line, calling to ready arms. They lifted their voices to join his, brandishing a mix of swords, war axes, hammers, and guns. They were a fearsome lot, thought Cyrus, and he was honored to stand beside them. The risen dead were frightening, he was sure, but the true passion and anger lay within the people who lifted their weapons to strike down their enemy despite the risk of dying.

There were Mages intermixed with the civilian militia as well. They stood with no weapons, trusting their brethren to protect them while they worked the energies of the land.

When all had rallied, he returned to Clio's side, waiting for the next command. Her hand remained held upward, holding off their attack. From the broken gateway, a flood of Kaburem soldiers poured out, taking a stand on the land before the castle, the threat of previous waves forcing them to open ground.

Clio nodded towards the Mage, and a second burst of light shot from her palm, this one illuminating the grey clouds with a bright blue hue, summoning the dragon swarm. They descended from the clouds in a massive wave of flapping wings and glimmering scales, and from their jaws came Zalder's wrath. Amongst the orange tendrils, Cyrus caught a glint of gold from Zuri, who barreled through the smoke.

The Kaburem soldiers fled in every direction, desperate to avoid the lick of the flames. Once rightly scattered, the dragons relented their stream, landing amidst the disarray to attack from the ground. Bodies glowed like torches, and their wails sliced viciously through the air.

"Forward!" Clio cried, and the final charge began.

Cyrus rushed forth with Patch riding hard at his side, spraying dirt and mud as their horses ran. Their mission was separate from the rest. They were to find Tempest with utmost haste. He whistled as they neared the fray, bringing Zuri to his side.

Few held courage enough to remain in their path. Kaburem fighters dodged left and right, fleeing the charge of Cyrus' mount, Patch carving a similar path parallel to him. Near the portcullis, one dared to challenge. He was a man much larger than Cyrus, and he reminded Cyrus of the giants in the stories his mother told him in his youth. Adding to the mythical ambiance of his stature were blistering burn marks that covered his left side. He'd fallen victim to the dragons' fires, yet swung the bladed tip of his gun with unfaltering strength.

Cyrus drove his sword through the man's flesh with the aid of the horse's strength beneath him. Giant or not, the man was mortal in the end. He fell in a heap on the blooded cobble, replaced shortly by another. This other had escaped the burnings, but he limped from a wound to the left leg.

A crack echoed from the barrel of Patch's gun, and the attacker roared in pain. It was a crippling wound, but not one to be fatal. Cyrus made note of this and respected Patch more for it. Even on the battlefield, Patch fought for the side of life.

No others thought it wise to face them, and the path cleared to the portcullis. Cyrus and Patch abandoned their mounts once they'd crossed its threshold. There were too many ever-changing threats to continue safely on horseback. Elephants ran, bellowing and roaring. The dead slaughtered, and the ground shifted as the Mages toyed with nature's energy.

In the seconds it took for him to process all this, another Kaburem soldier stepped forward, feet planted, swinging their blade towards Cyrus' back. He noticed it on the downswing, too late to do much about it. To his fortune, however, Zuri reacted quickly. Before the blade landed, the Kaburem soldier was set aflame. He didn't stay to see what happened next.

"Do you know where the throne room is?" Cyrus asked, turning his back to protect Patch's blind side.

Patch pointed to the sky with the tip of his gun. "Follow the smoke," he said. "Come on."

Side by side, they fought their way into the castle, neither one able to make it through alone. Patch made a notable companion on the field, thought Cyrus between swings. The healer's blows landed with swift precision, boasting a unique knowledge of the human flesh. Patch knew well how to maim without killing.

Cyrus took a different approach. He was more forceful in his strikes, and he tore down any man that stood in his way. "This way, I see the flames," he said, spotting thick smoke down the hall.

Within minutes, they found the burning door. It was splintered and nearly destroyed. Cyrus threw his coat across the shards and crawled through a slight opening, emerging in the throne room with Patch close behind.

The room was ablaze, cloth banners melting into ashen piles while the wood smoked and groaned under the stress of the heat. On the floor, Cyrus counted four bodies, two of which lay side by side in the center. "Tempest," he muttered, watching as Neymar spread his wings over her, bared his teeth, and snarled.

"Can you calm him?" Patch asked, looking warily towards the wrathful beast.

"I can try." He approached slowly with Zuri at his side, palms held forward in submission, eyes staying locked in the mental dance that occurred when a dragon tested a man.

Neymar whipped his tail and spit flames with every step Cyrus took, but he replied to these assaults with soft whispers that soothed the beast to surrender long enough for Cyrus and Zuri to be recognized. The dragon's head tilted, then he backed away slowly, opening access to Tempest's limp body.

Patch dropped quickly to his knees beside her, fingers placed at the crease of her neck in search of a pulse. "She's still alive, but she's struggling," he deduced. He tore a cloth and did his best to cleanse and bind the wound with what little materials he had in his pouch. "The bullet is lodged too deep. I can't help her here. Get her onto a plank while I check the others."

Cyrus nodded and did as Patch bid, using the task to keep his mind focused. He reached into the ruins of the door and pulled a large fragment from its pieces. The edges were blackened, and fire ate at the corner of the wood. He set it on the ground and beat the flames out with the foot of his boot before carrying it over to Tempest's side.

He crouched beside her and scooped her carefully into his arms. She looked at peace, eyes closed and muscles loose. Her breaths were labored, but every shaky inhale was a beacon of hope for Cyrus. He laid her gently on the plank and brushed a lock of hair from her face, distracted for a moment from the sounds of warfare outside.

A new set of footsteps broke the silence of the room, and Cyrus looked up to find Clio standing in the threshold with a large white cloth in her hand.

"Is she alive?" Clio asked.

"For now," Cyrus replied, taking Tempest's hand.

A look of relief washed over Clio's face. "Where's Lazareth?" she asked, scanning the various bodies in the room.

Cyrus looked over his shoulder to Patch who'd stopped over the Kaburem king. In his hand was the dragon hilted dagger, blade red with blood. "He's dead," Patch answered, wiping the blade on a piece of cloth. "The blade mortally wounded him. The fire finished him off."

"I'll spread the word," said Clio, lifting the white cloth up for them to see. "Kaburem surrendered. Victory is ours."

As though to confirm her words, bells chimed throughout the city, singing a song of freedom. Cyrus hoped Tempest would wake to enjoy them. "Ready?" he asked Patch, not wanting to waste a moment.

"Let's go," said Patch, moving to stand at the other end of the plank. He nodded, and the pair of them lifted, carrying Tempest out of the treacherous room and through the battlefield.

Rubble, loose rock, and bodies littered the ground, but Cyrus managed to keep his footing strong, and so too did Patch. They moved with unhindered speed through the field, stopping only when they reached the hospital.

Voices roared within the room. The war wasn't over yet, thought Cyrus. It'd only moved to a grander scale. A battle between life and death. At the center of the room, molding the chaos into something resembling order was a woman working fervently.

A few Necromancers lurked about, watching for the summons of death. One drew close as Cyrus and Patch entered. She seemed to sense death's nearness in Tempest, and Cyrus wanted to send her away for it.

"Liz!" Patch called as they set Tempest down on a countertop. The leading woman turned, eyes wide. She abandoned her task and joined them, rinsing her hands in a bowl of alcohol as she passed.

Screams, moans, and the stench of the dying filled the room, overwhelming Cyrus' senses. The horrors of each made their presence known the moment he passed Tempest's safe keeping to the Medics. It was one thing to experience it all on the battlefield where the wind carried the sounds and smells away, thought Cyrus. It was another to have it all shoved into a tightly packed room. All of it together made him dizzy.

He leaned against the wall, hand clutching Tempest's as Liz and Patch set to work. Cyrus had never been one to pray to the gods. He'd always found them more present in nature than in his words, but praying seemed to be the only thing he could do in this moment. He said the words silently in his mind, eyes focused on the weaving hands before him. They worked magic over the wound, removing the bullet and suturing the entry point.

Beads of sweat decorated Liz's brow like gems, shimmering in the low light of the room, but she never once let the exhaustion show. Watching over it all was the Necromancer in waiting. She was dark skinned and had warm brown eyes that watched intently, monitoring the state of the soul. With a huff of breath, Liz sat on the bench that stood against the wall, rubbing her palms together. "I've done all that I can," she said. "It's up to Tempest and the gods now."

Cyrus nodded, a line of worry creasing his brow. She looked so fragile lying there, but he knew she was strong. He knew she would survive.

"Cyrus!" Clio called, aiding an injured man into the hospital. "I need all able hands on the field. Can you be spared?"

His lips pressed together. He didn't want to leave Tempest, but he knew there was nothing he could do at present. Patch placed his hand on Cyrus' shoulder, supporting whatever decision he made. "I'll take care of her," Patch promised, sincerity in his eyes. "If anything changes, you'll be the first to know."

"Thank you," Cyrus said, laying Tempest's hand on the table's edge. "I won't stray far."

Patch took Cyrus' place by Tempest's side, and Liz left to continue her own battle at the lead of the Medics. Once Clio had seated the injured man, Cyrus followed her out, leaving the two dragons to stand guard by Tempest's side.

Gaslights illuminated the evening streets, lit by a young boy walking the cobble road. The boy reminded Cyrus a bit of himself. Dark features shadowed by the fading light, eyes bold in contrast, looking around with unbound curiosity. These eyes followed Cyrus as he passed, and the boy's head tilted, a thought forming behind the telling lines of his face.

"Is it over?" the boy asked, catching Cyrus off guard. It was not a question he'd expected. The king was dead, and Kaburem defeated. It seemed an obvious answer, but his agreement never left his lips.

"It is only beginning," he said, thinking of Tempest, whose life still lingered in dreadful uncertainty. Whether she lived or died, he knew nothing would ever be the same. Cyrus took a deep breath, accepting this knowledge, ready to brave whatever was to come, and hoping beyond anything that Tempest would be by his side when it was faced. He pressed forward, following Clio to the crest of the hill, leaving the young lad to his own.

There was death in the air, and it made his skin crawl. Memories of the battle lay everywhere he looked, fresh and festering. He could hardly recognize the castle. It stood as a shattered relic to the world that once was.

"We took their cannons and turned them inward," said Clio, explaining the excessive damage. "With their final advantage gone, they accepted their defeat." She pulled a jar of ochre paste from a pouch hanging at her side and handed it to Cyrus. "Mark the dead with this. An X on the forehead like so," she said, tracing the shape just above her brow.

Cyrus took the paste and turned his gaze to the carnage, watching Clio as she departed. Her presence held a humble command, and she fell into the motions of leadership with ease. She stopped beside a man of her trust, a head shorter but bolder in stature than he was, and she monitored the line of prisoners being escorted to the temple.

The prisoners were stripped of their guns and weapons before they were marched single file down the hill. They looked exhausted in mind, body, and soul, their heads low with the grief of defeat. Cyrus wondered what would become of each of them. He wondered what Tempest would do to them. For a moment, looking at their solemn despair, he selfishly thanked the gods he wasn't one of them.

Neither, he thought, crouching down to the pale woman who lay bloodied before him, was he one of the dead. Her eyes stared upward, no longer seeing, and any sign of life had long drained from her features. He took her hand and touched the Siam ring that marked her a Mage.

Cyrus reached up with his other hand and closed her eyes so that she could be delivered to Xudor's realm with ease. He marked her with the paste, then said a soft prayer that he repeated for the souls of every dead fighter he found, paying no mind to which side they'd fought for.

Just beyond the portcullis, he heard the muffled sounds of a man groaning. Despite it being a sound of great pain, it comforted Cyrus. It meant someone was alive.

He followed the voice for some time until he came upon a fallen horse from which the groans seemed to be coming from. A hand reached around the creature's torso, pushing with feeble effort.

"Are you injured, man?" Cyrus asked, stepping closer to inspect. The man's lower half was pinned beneath the horse's body, and his face had a ghostly pallor. He gave no response but for a simple nod. Cyrus turned and called to the nearest Medic for assistance. "Help me move this horse," he said when the Medic was near enough.

The Medic asked no questions, just crouched down and helped Cyrus lift the beast enough for the injured man to drag himself out. His right leg was bent unnaturally, and the man was unable to move it without pain. The Medic ran his hands along the shape of the leg, straightening it where he could. "It's broken in a few places, but it isn't anything that won't heal," said the Medic. "Help him down to the hospital and don't let him use his leg." The Medic had addressed Cyrus with that last bit, but it was the man who replied.

"I couldn't if I tried," said the man with a grunt, staring down at the limp limb with mild amusement. "Leave it to me to fall beneath my horse," he muttered.

"You made it quite a ways before you did," Cyrus said, extending his arm to help the man to his good leg.

He used Cyrus' aid to pull himself up, and together, they hobbled down to the hospital where operations had expanded to the streets. There was music and singing in the air, distant celebrations of the battle won, kept time by the soft patter of fresh falling rains. Cyrus wished he could join in their jubilation, but victory seemed so far away.

"Here will do," said the man, pulling Cyrus from his thoughts.

Cyrus helped seat him on an empty crate that sat in a pile along the alleyway. There were others waiting here as well. They were those whose injuries were less urgent in their needs. "I owe you greatly, young sir."

"I only wish I could do more," said Cyrus, feeling a bit helpless in the sea of casualties. "You'll be fine here?" he asked before departing.

"I will," said the man, and Cyrus turned to leave.

A figure stood shaded beneath an overhang just across the way, green eyes illuminated by the flickering light of a lantern. It was Patch, Cyrus realized, gut suddenly twisting. Something had changed in Tempest's health, and from Patch's stoic expression, he couldn't yet determine if it was for better or worse.

Patch lifted the lantern and gestured for Cyrus to follow.

46

rom the depths of unending darkness, a light began to form. It was the warm glow of a thousand flames that seemed to swallow Tempest's being. She felt none of them, too numb to feel much of anything.

Through the red haze of the fires, the world took shape, abandoning the flames for the strange remnants of her world. She felt as though she were walking through a dream, the world around her not quite present, yet still recognizable.

Beside her lay a humanoid figure that stirred memories to the surface of her mind. *Atticus,* Tempest realized, crouching down to see his face. It seemed warped and inhuman in her state, but she knew it to be him. Shattered fragments of the bone crown lay ornamentally around his head.

Tempest stood, contentment flooding her heart. Her people were free, and so, it seemed, was she. Free of earthly bounds for the moment, at least, but not completely lost. She felt weightless, yet grounded all at once, tethered to some distant root that kept her drifting soul planted.

It was all a mess of contradiction that mirrored the state of the room. The stone walls of the throne room lay in ruins while also standing perfectly erect. She seemed to be a voyeur in two worlds at once, one frozen in the eye of eternity, the other a glimpse of actuality. The former was warm and endearing, and her heart begged to accept it as the only truth, but her mind fought its temptations. She knew where it would lead, and she wasn't quite ready to face it.

Instead, she turned her focus elsewhere and made her way down the familiar path to the library. The tugs of each world felt most balanced in this spot. Memories of her youth mixed with the clarity of the present. Like the rest of the castle, in one world, the books lay disheveled and scat-tered. In the other, it was just as she'd remembered it, corridors of books waiting to be read.

Tempest wondered if this was how the ghost, Seraphine, existed, trapped within Mortem with a foot in each world, yet never belonging to either. She found it difficult to keep the two worlds separated and wondered how Seraphine managed to slip between them with such ease.

Wanting to make sense of each world, Tempest took a seat at the table where her magister used to teach, and she began to note the things present. On the corner of the table sat a rolled up scroll. In it, she knew there'd be a list of those born to the various Royal families throughout history. *Not real,* she decided, placing the object in the world of memory.

To her left was a bookcase, shattered with its contents strewn. This library had always been well cared for. Damage to it was rare. *Real,* she thought, sounds of gunfire echoing in the back of her mind, bringing forth thoughts of battle. She wondered how it'd all unfolded, what it'd looked like when the castle came crumbling.

Another object on the table caught her eye. This one a book laying open to a memory. Tempest reached forward and touched the page, remembering. *"What is Odemus the god of?"* her magister had asked.

"Death," she muttered to herself, and the worlds shifted, the disheveled aftermath of war fading to the comforting solidity of death's reflection. She found her mind succumbing to it. Death's realm felt safe, and the people she'd lost waited within it.

Curious, for a moment, Tempest lifted the page. On the back, she caught a glimpse of Ides, and the faces of the living joined the dead in her mind's eye; Patch, Cyrus, and all her friends amongst them stood as a barrier between her and death's lure. She felt oddly like the thin edge of the paper at her fingertips, existing on a plane of her own while acting as a bridge between the two sides.

Life and death. Her father had deemed them eternal lovers in a time long past.

"Is that what we are, then? Lovers?" Cyrus' words echoed in her thoughts with prominence. She could almost feel his lips on hers, skin meeting with a phantom's touch. They'd hardly had time to truly know each other, but the easeful path of discovery had made her giddy. Flesh and minds entangled, he'd taught her time and time again to see the wonders of life.

From the poetry of nature's symphony, to the flames of growing passion, she'd fallen for the way he saw the world, and she longed to maintain a presence in it. *"Promise you'll come back to me,"* he'd said before their final parting. She recalled Cyrus' voice so clearly, and even in this dream-like realm, she felt his presence near. His and another.

She looked up, met by a Necromancer with two lions at her side.

"Am I dead?" Tempest asked, feeling foolish for it. It was a question she thought one normally knew the answer to.

"That's for you to decide," said the Necromancer, stroking the black lion's head. "I suggest making it a quick decision, though. The gods don't like to be kept waiting."

Tempest looked down at the page she held in her hand. The faces of life and death gazed outward on either side of it, suspended momentarily in her grasp. Both sides called to her with unrelenting gravitation.

Death promised a nurturing bliss. It promised a reunion with her parents. There'd be no more pain, no more sorrow. On the other hand, life promised adventure, but she'd had enough of that. Peace seemed far kinder.

Both sides promised love, one an eternal link that'd been with her since birth and would wait until her dying days, the other more fleeting, freshly cultivated, and bound presently to the realm of the living.

With a smile, Tempest released the page and watched as it drifted down and settled with the others. Now, staring back at her was the face of life.

47

There was a freedom in flight, thought Tempest. One understood deeply by the birds and the dragons. Wings outstretched, the creatures caught the wind and knew nothing but salvation. She thought that was what dying would have felt like, but she had chosen to live, and there were no wings to catch her here.

She felt as though she'd been falling forever, heart floating weightless in her chest as she plummeted through the void to an unknown landing, though, in truth, the feeling only lasted a matter of seconds. It wasn't a foreign sensation. She'd felt it before in dreams. When she was a child, her mother had theorized it to be the feeling of the soul returning to the body after a dream took it too far astray.

There seemed to be truth in that idea, for suddenly, Tempest's soul landed, struck ruthlessly by the overwhelming sensations of being human. Voices murmured like roaring ocean waves, and a fowl stench made her insides twist. She could feel hard wood beneath her and a hand clutching hers. Above it all, though, she felt a searing pain in her ribs that throbbed with every heartbeat.

A groan escaped her lips, and her eyes fluttered open, locking with Cyrus'. He was alive, and so was she. That much she knew to be fact. Everything else seemed still unnatural, warped by the dizziness of waking. "Did it work?" she asked, voice coming out in a raspy whisper. "Did they surrender?"

"They did," said Cyrus, a smile on his lips. Seeing it brought joy to Tempest's heart.

"I killed him," she said, equally shocked and prideful for the statement, though a hint of mourning latched to her words. In the end, Atticus had been her last of kin.

"I know." Cyrus leaned forward and pressed his lips to her brow. "Rest now."

Tempest closed her eyes, memories clashing like flaming swords in the back of her mind. She wanted to fight the pain of it all, stand despite it, and be with Cyrus, but she knew she couldn't. The worst of it was over, and her body needed time to recover. Somewhere distantly, Cyrus' voice soothed her troubled soul and guided her to the realms of resting.

~~~

Songbirds chirping in the nearby window stirred Tempest from her slumber. It was a peaceful sound in a room filled with the despairing cries of the injured and dying. Her senses were sharper this time, and the usage of them no longer overwhelmed her.

With effort, Tempest pulled herself to an upright position, taking a moment to gather her thoughts. It was all over, she realized, hardly able to accept it as true. How long she'd waited for this day.

Tempest flexed her fingers and clenched her fists, testing her mobility. As she watched her fingers move, she noticed for the first time that there was a ring on either hand. On her right was the emerald ring of the Dragon Keepers, and on her left was the amethyst ring that'd belonged to her mother. It'd been returned, she assumed, by Patch while she slept.

Patch himself stood no more than a few paces away, tending to a wounded man on a straw pallet. He turned his head, seeming to have felt her gaze. "Welcome back," he said, setting a wooden bowl of dressings on the table by his side. After a final glance to his patient, he turned to face her in entirety. "How do you feel?"

"Like I've been shot," she said with mild humor, touching the fresh bindings around her ribs.

"Good," said Patch. "You're supposed to." He stepped closer and held out his hand. "Can you stand?"

Tempest grabbed his hand and took a deep breath. "We're about to find out," she answered and hoisted herself to her feet, dizzied a bit by the action. Her legs wobbled, but otherwise, she managed to keep her stance.

"Come on. Let's get you some fresh air."

Patch guided her slowly to the street. Each step was a bit precarious, but with persistence, her body fell into the basic rhythm of walking. The air outside was thick and humid, and petrichor diluted the scents of the city. It was a welcome change to the stuffy confines of the hospital.

Down the road a bit, her eyes caught sight of Neymar. He had his nose up, jaws snapping at a rabbit haunch Cyrus dangled above him. A sniff of the air changed the dragon's focus, however, and the beast turned his head to her, chirping contently as Zuri took his share of food. Cyrus' gaze followed Neymar's and he strode forward with a smile.

"I'll be in the hospital if you need me," said Patch, and he bowed his head and parted.

Without a moment's hesitation, Cyrus took her in his arms and seized her strength with a kiss. Tempest put up no restraint, she simply closed her eyes and melted into his hold. It was a kiss like none he'd ever given, mixed with desperation and the promise of tomorrow. She returned its passion willingly.

"Gods be good," said Cyrus when their lips drew apart. "I feared I'd never get to do that again."

"So did I." She clutched the fabric of his coat and sighed, wanting to give her heart to the giddiness bubbling inside it, but a wail burst from within the hospital and sobered her gleaming soul. "How many did we lose?" she asked, looking at the blood stained trail that led to the door.

"A good many," he admitted. "Kaburem did not surrender easy."

"Will you take me to them? I want to see."

Cyrus held her steadily with his arm and helped her to the hilltop where the dead had been laid out for burial. Necromancers wandered the lines, blessing the souls of each of the dead. Amongst them stood a group of familiar faces.

"Benjamin and Marius were killed," Cyrus said before they got close enough to see.

"Oh," said Tempest, unable to form further words.

"Clio found them last night. From what I've heard, they both died with honor."

Felix stood with his head held high beside Jensen as Clio spoke words for both of Tempest's fallen friends, but tears streamed down the child's face, and his eyes were red and swollen. When Clio's speech was finished, the boy reached forward and set a small object on Benjamin's wooden deathbed. It was the elephant figurine he'd gotten in Isigodi with his brother's name carved upon the leg.

Tempest walked forward to join them. "I'm so sorry," she whispered, taking in the faces of the dead one last time. Marius' features showed hardly any signs of age. She could still see him in memory, standing so lively on the tavern table, urging folks to join their cause. He'd had so much passion in him, and now it'd been extinguished.

Beside him was Benjamin, grey streaks in his hair, and skin creased with wizened age. He'd told a million stories in the short time Tempest had known him, but she longed to hear one more.

"He knew the risk," said Jensen. "He knew what we were fighting for."

"Marco and the village people will have missed him. It'll be a great reunion," Felix added.

"It will, indeed," said Tempest, a somber smile on her lips. "Benjamin with his people, and Marius with Sarah. They'll both be happy, I think."

A murmur of agreement left the lips of those gathered, and Tempest bowed, leaving them to their mourning. Cyrus took her hand with tenderness and guided her through the remaining lines. She looked upon the faces of them all, vowing to remember their sacrifices.

At the end, one body lay apart from the rest, shrouded in a white cloth. "It's Atticus," Cyrus explained. "We didn't know if he should be buried with his family or sent back to Kaburem."

"He should be buried here," Tempest said. "This was his home."

Nearing footsteps drew her attention behind her where Clio now stood. "Are you well?" asked Clio, eyes flitting to the bound wound.

"Well enough," said Tempest. "Will you call a meeting? There's much we should discuss."

~~~

The cloth of the canopy snapped and rippled with the wind as a group of militia men set it up. When it'd been secured, Tempest took a seat in a chair beneath it, joined shortly by her council and commanders. Amongst them was the Mage who'd taken Avery's charge and a Kaburem soldier who'd been elected to discuss the terms of their surrender. Tempest lifted her hand, and the group's attention turned to her.

"It is a great honor that I stand with you today," she said. "One that will not be taken lightly. I made a promise to each of you when you joined me, and it's time those promises are upheld. But, before we begin, Kaburem's fate must be decided." She turned to the Kaburem officer. "Have you anything to say on behalf of your people?"

The officer lowered his tricorne hat and bowed his head before responding. "M'lady, while many of us came under orders of occupation, war was not something we wanted. This land, your people, we have no quarrel with you. We accept our defeat humbly and hope a relationship between our nations can grow."

"Intended or not, damage was done. I watched as a child was shot cold blooded for suspicions of treason. I watched as houses were burned with no intentions of extinguishment. I watched as you slaughtered innocent citizens and set the blame on us. These people that stand with me today have seen all these things and more. We cannot let it slide."

The officer nodded. "Rightly so. Kaburem can never right the wrongs that happened here, but at your bidding, we shall work to make amends."

"Indeed, you shall. Kaburem will pay reparations to aid in the healing of our nation. You will help rebuild the land you very nearly destroyed, and those who are known to have committed barbarous acts shall be tried and incarcerated.

"Once all this is done, a trade relation will be formed as was intended in the beginning," said Tempest. "Both our nations will find benefit in the unity that comes from such trades."

"I agree," said the officer.

"Good. I'll have a treaty drawn before your ships set sail. Are there any oppositions?"

Eyes met hers with no comments or debates, but Jyles shifted in his seat. "I'd like to give consideration to those who wish to stay here when the treaty is written. There are a few who've taken a liking to this land from what I've heard, Morris included."

This surprised Tempest. She'd not thought any of them would want to stay. From what Morris had told her of his homeland, they seemed to have a vastly different way of life than was custom on this land. After a moment's contemplation, she gave her answer. "Those who wish to stay will be allowed to, so long as they respect our laws and our methods," she decided. "Morris will be given trial by our Law Enforcement. If found honest, he'll be welcomed into our nation." She reached forward and brushed the wrinkles from her gown, gaze meeting once more with the Kaburem officer. "If that is all, take this news to your people and make the agreement known. We'll meet again when the treaty is drawn."

The officer bowed, then left with a small militia guard. "As for the rest of you," said Tempest when the officer had gone. "Payment is long overdue. I'll be needing a crown treasurer to divvy up funds for both past and future services. Jyles, I hoped that could be you."

Jyle's face twisted. "Me? Are you certain? Given my history…"

"Given your history, you're no stranger to the handling of coin. Yes," said Tempest. "I'm certain."

"Where shall I begin?"

"With a stipend for every rebel who fought for our cause, including each of you. We'll set up posts throughout the city for them to collect their wages. The vaults are beneath the throne room. You'll find sufficient coin in there. We'll need to set funds aside for some other projects as well, though.

"Cedric and Emil, you have both upheld your end of our bargain at what I hope was not too great a cost. I wish to grant you funds enough to rebuild the elephant sanctuary, and to help it grow. With your instruction, I will write laws to help protect them from any harm that may come their way. Together, we can help their species recover."

Cedric's eyes widened, and he grasped Emil by the arm. "You're too kind, m'lady," he said with an unguarded smile. "We can't thank you enough."

Tempest turned next to Patch and gave a pleasant smile. "Patch," she addressed. "The elephant sanctuary isn't the only thing I want to build. You and I made a vow to help the children on the streets. With your assistance, I want to build a crown funded orphanage. We will help them to their feet and give them opportunities that have been denied to them for far too long."

"I'd be honored to be a part of it," said Patch

"That isn't all I want you to be a part of," Tempest added. "I need you to be the voice of the people. I want your council on public affairs, if you'll give it."

"Of course. What kind of friend would I be if I abandoned you in your studies after all this time?"

"A terrible one," said Tempest with a chuckle. "I figure the rest of you will want to return to your homes. You and your groups will be sent with proper provisions for the journey. Any of you who wish to stay in Alyria are welcome in my court. I will find you land in the city or wherever you please. You've all earned much more than that. Those whose homes were destroyed by Kaburem receive the same offer. You may stay, or I will send you on your way with funds to start again. Are there any questions?"

"None, m'lady," said Jensen, and the rest echoed his response.

"I'll see you all when the dust settles, and I look forward to revisiting your cities. Until then, I'll hold the memories of each of you dear to my heart." She stood and bowed.

Each of her friends rose in turn, mingling together to utter farewells. First to approach her was Tegan. "I'll be leaving in the morning with the Necromancers and the Mortem knights," she said, reaching out to grab Tempest's hands. "It's time they're laid to rest."

Unwarranted tears welled in Tempest's eyes. She'd been so caught up in the verdict of the war that she hadn't prepared to say goodbye. "None of this would have been possible if it weren't for you. You were the first tendrils of this army. I'll never forget that."

"Neither will we," said Tegan.

Others came also to voice well wishes and parting words. Adrian, Sagua, Jensen, Ivy, Callum, Cedric, and Emil amongst them. She'd miss them all terribly.

At the end, Cyrus stood before her, arm outstretched, inviting. "May I steal a moment of your time?" he asked, and Tempest accepted.

With her arm locked in his, she walked beside him, leaving the canopy and those beneath it behind for a moment of escape. Behind the pair of them, the tapping talons of their dragons beat a steady rhythm. This and their combined steps were the only sounds made until they reached the edge of the castle ruins.

Tempest was content with the quietness. It was something that came in rare doses these days, and the silence between them was a communication of its own. Once through the castle walls, however, it became unnerving. She tightened her grip on Cyrus' arm and stopped, mind dancing between the present and the memory of death's cusp.

"I'm sorry," said Cyrus. "I shouldn't have brought you here. I only meant to find some privacy."

"It's okay," she assured. "It's only my mind playing tricks on me." To prove her stability, she stepped forward, grazing her hand along the stone walls as she went. The roughness of its surface kept her thoughts anchored to reality. Cyrus walked behind her, presence calm and comforting. "Come down this way."

The halls were dim where they were whole, small beams of light breaking through cracks in the stone. Some parts of the castle were hardly damaged, while other parts hardly remained. Despite it all, Tempest found her way to the library. It was as she remembered it in the ruined realm of her dream-like state, splintered and scattered, but still mostly intact. Many of the shelves stood upright, books only slightly disheveled, but on the floor lay one shelf completely destroyed.

"I used to spend hours in this room," Tempest said upon crossing its threshold. Cyrus followed her through, and she turned to face him. "You'd think I'd have been more cautious about living a life worth a story after reading about the hardships that came along with one, but I was naïve and longed for adventure."

Cyrus stepped gingerly over a pile of books and stopped only inches from her. "After having lived such a life, would you change it?" he asked.

Tempest touched her fingers to the curve of his jaw and gave him a tender kiss. "Never."

"Neither would I." He crouched down and picked up a stack of fallen books, setting them aside. "Though I imagine this place would have fared better if you'd done so."

Tempest laughed at that, but one of the books he'd gathered pulled her attention away from his remark. She picked it up with care and inspected its scorched and tattered pages. Near the center, she found the familiar page, one side bearing the face of Odemus, the other bearing the face of Ides. She closed the book and held it tight to her chest, feeling somehow that a part of her lived within it.

When she looked up, Cyrus had wandered through a large hole in the eastern wall. She followed him through it, watching the ground for the threat of loose rocks.

The light on the other side of the wall was blinding after being in such dark quarters, but soon, her eyes adjusted. Just ahead, she saw a fragment of the rampart standing in stubborn defiance with a stairwell at its center. She didn't know how sturdy it was, but Cyrus reached the top with ease, so Tempest joined him.

He extended his hand and helped her up the final stair; it was broken and lay diagonally, but the stone wall held true, unmoving beneath their weight. "Your kingdom," he said, bringing her hand to his lips and pulling her forward.

Neymar and Zuri abandoned the stairs and flew to sit beside them, each perched on either side of the parapet like gargoyles, guarding them in this fleeting moment of shared bliss.

The view from the parapet struck her with sudden awe when she reached the wall's edge. Off in the distance, she could see most of the city laid out across the land. She'd seen it many times, but it and its people had always seemed so foreign to her. Now she'd lived amongst them, and she no longer felt estranged from those she'd promised to lead.

Tempest leaned against the battered stone, a nostalgic warmth building in her heart, and she smiled, home at last.

THE GODS AND THE MONTHS

The Gods and the Months:

Month One: *Wynris: Goddess of Winter and Ice.*

Month Two: *Odemus: God of Death.*

Month Three: Izasel: *Goddess of Spring.*

Month Four: *Rhumir: God of Rain.*

Month Five: *Ides: Goddess of Life.*

Month Six: *Fejun: God of Nature.*

Month Seven: *Zalder: God of Summer and Fire.*

Month Eight: *Aborh: God of Harvest.*

Month Nine: *Arasil: Goddess of Autumn.*

Month Ten: *Xudor: God of the Underworld.*

Month Eleven: *Ammos: God of Prosperity.*

Month Twelve: *Jukion: God of Time.*

THE GUILDS AND THE RINGS

The Guilds and the Rings:

Royal House: *Amethyst*

Kaburem: *Blood-Stone*

Dragon Keeper: *Emerald*

Mage: *Siam*

Necromancer: *Jet*

Navy: *Aquamarine*

Army: *Olivine*

Law Enforcement: *Sapphire*

Fire Keeper: *Fire Opal*

Medic: *Amber*

Blacksmith: *Black Diamond*

Merchant: *Burgundy*

Farmer: *Jonquil*

Priest: *Fuchsia*

Undecided: *Clear Diamond*

APPENDIX

THE CHARACTERS

The Characters:

Dasha/Tempest: heir to the Throne; daughter of the Royal House

Neymar: King of Alyria; Tempest's father; Tempest's dragon

Prince: the king's squire

Patch: orphan; Tempest's right hand man

Sepora: Necromancer guild leader

Sagua: Dragon Keeper guild leader

Vitani: Mage guild leader

Liz: Medic; owner of hospital

Tanith: former convict; harlot; secret trader

Lazareth: the usurper; King of Kaburem

Adrian: turncoat

Markus: drunkard at the Smokey Inn; storyteller; seer

Mereb: enlisted Dragon Keeper; Tempest's first friend in Firethorne

Sparrow: Mereb's younger sister

Tyce: enlisted Dragon Keeper; Mereb's friend

Zeke: enlisted Dragon Keeper; Mereb's friend

Theria: enlisted Dragon Keeper; Mereb's friend

Ari Paxton: Mereb and Sparrow's mother

John Paxton: Mereb and Sparrow's father

Colonel Atheris: Army officer; leader of the western province

Lyra: Dragon Keeper recruit

Cora: Dragon Keeper recruit

Reuben: Dragon Keeper recruit

Klaus: Dragon Keeper recruit

Cyrus: Dragon Keeper recruit

Paris: Dragon Keeper recruit

Luke: Dragon Keeper recruit

The Characters:

Sage: Dragon Keeper recruit

Jax: Dragon Keeper officer; recruit mentor

Seraphine: ghost of Mortem; Sepora's sister

Tegan: Necromancer officer; advisor to Tempest

Benjamin: leader of Umoja village; the storyteller

Felix: member of Umoja village; the young dreamer; Tempest's squire

Jensen: member of Umoja village; the warrior

Nikita: leader of Isigodi

Emil: member of Isigodi; elephant aid

Callum: Necromancer officer

Ivy: Necromancer officer

Cedric: leader of elephant sanctuary

Jada: Tempest's seamstress and swordsmith

Ava: Tempest's squire

Marius: militia spokesman; rebellion advocate

Clio: leader of militia group; Tempest's war advisor

Jyles: smuggler

Morris: Kaburem prisoner

Avery: leader of Mage rebel group

Amir: rebel aid

Elias: rebel aid

Arthur: Amir and Elias' father; town leader

Acknowledgements

To Neal, for everything. Late night lessons and quotes, advisement throughout the process, controlling the semicolon plague, sifting through the tragedy of the rough draft, loving the characters as much as I do, being there for every question and concern, the dragon of Wales, random history lessons, shared wisdom, and so much more.

To Rachel, for helping me through this entire publication process and answering every question I had, no matter how many there were.

To my Mother, for not only supporting me in all my wildest dreams, but doing everything in your power to help me reach them. I love you.

To my Father, for the endless love, support, and pride you've given me. I love you.

To Janie, for being my fan since the beginning. You've inspired me more than you know. I love you.

To my family, we may be scattered, but your love and support never fails. I love you all from the bottom of my heart.

To Dani, for being there for me through anything. You're amazing. Never forget it.

To Ashlee, for all the epic adventures you have taken me on, for random synchronized dance breaks, for teaching me to get my head out of the books and live a little, for supporting me until the end, and for everything in between.

To Feist, Frost, Gaffigan, Pitts, and Reardon, for making the Sycamore English hall one of my favorite places.

To Alyssa, for sitting beside me in sophomore year creative writing class and asking, "When on earth are you actually going to start writing this thing?" Wherever you are, I started, and now I've finished.

To David, without your careful advisement, this book would not be what it is today. Thank you for everything.

To Tahshae, Sam, Alexis, Selena, Krista, and Andee, for your constant support and the never ending questions of, "Are you finished yet?" Because of you, I can proudly say, "I am."

To Anneka, for all our creative collaborations, your continuous support, and your help with the beta reading process.

To the Writer's Block Discord community, for keeping me motivated and helping me push through every obstacle.

To Avery, for supporting this story endlessly in all its abstract forms.

To everyone else who has helped me throughout this journey, I can't thank you enough.

To you, dear reader, for joining me on this adventure. May we meet again on another.

About the Author:

Calista Robbins was born and raised in the Midwest but now resides in Nevada to pursue her dreams in the world of entertainment. For her entire life, she has been fascinated with the idea of storytelling, and ever since she learned to sweep letters across pages, she's felt the need to write her stories out. Tempest is her first published work. It began as a quest to combine all the things she found intriguing in this world with the things she loved in the worlds of others. In the end, it became a journey of a lifetime that spanned over seven years in the making.

Facebook.com/CalistaRobbinsLD
www.calistarobbins.com
@Robbins_Books

Printed in Great Britain
by Amazon